INK AND SHADOWS

RHYS FORD

DSP PUBLICATIONS

Published by

DSP PUBLICATIONS

5032 Capital Circle SW, Suite 2, PMB# 279, Tallahassee, FL 32305-7886 USA
http://www.dsppublications.com/

Ink and Shadows
© 2015 Rhys Ford.

Cover Art
© 2015 Anne Cain.
annecain.art@gmail.com
Cover content is for illustrative purposes only and any person depicted on the cover is a model.

ISBN: 978-1-63476-016-4
Digital ISBN: 978-1-63476-017-1
Library of Congress Control Number: 2014920708
First Edition July 2015

Printed in the United States of America
⊚
This paper meets the requirements of
ANSI/NISO Z39.48-1992 (Permanence of Paper).

Readers love *Black Dog Blues*
by RHYS FORD

"I devoured all 246 pages of it as quickly as I possibly could… Rhys strings descriptive prose together in a way that I loved."
—Boy Meets Boy Reviews

"Dark, gripping, intense and imaginative… I thought this was a great read."
—MM Good Book Reviews

"Rhys Ford is an artist; her words are dredged off the palette and brushed on the pages, creating a world that overwhelmed my senses for days after I read the last words."
—The Novel Approach

"This author plunges you straight into a gritty scene that totally showcases her ability to create sounds, smells and the essence of a scene from mere words."
—Sinfully… Addicted to All Male Romance

"This story is everything a fantasy should be… not only a fantastic story, its technically excellent and smartly edited. It's definitely an example of the brilliance I've come to expect from Rhys Ford."
—Love Bytes

"I'm in awe over this Urban Fantasy world that Rhys Ford has created and I want more!"
—Rainbow Book Reviews

The Four is dedicated to… the Five, Z.A. Maxfield, and LE Franks.
For the Five because they are the foundation of every work I've ever done.
For ZAM, who is convinced she loves me.
And for LE because apparently she licked the pixels and declared it hers.

ACKNOWLEDGMENTS

TO THE FIVE who are everything—from Dragon to Rat: Penn, Lea, Tamm, and Jenn. And to my hanai sisters: Ren, Ree, and Lisa.

There are never enough words of thanks for Elizabeth North and everyone at Dreamspinner Press. Everything that is good is because of them. I cannot thank Grace and her crew enough for herding me like the nipped-up one-eyed cat that I am.

As many thanks to my beta readers and the Dirty Ford Guinea Pigs who put up with SOOOOO much of my crap and whining and damn, don't read that—I've got another idea. So much patience.

Lastly, to every single artist in my music library. God, thank you for keeping me company.

CHAPTER ONE

DEATH SELECTED a ripe orange from the fruit bowl, hitching himself farther back onto the kitchen counter, the marble cold under him, even through the thickness of the low-slung cotton pants he'd tugged on after his workout.

The sudden screech of thumping music had broken the quiet of their penthouse, but Death didn't mind. It was good to have Mal around, and Death was willing to make adjustments for their youngest. As their new Pestilence, Mal brought a youthfulness to their Four that was long missing, although the other two didn't see it as quite as much of a good thing as Death did. At least this time the volume hadn't been loud enough to rattle the windows. They'd replaced a broken mirror recently, a victim of Mal's music.

When the eldest Horseman bent over, his inky hair curved down over his strong jaw, nearly hiding the sharp angles of his cheekbones. Behind him the city glowed under the waning sunlight, holding back the San Diego night creeping in from the horizon.

Sliding his thumbnail against the dimpled orange skin, Death inhaled the sharp citrus oil of the pierced rind. Curving his nail carefully around the rim of the navel, he pushed down gently to barely break the surface. The fruit still lay under in its bright rind, seemingly immune to the immortal's fingers. A door opened down to the left of the kitchen area. Then Ari strode into the common area, fresh from a shower.

Ari's rib cage ran thick in one spot, a cicatrice blooming on a stretch of tanned skin. The sunburst peeking over the towel's edge caught Death's attention, pulling him away from his orange and the problem that had landed in his lap. War's scar was as familiar to him as his own but much more intriguing, rays of thinner lines spiraling out from a single spray, and still it tugged at his imagination. He gave the thin scar running down his left eye ridge and over the bridge of his nose much less thought.

Death wondered if their scars were from their deaths, one of the few times he'd given himself permission to wonder about where the Horsemen all came from, but the answer, like so many others, was out of his reach. Pestilence, the most recent of their Four, had none on him. Death was amused at the irony of a Pestilence dead from a disease. Min's flat belly was carved with a half-moon arc between her hip bones, nearly a pinkie width of tangled skin.

"Ah, we're alone. Okay, maybe not totally alone, but unless Cooties comes out of his room, we're alone enough. Want to neck and have some fun?" Ari's white teeth nipped at the dark-haired man's ear, barely skimming the soft flesh before Death pulled away and gave him a muted disapproving look Ari was quite used to. Eyes slanted slightly upward, he glanced a black warning at Ari's familiarity with his body.

"Stop it." His gaze dropped, voice soft in a whisper, a reluctant protestation made out of habit. Looking at the recalcitrant fruit, Death worried once more at the rind, crushing the pulp inside. "I'm thinking."

"You think too much sometimes. And give me that. I'll open it for you." His rough voice broke Death's study of the fruit. Disgusted at the mess made of the orange, he reached for it, tugging at the fruit until Death let go.

Death gave up the orange reluctantly, long fingers opening under the press of Ari's callused hand. Ari met the other immortal's contemplative dark eyes with a steady stare, refusing to give in to Death's stubbornness. Looking down, Death avoided the other man's frank gaze, staring instead at the towel knotted about Ari's waist.

Ari's flat stomach was bare except for a faint dusting of blond hair around his navel, the down darkened from spots of water, burrowing down past the towel. Moving forward, Ari's thick and powerful legs straddled Death's knees as the blond savagely worked the orange free from its skin.

Standing against one another in the kitchen, they touched casually, although Death was cautious, knowing Ari would take even the slightest hint of intimacy and run away with it. Ari had laid siege more than once around the dark-haired immortal, each time falling back and licking his wounds while promising never to approach again, then swearing under his breath when he renewed pursuit. Now they were at a rare peace, Ari circling and looking for an opening while Death was seemingly unaware.

Old arguments hung between them, heated tensions folded more times than they could count and tempered by the passions of the blond man, who sometimes pushed too hard. Death was a contrary player in Ari's games, permissive just far enough to whet Ari's appetites.

The fruit's rind parted under Ari's thumbs, tearing free from the flesh with a gush of juice.

Sucking at the white membrane left on his thumb, Ari handed the fruit back, grinning widely at Death's wrinkled nose at the bruised segments.

"You've killed it." Pulling the juicy sphere apart, Death gave a mock grimace at the shattered cells, popped from Ari's aggressive tearing.

"You're too gentle with things." Ari sniffed, tugging the towel closed where it threatened to tumble from his hips. Most of his body was still damp, his long dirty-blond hair just starting to dry at the ends. Leaning on the marble counter, the tips of his fingers dragging along the outer edge of Death's knee, Ari quirked one eyebrow at the immortal. "Sometimes you just have to tear things apart. It looked like you were making juice inside of that rind."

"Sometimes you have to coax them along," Death replied, trying to separate out a piece of orange.

"I've tried coaxing. It doesn't work as well as tearing," Ari said.

Turning, Ari gazed at the city below, the penthouse's west expanse of windows reaching out over downtown and toward the bay. "City looks nice tonight. Fog might roll in early."

"It might." Death nodded.

A shuddering wraith wove past the window, then slammed into the glass, startling the two Horsemen.

Its reptilian face was screwed up into a pout, eyes running down an elongated face as it howled soundlessly at them. White and pasty, it pressed hard against the glass, wanting some sort of recognition from the men living just beyond its reach. A flash of opal, and the Veil thickened, shoving the specter away from the immortals. It plunged it back into the shadows where other creatures lurked, then circled back around, a wisp of pale gray against the sky.

"What the fuck?" Ari straightened, sliding his hand around Death's waist, ready to pull the other Horseman off the counter and into safety. "What the hell is that doing up here?"

"It's been hitting at the windows for the past half an hour." Death shrugged. "I thought I'd worry about it if it breaks the glass and gets in."

The creature circled around the upper floor of the building, drawing in close to Mal's windows.

Ari grinned at the youngest's startled shout, dangerously excited by the wraith popping in and out of the darkness outside. He laughed into Death's shoulder, a wicked grin on his face. "Guess it surprised Cooties."

Inside his room, Mal struggled to turn down the volume of his stereo, leveling out the bass before it broke the glass of his bookshelves with a resonant thump. Guided by the flickering green of the remote's display, he fumbled for the right knob, his vision fuzzy. Barking his knees on the coffee table, the youngest Horseman yelped, biting the tip of his tongue.

Searching about on the tabletop, he found his spectacles mostly by sound, his wire-rimmed glasses rattling when his fingers hit the earpiece. Putting them on, the world came into view, his messy study littered with open books and more than a few empty tumblers. Mal shoved his pale hair off his face, stray chunks falling forward into his eyes.

"Did you see that?" Mal poked his head out of his bedroom door, gesturing wildly behind him, then realized neither man could see through the solid wall to where he was pointing. "That was a wraith. Up here!"

"Got to hand it to the boy, he's sometimes got at least half a brain cell working." Ari leaned his hip against the counter. "Wraiths aren't that bold. That thing shouldn't have been able to come this close."

"It's rather daring. Maybe it feels safe behind the glass? But then why would it try to get in?" Death agreed as he worked off another piece of orange. He'd been troubled ever since he'd first gotten the message that the Four were needed for a task. "I think something near us is thinning the Veil. I've gotten some rumors about things happening, and well, then…."

"How thin?" Ari frowned.

"I've heard about things leaking out." Death watched Mal as he bounded into the living room, the young immortal following the wraith's progress as it looped around their penthouse. "You can go into my rooms if it's heading there. If it starts to look like it's coming through, let us know. We'll take care of it."

"Thanks." Mal strode past Ari, ignoring the other Horsemen. "I thought it broke one of my windows, but the pane held."

"Just don't open a window and let it in," Ari shouted at Mal's back as the young man headed to Death's rooms, looking for the phantasm. "Hell, it might eat him, and we can get a new Pestilence. One that knows how to hold a sword or something."

"Leave him alone, Ari," Death replied. "We have other things to fret about. Wraiths outside of our windows are the least of our worries. I tried asking around a bit, but mostly it seems to be just talk. I can't get anything solid."

"Crazy people talking to themselves is normal." Ari reached for the mangled bits of fruit in Death's hands, his thoughts as tangled as Death's fingers around the orange. "Now you're the one killing that."

"I'm Death. What else were you expecting?" Death gave Ari a bruised look, making the blond laugh, a burst of booming warmth.

"For you to eat it. You don't eat enough."

Ari's belly clenched when he held out a slice and Death leaned forward to bite into the offering, his teeth barely grazing Ari's fingertips. When the other man pulled back, chewing on the orange slice, Ari sucked his fingers clean, hoping to find some taste of Death left in the wetness.

The world paused for Ari, holding its breath before turning again as Death chewed. After swallowing to bring moisture back into his mouth, Ari spoke. "What kind of stuff are you talking about? Or is it the normal *God help us, someone is probing the cows*? And who's telling us this, those idiots beyond?"

"Those idiots, as you call them, are helpful. I got a message yesterday afternoon. I needed some time to think about it," Death remarked. Dealing with directives from beyond was a major reason Ari wanted nothing to do with guiding the Horsemen. "They want us to hunt down something."

"Every time you get one of those, I'm reminded how happy I am that you're our leader." Ari spit out a sliver of seed caught on his tongue. "I hate those things. Everything is cryptic, and they remind me we're just puppets. They make my skin crawl."

"I'm used to them, I suppose." Death shrugged, picking the threads from the fruit. "It's better than it used to be. I'd rather have my dieffenbachia catching fire and speaking in tongues than my horse starting to paw out runes in the dirt. Somehow that's more disturbing."

"Your plant okay?"

"It's fine. They possessed the television this time." Death gave Ari a grin.

"What did the flaming television want this time?"

"Something's unbalancing the Veil. Things are bleeding through. Things from our side." Death leaned back on his hands, slick with citrus juice. "They didn't give me much in the message. You know it's hard for them to see into the mortal world."

"Omnipotent but blind. Interesting combination. It's funny how they always cop the *we're blind to things in the mortal world* whenever they give us squat to go on." Ari rarely kept his own opinions about the unseen puppet masters to himself. "What exactly are we looking for?"

"I don't know. I know it's tearing the Veil wide open. Maybe something big got loose. Might even have been something let loose by someone playing with things they didn't understand."

"Someone being a seer or magus? They're always pains in the asses." Ari mulled over the possibility of the world returning to an older time when humans were accustomed to the Veiled walking among them. "Be a bitch if we have to spend all of our time chasing down shadows."

"Those we could handle. I was told that things are crawling out of the Veil, and humans are able to see them and touch them." Swallowing another bite of orange, Death wrinkled his nose. "San Diego seems to be hit the hardest, from what I can tell."

"So it's probably starting here in the city." Ari helped himself to another slice of Death's fruit, sucking the pulp free.

"It could be," Death said. "Whatever this is, it's even making the Fae nervous. Last thing they want is to be spilled out into the mortal world. It's been a long time since they've been exposed to humans. I don't think they would be able to handle it now. People these days would hunt them rather than worship them."

"Do you think there's something in the water doing it?" Ari asked, playing with the folds of his wrapped towel. "You remember that one time in Montana when there was a wheat fungus that made entire towns see the things that go bump? We were there for days until Pestilence… Batu… figured that out."

"I don't know what it is. I wish we had more help in this, but the Others aren't willing. I've asked." Death shook his head to stop Ari's railing about the other immortals. "The television flared on again this morning, but it wasn't any clearer."

"Maybe it won't be anything, but hell, it'll be nice to get out and do something else, huh?" Stretching his arms up, Ari felt the kink pop out of his neck. "Good time to be hunting. Night's cool, and the moon's a bit thin. Good time to break legs and suck the marrow clean from the bone."

"I was trying to get a feel for what is going on, but I didn't have much luck," Death replied, leaving off picking through the orange. "The humans that can see us tend to avoid me."

"Mortals." Ari leaned over and picked at a scab on Death's consciousness. "Don't feel bad about not liking to talk to them or them not talking to you. One doesn't make a pet out of the pig that's going to be the Christmas ham. Besides, it's better if you're all mysterious and aloof."

Death snorted. "We are what we are."

"True, but you skulk. People like that. All spooky and shadows. That makes you more legend-like. I blunder, stomp, and whore my way through it. Not much mystery there." Ari grinned, flashing a bright smile at his oldest friend. "And I happen to like blundering and stomping."

"And whoring," Death pointed out.

"True, whoring's a good bit of fun," Ari agreed. "Let me get dressed, and we can go hunting for rabbits."

"I can't."

The pain in Death's eyes stopped Ari in his tracks. The cinnamon shade held in them burned from a fire inside of the immortal.

"I've got a calling to attend to in Asia."

"You've got souls to look to?" Canting his head, Ari drew back to his friend's side. He knew what was coming, what was out there waiting for Death, but his mind denied wanting to look any further, trapped by conflicting emotions. "Bad time for it if you want to go out hunting for this mess."

Ari ached to touch Death's face, to feel the strength of bone in the cradle of his palm. Ari loved his role in the Horsemen, but Death dreaded his, seducing souls to pass. Most went without Death's attendance, carried on to unknown places. No one living behind the Veil, a shadowy existence just beyond the Mortal world, knew what lay beyond. Where an immortal went after their service, no one knew, not even Death.

"Do you really need to go?" Ari knew the answer to that question before the words fell from his mouth. Death answered with a silence steeped in duty. "I mean, do you have to go right now?"

Of course Death would go, Ari scolded himself. If he didn't, who knew what the world would become. Souls torn from their bodies, usually from tragedies or conflicts, roamed the area and threatened the Veil's ability to hold back the other things that fed on mankind. Single specters were not much of a problem, but a large concentration often proved troublesome. If not persuaded to sever the ties to the mortal world, a resonance would linger… sometimes drawing others to stay behind or try to reach out to the people around it, not understanding that its body turned it out.

Drawing out his breath, Ari asked, "How soon?"

"Soon." Death found his voice and picked at a piece of rind on the counter, smashing the skin between his pinched fingers. "A fire in the slums of lower Hong Kong. I don't know how many yet, but I'll want to be there."

"You don't need to be there when it starts. There's hours after their passing until they're stuck here." Ari gritted his teeth, chewing on a point of argument ages old. "Go after. Spare yourself that pain."

"Someone needs to be there when they die. No one should pass unseen, untouched," Death said. Ari's anger was thoughtless most of the time, but now Ari held it rigidly in, something Death appreciated.

"If not me, then who? It's what I'm here for. So they don't wander, alone and forgotten."

Ari placed his palms flat on the cold counter, his hands resting by the sides of his friend's hips. "Yeah, we're the Horsemen… the Four. But there's no one here telling you that you have to drink from that cup every time it's poured hot. Let it cool first."

"We've talked about this, Ari." Death's voice was a whisper, husky from Ari's closeness. "I have to. It is who I am, what I am. I need you to take a look around tonight. Something in my gut says that it can't wait."

"You're the brains. I'm just the muscle," Ari said, pushing free from the counter, tucking the ends of the unraveling towel around his waist. Ari was reluctant to give up this fight, to let Death loose into the slums where he would wander for hours, reaching into each soul to see if they wanted or needed assistance in shedding the mortal world. "But I'm definitely sexier."

"Take Mal." Death held up a hand, fending off Ari's yet unspoken protests. "He's one of us. He needs to know what we do, and not just from stories told around the dining table."

"Oh, you've got to be shitting me." Ari hissed with frustration. "Look at him. He's chasing a wraith around the apartment like he's a goldfish looking for flakes."

"He needs to feel like he's a part of us." Death's dark eyes were distant, running along another train of thought. "Mal doesn't feel like he's one of us. I know losing Batu was hard on you. It was hard on all of us. He was a good friend."

"Batu was a damned good friend," Ari grumbled, crossing his arms over his bare chest. "And a damned good Pestilence. Mal's…. Death, the kid's useless compared to Batu."

Mal stopped before entering the living room. He'd heard Batu's name whispered about when the others thought he wasn't listening. Ari's words hurt, deep in his chest, and the young Horseman gritted his teeth to keep from biting Ari's head off.

"That isn't Mal's fault. New ones feel excluded for a long time," Death reminded him. "And that's not something that I can have between us."

"He feels outside of us. Min, she fit right in. Not a problem. She's a good Famine, skinny little twit but vicious. I like that in a Famine," Ari bit back as Death's gaze slid over him, and he felt the reproach there. "He's different than us. Too different."

"We needed different." Death leaned forward, their bodies close and his eyes still on Ari's tanned face. "So they gave us Mal. You and I, we've been here forever, but the others need changing sometimes. You know that. Even if we want them to stay, they have to move on. Mal's here because we need a Mal. And maybe he needs us. We don't know."

"Batu just worked. No fuss. No massaging little-boy egos and hurts. He just slid in and did what Pestilences need to do." Ari's mouth twisted sourly at the thought of spending hours with the youngest Horseman. "Mal's like a sheath that's too tight for the sword it was made for."

Mal, the new Pestilence, seemed to have a knack for getting in the way, and the constant questions drove Ari to distraction. Most of all, and Ari hated to admit it, he plainly missed the last Pestilence.

The last Pestilence was a lean-boned black man with twisted dreads that hung down his back and had been one for a good laugh or a shared quiet joke over a beer. When Batu decided it was time to leave the Horsemen, Ari spent days grieving, staring up from bottles of whiskey and vodka. Min joined Ari for a day or so before moving on with her work, but her eyes were always drawn to the small ebony sculptures Batu had spent hours carving and left behind. Death sat and prepared for the new Pestilence that would arrive, naked and confused, with a head filled with an immense knowledge of how to inflict the worst kind of suffering on mankind.

Batu was replaced like he replaced the Pestilence before him. Within two hours, a fresh-faced innocent arrived, a myopic blond with a guileless face. A studious-looking young man with wire-rimmed glasses, a mess of straw-colored hair, and a curiosity that seemed to well up from a bottomless pit, this new Pestilence also arrived overflowing with technological babble and other modern ideas.

"Are you talking about me again?" Barefooted, Mal approached nearly silent on the polished wooden floors, still holding a third-filled cup of cold coffee in his hands. "Don't you have anything else to keep you occupied? I hear they invented coloring books."

"Death wants us to go sniffing around for something. And somehow I pissed him off enough that he's making me take you along." Ari took advantage of his friend's distracted glance at Pestilence and brushed a light kiss along Death's jaw. "Talk the boy into listening to me for once and maybe getting some shoes on."

"He listens to you better than you listen to *me*," Death grumbled as Ari walked off.

Mal snarled at Ari, biting back more words when he felt Death's eyes fix on him. Turning to the eldest, Mal pursed his mouth and mumbled, "There's nothing I can say without sounding like a whining child."

"He's better at arguments than you are," Death replied. "It's what he does."

"He hates me." Trying to choose his words carefully, Mal still grimaced when he heard himself speak. "No, I still sound like a whining child."

"Ari's a simple creature." Death contemplated that notion for a moment. Ari brimmed with strong emotions, a stormy tempest blowing through the quiet. "He growls at things or people he doesn't understand. He doesn't understand you. Did the wraith leave?"

"You sidestep well." Mal grinned at the older Horseman. "And it disappeared after a few moments."

"I've had millennia to practice sidestepping," Death said, the thin scar over his cheek nearly invisible when he smiled in return. "Ari's going to grouse if you keep him waiting."

Mal chewed on the inside of his bottom lip, unsure of what to think. He'd already made a mess of things among humans once. The world was still reeling from his need to prove himself to the older Horsemen. He wasn't quite ready to jump back into the thick of things when his first disaster had crept through entire regions, wiping out innocents without any regard to race or gender.

"Are you sure about me going?" Mal glanced up, a sheen of light sliding over his glasses. "Can this thing with Ari wait until you come back?"

"I have to answer a calling in a few hours," Death replied, sweeping the discarded rinds into the palm of his hand. "You and Min might have to follow my trail in a couple of days. We'll have to see how it goes."

Death's face stilled, a placid mask of nothingness that hid more secrets than Mal could even imagine. He knew why Death would not be coming with them and why Ari bristled and walked away.

Only one thing brought out a brittle anger from Ari. Something large and horrible would happen during the night, and Death would be forced to walk among dying humans to pull them out of the now and into the beyond.

Mal knew about horror, but not on the scale that Death dealt with.

Mal had been jubilant when his first plague struck. As thousands died, he knew those deaths were necessary, sacrifices made to bind humanity together. The world should have rallied to beat the virus Mal developed and let loose.

Instead, as more died and tolerance waned, leaders rose up, proclaiming the sick deserved their deaths. Soon no one was safe from the disease, and Mal then realized what he'd let loose, an illness twisted into hatred. Mal took a good hard look at the chaos and where it would lead.

And wept hard.

Death was there. As everything crumbled and his wondrous plan to shape society into a kinder, more giving community shattered under a zealous condemnation, Death was there for him, for the shattered Pestilence who had let his ego and arrogance overwhelm him. Death gave comfort in words, with cups of hot steaming tea, and reminded him that they were to be outside of humanity, to be above changing society and to let mankind evolve or devolve as it needed to. Free will drove mankind. The Horsemen could only react and sometimes influence.

"Remember that you… we… are human, even as we're now, for all intents and purposes, immortal. We have their flaws. We have their strengths. We are pulled from our deaths to serve," Death told him then. "None of us are perfect. The Horsemen are here to give mankind an avenue for hope. We do despicable things and try to have faith that mankind will rise to that challenge we have put down before them. That is our purpose, Pestilence."

"I'm sorry." Mal stumbled over his words. "I wasn't thinking. It'll be good to get out even if it is with Ari."

"It's about time you pulled your weight in things." Ari rejoined them, hair tousled dry. Pulling on a leather jacket, worn soft from years of wear, Ari walked into the kitchen area. Nodding at Death, Ari tossed a set of keys in the air and caught them. "Sometimes we have to go chase down shit that nobody else has time for."

"He knows that, Ari," Death replied softly. Sliding from the counter, he let go of Mal's shoulder. "People who see us tend to shy away from me. With good reason."

"Not if they knew you." Mal leaped to Death's defense.

"If they know me, then chances are they've been long dead and are looking for conversation. And the dead tend to be very poor conversationalists." Death grinned, an easy humor on his face. "It's okay, Mal. I'm used to people running from me. It's a fight-or-flight response in humans. Just go with him and try not to let him bully you too much. Or anyone else for that matter."

"Come on, Pest." Ari bumped Mal's shoulder with his own, nearly knocking the younger immortal off his feet.

"I hate it when you call me that." Mal grabbed at the counter, glaring at War. He stepped away from the kitchen area, locating a pair of sneakers he'd left near the sprawl of couches in the main room. Tugging his discarded socks over his feet, Mal listened with half an ear to what the other two were talking about in the kitchen.

"Probably why I do it," Ari muttered, his voice barely dropped to a whisper. Drawing close to Death, Ari stood nearly nose-to-nose to him, breaths intermingling. "I don't know if you'll be here when we get back."

"Probably not." Death shook his head. "I'll be gone for hours, maybe. That area is packed with people, and they're disposable to the government. I'm guessing that there will be little to no emergency response."

"So it'll be bad, then." Ari hooked his thumbs into the belt loops on his jeans. He didn't trust himself to touch Death. Anger trembled in his belly at the thought of the Horseman wading through dying bodies, trying to sort out who needed to be convinced to move along. Sending a small prayer to what he suspected was a deaf God, Ari hoped for a heavy rain to slow down the fire's progress and give people a chance to escape. "Do you want me to join you if we get back before you do?"

"What can you do there?" Death cocked his head, a play of shadows and light. "Tensions and emotions will be high. Your being there might lead to riots."

"I'll be glad to start a riot for you—" Ari cut his words off with a salacious grin. "But that can wait until you come back. Let me just take the kid with me and see how much trouble we can get into."

"Please don't get arrested." Death reluctantly pulled himself away from Ari's warmth, heading down the hall toward his own rooms. "You'll have to wait until I can bail you out. Min's off in Africa doing something horrendous and probably won't be back until tomorrow."

"Just take care of yourself, Shi," Ari muttered as he watched Death disappear into his rooms. Glancing at Mal, he sighed heavily. The last thing he wanted to do was drag the young immortal along. "Guess I'm stuck with you."

"I'd tell you Death said to play nice, but that'll just piss you off." Mal fell into step, trying to keep up with Ari, whose strides outmatched even Mal's long legs.

"I'd know you were lying." Ari punched at the elevator button. "Death gave up telling me to play nice eons ago. Now he just tells people I'm an asshole, and they have to live with it."

Chapter Two

Butterflies.

Simple creatures. Innocuous. Spending their days looking pretty and sipping sugar. A simple life.

Sweet and harmless.

They never crawled back out of the skin once they were inked. Nope, Kismet thought as he added a bit of red to a wing, butterflies always stayed where they were placed. They remained under the skin, never unfurling spiral tongues to lap at the blood welling up around the tattooed lines.

Kismet hated butterflies. Hated tattooing them. Hated seeing them.

There was no life to them, he decided, cocking his head to look at the spray of insects he'd laid down on a blonde's hip. Slender creatures, barely able to take the brunt of a strong wind. It was ironic that people melted at the sight of a butterfly on the wind. Cockroaches were more admirable. Survivors of hatred and stomping feet. A butterfly's life was a short, easy thing. Roaches were probably plotting their downfall, a massive genocide of the prettier brethren.

Either that or coming up with ways to make themselves prettier. For the most part, pretty survived brutality.

And usually attracted it.

Oh, he knew how much beauty attracted the cruelties of predators, Kismet snorted under his breath. Lost in his own thoughts, he concentrated solely on the stippling of hues across his unforgiving canvas. Another dash of blue and then a deeper shade to pull the wing out of a stilled flutter, giving it depth.

His client murmured under him, a low moan that sounded sexual. Her fingers touched the nape of his neck, stroking at the long brown strands. The touch made him start, jerking him from his contemplation of butterflies and roaches. A smile was on her face, a heavy-lidded look thickening her eyes. He knew that look. Kismet knew it too well.

"I'm almost done." Pursing his lips, he turned back to the paper cups of ink he'd placed on top of the plastic cabriolet, then cleaned off his machine before dipping the needle tips into a vibrant yellow. The book of butterflies she'd brought with her gave him some idea on how the hues would look against one another, nature being generous with the nectar-drinkers' clothing.

"Good, because this really hurts." A toss of her hair over one shoulder was an invitation of sorts, he figured. So was the trailing touch across his lips. He could feel the shift of heat over her stomach, the scent of her sweetness in his nose. "What are you doing tonight? We're having a party. You could come over. I can introduce you around when I show off my new tat."

"Ah, I don't know. I've got some things I have to do tonight." Kismet shook his head, keeping his eyes down.

That was a mistake. One he realized as soon as he did it. Curled under the counter ledge was his brother, Chase, his young body pulled in so his knees could serve as mountains to the ponies he made with his fingers. Enormous eyes peered out from under Chase's mop of hair, a little boy's innocence that Kismet had lost long ago.

He knew exactly when he'd lost that naiveté. The morning he woke up and found his brother's cold, lifeless body next to him, Kismet felt every scrap of innocence whisper away in the morning light. His childhood washed away from him in the shower when he'd stood under the water, watching the crusted remains of Chase's blood and his own turn the tiles pink.

The innocence in the ghost's eyes never left. It was the only thing Kismet was truly glad for.

The specter continued playing with his imaginary pets, stables of long-legged mounts galloping over rugged hills. As Kismet's feet passed through Chase's leg, the clustered shadows stuttered, broken into slats of darkness before righting again, leaving the gray-faced boy as solid as he ever could be.

"You're cute, you know." A whisper of an offer lay in her voice. Kismet knew that game too. "Like one of my butterflies."

"I'd rather be one of the roaches," he muttered, keeping his dark brown eyes down. Finding the spot he wanted to dash over with a buttery yellow, he stretched her hip taut, the black of his gloves a latex bruise on her pale skin. "Stay still for a bit. I'm almost done."

He avoided talking while he inked, much to Nick's disgust. The shop owner constantly hounded him to keep up a patter with his clients, but Kismet found it too distracting. It was hard enough painting with needles. Talking to his canvas was more trouble than it was worth. People tended to move when they talked. He couldn't paint over a mistake when he tattooed. Acrylics were much more forgiving but definitely didn't pay as much.

If he could figure out a way to make tattooing dead people profitable, he'd be all set.

"I'm doing this for my mom," the blonde said suddenly. "She loved butterflies. She died when I was young."

"Shit. Fucking Nick." Kismet nearly lost his grip on the machine, pulling it back before he did any damage. "Should have told me before. I don't do portraits or memorials."

"He told me that, but I thought I should at least tell you." She blinked, her eyes watering. "So you knew how much this means to me. Doesn't that make it better? You're not going to stop, are you?"

Kismet wanted to stand up and walk off, his fingers clenched tight around the stilled machine. Closing his eyes, he took a deep breath, trying to find some sort of calm in his thoughts. *The only thing hanging around you today has been Chase*, he scolded himself. No other shadow. No other faces peering out from the darkness. *Her mother is probably long gone, left someplace else.*

Not everyone carries their horrors with them, Kismet's mind whispered. Only the guilty drag their ghosts behind them.

"No, it's okay." He shook off the crawling pinpricks under his skin. "I understand what it's like to miss family."

Opening his eyes, he stared around her, finding nothing but dust motes floating in the late afternoon sun. The studio was quiet except for the low tick-ticking of machines and an occasional burst of laughter from one of the other artists as they talked to their clients. He could hear Nick on the phone in the front, a clear shower curtain painted with flash art blocking Kismet's view of the waiting area and high reception counter.

The last thing he wanted was to embed someone's ghost into their skin. He knew people lied about how much they loved someone. He knew that oftentimes, people lied about how their loved ones died. Kismet heard more tales of heroic tragedy than he cared to admit. Those customers were usually accompanied by the tattered remains of a human being lurking behind them, faces battered apart from angry fists or torn open from gunshot wounds.

He'd refused to do portraits on the day he saw a little girl standing behind her mother, her legs sticky with blood and her eyes swollen from tears. The woman's story of her daughter drowning didn't persuade him. Nor did Nick's promise of a full take from the ink. It was the pain in the girl's eyes that turned him away. It made him thankful for Chase's ignorance.

It also made him believe people wanted trophies for their pain. Either from guilt or in some sick, triumphant thrill. He wouldn't be a part of cementing that little girl, or any of the dead, into someone's skin. He still had hope that Chase would move on one day.

He'd long wondered if he forced Chase's soul to stay with him, either because he'd been way too young to understand that his brother was dead or because the ghost, like Kismet, had no one else to be around. It was hard to let go of the only person you'd ever felt love for, Kismet reasoned.

"Hey, you okay?" The girl touched him again, the chill of her fingertips a shock against the flush of his cheeks.

Jerking away, Kismet swallowed hard, his hands trembling. Exhaling, he nodded. "Yeah, I'm fine. Just don't tell anyone that I did this. If I make an exception for you, then I've got to do other people. I'll take it up with Nick later."

"I didn't mean to get him into trouble."

"How much trouble could I be?" Kismet laughed, a bitter sound. He shifted his long legs until they were firm under the massage table he used to ink clients on. "Nick owns the place. I'm just a squatter in one of the stalls."

The cleanup was quick, a wash of antiseptic and the requisite explanation of how to care for tattooed skin. He spent a few seconds explaining the scabbing process and that it was going to look like she had ink coming up for a couple of days. She'd not liked that. She liked it even less when he suggested she keep it covered for a day or two so the scabs could form without getting her clothes ruined.

"People like to look at their tats, Andreas." One of the other artists came out of his area, looking with disgust at the sterile packing pads Kismet used to cover new ink. "Plastic wrap is the way to go, Andreas."

"People aren't sandwiches, Mike. They don't need to be kept fresh," he replied, stepping around Chase's feet. When possible he avoided the ghost. It was hardly ever possible. "New ink under wrap looks like a fucking fruit cocktail Jell-O mold gone bad."

"Just saying, princess." Mike leaned on the half wall between them. "People like to show off that they've just gone through a lot of fucking pain. It's human nature."

Kismet ignored him, dropping his gear into one of the autoclaves. He'd been called worse things since he'd first started working at Steel Sin. Some of them he even agreed with. He finished cleaning up, crumpled the table's paper sheeting, used inking cups, and towels together, then dumped all of it into the biohazard can.

"Hey, baby." He felt Nick's hand on his side. The older man's fingers lifted the hem of his shirt and slid under the fabric, his touch running along the dip of Kismet's spine. "That was a nice piece you just did. I got a picture of it for your book. I even put the packing back."

"Should have told me it was for her mother." Kismet stepped free, breaking the contact. He knew it was pissy of him to stay mad at Nick. The man didn't understand the reasons behind his revulsion. He couldn't expect Nick to respect what seemed like an unreasonable quirk.

But then how do you tell someone that you feared sealing a soul to someone else's body?

Nick was too realistic of a person to accept that as a reason. Better to lay his oddness at just being crazy. Kismet figured he might as well use the reputation for insanity that seemed to dog him.

"You wouldn't have done it. And kid, you need the money." Nick produced a sheaf of bills from his pocket. "Here, no take for the studio. It's all yours."

"They're going to be pissed off when they find out about it." Kismet glanced over his shoulder, as if the other artists were peeking into his area. Nick had closed the curtain behind him, leaving them secluded and hidden from view. Despite his protests, Kismet slid the cash into his pocket. His wallet was too lean to worry about how the others felt about him pocketing the whole take.

"I own the place." Nick leaned against the counter, his feet passing through Chase's legs. "They can go fuck themselves."

The waning afternoon sunlight backlit the older man's dark hair, plunging his face into shadow.

Nick pulled at the inker's wrist, dragging him over to stand between his legs. Nick's teeth flashed wide in his tanned craggy face, his broad body dominating Kismet's slender frame.

"Thanks." Kismet meant it. He had nothing but gratitude for the things Nick did for him. The man apprenticed him and let him use a stall when he needed cash. "I owe you."

"I like you owing me." Nick maneuvered Kismet closer, weaving his fingers together behind the young man's back. "You doing okay?"

He wasn't surprised at Nick's seemingly sincere concern. Nick would prey upon any weakness shown. Admitting to weakness would be like a pig handing the butcher a newly sharpened knife. The older man grinned at Kismet's slight frown, quirking his thin mouth. Nodding, he tried not to shiver when Nick's hands wandered, the man's fingers reaching down past his waistband. "Yeah, I'm fine. Just getting the itches, you know?"

"Ah, got something for that." The man grinned, leaning in to nibble at Kismet's earlobe. "Check my front pocket."

They'd played this game for years, starting when Kismet was around eleven and Nick came around to party with Kismet's mother. The man's pocket held candy or gum back then. Now it held a different kind of sweet. Kismet dug into the denim sleeve, finding the latex roll inside. After tugging the heroin pack free, Kismet weighed it in his palm, gauging how much he'd have to owe Nick for the drug.

"How much?" It was another game they played, guessing of how much money Nick would want back from the take. For all of his gratitude for what Nick did for him, Kismet was very much aware that the man's kindness often came with a high price. Sometimes money wasn't what Nick wanted. Kismet was too tired and on edge to fall into that kind of payment. He wanted to go home, take the need down, and paint on something that didn't move.

"Stick around for a bit." Nick's mouth was hot on his throat, a searing trail of wet Kismet wanted to wipe clean. "I'm sure I can find a few things for you to do for it."

"You've got me confused with my mother." Kismet stepped away as far as he could, disengaging himself from Nick's embrace. "I'm not a whore."

"If your mom hadn't been a whore, you wouldn't be standing here right now. You should give thanks to your mom's whoring. Besides, without me sniffing around looking for some, I wouldn't have gotten to know you. Then where would you be?"

"I'm not her. Just don't confuse us. I pay for what I take. I don't do people to get shit handed to me."

"You look like her, you know. All long legs and soft brown eyes. She was blonde, though. I like the brown hair you got. It's like coffee." The older man stared at the lean young artist standing in front of him. "You're as pretty as she was. Although you're probably better in bed than she ever could be. Your mother was a frigid bitch. Even as cold as you are, you're a better lay than she was, Kiz."

"Focus, Nicky. How much?" Kismet dangled the latex ball from his fingertips. "I don't want to owe you anything."

"You owe me everything, Kizzie." The caustic reminder burned nearly as much as the kiss Nick stole from him. "Keep it. You don't owe me anything for it."

"You sure?" Nick's generosity made him suspicious. The roll had to hold at least five hits, more than enough to tide him over for a week, maybe two if he was careful. "How come?"

"Nobody but you likes this shit. It makes everyone else nuts. You're the only one who doesn't get weird on it." Nick shrugged, his gaze following Kismet's. "I told the guy I didn't want to deal it for him anymore. Hard to unload it when I've only got one customer that does it. Baby, I don't care how hot you are, I'm not taking some shit in that I can't sell off."

"Guess it helps to already be crazy." He tried to keep his fingers calm, but the tremors working down his arm were difficult to control. The bite of his addiction was rising, uncoiling into his blood. He'd have to feed it soon, or the sweats would start and then the clenching in his guts.

"Don't kill yourself. That's all I ask." Nick pushed away from the counter, trapping Kismet's wrist in his fingers. The grip was hard, nearly bruising the young man down to the bone. "Don't want to lose you to this shit."

"Shouldn't have gotten me started on the stuff to begin with, then," he shot back, tilting his head to stare up at the taller man.

The first time he'd taken a taste, he'd been in Nick's bed, sprawled on dirty sheets and wondering why there was a party going on around him. With every breath the darkness circled closer, the ghosts and faces caught in the folds of shadows nearly drowning Kismet. Fear paralyzed him, and alcohol was no longer enough to keep the monsters at bay. His body ached in places where claws dug down into his skin, red furrows that disappeared after a few minutes, but the burn remained, invisible agonies that drove Kismet insane.

A bite of steel into his vein cured that. The floating nirvana left behind a detached peace that Kismet clung to. Drops of pearled powder became his salvation as the world grew darker. His mind begged for the cessation of nightmares that stalked him, and soon his body wept for the taste of bitterness a needle could bring him.

He owed his sanity to Nick. Hell, Kismet thought, I should kiss Nick's feet for pushing that needle into me. There were days when he thought the drug was the only thing keeping him alive.

Those were also the days when he wondered why he was even trying.

KISMET TUCKED his hands deep into his jeans, feeling at the money he'd shoved up in his pocket. The ball of latex rubbed on his thumb, a promised calm in its crumble. At the moment all he wanted was a lungful of sweet smoke and sleep. His stomach and veins could wait until he woke up before he took care of their needs. Well, maybe his stomach, Kismet thought. He'd have to see how much longer he could go before he cracked open the knot on the packet.

The College Area hadn't changed much since his birth, a cesspool of the hopeless and unwashed for as long as he could remember. Much of his childhood had been spent within a five-mile radius of where he lived now, sometimes sheltered by four walls. Other times they huddled in the front seat of a parked car trying to sleep while his mother grunted out slack pleasure for the man lying soft and wet on her skinny body.

Kismet felt like as much of a street fixture as the transient population of whores and their keepers.

He'd grown up among them, and now as an adult, he could walk casually through the familiar grime, draped in loose T-shirts and jeans splattered with painted bruised acrylics, a pale ghost drifting past lives more broken than his own.

A grim-faced Latino stepped out from a doorway niche, his face ripe for a challenge. His companion grabbed at his elbow, nodding at the artist, his voice a low whisper. Kismet knew the whispers well… knew what was being said, often while he was still in earshot. He didn't think there was anyone left who hadn't heard that he was insane. All in all, it wasn't a bad reputation to have among people who were looking for a warm body to take money from. Crazy seemed to keep people back. In Kismet's mind, he couldn't have asked for a better set of armor.

"Kizzie."

Kismet kept walking, his eyes fixed on the storefront at the corner. He paced off his steps, counting each break in the sidewalk in silent progression. Kismet no longer searched for the slip of darkness hiding in the side of his vision. He knew where Chase would be, lurking and stalking his waking thoughts. The ring of a bell sounded when he entered the convenience store, an electronic blip signaling his entrance to the clerk sequestered behind a steel cage.

The swarthy man nodded at him as he entered, pulling a pack of clove cigarettes from a slot on the wall. Kismet motioned for another, unsure of when he'd be as flush with money as he was right now. Placing the packs on the counter, the clerk moved to ring up the purchase, stopped by the contemplative look on Kismet's face.

"You want something else?" The man glanced at the locked cabinets of alcohol behind him. "Maybe something to put the color back in your face? I still got some of that Buckfast."

"Yeah, that'll work." Kismet cleared his throat. The clerk didn't hear the shuffle of tiny feet on the broken linoleum floor or see the bouncing head of hair as Chase gripped the counter with ghostly hands, springing up and down on the balls of his bare feet.

"Candy. Candy. Candy. I want some candy." Kismet closed his eyes for a brief second, watching the man turn his back before acknowledging the apparition next to him. Chase's round eyes were as gray as the rest of his body, a whitewash of nothingness turned ashen in death. "Do we have money for candy?"

The ghost wouldn't go away until Kismet acknowledged it, a puppet his sick brain strung through the theater of his thoughts. Faded, the specter pushed and pulled through the air, struggling to maintain cohesiveness while Kismet attempted to bury his madness behind a solid wall of logic. Drugged or drunk, the phantasms hounding him faded into the background. When he was sober, they took on full form, his young dead brother being his most constant companion.

He needed to take care of his sobriety. At the very least, drink the edge off it.

"What kind do you want?" The click of a key in the cabinet lock and then footsteps warned Kismet of the man's return. He kept his voice low, not wanting the clerk to hear him. His dead brother's face lit up, and Kismet busied himself by looking over the selection of sweets set under the counter's edge, his hand hovering over the boxes. "Pick one, Chase. Before that guy comes back."

"Chocolate. A big one." Chase bounced again, his body wavering at the edges with a smoky mist.

Kismet grabbed a bar wrapped in brown paper and foil, then slid it onto the counter next to the cloves. Tossing down the cash, he took the bag from the clerk's hand, nodding a farewell before heading out the door, blinking at the tears in his eyes.

Cutting through the parking lot, Kismet turned into the alley behind the store, Chase's singsong chant of chocolate echoing in his ears. The blue roof of his motel poked out coyly above the squat buildings nearby, the sky hue vibrant amid the gray. As he approached the motel, Chase's voice softened before falling away, hiding from the light.

A lean form huddled against one of the dumpsters at the side of the motel, the battered hunter green metal providing little shelter from the elements. Her tobacco-tinted hair a tangled mess around her worn face, the woman blearily looked up from picking at her fingernails, the cuticles raw and bleeding.

Black stumps poked up from her gums, teeth rotten down into the root. She waved out a bony hand, sun-dried fingers stained sienna from cigarettes, her gaze dropping to the pavement. Kismet stepped in close, crouching at the woman's side, placing a five-dollar bill in her outstretched palm.

"Hey, Lucy." He spoke softly. Kismet kept his breathing low, trying not to pull the stink of her unwashed body into his nose. Dried urine caked dirt at her crotch, the stale clotted grease of human skin rank in his throat. She was a familiar sight. He hurt every time he saw her.

The woman raised her face, weathered and beaten skin stretched thin over her blunt facial bones. There was nothing left of the laughing beauty who had slipped him money for a hamburger or candy, one of his mother's many casual friends who were quick to baby the pretty-faced boy running wild among them. Now she just looked wrinkled and parched dry of life.

"Kizzie!" she exclaimed, her breath fouled by the drugs eating off the enamel on her teeth. Lucy patted the damp ground beside her, more comfortable sitting in a garbage-strewn alley than most women would be in a fine parlor. "Sit down. You shouldn't give me money. Keep it. You need it more."

"I got some ink done today. I've got enough," he murmured. She'd given him a place to crash when he'd first been turned out by one of his mother's lovers. Money was the least he could give the broken woman sitting at his feet.

With her face turned up to him, Kismet spotted the writhing black tadpoles eating away at the sores in her skin. Without anything in his system, he saw the shapes clearly, vicious chewing shadows wiggling to pull bits of her flesh into wide, razor-lined mouths. They consumed her sanity; Kismet was sure of it. One in particular nearly pushed in through her cornea, its head enveloped by the clear membrane. Kismet cracked open the fortified wine nearly hidden in the sack, took a hefty swig, then passed it to Lucy, his teeth worrying at his lower lip.

"You're not taking your meds, Luce." Kismet swallowed the mouthful, grunting at the burn of his soft throat tissues. "You know you have to."

"They make me… crazy, Kizzie." Lucy held the bottle with both hands, trembling as she raised it to her mouth. Widening her jaw, she splashed a dollop into her gullet, not touching the mouth of the bottle to her lips. "I can't think when I've got one of those things in me."

"Lucy, you have to take them. And you're supposed to keep taking them until your body gets used to them. You just can't stop because you're feeling better." Kismet helped Lucy take another swig, holding the end of the vessel before taking it back, filling his mouth with the numbing liquid. "Stay still. I've got to get this crap off of you."

When he was young, he'd watched the small shadows eating away at his mother's breasts, slithering trails of eyeless creatures working under her skin until nothing remained but very real pocked scars and a burned blemish on her pale flesh. Over the years, the people who drifted through his life were often riddled with the inky dollops, sometimes dripping from sores on their faces or arms, all the while oblivious to the creatures feeding on them.

Kismet still checked his own body when he was sober enough to see, looking for the telltale divots of forming tails over his crotch or heart. He hated the things. More than hating the touch of them on his skin, he hated the stink they left behind when he pulled them off someone, their wriggling and screaming shapes twisting between his pinches.

Steeling himself, Kismet plucked at the one fixed under Lucy's eye, peeling it free from her lashes. As he pulled it off, he crushed it between his fingers, its high-pitched squeal cut off in midscream. Gagging at the rank odor, he worked carefully over the woman's face and shoulders, removing what he could see. Fighting an overwhelming urge to puke, he dug through the matted, greasy locks around her neck, unwinding a long, serpentine trail from behind her ear.

With a final inspection, Kismet dug through Lucy's belongings, a faded crocheted knapsack run brown with dirt. She protested the intrusion, silenced only when Kismet passed over the bottle, muttering under his breath for her to keep it. The woman squirmed about, her legs hooking around Kismet's ankles, nearly toppling him into her wastes. A brown plastic container rattled when he grabbed at it, the pills inside dusty from being tossed around during her daily travels.

"Here, take one." Kismet steadied himself, resting a kneecap on the wall next to Lucy's head.

He shook out a dose, then held it for Lucy to take.

"I only have the stuff here." Lucy held up the bottle, her trembling hand shaking the container. "Doctors said I shouldn't drink as much."

"Yeah, well, chances are I won't tell the doctor that you've taken a hit with your drugs." Kismet stroked at the woman's temple, weary to his bones. She slurped at the bottle, cradling the wine to her chest and burping delicately behind her free hand. "You doing okay, Lucy?"

It wasn't hard to reconcile the beaten, sparse woman sitting in cast-off clothes and runoff fluids with the brassy, come-hither flirt who ran around with his mother. He'd seen others decline, a well-traveled path they all seemed to take. Kismet figured Lucy was merely keeping his own place warm in the meantime, the alleyway sheltered from the wind, although the flat side of the building offered no protection from the harsh San Diego sun. One day she would drop out of sight, a rumor of a person leaving nothing behind but a drying stain.

"You tell your mom I said hi. And tell her not to be a stranger." Lucy's faded brown eyes peered up at him, a flicker of something in their depths. It was funny how often she'd spoken of the woman they both barely knew, never seeming to remember his mother died years before. "You take care of her."

"Sure, Lucy." Kismet forced himself to kiss her forehead, tasting the smear of rank shadow on her skin. It crept into his tongue, burning bitter and spreading thin in his spit. Taking only the cloves, he left her with the Buckfast and chocolate.

The side gate let him into the cracked paved courtyard a few doors down from his room. At some point in the motel's history, someone optimistic tiled the edge of the sidewalk with festive turquoise tiles. Time had faded most of the colors, but a glimmer of sand-frozen sky remained in the traces along the wall.

Closing the wrought iron gate behind him, Kismet stood in the cold, the sky nearly burned free of the day.

Opening the door, Kismet reached for the light switch, driving back the dimness in the room. The stench of the wraiths clung to his hands, foul and greasy when he rubbed his palms together, hoping to get a hint of warmth under his skin. A quick washing in the tiny bathroom took most of the stink off. Just a lingering moldy smell caught under his nails, the shadows' rank ooze spurting under his pressed fingers and staining his nail tips.

A dresser drawer held a stash of half-full bottles, a vodka, cheaper and rawer than the Buckfast he'd given Lucy, and a few off-colored tequilas. Kismet seriously doubted agave had any part in the making of the tequila, its taste more like the thinner he used when oil painting than anything else.

His back ached from being hunched over, and his arms throbbed from the rattle of the machine. The stress on his shoulders tugged along the ache in his muscles, tight and knotted from staying in one place too long. If he made more money, he would get one of the chairs the others used. Of course he'd have to work more to make more money. Kismet wasn't sure if he could stand the assholes working at Steel Sin long enough to earn enough for the chair.

He snagged the vodka from the drawer, then unscrewed the top. Kicking off his shoes first, Kismet slouched down on the lumpy queen-sized bed dominating the room. His paintings took up most of the spare space near the bathroom door, stacked like tossed-away card soldiers. The canvas he currently argued with sat waiting on the easel, pencil marks loosely creating a framework for the nightmares that crawled out of his imagination and onto the stretched white fabric.

The first gulp kicked him back, nearly making him choke. He needed to hold off the needle until he'd gotten some sleep and food so he could spend the night painting. If he was lucky, he could get one of the large pieces finished. The blankness bothered him. There were things that needed filling in.

The nightmares waiting in the darkness had other ideas for his evening.

A stygian mass curled up over the edge of his bed, weaving through the broken filament stitching of the bed's comforter. Kismet swallowed, pulling his feet up, hoping to keep his toes out of the creeping shadow's reach. Talons clawed free of the shadow, a sibilant menace gleaming in its crimson eyes.

Blinking, the young man shook off the dread in his belly, willing the figment away with a whispered prayer.

"Shit." He nearly fumbled the bottle over the edge of the mattress, a large splash of the potent liquor soaking into the battered industrial carpet. Licking at his fingers, Kismet suckled the coarse fluid, choking at its sting. "Come on, Kiz. Keep it together. This shit's not real. It's never real. Just crap that your brain makes up."

Kismet gulped at the bottle, and the acidic liquid hit the back of his throat. The oozing dark crawling toward him shimmered, pieces of the flotilla roiling beneath the slick, oily surface of its skin. The thing pulsed, growing thicker until it formed a wide, flat body. It approached cautiously, sinking into the bedspread as it hooked its claws into the fabric, a trail of loose soot marking its progress.

When he was young, the shadows were a welcome diversion at first, a break from the hunger in his belly. When the faces took on familiar forms, hands reaching inside of him and pleading for surcease, he turned to the mind-numbing comfort of his vices, keeping the shadows at bay. Now they took the shape of monsters, fangs and red eyes glowing out from pitch molasses, snapping jaws or reaching talons raking at his vulnerability.

The vodka would serve as a stopgap, a foul-tasting placebo compared to the bite of steel into his veins. Heroin gave him some space from the shadows, but used too much, it would blunt the river of images he needed to paint in order to clear his mind. Used too little, the shadows would feed on him while he lay helpless beneath their raging maws, little bits of his soul consumed in pinprick appetizers. He just wasn't ready for the drug yet. If he took it now, the early-morning hours would be haunted by demons he couldn't get away from.

But the shadows rarely attacked him until all of his defenses were worn thin. He wasn't so far along that he needed drugs. Kismet knew he'd had hours before they would have closed in. The rules were changed. And no one had told him.

A man's voice hid under the creature's low, rumbling growl. Kismet heard snatches of conversation, a low drone buzzing behind the words. Kismet's bare ankle burned where claws ran over his skin, red welts bubbling to raised peaks with frightening quickness.

Choking on the mouthful of vomit on his tongue, Kismet spat, gasping for air. He hurt. Deep inside of his skull, a hurt burned away his thoughts until he wanted to claw his eyes out, anything to make the pain stop. Another sharp stab of agony lit up the back of his head, and Kismet cried out, twisting as he grabbed at his hair.

Fighting to stay above the pain, Kismet forced himself to swallow again, the bile in his stomach rising to fight the influx of vodka. Willing the creature away, he felt something shift inside his brain, a breach of fluids popping suddenly behind his eyes. Fiery agony ran loose in his nerves, hitting the soft spots of his temples and curdling his testicles up into the hollow between his thighs. Crying, he struggled to be free of the creature, flailing wildly. The bottle tilted over, its meager contents splashing out and running into puddles over the moisture-resistant comforter.

He followed the bottle with a tight-boned tumble onto the floor.

The smell of the carpet hit Kismet's face, a stale sourness reeking of puke and piss. A hiccup brought up a mouthful of his own belly's fluids, the rough scratch of the rug pile harsh against his skin. Slithering over the edge of the bed, the creature's mouth reached for the front of Kismet's face, its lower jaw unhinging to bite at his skull. Kismet barely heard the echo of the man's voice again, a barking order stopping the large wraith.

The air folded up around the creature, spines of wind snapping through its body and shoving it back into the curtain of shadows. It left nothing behind except the stink of its oily scent.

A final burst of white washed his vision clear, and Kismet felt his body surrender. Welcoming the numbness seeping into his bones, he let go, allowing a heavy slumber to settle over him. If the creature came back, he thought before the hard blackness tugged him under, it could have him.

CHAPTER THREE

THE ELEVATOR air shifted cold as the Veil thickened around them, a perceptible chill in their bones. Ari no longer felt the slicing cold, but Mal still shivered at its touch. Glancing at Pestilence, Ari kept his grin tight and began humming, a short ditty about a girl from Brazil, as the lift slid down into the garage.

"That's annoying," Mal commented, stepping from the elevator when the doors opened into the garage.

"Yep." Ari jingled his keys. "That's what makes it so fun."

Mal wasn't sure who paid for the private garage level or, for that matter, the two-storied penthouse they lived in, four quarters divided around a large living space and kitchen area. The enormous dining room meant to host dinner parties instead was a training room for the Horsemen, its walls pitted and scored from mock battles. When asked about finances and the like, Death shrugged and told him it was taken care of.

Mal hated secrets, and Death had many.

The garage's low lights glowed a sickly tangerine. The level's retaining walls came up nearly to Ari's chest, thick expanses of grooved slats, nearly blocking the skyline vista. Shadows pooled thickly on the ground and lapped at the occasional column, dust blurring the white painted lines on the ground. As they walked, the Horsemen's shoes made hollow sounds, echoing against the emptiness of the private level.

Ari's sleek red Mustang chirruped in response to his thumbing the alarm. He missed his old one, a broad Grande Coupe from the '60s, but it met a tragic death. He'd fallen in love with the reissued Pony, grinning like a young boy with a new plaything when he brought it home. Death properly admired it. Min showed her disgust at being dragged down to the garage to look at a chunk of steel. He'd not asked Mal his opinion, and he'd tried to pretend it didn't matter, but Mal beamed when Ari took him for a drive down to Ocean Beach, the car screaming around the tight curves of Point Loma in the middle of the night.

"I could drive," Mal offered, longingly glancing at his reliable SUV, a squat monster of hammered steel and much safer on the road than Ari's car. Min's motorcycle leaned on its stands next to Death's ashen Aston Martin, a fine layer of dust coating the Vanquish's gleaming waxed metal skin. Ari snorted at Mal's suggestion, hooking his hand into the Mustang's door handle.

"You could walk." Ari cast a glance over his shoulder, jerking his head toward the passenger side of the car.

"I think you're scared of my driving. Big bad Ari is frightened of my SUV." Mal stepped toward the Mustang.

And slipped on a puddle of shadow.

Arms flailing, Mal fought to regain his footing as a hand rose from the inky black. The hand's claws stretched upward and tore into the cement as the creature pulled itself up. Elongated arms, spindly and thin, snapped forward, digging long hands into Mal's leg. A head appeared, red eyes nictitating in a featureless oval. Its skull stretched out into a point, a jutting jaw bristling with brilliant white teeth.

The creature's squat round body swallowed the light, shaking itself free from the ground and opening its maw to snarl at War. Pulling free, its legs shook out, three truncated limbs ending in nearly flipper-like appendages, wide to balance its heavy body. Keeping a firm grip on its captured prey, the Veiled creature licked its lipless mouth, a dusky serpentine tongue dripping saliva on Mal's sneaker.

Mal twisted, his leg burning where the creature's nails dug into his skin. Shouting for Ari, Mal clawed at the creature's hand, working his fingers under its talons to break loose its grip. It tightened its hold, bending Mal's fingers back until they strained under the effort of fighting the creature's strength. He kicked out with his free foot, slamming the wraith across the forehead. A tilt of its jaw giving under the blow gave him little comfort when its head slid back down, mouth widening over his stomach. A popping noise drove panic though Mal as the creature's distended jaw opened wide, easily leaving more than enough space to fit his rib cage into its mouth.

"Shit," Mal hissed, eyes widening, shock creeping into his limbs. Nearly numb from the pain in his leg, he caught a blur of movement to the side of the creature. Relief flooded through him when he saw War easing around the Mustang.

The wraith's right eye jerked to the side, catching sight of Ari, a single crimson orb bright in its deep sockets. The creature growled deep in its chest, warning the immortal off its prey as War circled, wary of the snapping mouth, sharp teeth glistening in the muddy light. Sliding a long knife from its sheath at his back, Ari drew near, testing the creature's reflexes.

Threatened by the more powerful predator, the creature reacted in a panic. It struck, flinging Mal at the crouching War. The immortal flew wide, his body loose from the shock of leaving the creature's grip, and he windmilled, trying to right himself. War lunged, trying to get a hold on him as the youngest Horseman flew by, his fingers a few seconds too late.

Mal hit one of the parking garage's cement columns, slamming hard into its solid mass. The world tilted sideways, and a shower of fine grit covered him as he slid down onto the garage floor, ending up facedown in a puddle of oil-slicked water. His lungs ached to recover his wind, desperate to get rid of the pressed-in feeling in his chest. Coughing, he tried to shake off the ringing in his ears, a high-pitched whining that seemed to fade in and out with each breath he took.

Swearing, Ari feinted to the right when the wraith surged forward. With a snap of its jaw, the creature's teeth nearly snagged War's arm. The wraith caught the back of Ari's hand, blood flying in spiraled curls from the cuts. Ari winced and shifted, trying to keep one eye on the creature and another to check on Mal.

"You okay, Pest?" He stabbed at the creature when it lunged, slicing into its cheek. An unearthly howl ripped from the creature's throat, the cold metal burning light down into its face.

Gasping still, Mal choked on his breath, lungs filling with paint flakes and head pounding from striking the column. Clearing his throat, he struggled to stand, hands shaking as he pushed off the floor. Nodding, Mal spat the blood from his mouth, slightly amazed that he retained consciousness.

The rippling pain far surpassed anything Death gave him during his rare sparring bouts.

Incredible aches formed under his throbbing flesh. The others always warned him to be careful. Being immortal didn't mean they didn't feel every bruise and shattered bone until it healed. Mal now understood what Min meant when she said sometimes it would be better if they died just long enough for their bodies to heal.

Cramped with the agony of his twisted body, sharp breaks in his bones knitting under torn skin, Mal wanted to pass out rather than suffer through the prolonged torture of healing, something not open to him at the moment. Ari would never let him live down passing out during a fight. Mal shook off the pinpricks of dizziness, hoping he wouldn't throw up if he stood.

"I'm fine. I think I broke a few things, though." Another cough produced a splatter of red-and-white foam, and his vision swam, refocusing on the small cracks on the garage floor. His hands ached from holding up his weight, and the shadows around him pulsed, pulling away from the Horsemen. "What the hell is going on? And what the hell is that? Is that a wraith?"

"Yeah, let's talk about that a bit later. I'm kind of busy right now, kid." Ari struck, feeling for the creature's reach. It dodged to one side, keeping its head low, tilting sideways to avoid the knife. Watching its reactions carefully, Ari moved in again, slicing upward and meeting empty air.

Bouncing away, the wraith moved in, trying to strike under the man's arm with its gnashing teeth.

Twisting, he drove his dagger down at the wraith's skull, finding a sweet spot between the creature's pupil-devoid eyes. The blade sank down a few inches, stopping short with a shuddering clang when it hit the creature's frontal bone. Its crimson eyes flared with pain when the steel bit down into the darkness of its ether-formed skeletal frame.

Reeling, it struggled to get away from War, claws hitting out in an attempt to injure him. The knife wound gushed, shadowy skin split apart, seeping a viscous oily liquid. Its vision blinded from the ichor pouring from its wound, the wraith thrashed wildly, talons scraping deep into the Vanquish's front quarter panel. Scorched paint, hot from the creature's hands, smoked and peeled off the metal below, the panel neatly folding back from the wraith's talons.

"Shit. Not the car. Come on, not the car," he pleaded. Rage took over when the wraith continued to drive its claws into the fender. Ari stepped in tight against the creature, plunging the dagger into its neck. He drove the blade upward past the swooping curve of its skull, hoping to find a soft spot to reach its miniscule brain. "Fuck, he's going to kill me."

Long strings of pitch mucus spooled out from the cuts, the dagger's runnel filling and emptying with each thrust. The splashing liquid burned, bubbling Ari's skin where it struck his flesh. Shaking off the sting of the creature's poisonous blood, Ari straddled its body, waiting for its final throes.

Keening, the creature gripped at the smoke-stained car, digging enormous grooves into the metal. It reached for Ari, eyes dulling as its essence leaked out onto the garage floor. Sticking its bony elbows outward, it dimpled the car door as it rose to its feet. Panting, straining to maintain its form, it lurched, its body jerking forward before toppling, a stretch of shadow slowly turning stagnant. The creature's remains oozed outward, leeched dry and flat.

Standing over the thinning puddle, Ari nudged at the length of shadow with his boot tip.

Encountering nothing more dangerous than the cast-off shape of Death's damaged car, Ari let out a hiss of hot relief. He flicked the dagger with a quick twist of his wrist, then placed the clean blade back into its sheath.

He spent a moment staring intently at the ruined Aston Martin, wishing he could kick at something, preferably the black nothingness at his feet. Resigned to the damage, he headed back over to Mal.

Mal staggered to his feet, head reeling from the attack. His temple throbbed, and his left leg threatened to give out under him when he put his weight on it. Wincing, Mal touched his forehead, feeling a stickiness under his questing fingers. Drawing his hand down, he stared in amazement at the blood filling his palm.

"I'm bleeding." Mal held his hand up for Ari to see.

"Yeah, I can see that. Won't be the last time either." Ari held up his own hands for Mal to see the healing blisters. "Suck it up, pussy."

Gripping Mal's face, he checked the younger immortal's eyes, peering into the other man's pupils.

Satisfied the boy retained most of his senses, Ari suddenly released him and walked toward Death's ruined car. The shattered bits of cement column crunched beneath Ari's boots as he circled around the crumpled Vanquish.

"Do you see what that thing did to this car?" Running his hands through his hair, Ari gripped the back of his skull, knitting his fingers together in frustration, and moaned low in his throat. "Death's going to be pissed."

"He can't blame you for this." Mal limped over.

Tugging at his jeans, he studied the holes made by the creature's talons. "This wasn't your fault. He won't blame you."

"That's what you think." War snorted derisively. "He still hasn't forgiven me for shooting his horse with a crossbow once."

Swallowing around the lump forming on his tongue where he bit into it, Mal gaped. "You shot his horse?"

"Killed it. An accident, but try telling him that, though." War dismissed the incident with a casual wave of his hand. "Trust me, he's hard to piss off, but once you get him there, he takes forever to forgive. Especially if you kill his horse. I don't even want to think about how pissed off he's going to be about a car. He loves this car. The horse was going to die anyway. I mean, it was a horse. But a car, that should last longer."

"Don't you think he'd be more concerned about a wraith openly attacking us in the garage?" Another mouthful of spit hit the ground, less speckled with blood than the last. Mal filled his tortured lungs with air, trying to catch his breath. "Do you think that was the wraith from upstairs? Should we go tell him?"

"No. Hell no." Ari turned, his face in profile. "We're both fine, and I really don't want to go upstairs to talk to him about his car. We can tell him about this later. We'll play up the saving you part. He likes you. It might make a difference."

Nodding carefully, Mal opened the passenger side door, taking a moment to catch his breath. Easing into the Mustang, he felt his body's tightness release against the cradle of the seat. Leaning his head back did wonders for the ache in his skull. Sighing with a quiet relief, Mal dared a glance at Ari.

"You think the thinning of the Veil's got something to do with that wraith being so aggressive?"

"I'm guessing yes." Face set into a grim mask, Ari started the powerful engine, feeling it throb through the steering wheel. "Wraiths don't attack immortals, certainly not Horsemen. That thing was huge, bigger than the one upstairs was. Must have just smelled the human on us and figured we were prey. I'm hoping there aren't more like that out there."

"We're not that human."

"Human enough. Human enough for it to want to eat us." Ari eased out of the garage, keyed up and watching each length of shadow clustered into distant corners. "Let's see what we can find and come back to Death with some answers. Maybe he'll forgive us about the car."

KISMET WOKE up to pain. It wouldn't have been so bad if it hadn't been a familiar pain. His body was craving to be drugged. It wouldn't leave him alone until he took care of its mewling demands.

Countless invisible spiders crept under his skin, torturous pinpricks digging into his nerves and muscles. His bones felt too tight, cramped up against one another. The dryness in his mouth stank of vomit and the sour taste of cheap vodka. He turned his head, his cheek hitting the hardness of the motel room's matted carpet, a pool of rank wet stretching from under his shoulder blades to the small of his back. It hurt too much to roll over, head pounding from the alcohol he had poured into his stomach the night before. Kismet blinked the grit out of his eyes and tried to sit up.

His belly rebelled, and his world tilted on a crazy axis, the mold-stained paneling on the walls swimming around him. From the smell of things, he had only emptied his stomach on the floor, although, if he didn't hurry, he knew his piss would soon mingle with the carpet's more disgusting fluids.

"I've got to stop waking up like this," Kismet muttered. His face felt bruised, runs of cobalt puffing beneath his eyes. Rubbing his hands over his temples, his fingers shook as the need kicked into his body, leeching his veins dry of every ounce of blood. Each of his twenty-something-odd years was rubbed into his skin, lines Kismet knew would disappear once he'd eaten and gotten some water into him. The bathroom's stained white tiles shifted, and dark splotches appeared in the mottled shower door. Kismet looked away, refusing to be captured by the moving images.

The shower door rattled, a skeletal hand reaching around to let out the specter of a pale-skinned woman who passed through the tub's molded plastic side. He'd seen her before, heard her stumble around in the bathroom as she prepared to walk through the outside door, heading to someplace she never would reach.

The ghost in his room reminded him of Lucy. Stick thin with flat, drooping breasts bleached gray in death, dusky pink nipples plucked hard from a perpetual chill. A large swath of scars marbled her belly and thighs, twisting her skin as she stepped out of the tub and reached for a towel no longer hanging off the bathroom bar, torn from one of its fastenings and dangling down toward the cracked linoleum floor. Broken trails of blue ink, dotted and run together, covered the inside of one of her wrists, a name of someone she once loved and possibly left behind. A patch of hair grew sparsely over her mons, touched with the sparks of gray she washed out of her hair with cheap dye, the straggling mop an intense, solid honey blonde with an inch of peppered black growth hugging her scalp.

She turned, her face caved in on one side, and smiled toothlessly at Kismet, fingers trailing down his naked back until the cold of her touch chilled his spine. Shuddering, he pulled away and swallowed the bile rising in his throat, unable to wrench his eyes from the dangling thread of gore suspending her right eye down over her cheek. He knew without looking that her tongue moved through the gash along her jaw, an entire chunk of her face flapping when she walked. Rotted, her teeth were punctuated with large gaps, gums swollen and purple from infection. He'd seen it all before, and Kismet was growing very tired of her walking through his room.

"Go away." The cold passed over him again and crossed into the main room, where she would disappear within moments of her feet touching the soiled carpet. "You're like every thing in every place that I've lived in. You're not real."

Panting, he pressed his face against his hands, letting the roiling screams in his throat lurch out in quiet sobs. The ache in his belly grew, and his arms throbbed where the nearly healed punctures wept with water, veins tapped dry until they collapsed under the sucking plunge of repeated needles. Kismet knew he'd have to get cleaned up and go looking for something to ease the dragon chewing away bits of him.

"I just need to see what Nick gave me," Kismet mumbled. "That'll take care of it."

He forced himself into the recently vacated tub, then let the lukewarm water from the room's complaining pipes wash over him, scrubbing at his disheveled mane of hair until his scalp tingled. The toothbrush he left in a plastic basket scoured away the fur on his teeth. He'd long since given up looking into mirrors for any length of time. Too many melted faces pressed up against the glass to look back, sometimes reaching through to grab at his face and screech their pain into his mind.

The few clean clothes he had left meant an impending trip to the Laundromat. The shower rod usually held up under the weight of a few jeans and socks. Drying cost too much money, and the woman who manned the coin machine had an eagle eye out for people who snuck their clothes into unattended dryers. He found a rumpled pair of pants under a stiff blanket, then pulled them up over his slender hips, buttoning them closed as he rummaged for a shirt.

"Andreas!" Pounding rattled the thinly constructed door of the room, threatening to shatter the frame and its pot-iron metal lock. "Open the fuck up."

Kismet debated leaving the door closed and staying silent until the man gave up, but he didn't have time to wait Carl out. A large pug-nosed man quickly stepped onto the threshold, arms bared and belly peeking out from under the hem of a too tight bowling shirt with its sleeves ripped free from the seams.

"You got some money for me?"

Kismet tallied up what he'd made in his head and winced at the idea of handing over some of it to the motel manager. He'd parceled out a hundred into an envelope. A quick search on the dresser came up with the monies, still tucked safely into the blue-hatched envelope.

Cracking the flap open, Carl counted out the variety of bills, calculating how much the young man still owed. "You got a couple of weeks with this, but you'll have to come up with the rest of it by next week or you're out. Understand?"

"Yeah, I know." Full lip jutted out, Kismet leaned on the frame, refusing to let Carl intimidate him.

The man often pushed his way into the room, going through Kismet's things while he was gone. Long used to the intrusions, Kismet no longer left anything of value out, squirreling away everything he owned into a footlocker with a thick padlock. "You need anything else?"

"You kill yourself with that shit you do, and I'm just tossing your stuff out and letting the fucking homeless pick through it like they do everything else." Carl poked at Kismet's chest. "Do me a favor and die someplace else."

"Go to hell," Kismet muttered at the closed door, shutting Carl out of view. His clenched fist followed his angry words, slamming into the wall. A deep breath rattled Kismet's lungs, stretching them out with the room's curdled air. The carpet's weave still bore the woman's footprints, wet splotches tracking through the room until they reached the edge of the bed. Struggling to get his wallet into the pocket of his denim jacket, Kismet stared down at the moist prints until they blurred.

"*Kizzie, are you going to leave me here?*" Chase grabbed at his shirt, the boy's hand passing through the fabric. The young man burned where his brother touched him, his back itching from the ghostly presence. Kismet reached for the spot, rubbing at the crawling sensation.

Chase's body was nearly firm, fleshed out and solid. Kismet could almost imagine his brother sitting there, not a day over five. The hardest thing to see was the innocence on his round face, wide eyes with long lashes, frozen in a time when life was a happy romp through empty motel rooms and sleeping under the stars in a park was an adventure. A blink of Kismet's eyes sent Chase off, and his ghost became a cloud of smoke wafted away from the wind coming through the cracked window.

Kismet stared up at the ceiling, counting slowly to regain his composure. His brother never aged, never fought with him or stole food from his plate. That sibling was long gone, and all that was left was a construct of the insanity that plagued their mother.

The itch in his arms nicked his attention, and Kismet fought not to rub at his tortured skin. He moved to close the curtain and spotted a police cruiser slowly working its way through the parking lot.

His face was known to the local cops, a throwaway child of a drug-using whore. Kismet didn't want company, and definitely not uniformed company. He'd been told more than once that he would end up like his mother, dying from too much liquid poison and disease in her veins while her body stiffened and crackled to a dry rot under San Diego's intense summer heat. The system picked him up and chewed on his ass for a while, spitting him out unceremoniously when he turned seventeen. He'd been one of thousands of faceless kids serving a sentence for a parent's neglect. Kismet figured he survived the experience. He knew there were others who weren't as lucky.

His mangled brain often reminded him he could have done without the ghosts his mother left behind.

They were everywhere, some of them with faces, just floating ovals with wide mouths and sharpened eyes. Others had full bodies, slithering around him in an attempt to pull Kismet with them as they walked in circles around the small tight spaces their memories lived in. More were just shapes moving in the corner of his vision, tidal pools of slippery forms that grew claws and teeth to score furrows on his vulnerable flesh. As a child, he bore more than one set of raking scratches on his face or arms from the nightmares that crawled into bed with him.

"Shit. Take your time, Kiz," Kismet scolded himself, teeth chattering under the pressure of his body's need. "Got to make this last."

Prepping the powder was easy. Working up the nerve to inject himself was harder. He hated needing the drug. Hated what it did to him.

But the nightmares were horrific. And were getting worse all the time.

The tiny vein proved stubborn, sliding around the needle tip. Working it around, the skin puckering as the metal slid farther down the vein's length, Kismet sighed with relief as a burst of blood stained the heroin darker. Holding the tubing taut, he slowly tapped at the end of the plunger, releasing small amounts of heroin into his blood.

Swallowing hard, Kismet dragged the needle free from his arm, and his body rode the euphoria. The wave hit him again, carrying him off with a burble of nonsensical sounds he couldn't follow.

His legs were unsteady under him as he turned, trying to crawl across the bed. Flailing, his foot hit the bed frame, and Kismet landed facedown on the wadded-up covers he'd thrown on the floor.

"Mess." Phantom toes nudged at his face, their nails covered with chipped lavender polish. They were wet, dripping with fading soap bubbles and water. Despite the obvious evidence of a recent washing, Kismet could see the caked layers of dirt caught on the nails' cuticles. The toes shoved at his cheek again, digging into the tender flesh beneath his eye. Tongue working free from the hole in her face, the ghost struggled to speak, a loose tooth jiggling in her gums as she spoke. "You're a mess."

The carpet moved under him, a rippling mass of fibers sliding him away from the bed. Grabbing at the open footlocker, Kismet struggled to remain flat, but the floor had other ideas, flipping him easily onto his back. The owner of the toes stretched up above him, her face a blank circle with no emotion. He recognized the woman from the tub, her nude body slack from use.

Behind her a man Kismet had never seen before loomed, the shape of him dark and foamy at the edges. His features were lost behind a haze of nothingness, dull sooty noise blinking in and out. The paneling played peek-a-boo through him, fists raised up behind the woman's head, danger paused for a short eternity. Kismet could feel the rage pouring from him, amazed the woman could be standing there without screaming. The man's hands rushed down, suddenly popping her head apart in a splash of brains, the wet splattering across Kismet's face.

Then they were gone, leaving him with the gore sinking into his scalp.

Fighting back a scream, he pulled himself up onto his feet, swaying until the bed hit the back of his knees. Tumbling onto the hard mattress, Kismet pulled a lungful of air into his chest, trying to shake off the vision of the woman's murder from his mind. His eyes bulged as the ceiling bowed, a single drop of black peeling out from the cracks in the plaster. It struck the mattress, a spot spreading out next to his ear, hissing as the bedding began to smoke and the inky shadows spread, edging closer to his tender skin.

"God." His teeth furred under his tongue, time slipping away from him. Kismet's eyes grew heavy, his limbs refusing to respond to the frantic screams of his brain knocking on the inside of his skull. The stink of burning fabric grew, filling his nostrils with a foul smell. The smoke curled up, billowing softly against the pulled peaks of the ceiling's cracked plaster. Faces churned out of the patterns, sightless eyes rolling to catch a glimpse of the sprawled young man, twitching uncontrollably as the drug took over his body.

Broken dreams plagued Kismet's mind, faces spinning out of misted-over wood paneling tightening around his bed. His throat was dry, and his tongue stuck to the roof of his mouth, a distinct clicking noise when he pried it loose. The room spun when he tried to sit up, a wavy whirlpool of sounds slamming against his eyes.

Loud voices splintered outside his door, a torrential spate of a local Spanish dialect. From the sounds of it, Luis's girlfriend found him in bed with another woman, fierce screams of anger tearing into the night. Briefly, Kismet pondered going outside and then thought better of it when his body refused to move.

Pinned to the bare mattress, he felt every inch of the scratchy cover through his thin T-shirt, knobby buttons digging into his skin.

The heroin held a firm grip on his senses. Aching, he tried to turn over onto his stomach, feeling the sick in his throat. The high was already departing, its remnants of paranoia and anxiety crawling in to rest in Kismet's brain. A quick glance at his clock's glowing red numbers said only a few minutes had passed, too short of a time for the amount of heroin he'd shoved into his veins.

Amid the chaos of sound, he listened to the world around him, hearing it breathe in and out like a living thing. Even the argument next door felt like something alive under his skin. With the numbness gone, Kismet could feel every little shiver through the air, each person's reverberation against his own.

Then the world went silent. Abruptly. Without warning.

The sounds of Luis and his girlfriend were gone. The chatter of people across the courtyard watching the fight, a pair of gossips soaking up every miserable second of other people's lives, was quiet. Even the rush of traffic just beyond the alleyway behind his room muted to a whisper, no sound of the cars pulling through the cut toward the other buildings along the way. Nothing but the sounds of Kismet's own breathing in his ears.

Nothing moved but the shadows around him.

"Shit, maybe this crap finally caught up with me." He gulped at the air, forcing the heat into his chest.

Something had changed. He felt it. Something was different in this trip. He couldn't put a finger on it, but the numbness and the honeyed flow of the world was altered. And so much scarier. None of the black, inky shapes melted away. If anything, the creatures lurking in the crevices of his room grew more distinct.

"It wasn't supposed to happen this way," Kismet murmured to himself. "I do this, you all go away. It's what happens. You're not supposed to get stronger." He struggled to regain some control over himself, trying to break loose of the drug's creeping lethargy. "What the fuck is going on?"

A heartbeat pounded in his ears, the single thump followed by another tortured skip. His body fought the release, refusing to give over to Kismet's demands. Grasping at every bit of melted powder in his blood, his limbs became dead weight on the mattress, and he stared up in horror as one of the shadows broke loose from the cluster and worked its way toward him.

Chapter Four

Mal stared out of the passenger window, watching the city roll by. They'd stopped at a few places, Ari getting out to talk to someone after ordering Mal to stay in the car. Mal was certain Death hadn't suggested that he go along with Ari for a silent tour of the city. Ari was somber after the attack in the garage, the teasing lilt gone from his voice when he spoke. His manner toward Mal was calm, nearly professional. A far cry from their normal relationship.

Mal nearly missed Ari's taunting. Nearly.

Not everyone they stopped to talk with was human. A few darkfae and a Sidhe. Before that, a very aware phantasm caught on the edges of the Veil, unable to cross. Death did not come for everyone. Trapped, the ghosts faded from existence or remained, watching the world pass and making note of its changes, while others refused to believe they were dead.

Death and Ari both said they didn't know what happened to a dead person's soul, if it continued on or merely ceased to exist. The mysteries of life and souls were as enigmatic to the immortal as they were to humans. Mal was fairly certain Death knew more than what he was telling.

Secrets annoyed Mal to no end. But Death was Death. No one could pry anything out of the eldest Horseman if he didn't want to say something.

Mal sighed as Ari disappeared into an alleyway, watching with hooded eyes behind his wire-rimmed glasses. He strained to see around a planter, but Ari was entirely out of sight, and Mal resigned himself to a long wait.

The parking lot teemed with the Veiled, snippets of shadows weaving in between humans going about their daily lives. Behind the Mustang, a couple of children played, cars ghosting through their wispy bodies in an odd game of failed tag. There were other specters, some nearly too transparent to see.

Those were the ones that tugged most at Mal's heart, echoes of people left behind.

A tap on the windshield glass made Mal jump. Peering at him from his perch on the car's hood, a squat lower fae tapped again, his face a curdle of flesh and straggling hair. The redcap's hat was newly soaked, tight against his tanned forehead. Red speckles dotted his cheeks where the blood drops hit, his pointed tongue darting out to pluck off the fattest dribbles before they rolled down onto his clothes.

Draped mostly in discarded clothes he'd found in a charity bin, the Veiled looked more like a lawn gnome cobbled together from leftover burned biscuits, with the sharp tusks poking up from his lower jaw.

"Horseman." Its voice creaked, a rusty nail scraping along an iron blade. "Wake up. I'm trying to talk to you here."

Mal cast a glance over his shoulder, hoping to spot Ari strolling out from the side street, but the parking lot held only humans and whispers of wraiths. A drop of blood from the creature's cap struck the Mustang, and Mal winced, knowing he would hear Ari rant for hours if it dried and ruined the paint.

Reluctantly, Mal got out, mindful of the redcap. They were unpredictable, one of the many creatures that lived behind the Veil, not like the echoes of children scampering around the Volvo parked nearby. Here was a creature that kept itself hidden from mankind, feeding on humans and their wastes. Something that could, if it had a mind to, do serious injury to another Veiled. Like an unsuspecting Horseman with a newly healed leg.

As he stepped clear from the car, Mal closed his hand around the short knife Ari left with him, its sheath shoved hastily into Mal's waistband. He'd never mastered the quick feints and sharp stabs Death and Ari tried to teach him. He was more likely to stab himself in the leg again before actually hitting an opponent. Pulling himself up to his full height and squaring his shoulders, Mal tried to look casually formidable, sternly reminding himself that he was one of the Four Horsemen.

"What do you want?" His words sounded childish to his own ears, a boy putting on his father's grown-up jacket for a game of pretend. Mal strained his facial features to control the wince he felt ticking behind his muscles. *At least I kept my voice from cracking*, he thought to himself.

"I need to talk to Death. Is he around?" The squat creature jerked his thumb toward Ari. "No use talking to that one. He doesn't listen much to people like me."

"Death's busy." This talking was easier if he kept to short sentences and the truth. Changing tactics, Mal went on the offensive. "You can talk to me."

"You?" The redcap's mouth screwed up, and he spat at Mal's feet. "You're Pestilence. Not even a real Horseman. You and the skinny broad, you're just filling space behind them."

Mal countered with something calmer. "I'm all you got here. Talk, or I go back into the car."

"Maybe I should go talk to War." The creature poked a stubby finger into the air. Mal could see it was tipped red from shoving his cap back into place. "Maybe I can get him to listen."

"He's busy too. Like I said, I'm here."

"I'm looking for someone who can actually do something." The redcap's beady eyes drifted to where a couple was arguing, drawn by the negative energy arcing between them. "I got some information I'll trade for."

"What kind of information?" Mal steeled himself not to step back when the creature jumped down from the hood, flat feet hitting the asphalt with an audible wetness. Steadying himself, the redcap craned his head back to stare up at the tall Horseman, his tongue darting furiously.

"Something that came out of the shadows. Something not good." The scent of fresh blood tugged at the redcap's nose. Sniffing, he honed in on Mal's leg, spotting the crusted holes in his jeans. "I'll want payment."

"I don't have anything to give you." Mal's brain crackled, thinking about what Death told him about payments to other Veiled creatures. He came up with very little, scant help to him now.

"Lick off your leg will pay for anything." Again, his tongue crept out, a hummingbird of movement. "I've never tasted a Horseman before."

The thought of the creature's tongue running over him gave Mal the shivers, and his stomach complained, the nausea scrambling at his throat. Swallowing hard, Mal shook his head. "Tell you what. I have a rag that I used to wipe off the blood. It's in the car. You can have that."

"That would be even better." Smiling, the creature proved even uglier, sharp teeth fighting for position in a too small mouth.

Reaching into the car, Mal grabbed at the towel Ari tossed at him when they left the garage, splotches of dried brown splatter marbling the pile. The redcap made a grab for it, brushing up against Mal's leg when the Horseman jerked it out of range.

"Talk first," Mal cautioned, feeling the length of metal against his rib cage. "Then I'll hand it over."

"Deal," the redcap grunted. "You're not much of a Horseman, but you are good for your word.

"Something came up behind me when I was scrounging down by the record store." The redcap hugged his short, burly arms, wrists clasped about his elbows, drawn by the scent of the Horseman's fluids. "The wraith's big, bigger than a mastiff. I haven't seen one like that in a long time, but that's what it was. You don't ever really forget what one that big looks like."

"How big of one?" Mal lowered his arm. He'd seen other specters pulled free from the Veil, sometimes taking the form of nightmares or animals, but a wraith was something entirely different, a bad omen from humanity's past.

A keening howl tore apart the air. Around them, humans continued to walk and chat, oblivious to the dangers lurking just beyond their eyesight. A thumping rattled the ground, nearly shaking Mal off his feet and sending the redcap tumbling onto his back. Mewling, the creature struggled to right himself, holding his soaking cap firm with one hand while trying to flip over. Another shuddering stomp rippled through the ground, crossing the Veil in a wave of motion.

Nearby, a fire hydrant popped its cover, metal shards flying. Mal ducked, a bolt barely missing his head. He didn't want to test out his immortality against a slab of steel in his temple. Gods knew how long it would take to heal from that.

Seizing the opportunity, the redcap made a grab for the towel, hooking an end over his tusks before galloping a few feet away from Mal. Rocking on his knuckles, the redcap mumbled around the gag, pointing at the enormous doglike creature shouldering past the hydrant's remains. The wraith was still nearly twenty feet away, but Mal choked on its foul breath, a sourly sweet curdled milk poured into a too ripe pineapple. Its shoulders rose nearly as high as Mal's elbows, rocky precipices of bony plating with chunks of brown fur growing between the cracks.

"Damn, that thing is big," Mal whispered, watching as a woman darted around the waterspout pouring from a crack in the hydrant's pipes.

The wraith snapped at the human, its nearly doglike muzzle passing through the woman's solid flesh. A rounded body, powerful under the scaly plating, was broad across the chest, narrowing down in the hips. It moved on all fours, prowling forward to sniff at the mortals running away from the torrent. The wraith twitched, as if to break into a run, but the scent of its prey didn't draw it out. Instead it circled the area, looking for something it couldn't find.

"What the…?" Ari came running out from the side street, the Veil pulled tight around him.

Invisible to anyone who might glance his way, he stopped short of the Mustang's rear end, nearly hitting Mal. He had already drawn his long dagger, cocking it away from the other Horseman.

"Shit! Where the fuck did that thing come from?" Ari matched the wraith's growl with one of his own.

Unseen by the humans avoiding the water pouring from the damaged fire hydrant, the Veiled creature snorted, frustrated at being unable to bite at anyone passing by.

"What the damned hell is going on? And get down. If that thing sees you, it'll come for you."

Mal ducked down behind the Volvo parked next to the Mustang, Ari crouching beside him. "The redcap said it was a wraith. Looks like a wraith. Sort of. If they were dinosaur-sized."

Another chunk of metal flew past and struck a truck camper, rocking the vehicle on its wheels. People screamed as the hydrant blew more water upward, their eyes fixed firm on the real world, not seeing the shadowy beast hunkered into a crouch. Pouncing at the fleeing humans, the wraith ghosted through a security guard trying to herd people out of the way.

"Yeah, I know it's a wraith. I've been doing this for a while, Cooties," Ari snarled, noticing the trail of blood on his car. "Lying bastards always leave a mess. And didn't I tell you to stay in the car?"

"He wanted to pass along some information about a disturbance," Mal said, jerking his head in the wraith's direction. "And he wasn't lying."

"What did you trade? They always want something." Ari ducked around the Volvo's squared-down front, trying to find the wraith's location amid the confusion of frightened mortals. Another hydrant nearby burst open from the overloaded water pressure, shorn bolts shattering through the windowpane of a used book store.

The air shimmered around its body, and the Veil thinned around its massive frame, then broke, allowing the wraith to pass into the real world. Howling, its roar shook the Mustang's windows. Coiling its powerful body, it struck out at the guard, its solidifying talons raking open the man's shoulder.

"Shit twice! Damn thing is out of the Veil," Ari growled "We need to kill it, and here I am stuck with you."

In the distance, sirens wailed, and blue-and-red lights bounced off buildings in the distance. The creature's dark shape hovered over the fallen man, his body too still for Ari's liking. Slavering at the man's torso, the wraith sniffed carefully, nosing the mortal aside. The creature's nose passed through the man's flesh, and streaks of sticky black caught on the mortal's skin. Strings of gummy pitch snapped off the wraith's muzzle, wriggling tendrils slithering back into the man's torso.

"How did you know I traded something?" Mal wondered if he should attempt to pull the man free from the wraith's attention. A large section of the hydrant's base rocked on its edge near the man's head, blood beginning to pool from the slashes across his throat. Mal watched as the redcap furtively shuffled from behind a nearby shrub to the dubious safety of a column, the redcap's tongue working hungrily at his lips.

"They don't give anything away for free and usually give you something you can find out yourself." Ari fixed a pointed glare at

Mal. "I'm asking you again, what did you trade? Nothing from my car, right?"

"No, he was happy with the towel I used to sop up the blood I was going to get all over your precious carpet," Mal snapped back. "I figured you wouldn't mind."

"You fucking idiot." Ari's fist clenched, and he told himself not to crack open Mal's skull. Death warned him off the last time he'd struck Mal into unconsciousness. "You gave him your blood?"

"Seemed like a good idea at the time. I wasn't using it anymore. I was done bleeding out. Didn't have any plans to put it back in me, being dried and all." Mal got up onto his knees, feeling each pebble under his shins. "It wasn't a lot of blood. How much could he have gotten from it?"

"A dried towel can be soaked with water to bring the blood back up, and there was a lot of your blood on that rag." Ari cursed the younger Horseman's foolishness. "Shit, why didn't you just stab a seraphim, pull out its wings, and give him those as well?"

"You know, I'm getting kind of tired of you thinking I know everything." A hedge went flying, sections of sidewalk being ripped up by the creature's claws, the water pipes below bursting as the shadow came into contact with the cold iron. The sirens drew nearer, and the shadow fed off the chaotic emotions streaming from the frightened crowd. "Besides, how much power do I have? I'm Pestilence, remember? You're always telling me I'm the least of the Horsemen."

"Quit your whining, Pest. That thing is tearing this place and those humans apart." Ari spotted the wraith. "Come on. Guess you're better than nothing."

Stepping into the main parking lot, the wraith crouched down and inhaled deeply, tracking something on the ground. The creature turned its massive head, following the scent, then with a sharp jolt, scrambled past the crowds and broke into a full run. Ari swore as the wraith tore past them. "Come on, it's moving. Let's follow it."

"Do you think that's smart?" Mal protested as Ari manhandled him into the Mustang. "Okay, so it's probably what Death would want us to do, but—"

"Shut up!" Ari cut him off, gunning the engine and pulling out of the space, barely dropping the transmission into drive before barreling out of the driveway. He handled the drifting end of the Mustang with a skilled ease, strong hands gripping the steering wheel. One of the back tires jumped the curb, giving the car a little bump as they hit the pavement and roared onto the street.

"Again, thinking this isn't the wisest thing to do." Mal grabbed at the molded armrest. "You think you can keep up with that wraith in this?"

"If I can't keep up with a wraith in this Mustang, I'll eat Death's Vanquish."

"You might be doing that anyway when he sees what happened to his car," Mal retorted, closing his eyes as they squealed around a slow-moving minivan. "You're going to kill us. Sometimes I think you like seeing how far you can take things just to see if you can kill me and blame it on something else."

"You know, for someone who is immortal, you sure spend a lot of time complaining that you're going to die." A motorcycle cut in front of the careening Ford. Ari slammed on his brakes and downshifted, zipping through a tiny space between two lumbering trucks. "Now let me drive. Unless you see that thing, then tell me where the hell it went."

"I think it went down that street." Mal pointed down a tight, curvy bend, lawn signs spotting the grass ponds bravely growing between lengths of sidewalk. "Either that or they're making VWs a lot uglier these days."

"Let's see if we can catch up with it." Ari pressed down on the gas, cutting the corner sharply. "It might lead us to where the Veil started thinning."

"How much thinner can it get? That thing came through it," Mal squeaked, slamming against the passenger door as Ari made another tight turn. "It just closes back up, right? Doesn't a tear just close back up?"

"It's supposed to. Sometimes it doesn't. Then shit happens." Ari slowed down, eyes scanning the area for the wraith. Spotting a quick-moving shadow cast on a building's exterior, he hurried the Mustang along. "One of the crazies behind the store—"

"Don't call them that, Ari," Mal muttered.

"So the crazy guy I ran into told me he's been seeing things walk through. Small things like spirits and bogeys, but still, that's not a good thing." Ari swore as another car cut in front of his path. "Where small things can come through, eventually bigger things can. That's never been a good thing in the past. Don't see that changing anytime soon. I'm worried that one over there came through uninvited. If it did, then we're fucked."

"You think a wraith that big came through without being summoned?" Mal's throat suddenly felt dry.

"No. Shit, maybe," Ari replied, jerking the wheel to the side to avoid a trash can lying in the street. "I think the Veil weakening isn't what someone wanted. If someone wanted to bring something over, something big over, it would be stretched in one spot just long enough for that something to cross over. Then it would snap back. A summoning is just a breach. It wouldn't thin the Veil. This is wrong."

"Someone bringing a wraith over isn't wrong?" Mal shouted as he spotted the canine-like creature pawing at the base of a streetlamp, canting its head as it tracked a scent. "What can be much more wrong than that?'

"A lot of things can be called from the Veil, but they can be controlled. Maybe not by us but controlled by someone," Ari said. "If nasty, big things can just walk through, this place is going to go to shit and fast. Those things don't kill easy when they're behind the Veil. Nearly impossible if they've crossed over."

He'd half listened to Death and Ari talk about the past, of enormous creatures formed from the shadows and feeding off entire towns before they could be killed. "This isn't anything but bad, then?"

"Very bad," Ari agreed. "Now let's find out where that damned monster is going."

THE CREATURE plunged for him, curving past his shoulder and slamming into the wood paneling behind him. Chilled, he shivered, a frost pouring over his right arm where the form touched him. His shoulder ached where its minute nails dug into his skin. Pulling up the sleeve of his shirt, he blew on the welts bubbling up, furrows of blisters running from his chest and over his forearm.

All around him, the room churned, once pitch-black shadows now separating into distinct shades of blue and gray amid swirls of dusky red. Eyes formed in the crevices of the walls, following the lines of the paneling, painted sienna highways for blinking orbs. Sometimes a nose would push outward, bending the fake wood around the protuberance, nostrils flaring as they sniffed at the air. Just the hint of a face, the side of a jaw or a cheekbone, dimpled with gouges that leaked more shadow. Fingers started to press at the cracks, forcing sharpened talons into the room, then snapping back, not quite strong enough to push through.

Kismet hooked his hands over the edge of the uneven mattress and stared at the blossoming world in his room. Thin shades of people carried on through the walls, some glancing his way and marking his presence before disappearing. He almost fell from the bed, found his balance, then headed to the door.

The cold air outside made him shiver, chilling the moistness of his sweat under his thin T-shirt. Wrapping his arms tight about his thin chest, Kismet stood still, drinking in the changes in the world he saw laid out in front of him.

The moon hung low over the far-off hills, poking in and out of a string of clouds. The neighbors were still on the walkway, their voices a scream of noise under a curtain. Kismet could no longer make out what they were saying or if they were doing any talking at all, their mouths moving in a rapid shushed whisper. Luis, a man Kismet knew rarely raised his voice, screamed soundlessly at his girlfriend. The heat of her anger was tempered only slightly by the irrational craziness set into the lines of her face, and she faced Luis to give him a piece of her mind.

"Hey!" Kismet rubbed at his arms, trying to get the chill out of his skin. "You guys okay? Luis, maybe you guys need to take a walk."

The woman struck at her boyfriend's face, the silent slap leaving an angry red mark over his whiskered cheek. Luis's mouth turned ugly, shouting back in a silent roar. She responded, eyes filling with fear when Luis stepped closer, body tense with fury. Her hands raised, a gold bracelet glittering on her wrist, she tried to push Luis away. Stronger and heavier, he didn't budge and shoved her back into the cinder-block wall.

Kismet moved forward a step, then stopped. A child-shaped curling smoke floated between the couple, growing brighter with each second, its face visible as it turned about in the air. Almond-shaped black eyes, lacking whites, wrapped about its triangular face, its features growing stronger with each breath that buffeted its body. Sharp teeth curled over its lips, a thin slash of menace above a pointed chin. The thing spotted Kismet, alarm widening its mouth into an *O*. It moved forward, as if to intercept him, then skidded to a stop, its spindly arms flailing back hastily as a shadow loomed behind the young man.

Luis grabbed at the woman, digging into her arms with his hands and yanking her against the building's side. Her mouth contorted in a noiseless scream, she tore at his face, burned red-painted fingernails raking into his cheek. They took no notice of the pale young man standing near them.

A hot wind burst on Kismet's shoulders, warming the chill from his body. It carried with it a faint odor of decay. While the heat was strangely welcome, Kismet had a strong suspicion that he wouldn't like what was behind him. The smoky wraith took one last inhalation of the argument and plunged down into the shadows at Luis's feet, disappearing into the black.

"God, what the hell is going on?" He wanted to turn around. To be honest with himself, he wanted to walk back into his room and shut the door behind him. "Look behind you, Kiz. Can't be anything worse than what's in front of you."

The heat was growing, and Kismet reluctantly twisted around, then immediately regretted it.

A doglike creature stood a few feet from him, massive feet spread apart to support its wide body. Panting, it ducked its head and sniffed hard at him, drool foaming along its folded-over lips.

Its head was nearly as big as Kismet's, a thick fur spottily spread over its skull, pointed ears flopping down to the sides. Kismet could make out its shoulders rising up behind it, its body sloping down to its narrow hips. Its nails clicked and caught on the artificial turf laid out along the walkway's edge, making a soft snicking noise as it walked.

"Oh, fuck me," he whispered under his breath, his panic rising in short bursts along his torso. The monster swallowed, its throat working its neck's strong muscles, its chest rippling with the effort.

Wrinkled brindle skin, spotted and flaking, covered its flanks, strands of wispy hair clustered on its hip bones. Its eyes glowed as it approached, and its rank smell assaulted Kismet's nose.

When the creature came closer, Kismet stepped back, his foot hitting the walkway and catching on the turf. Caught on the uneven edge, he went down to his knees, the plastic faux grass skinning his palms. The violent motion wrenched his already touchy stomach, and he retched, choking on his own vomit as he tried to get back up onto his feet to run. Wanting to disappear like the smoke thing he'd seen, Kismet twisted onto his back, prepared to kick out at the monster.

A spindly thread of drool clung to its muzzle, stretching down to drag along the cement sidewalk. The rough walk crackled under the spit, small chunks of rock pocked where the end struck. One chip struck Kismet's face, searing a line across his cheek. Another step brought the monster even closer, its eyes fixed firmly on the artist sprawled out before it. Taking a deep breath, Kismet drew his legs up, waiting for the monster to come near.

Sound returned. Suddenly and overwhelming.

It was too loud. Everything flared to a brilliant volume, shrieking and mingled. Amid the cacophony, he strained to filter out what was immediately around him. He could hear the monster's heavy breathing, a deep, growling pant in its chest as it stepped closer. Behind him, the couple continued their intense, violent argument, Luis's fists flying across his girlfriend's face.

The woman's screams were loud and pleading, as were the heavy wet thumps of Luis's hands striking her pummeled flesh. Kismet stared in horror, caught between the descending menace of the growling creature and the woman's death.

He cried out when her screams suddenly stopped, the rest of the world's noises continuing on as if nothing had happened.

Her blood splattered on the faded ivory motel walls, a vivid splash of red that dripped onto the sidewalk. Luis's sweatpants soaked up the blood, red trails creeping up to his knees. He ignored that as well, his knuckles now torn from continuously striking hard bone and muscle. The woman's corpse began to bleed out, pools of fluids creeping down the slanted walkway.

Nose twitching, the monster stopped in its tracks, drawn by the scent of death nearly as much as by the young man it identified as its prey. Kismet tried to work his legs free from the lethargy of his brain, hoping to be able to reach his room door before the creature caught him.

The monster saw the movement and pounced, its jaws open and its giant paws slamming down beside Kismet's head.

A rumbling sound drew the creature's ears back, the points swiveling around. A growl threatened to break apart its rib cage, nostrils flaring as it sniffed at the air. The growl deepened, jaws closing down over Kismet's neck. The young man tried to scream, but nothing came, his air supply cut off by the canine's fangs sinking through his throat. Choking on his own blood, Kismet thrashed about, convulsing around the wraith's powerful mouth.

His hands pushed uselessly at the immovable weight straddling his chest, unable to budge the heavy monster. White pain coursed through his body, his mind overloaded by the aching waves. His blood pooled on the fake grass, a small bog filled with miniature green plastic clusters. Where the monster's teeth broke through his skin, he burned from the acidic dribbles of the wraith's saliva, a faint popping sound as he cooked around the monster's hold.

The monster released him, only to bite back down again, firming its grip. As the feeling left his face, he laughed, a chuckle wheezing through his punctured throat when an all too familiar numbness stole into his body. If he'd only been willing to die, the pleasant scary feeling of nothingness that he chased with pills and needles could have been his.

Kismet made a trail behind him, a wetness darkening the cement where he bled. The monster's legs surged, dragging its prey down the walkway and toward the parking lot. Panting, he struggled, refusing to be carried off like a chicken. The monster growled and shook him, hard.

"Not dying like this." Kismet fought, his weakening hands nearly useless against the creature's greater strength.

Checkerboard squares swam in front of his eyes, and his stomach clenched at the pain. Every breath became torture, a struggle to pull in air. He vaguely heard the roar of an engine behind him and then nothing as his body began to shut down. Balling his fist, he struck at the monster's muzzle.

"Fuck you, bitch." Each word was a torture to mutter, and his hand throbbed where he'd struck against the creature's hard skull. Pulling his fist back, he was determined to take out at least a tooth before he died.

CHAPTER FIVE

ARI PULLED himself free of the car, going for his weapon. The hilt slid into his palm, settling against the ridges when his fingers closed over them. Ari moved swiftly. He noticed a ghost watching him through a part in the curtains. She faded when spotted, leaving the imprint of her face against the glass.

The huge wraith snarled, an ominous sound close to Kismet's numb hearing. He could barely feel his fingers or anything below his waist. The wraith shook him, tossing Kismet's limp body back and forth on the turf. Clamping down further on Kismet's neck, it continued to drag him, unmindful of the Horsemen coming its way.

"He's got that kid," Mal shouted at Ari, circling around the wraith to its right. The monster's gleaming eyes tracked Mal, keeping the Horseman in sight. Stopping in its tracks, it sniffed at the air, then dismissed Mal as a threat. It jerked against its prey's weight, pulling Kismet along another foot.

"I can see he's got the kid. It shouldn't even be able to get a hold on him," Ari yelled back, grabbing at the Veil with his mind to pull it over the wraith. Shadows around them thickened, enveloping the wraith. It shivered from a brush of cold over its body, then adjusted its mouth around the boy's throat. The air shimmered again before falling back into place.

Ari stood there for a moment, slack-mouthed with surprise. The wraith should have let the boy go, the Veil's touch overwhelming the creature. He glanced at a sobbing Hispanic man curled up over the bloody body of a dead woman. "Nothing. Shit, this thing is fully Veiled. Let's see if we can get it to drop the boy."

To Ari's experienced eyes, the woman looked recently dead, her limbs still softened with slack muscles. There was too much blood for Ari to tell what happened. Either the monster somehow attacked all three and was only now finishing up with the boy, or other things were at play.

"See if you can get around to the front of it," Ari directed Mal. "I'll take it from the back. They're more vulnerable from the back. Less pointy teeth. You can be bait."

"I didn't bring the knife," Mal reminded him, holding up bare hands. "Look, no pointy thing."

"What happened to the knife I gave you?" Ari hissed. "I gave you a *perfectly* good knife. What the hell did you do with it?"

"Left it in the car. It's not like I'm any good at that kind of stuff," Mal said, taking a tentative step onto the covered cement walkway.

"What the hell are you thinking, going out without at least a knife?" With a disgusted look backward, Ari dismissed Mal with a wave of his hand. "Shit. Fine. I'll deal with it. Go in to distract it. I'll get it from the other side."

Mal approached cautiously, but he was fairly certain the boy held in the wraith's mouth was dead. A human wouldn't be able to survive the damage inflicted by the creature. The young man's face still held flickers of life, a soft moan creaking from his parched lips. He was older than what Mal originally guessed, and his heart convulsed at the pain etched into the man's pretty features. The monster's jaws had made nasty work of his neck, delivering fatal punctures to the arteries along his throat. Mal was surprised he'd not yet bled out. Death's touch wasn't far from the young man's soul.

Ari growled at him, "Just fucking kick the thing."

Focusing a hazy stare on Mal, the boy called out to the immortal. The words were garbled, nearly unintelligible, but the young man's intent was plain. He wasn't going to go down without a fight. Swallowing, Mal nodded and started to move closer, stopped short in his tracks by Ari's warning shout.

"Mal, wait a damned minute! That kid's not going anywhere," Ari yelled at the Four's youngest. "Gods, Pest, you're such an idiot."

Looking over the wraith's body, Ari worked on how best to kill the creature quickly. The bony plates covering its flanks and underbelly promised to be a problem. He debated driving the dagger into its skull, as he'd done with the wraith in their garage, but the wraith's bony forehead and heavy brow ridge gave him pause. "This thing is built like a tank."

"He can see me." Mal stood still, whispering in astonishment. Speaking louder, he repeated himself to a distracted Ari. "War, the boy can see me."

Mal was certain that no sane mortal saw the Horsemen behind the Veil. They had to push past the Veil to be seen, and he'd always carefully chosen the times he made himself visible to humans. He enjoyed the contact when he did but never once interacted directly. Mal never felt more alive than when he spent an afternoon in a coffee house listening to chatter or in the relative silence of a movie theater. Humans were invigorating and fascinating to watch.

But an effort had to be made. Mortals just didn't see their kind, but here was one, one seemingly untouched by the madness that poured out in a rankled stench from the insane. To Mal, the dying young man didn't smell insane, just of sour poison and the acrid oil of fear on his skin, and he most definitely saw Mal.

Ari struck at the wraith, sparks flying from the dagger's edge when it hit the plated armor along the monster's rigid backbone. A speck of blood boiled from the crevices along the plating, the weapon's point finding a vulnerable spot between the sections. Fed by the boy's fluids and fear, the wraith surged forward, a powerful concentration of force barreling past Mal. The boy's body bounced along, one of his arms catching around an awning post, yanking at his shoulder and stopping the monster's momentum with a shuddering jerk.

Trying to work its prey loose with a mighty shake of its head, the monster didn't see Ari moving in, dagger low. With the weapon's point tipped up, Ari aimed for a soft spot beneath one of the wraith's front legs, hoping to get at the shoulder muscle to cripple its movements. Nearly slipping on the blood pooling on the cement, Ari's thrust lost some of its power, the blade slicing up enough into the soft tissue to catch the wraith's attention. Scenting its prey, the wraith whirled about, jowls dripping with speckles of bloody foam. Head low, it rushed War, intent on the kill.

The young man's moan tugged at Mal's resolve. Deciding Ari would be better off without the human in the way, Mal reached in and grabbed the young man's shoulders, grunting at Kismet's slight weight.

He'd seen enough death in humans' eyes to know the young man wasn't going to survive his wounds.

There was too much blood loss, even if the shock didn't kill him. The boy's gore spilled onto Mal's hands, staining them dark. Still, Kismet's limp form was warm in Mal's arms, the sticky mess of his life clinging to the Horseman's cheek when Mal held him up to listen to Kismet's tortured breathing. Behind them, Ari moved in to protect them, the wraith raging at the loss of its prey.

"What's your name?" Mal bent close. If the boy died, he would at least know the human's name. He'd never held a dying human before. His purpose rarely gave him opportunity to see death up close, much less touch it.

"Kismet." Gasping, the young man choked on a burble of blood spilling up from his lungs.

"I'm Mal." The absurdity of the conversation struck Mal. Cradling the young man, he tried to make Kismet comfortable.

"There's a monster," Kismet croaked with a gulp, swallowing painfully around the holes in his throat. "Watch out for it. Mean fucking thing."

"We see the monster. Don't try to talk. You'll need your strength." For what, Mal didn't know. Little by little, death crept into the young man's body. Mal figured he would be holding a corpse in a matter of minutes. The thought of the boy dying hurt Mal. Something in the jut of the young man's jaw, defiant and vulnerable at the same time, touched Mal inside. "Hold on. I won't let you go."

Mal tried gently to pull Kismet's blood-matted hair out of his wounds, trying to see just how severe the damage was. He was beginning to think he'd misjudged the severity of the wounds when the young man drew in another rattling breath, easier than the last. The young man's color was returning to his cheeks, a flush of pink under his skin. Sticky black with drying blood, Kismet's brown hair was difficult to remove, catching on the jagged ends of the punctures. Hoping he wouldn't hurt the dying young man even more, Mal pulled harder, risking tearing the tender skin beneath.

With the boy's hair out of the way, Mal's breath left his chest, shocked at what he saw. The young man's wounds were closing. Even more amazing were the wounds on his torn-open throat, healing slowly but definitely sealing together. Mal watched, awestruck, as the damaged tissues knitted, tendons edging closer and binding back together.

A cough worked a clot free from Kismet's lungs, forcing it out through a shrinking space between torn skin. Kismet's dark brown eyes rolled back into his head, consciousness leaving him. Mal bent over, finding a steadying pulse and labored breaths being pulled into Kismet's chest. With a sigh of shocked relief, Mal worked his arms under the young man's body, trying to lift him clear of the blood puddle under them.

Ari dodged the wraith's lunge, stepping aside. Turning, the creature snapped its teeth, catching the back of Ari's thigh. Grunting from the ripping pain, the Horseman regained his balance in time to see the wraith making a tight turn, nails scrambling to gain purchase on the bloodied cement. Ari crooked his head to the side, trying to get a good look at the wraith's neck.

The plating around the wraith's neck gaped as it brought its head up, leaping in an attempt to close its slavering jaws about Ari's face. Mindful of the edge of the concrete walkway, Ari balanced on the ball of his foot and turned sideways, letting the creature's momentum carry it past him once more.

The wraith's response was swift, its turn tighter, nearly doubling its spine back over. Screaming a yowl of rage, it built up speed in its powerful legs, pounding the ground with long strides. Ari jumped back, giving himself some distance from the edge of the raised walkway. The wraith leaped, springing upward. Its back legs struck the cement, nails scraping the rough surface. Ready for its attack, Ari placed one palm on the pommel of the long dagger, the other hand cupping the bottom of its cross guards.

When the wraith's massive head nearly reached his chest, Ari shoved the dagger between the gaping plates on its neck. His shoulder muscles bulged with the effort of working through the creature's thick body. Digging through the tightness of its moving neck, Ari struck bone. Swearing, he twisted the hilt, mindful of the wraith's thrashing body. Smoking blood poured over Ari's hands, scalding his tanned flesh. He set aside the pain, intent on killing the thing. Ari felt his knee pop from the creature's weight, his leg unable to withstand the unnatural twisting of its muscles.

The creature struggled to get free, its back legs kicking furiously at the Horseman. With a stumble, they both went down, the wraith's greater weight driving Ari to his knees, then onto his back as it attempted to eat its way through the Horseman. The flecks of spit flung from its mouth were nearly as caustic as its blood, leaving bubbling water blisters on Ari's face and neck. Pushing up, Ari strained to put his weight behind a final thrust, nicking past the bone and into the base of the wraith's skull.

The pop of vertebrae and the wraith's choking gasps made Ari sigh with relief. Giving the wraith one final shove, he placed a foot on its stomach, kicking it away from his acid-splattered face. The monster's body went limp, landing on its side. Legs twitching, it growled and tried to move, chest heaving with the effort. In the dim light, the wraith's teeth glistened malevolently in its bloodied muzzle. Its fangs gnashed together in a final threat, a hideous snapping sound, and then the gleam faded from its eyes, its shattered neck sagging on the cement walk.

Limping, Ari walked over to Mal. His face burned, the reddened blisters bursting and soaking trails of salted water into the neck of his shirt. His jacket was a loss. Ari picked at the expensive leather with mournful fingers. The monster's spit had left massive holes in the soft, buttery hide, the wrist lining torn out from his earlier fight with the shadow wraith. Gazing over his shoulder, Ari gave a cursory glance at the sobbing Hispanic man, a few feet behind the dead wraith lying on its side.

"Leave him, Mal. We've got to go before the police come and find the kid." Sighing, Ari crouched next to his brother Horseman, touching Mal's light blond hair with gentle fingers. "They won't see us if we slip behind the Veil, but they'll notice the Mustang. I don't want to leave her here. She'll get impounded, and then I'll have to answer to Death. I have enough to explain away tonight."

"We can't leave him." Mal cradled the unconscious artist. "The wraith hurt him."

"Yeah, it obviously grew strong enough to hurt a human. It grew strong enough to hurt me. That happens sometimes. We've got to get back and tell Death what happened." Ari tugged at the back of Mal's shirt. "Come on. Drop the kid and let's go."

"I'm not leaving him." Mal struggled to get to his feet, Kismet's limp form an unwieldy weight in his arms. "Help me pick him up."

"Mal, we can't take him with us. He's human." Ari clenched his fists at his sides, the urge to strike Mal down and drag him off into the car nearly overwhelming him. "Leave him, already. He's not going to live. The cops will think that other guy got to him as well. We've got to go. Now!"

"He can see us, Ari." Mal's words stopped Ari as he turned toward the car. "I remained behind the Veil, and he saw me. Spoke to me. Warned me about the wraith."

"So he's crazy. Even better. Now drop him."

"Ari, help me get him into your damned precious car. I'm not leaving him behind."

Mal's temper flared, striking Ari full in the face. Ari tilted his head back, slightly unsure about what to do with an aggressive Mal.

"I. Am. Not. Leaving. Kismet. Behind."

"Great! You made friends with it while I was fighting off the wraith?" Ari snapped back. "Shit. Damn it. Fine, go grab the door."

Sirens carried through the neighborhood, a mournful, shocking wave riding the wind. Bending over, Ari took Kismet from Mal's arms, nestling the lithe body against his broad chest. Growling as Mal opened the Mustang's door, Ari shouldered him aside, then tumbled Kismet into the backseat.

"Get in. We've got to go." Ari started the engine, and Mal scrambled into the passenger side, tucking his legs in quickly. The car lurched backward, and Mal steadied himself with one hand on the dashboard, worriedly looking at the curled-up mortal bleeding on Ari's backseat.

"You're cleaning that up," Ari muttered darkly, the burned spots on his hands crackling when he clenched the steering wheel to maneuver the car onto the street. "Every single fucking drop of blood that he spills onto my carpet and upholstery. You're cleaning it up. If you have to lick it clean."

"Understood." Mal hid the smile that threatened to swallow his face.

"No smiling, and you're telling Death why we couldn't leave him behind." Ari pounded at the wheel with his fist. "And the Vanquish.

You're telling him about the car and that you're the reason it's all fucked up."

"He'll understand about the car," Mal said softly, taking one last look at the young man before settling back into the seat. "And about Kismet. He'll understand."

Snorting, Ari slowed the car down, moving into the stream of traffic leading to downtown San Diego. "That's what you think. The boy, maybe. The car, never."

MICHAEL BECKETT waited among the gathered curious, impatient for the cops to finally leave the motel parking lot, tracking the frenzied dogfights between different detectives, each offering up their own opinion of what happened. Trails of blood shone dully on the concrete walk, small yellow cones marking a flat slalom around the drying gore. A photographer's flash went off periodically, leaving stars in the bald man's vision when he stared too long.

From his vantage point, Beckett could see into the Veil, pushing his Sight nearly to the edge of its limits. The wraith he'd been able to pull free from the Veil decayed rapidly in the rising sunlight, a failure in his eyes. The man gritted his teeth, trying to keep the emotion from his face.

"Should have been here sooner, sir," Frazier murmured softly, his larger frame looming beside his employer. The man felt the loss of the boy personally. If he'd been there a bit sooner, he would have been able to deliver the boy to Beckett.

Beckett waved the apology off. Neither one of them could have predicted the chaos that had happened. "Don't worry about it, Frazier. We'll find him again. His kind always circle back to where they feel comfortable. I'm guessing that it won't be long before we stumble over him again."

"The compound seems to be working," Frazier commented. "I think I can see what you brought across. It's a mess."

"Good." Beckett smiled broadly, his face tight around the gesture. "You at least have the Sight developing. That's a step in the right direction. It won't be long, then, before you'll be like the boy."

He was taking a risk giving Frazier the concoction, but Beckett was willing to sacrifice the man. Losing Frazier to the madness that lurked behind the Veil would be a small price to pay if the mixture actually worked, and Frazier knew what he was risking, willingly becoming Beckett's guinea pig for the immortality the elixir promised. Once they had the boy, Beckett could confirm the effects and make any small corrections that he might need to before he took it himself.

"I'll see if I can get closer." Frazier didn't wait for Beckett's approval, stepping into the fray of people with purpose. The man knew how to work around authorities, easing his way through the crowd of policemen as if he belonged. He soon struck up a conversation with a detective, intent on drawing out information to take back to his employer.

From the condition of the wraith, Beckett guessed the addict not only could see into the Veil but could affect it, something Beckett wanted badly. For a drugged-out wastrel to cross over the elusive curtain of shadows seemed sacrilegious at best to the fuming man, but it was something he'd accepted could happen. Sacrifices had to be made. A blow to his ego seemed a small price to pay in the scheme of things. He would just have to wait things out. The addict could be dealt with later.

The heat burned moisture trails off the parking lot, running black around streams of tire tracks.

When more and more police sirens cut into the waning night, the asphalt square nearly emptied of vehicles, doors slamming shut and curtains drawn. In the dusty daylight, the motel looked abandoned, cracked stucco peeling off chicken-wire-framed walls. Oceans of rust from the exposed metal dying in the open air framed the blood splatter from Luis's hands and the puddles left from Kismet's wounds.

Footprints added their own splatter, a literal stampede of shoes and sneakers through the crime scene from motel residents deciding to leave before the police arrived and asked questions.

Beckett longed to get closer to the wraith before it whispered away into the nothingness that formed it. The blue-uniformed police were walking clean through it, some of the more sensitive unknowingly giving the area a wide berth, their feet circumventing the bony carcass wasting away under their noses. Its stink permeated the area, a blend of sweet decay and putrid offal. A flicker of a shadow poked up through the monster's head, some form of wraith drawn by the creature's death.

Small and squat, it scurried over the wraith's body, furtively glancing about with round yellow eyes slitted with rectangular pupils. It froze when a cop approached, holding still as a human leg passed through it and the carcass. Pert ears, points slightly bent, rotated with each sound, the tiny wraith keeping watch while it contemplated where to start its meal. Hooking its talons into a wide gash along the monster's rib cage, it buried its round face in the meat, only the tip of its truncated tail showing a mottled gray stub outside of the wound. Coming up with a mouthful, it chewed around fat cheeks, clotted blood circling its thin lips, a mockery of sienna lipstick. The scavenger dove in for another bite, keeping its eyes level with the gash as the movement through it increased.

"It's fascinating that the food chain exists no matter what side of the Veil one is on," a beloved voice whispered into Beckett's ear.

With other humans packed tight against his body, he hated that he couldn't answer her. Working himself free of the clamor, Beckett found a spot near a cluster of bedraggled trees, still keeping an eye on the ravaged wraith. She followed him, passing through the crowd with a blissful saunter. Several shivered as she walked, their hands moving across their chests and over their faces to ward off the chill creeping upon them.

Safe from eavesdroppers, Beckett tried to keep his eyes from wandering to the woman shimmering next to him. He'd not seen her in nearly a week, and he ached to reach out, running his fingers through her hair or touching the soft, downy skin along her exposed neck. Want tightened his throat, and he swallowed, trying to dislodge the lump that seemed to root there every time he thought of her.

He recalled the first time he saw her, walking through a graveyard of mourners, drawn by the words spoken over the dried husk of his father. He'd gone over to her after the procession began to pay their respects, more interested in the woman than in the man he'd spent a lifetime loathing. Before he reached her side, she disappeared into the fog, swirls of raindrops pounding the already moist ground.

Beckett kept the image of her in his heart, stoking his memory with the fantasy of her against him.

When she sought him out years later, she looked and felt as he imagined. Now he treasured every moment they could spend together. He'd have an eternity with Faith once he found the right elixir.

"What happened?" she asked, turning soulful eyes toward him. Faith drew near, rubbing her cheek against his, her ghostly flesh skimming just under the surface of his skin. "Did the drugs work? Are we successful?"

"I think so." Beckett touched his face where she'd been. She'd already drawn away, attention shifted to the wraith's body. "I don't know yet. One of the men that I passed them on to told me that one of his buyers wasn't affected by the heroin. He came back several times."

"Was it ineffective?" Faith turned back to face him. "Could the agent… it's called an agent, right? Could it have gone inert… dead? Do you think it's not working anymore?"

"I don't think so," Beckett replied. "Others using the same batch went insane, but I knew it would happen. I was hoping to find just one person that it would work on."

"Wouldn't someone miss him if he disappeared behind the Veil?" She frowned. "People would notice him being gone."

"No one would miss a druggie if he went missing. They would just think he overdosed somewhere and died," Beckett said, his eyes drifting back to the wraith's remains. "I'm thinking the boy could have already been very much aware, more than anyone else we've tried it on, and it crossed him over to the Veil. I'll have to get my hands on him before I can tell you exactly. But I can't imagine how he killed a wraith. Unless he had some sort of weapon."

"He would have had to have a knife." She walked closer, drawn by the amount of blood. The scene was different from the places she was called to. More personal. It spoke to something inside of her, and not for the first time, she wondered if she'd been made the wrong immortal.

"He might have had a gun," Beckett supposed. "I wouldn't be surprised about that."

"A gun wouldn't have worked. It would have passed right through the creature or any one of us," she replied softly. "Once the bullet left the gun, it would cross over and only be deadly to something mortal. Crossbows, any kind of projectile weaponry, it is all the same. It could only be killed with something anchored to the Veil."

The small wraith chewing on the wraith's corpse stopped, its head popping up, spotting the immortal in the Veil. She waggled her fingers at it, bursting with a giggle as it popped out, a wisp of smoke dust trailing behind it. Swallowed back up, it left nothing but its scent behind, a trace of nothingness conjured by some human emotion. Either it would find something else to eat or quickly die of starvation, its existence an eternal struggle between its burgeoning consciousness and its horrific hunger.

"I'm glad we found him, but we've lost him again." She looked about the motel grounds, not understanding what would draw anyone to live in its broken-down squalor.

"Frazier tracked him down to here," Beckett said. "Maybe there was a gardening tool or even something on the illegal they dragged out of here. Unless the drug changed him, made him stronger…."

"It could have." She sounded unconvinced. "That would be something unexpected. None of us seem any stronger than a human. If it has ill effects, then I'm not certain we want to continue."

"Nothing's certain," Beckett replied. "Let's wait and see. It could just be chance."

Her wavering made him unsteady. The last thing Beckett wanted was to jeopardize everything they had worked on. Something unexpected meant something unplanned, something neither one of them could control. If that were the case, there could be other unwanted surprises, and that definitely wasn't something Beckett wanted to risk. The crossing over had to be perfect for both of them.

"I'm sure you can solve anything that might come up." The woman gazed up at Beckett's open face, shining under his crooked smile. "Do you think the boy will return here?"

"I don't know. Frazier went to see what he could find." Beckett sighed as yet another round of official-looking vehicles arrived, including a black van with Coroner painted on its opaque panels. "I would think so, providing the police don't scare him off. I can't imagine he could have gone through everything he bought last night."

"That would be unfortunate." She cocked her head. "But then, if he can't come back here, he'll be forced to find more drugs, yes? Isn't that how that sickness works?"

"It's not a sickness. It's a weakness," Beckett scoffed. "He's a coward. Running away from his problems with drugs. He probably can't go for a day without them. People like that make me sick."

"People like that are helping us bring you over to me." Reminding him of their plan, she drew up close to his chest, hovering near enough to hear his breath in her body. "But that is how it works, yes? He has to have this drug?"

"Yes, and we know who he goes to. We can make it easy for him to get more," Beckett agreed. "He'll go mad without it. I'm certain Frazier will get the manager to tell me something about the boy. At least which rat-hole he lived in."

She gazed into the crowd, seeing past the stink of death and into the pool of humanity. "If the boy is his friend, perhaps he won't help us."

"Money will make him cooperate," Beckett replied. "I'm sure a few well-placed hundreds, and he'd chain the boy to a chair until one of us gets here. The kid could be the son he never had and he'll cooperate. These kinds of people don't have a lot of faith or loyalty."

"That's the problem with humans, isn't it?" She began to drift off past the Veil, becoming a shade in front of his eyes. "There's no effort to be better."

"I'm sorry, Faith." Beckett reached out, his hands momentarily snagging on what little there was to touch.

"I have to go. I have a calling to attend to." She smiled at the sound of the name she'd chosen. It was nice to hear it spoken aloud, as if hearing it in the air made her more real. "See if you can find him, Beckett. If he's the answer we're looking for, it would be the end to all of our problems. It's lonely here. I want you with me."

"I want to be there," he insisted, talking to empty air as she ghosted away. Anger clenched his guts, rolling frustration tangling up his feelings of affection and the anger at the Veil that kept them apart. "Just give me time. I'll find him. I promise."

KISMET WAS still unconscious when Ari carried him into the Horsemen's penthouse, Mal hovering close by. A thin Chinese woman stood at the far end of the open space, carrying a bowl of noodles into the living area. Nearly as pale as the young man Ari carried, she scratched at the rise of her collarbone, mouth twisting into a frown.

Dressed in a pair of loose cotton pants and a thin white tank top, Min was prepared to settle in for a peaceful night, a tumbler of iced green tea already waiting for her on a low table set in front of one of the couches. The noodles' steam clouded her features, a face of all sharp angles and hardness. With her thin mouth fully set with disapproval, she paced around Ari, taking a good look at his burden. Setting the *somen* down, Min placed a hand on her hip and stared at Ari, her black eyes glittering with harsh annoyance at Kismet's presence.

"What the hell is that doing here?" Min pointed at the young man. Her spiky hair stood straight up, a few inches of black sprouting up over her skull. She'd left the front a bit longer, shoving the fringe aside with impatient fingers. "What are you thinking, Ari?"

"This mess is Mal's idea." Ari cast about, looking for someplace to dump his burden. "Open your suite door, Pest. I'm dumping him in there."

"Him and his damned ideas. Does he have any idea what he's done with this?" Min's fury raged, a tempest barely contained in her voice. Min strode over to Mal's bedroom, then pushed the door open. "Gods, this is worse than that disease he let loose. What the hell is he thinking?"

"He doesn't think." Ari strode past, looking for someplace to dump Kismet. "You try talking to him. He seems to think he's above the rules. I either left him and the boy, or I took both of them. I didn't want to have to explain to Death why I left his latest Pestilence bchind."

"I'm standing right here," Mal muttered, closing the front door behind him.

The impact of what he'd done, bringing a human into their house, sank in. The young man's body still bore the bruises from the attack, a purple quilt of pain stitched over his pale body. His clothes had suffered in the fight, torn from his slender torso. The worn pair of jeans hitched down over his hip bones probably weren't much better looking before the wraith got ahold of him, but the dried blood had turned black in spots, acidic spit burning enormous holes into the denim.

"Is Death home yet?" Ari cocked his head at Min, moving her aside with a jerk of his chin.

Mouth pressed even tighter, Min moved the throw Mal left on the couch in his upper room, mindful of the ichor on the young man's body.

"Not yet. He's still in Hong Kong. I'm glad you're here. I think he needs to be brought home." Min sighed with exasperation. "And I saw the Vanquish. He's going to kill you."

"Tell me something I don't already know." Ari dumped Kismet onto the couch, then caught the young man before he rolled off. "You deal with this. I don't care how you deal with this… just deal with this. I don't want Death to see him. You keep him out of sight until we can figure out what to do with him."

"What did you want me to do?" Mal drew up close to War, nearly in his face. The light caught on Mal's glasses, a shimmering white running over his eyes. "I couldn't leave him."

"Why not?" Min poked at the prone Kismet with her bare foot. Her wiry form held a hidden strength, and the artist rocked slightly with the prod. "He looks fine. A bit beat-up but fine. Okay, so he looks closer to death than fine, but they do that. Sometimes they die. You just leave them where you find them. You don't bring them home like a lamp you found at a garage sale."

"A wraith got him," Ari muttered. "Biggest wraith I've seen in a bit. If I'd known we were going to be bringing Mal's pet home, I would have let the thing eat the boy and then killed it."

"Well, at least it's dead." Min's eyebrows rose. She noticed Ari's clothes and healing face for the first time, whistling under her breath as she walked around the tall Horseman. "I take it you kicked its ass. Well, after it kicked yours. You look thoroughly ass-kicked."

"It's dead. Had to leave it there because of this shit, but it should rot behind the Veil, and no one will be the wiser. Oh yeah, by myself, no thanks to Mal." Ari grunted. "He's no help in a fight. He didn't even bring a fucking knife with him. Sat there and wailed about the human for the most part."

"Fuck you." Mal turned on Ari, biting back. "I don't fight. You know that. Shit, you're the one that's always telling me I just get in the way. Don't start on the 'Mal didn't help me out' shit now."

"If you…." Ari bristled, stepping away from Min and ready for an argument.

The room grew hot, the air closing in on Mal's face. He cocked his chin up, daring Ari to hit him. Mal had no illusions of being able to stand up to the older Horseman. Ari had muscle and skill on his side.

"War, you need to go to him. Just grab him and come back. We'll still be here."

"Deal with that thing, Pest. Keep it hidden, and don't let it out for Death to see." Ari jabbed at Mal's chest. "I'll be bringing him home. I don't want more trouble."

"I STOPPED in Hong Kong before I came home." Min finally spoke, her voice troubled and muddied. "He couldn't get some of them to release. Humans are so unwilling to let go of what they have… even after they're dead, they grip onto what they know too tightly."

"How many?" Mal asked softly. "How many died?"

"I don't know. Hundreds," Min said, sitting down on the sofa, tucking her feet up. "He said he had to touch nearly all of them. I wouldn't want to tell someone that they're dead. That's got to piss people off."

"I couldn't do it." Mal sat down near Kismet's head, stroking at the tangled mass of hair hiding the artist's face. "I don't know how he does it. After as long as he's lived… it just makes my head hurt."

"Your head's not going to be the only thing hurting if you don't come up with a way to get rid of this human." Min motioned toward Kismet. "This is probably one of the stupidest things you've ever done."

"I couldn't leave him, Min." Mal moved to the edge of the cushion, trying to make her understand. "He can see us."

"A lot of them can see us," Min said, shaking her head at her brother's foolishness. "It just means that they're crazy. You know that."

"No. Not him. Well, maybe just a little bit, but that's from seeing past the Veil," Mal insisted. "He looked right at me and saw me plainly. None of the delirium or visions were in his sight. There wasn't any madness in him.

"I don't understand why I felt like we had to take him," Mal admitted. "I just ached when I thought about abandoning him. Something in me understood that I had to get him out of there. Take him someplace safe."

"So you brought him here," Min said with a sigh. "Ari's right. You're a fucking idiot."

"Here's the safest place I know," the youngest replied. "It became my problem. He became my problem."

"Your problem is not understanding how things work. You expect us to watch you crap, dig through your own feces, and then worship what you end up holding in your hands like it's some golden egg." Min let out her exasperation. "Death lets you get away with it because he feels sorry for you. Hell, I feel sorry for you, but this shit has got to stop, Mal. Even if he can see us, why bring him home? Others can see us. You don't see me asking them up for a cup of tea and a cookie."

"Nearly all of those people are crazy," Mal said. "The ones that can see us are usually cracked and slip between the folds in the Veil. He's not crazy. I just know it."

"Just because you think he's sane doesn't mean he's still not sensitive to the Veil," Min countered. "Doesn't mean he's not going to turn crazy. You've been at this long enough to know the differences between mortals. He's a human. Mortal."

"He healed up. Like we do. A bit slower, but still, healed right over," he told her, meeting Min's shocked gaze with a shrug. "The wraith tore him up, Min. There were pieces of him hanging out of his body."

"You were probably just thinking he was more hurt than he was." The boy's clothes were tattered and brown with dried blood, but she couldn't remember seeing any visible wounds on him. But then, Min admitted, she was much more concerned about Death than the flotsam Mal found in a gutter.

Pushing up Kismet's shirt, Min examined the boy's thin body, noticing the punctured, deflated veins in his arm and the bruises mottling his pale skin. "Nothing left of the wraith on him. Death's going to want to know about that in the morning. This isn't right, Mal."

"It didn't feel wrong, Min. I didn't feel like it left me sick to my stomach. His healing just felt… natural." Mal rubbed at his face, tasting the salt of his own sweat from his hands "I only looked because I thought that he was going to die and I might have to call Death if he got stuck. He was mine. I didn't want him trapped here because he was too far gone to realize he was dead."

"You'd call Death just for one human," Min said in disgust. "Even knowing he was called elsewhere and he would be dead tired and emotionally drained, you would have done that?"

"He would have come." Mal realized how selfish he must have seemed, but he had been past caring. All of his thoughts had been on the young man writhing in pain. He'd never been so close to a mortal dying before, and the shock of seeing the light fade from those luminous brown eyes would have killed him inside. "Death would have come if I asked."

"Only goes to show that you're not right in the head yourself," Min replied. "And Death's not too stable either for humoring you. You need a good kick in that soft-hearted ass of yours, Mal. Ari might have to do it, because you're just not listening to me."

"Ari kept telling me to dump him," Mal responded, pulling Kismet's tangled mane back. "It looked like he was bitten clear through his neck. But when I held him, he got better, became more alive. There was so much blood. Then everything just began to come together. He's still bruised to hell, but there were gaping wounds there… huge holes you could stick three fingers into, and they're almost gone."

Min stared at the reddened spots, skin bright with circles. She sat down hard, running nervous hands over her thighs. "There's something wrong here, Mal. Humans don't heal like this. Maybe he's a Changeling left by an UnSidhe?"

"Maybe he's immortal, like us?" Mal responded with a nod. "I'm telling you, something happened to him to make him like us. I don't know what."

"Yeah, something definitely happened. I'll give you that. If he's immortal, then he'd have a calling. Did either of you feel anything when he was awake?" Min asked, wondering if she'd ever get back to her dinner.

"Ari was the one who carried him into the car. He wouldn't show it, but I know he was worried about Death and just wanted to get back here," Mal answered. "Honestly, I didn't ask Ari about what he thought."

"He doesn't have any ideas unless Death clears them first," Min replied. "He gets into trouble otherwise. I wonder if any of the other immortals have any answers. Maybe he belongs to one of their groups."

"I don't really know about any of the others, other than Hope." Mal stood, stretching out the knots in his shoulders. His leg still ached from the encounter with the wraith in the garage.

"They stay away because we do nasty things to people. They don't care that we're here for a reason too."

Min retrieved her noodles and stood in front of Mal's doorway. Drawing out one strand and letting it fall back into the stock, she dug out a slice of pink-swirled *kamaboku* and bit into it. Grimacing at the cold mouthful, she returned to the kitchen and dumped the noodles into the garbage disposal.

She picked up her iced tea, cubes tinkling against the glass, and spoke to the younger immortal through the open door to his suite. "You might just want to leave him on the couch. It doesn't look like he's going to be moving any time soon. I'm going to catch some TV and then hit the sack. I'd suggest you do the same. It's nearly sunup."

"Thanks, Min," Mal said.

"For what?" Min sipped at her iced tea, making a face at its sugary sweetness. If she could, she'd take over making the iced tea just to save herself from Death's sweet tooth.

"For being nicer than Ari, I guess," Mal replied. "It's hard, you know, doing this. I feel like I'm not learning fast enough."

"You're not," Min agreed. "But you're less of a dick than some I've met. Not as much of an asshole as Ari, so I guess you're okay. Just try not to fuck up anymore. I'd hate to think you'd be the first one they fire. If anyone is going to screw up that bad, I'd rather it be me. I'd be famous."

CHAPTER SIX

THE DEAD were everywhere. They clouded the landscape, walking through burning buildings and smoking embers. With the slums of Hong Kong on fire, they clustered around the dying, calling out to other souls or people who could no longer hear them. The ghettos were towering stacks of makeshift dwellings made of cast-off wood and rusted iron roof sheeting, lining the narrow streets. In places there was barely enough space between them to see glimpses of the night sky.

Ari figured that, as slums went, it was better than most. And like nearly all slums, it burned as easily as a bundle of dry kindling.

He'd come out into a firestorm, flames rising into a tornado of sparks and hot winds. The Veil parted before him, sliced open as he pulled on Death's presence. He'd only had to part the shadows and step in, concentrating on finding the other immortal's resonance. Ari was certain the Veil had a wicked sense of humor, seeming to deposit him in the most dangerous of locations instead of at Death's side.

Fire gave death a pungent odor. It had been an honest one, at one time. Now plastics and other man-made materials curdled its honesty. Sniffing at the air, Ari gagged on the burned-peanut smell of polyesters and other melted substances, covering over the more familiar charred human flesh. The sourness of burning garbage warred with the powdery scent of smoking mold, an underlayer to the acrid smoke rising around him. Pulling up the collar of his shirt, he covered his nose, hoping to filter out some of the rankness in the air.

A ghost floated by, her arms wrapped around her thin body. Ari let her go by unmolested. She was long past Death's touch. There would be no helping her pass into the void that lay behind the Veil. Sighing, he resigned himself to searching the slums, keeping the Veil's influence around him. The last thing he wanted to do was be pulled into a rescue attempt or subject himself to the anger of a mob.

His nature encouraged the organization of mobs. He rather liked mobs, although the others frowned on them. In this case, he was sure Death would frown upon an uprising in the middle of a disastrous fire. His friend disliked riots in the middle of his work.

"Ari?" Death's tired voice called out to him as he picked his way through the ruins. "Is that you?"

"How many other tall blond men do you find wandering around Hong Kong ghettos?"

He approached Death with long strides, nearly running in his haste to reach the other man.

Placing his hands on his friend's shoulders, he stared into the immortal's weary features, not liking what he saw. Fatigue set itself firmly into the other's face, and Death looked drained to Ari's prying eyes.

The other man's fingers lightly brushed along the healing acid drops on Ari's cheek. Ari's jacket wrinkled when Death's hands dropped, clenching tightly at the leather. Their foreheads touched, Ari's face awash with turmoil, bare and unseen before Death's closed eyes. They stood there together for a moment, broken apart by internal battles. Ari drew away first, feeling the other man's shifting weight against his chest.

"You look like shit. You've got smears of smoke all over your face." Ari wiped at a line of black along the other's cheek, succeeding only in widening the dark streak. Grimacing, he wiped his hand on his torn jeans. "Is it bad?"

The immortal nodded, still mired down in the mud of his thoughts. Taking a deep breath, Death steadied himself, trying to shake off the weariness and the smell of crackling bodies from his mind. Giving Ari a wry smile, he poked a playful finger through one of the holes in the other's jacket, commenting softly, "Bad enough. From the looks of things, we've both had trials by fire tonight. What happened to you?"

"How bad is it, Shi?" Ari asked softly. "How bad?"

"Not Pompeii bad." Death's cheek dimpled hearing the old nickname given to him by a past Famine. It never sounded strange coming from their War. Maybe in time he'd accept that as his name. "But still bad. A lot of the dead didn't want to leave. Why are you here? You're going to cause problems."

"I'm known for that," Ari teased his friend.

"Ari, I'm serious. With you here, the dying will fight me. I can't have that."

"Shi, there's no one here left alive." Ari cupped Death's chin. "Any fighting that's going to be done will be by people punching each other out as they loot."

Death grew somber, still hearing the souls of crackling bodies crying out for their lost families.

When he closed his eyes, he saw burned children begging him to help look for parents buried under mounds of ashes, suffocating slowly beneath the weight of fallen houses. Offering promises, he cajoled distraught spirits to pass on through the Veil, hoping that some would stop digging at piles of burning shambles, wraith hands passing helplessly through the rubble. Then the whispering nothings of their spirits were trapped in the folds, set to wander as time fixed them in place, butterflies half-alive and pinned fast to a moving world.

"And you? You found something?" Death's voice trailed off. "You never answer me when I ask you a question."

"We found something alright." The Aston Martin was foremost on his mind. That and the boy Mal dragged home, but the fatigue on Death's face kept him quiet.

"What happened?" Death asked.

"Long story. We can deal with it later." Ari slid his arm around Death's waist. "Come on. Let's put you to bed. We can talk there."

"Talk? You never want to just talk." Death stood still, a motionless statue of anguish cast in bone and hair. There was humor in his voice, a flat thread of silver in the gloom. "I'm not ready to go home yet, Ari. I have to go through the ashes one more time. I might have missed someone."

The fragile truce between them wavered, threatening to fall. He wouldn't be able to deal with any of Ari's teasing propositions or wandering hands. Death wanted nothing more than to rest in the quiet of his own thoughts, mulling them over until the dead were driven into the back of his mind.

"Just talk," Ari promised. "And if you want to go through this shit hole one more time, then I'll do it with you."

Death searched Ari's face, digging at the countless lies told over so many centuries. Emotions raw, Ari felt his heart break at the reluctant nod Death gave him, a helpless little gesture offering up trust.

"Why?" Death asked, gently pushing Ari's control with the softness of his voice.

"Because you need me to. Maybe just because you need me," Ari said. "When we're done, we'll head home. I know Min set you up with some hot tea. Lots of sugar. She probably didn't even poison it."

With a soothing patience, Ari guided Death along, the dark-haired immortal tucked under his arm. Their mingling voices dropped into a whisper. Then Death stilled, frozen against the smoke.

"Did you hear that?"

"Hear what?" Ari stopped, listening for something human. "I didn't hear anything."

"Did you not hear anything because you didn't want to or because you really didn't hear anything?" Death pushed the other immortal away, his long legs quickly putting distance between them.

"Why do you always assume the worst from me?" Shouting at the other's back, Ari gritted his teeth against his rising anger. Muttering mostly to himself, he followed, carefully avoiding piles of embers. "I came looking for you, asshole. Doesn't that count for something?"

"I want to do a final cleanse. I think I got them all, but I'm never sure. Not with so many around me." Death glanced over his shoulder and Ari staring at him. "Are you going to help me?"

"You know I will." Ari mumbled curses under his breath, coming to Death's side. "I'll always help you."

Crossing over to a clear space in the street, Death drew a knife from a sheath at his thigh. The bronze blade was dull, its edge bent from years of use. He didn't need it to be sharp. The Veil responded more to the ritual of the blade than anything else. Raising his hand, Death drew the Veil up, thickening the shadows at his fingertips. As the darkness pulled together, he raised his knife and sliced into it, cutting away an opening.

The knife was an old companion, a remnant of a day when they actually rode horseback through the countryside, looking for travelers lost in their own death. He didn't remember where he'd gotten it, either a spoil from one of Ari's campaigns or a gift one of the other Four gave him. Either way, the hilt fit nicely into his hand, and the curled-around bone guard rested easily against the knuckles of his fingers.

He'd been fond of bronze, saddened when new metals rose to take its place. None of the darker sheens held the brightness of a good bronze, although their edges were much sharper. He'd kept the blade for this one purpose, to aid the dead in their passing.

As the Veil tore open, a rush of hot air struck his face, winds driven up from the depths of some unknown heat. The passage into the shadows always ran warm, sometimes a welcoming embrace, other times an inferno. Death placed no thought as to the heat. That storm raged long before the concept of Hell had come along. He sometimes wondered if the warmth led to the myth of a raging fire waiting to consume unlucky souls.

The tear brought down the wrath of the dead still left in the mortal world. As the afterlife seeped into the surrounding area, enraged howls cut through the air. Shrieks belled from the wreckage, long-dead ghosts rising from the ground, upset at the violation of their self-made prisons. Death was ready when a wraith spun down from the upper reaches, her hands hooked into claws, trying to rake at his face. Ari moved to intercept it, but Death shook his head, hoping the dead woman would pass through him.

"Let her be, Ari." He patted the immortal's forearm. "She can't hurt me."

"They're like roaches." Ari stepped closer to his friend's side, alert for any other attack. "Skittering things. Gives me the creeps sometimes."

"You're not very helpful here." Death shooed the other immortal off, pointing to the side. "Go stand over there. Out of the way."

"You could need me." Insistent, he brushed his hand along the back of Death's neck.

"I do need you. Oddly enough, having you nearby is comforting." Spoken aloud, the words were soft, but they burrowed with sharp claws into Ari's mind. "I just don't need you standing on top of me. Please, Ari."

Grunting, the immortal nodded, then walked back a few feet, still within reach if Death needed him. Turning back to the tear he made in the Veil, Death dug the blade back into the shadowy curtain, carving out another slice.

"Why do you always make triangles?" Ari wondered aloud. "Do something different for a change."

A ghost wandered around them, wringing his hands. Left with nothing to do but wait for Death, the specter periodically glanced back at the wreckage of his home, as if debating returning to his task.

Ari edged the ghost forward, placing himself between the ruined hovel and the dead man's spirit. "You stay right here. No heading off. You've got someplace else to be."

"I like the shapes. They feel like they can lead souls somewhere." After putting the knife away, Death folded the shadow slices back with his hands, struggling to affect the Veil. Tired, he strained against the curtain's resistance, manipulating it into a portal large enough for a man to pass through.

"It looks like a river." The dead man spoke, marveling at the wide thread of silver undulating beyond the velvet black slice. "It sounds like water flowing."

Death had heard many of the dead exclaim nearly the same thing, their eyes finding something substantial in the silvery ribbon cutting a swath through the hot darkness. Some saw a river, while others spoke of a wing. Still others saw clouds or just a stream of light.

Every immortal could step into the black spirals behind the Veil, sliding over to places on Earth that called them, but this was the one line none of them could touch. Death hoped it led to some place human souls could find peace. He'd not spoken to anyone who'd come back from the journey. He could only have faith in what he believed to be true.

Nervous, the man asked, "Can you come with me? I mean, aren't you supposed to come with me? To show me the way?"

"No, I'm sorry. I can't go where you need to." Refusing the man was hard, especially seeing the desolation in his face. He placed a hand on the man's ghostly shoulder, pushing him toward the shining ribbon. "You just need to step in. It will take you along to where you should be."

The soul hovered, sliding halfway through the opening Death had made into the Veil. Rising, the winds hit them, as hot and wild as the firestorm burning in the next district. The man hesitated, instinct telling him to hide away from the pull of the odd river, but the memory of his children's faces burned hotter than his fear, and he stepped further into shadows. His head disappeared, his shoulders frozen at the triangular opening, hanging onto the edge with tightly clenched hands.

"Don't you just want to stand behind them sometimes and give a hard push?" A torn fingernail caught on Ari's jeans, and he chewed its edge off, spitting the shredded nail out from between his teeth.

"Ari," Death growled, his patience unraveling to a single thread.

"Yeah, I know, shut up." The other man shrugged off Death's irritation. "Don't give me that look. I'm not even speaking his language. He can't understand me."

"I can understand you," Death said. He watched the man step into the dark, sparks of light swirling up from the silvered path. The current caught, dragging the soul off into the churning light at the horizon.

The man began to unravel around the edges. He glanced back, looking down at the blackened remains of his body, dark eyes tearing up. Reaching for Death, his fingers vanished before he could touch the immortal, falling away to the nothingness beyond.

"Let go," Death said. "It will be fine. I promise."

He finally went, falling into the quiet of the Veil. The man was gone in an instant, barely a whisper of a voice carried along the gusts of hot air. Death exhaled hard, relieved at the man's passing, and stood silent until Ari cleared his throat, a harsh, gruff noise that sounded a bit like disgust to Death's ears.

"What?" Ari widened his eyes, innocently staring back at his friend.

"You could be a bit more respectful."

"Why? They go on. We move along." The immortal shrugged, holding a hand out for Death to steady himself with. "It's what they do. It's what we do."

"One day, I'll make you understand this," Death said, gripping at Ari's wrist, allowing himself to be pulled to his feet. Slapping at the soot clinging to his pants, he stepped clear of the fallen walls.

"I'd rather just get you home." Holding onto the other man's waist, Ari reached out to find their sanctuary, drawing on the presence of the Four's resonance along the shadows running through the Veil. "And a shower. Because you, my friend, stink."

"You're not much sweeter," Death replied, wrinkling his nose at the scent of Ari's shirt. "What did you roll in? Dog shit?"

"I would have counted myself lucky to have rolled in dog shit," Ari laughed. "Come on. You strong enough to get there on your own, or do I have to piggyback you?"

"I'll be fine." He shook off Ari's hand. "But when we get home, you take a shower before you come to bed. I'm not having you on my sheets, smelling like that."

MAL RETURNED to his room and sat on the couch, careful not to jostle the young man. Alone except for the sleeping Kismet, Mal burrowed down against the soft cushions, wondering what to do next.

"Hey," Kismet said softly. Awake and pale, he blinked, trying to focus on his surroundings.

The human's husky voice startled Mal, and he jumped, knocking his knees against the low coffee table. Kismet's brown eyes were full of life again, and vivid bruises were beginning to rise on his cheekbone.

"Hello." Mal pushed his glasses up the ridge of his nose. Reluctantly, he eased away from the young man's welcome warmth, letting the cushions rise up and flatten under Kismet's body. "How do you feel?"

Coughing, Kismet tried to turn, stopped by a wave of pain in his head. Resting back down, he blinked away the tears in his eyes. "Fuck, that hurts."

"No, don't move, Kismet." Wincing in sympathy at the anguish on Kismet's face, Mal reached under to pull at a cushion to straighten it. "How much do you remember?"

"I'm better than I thought I would be, considering I was eaten alive by a huge dog-thing." Kismet winced as he shifted his legs, calves tight with contractions from being tucked under him. "I think it was trying to kill me. And I remember you guys coming. Then things started getting fuzzy. Oh, and I hurt."

Sitting on the coffee table's edge, Mal looked over the young man's bruises. He'd not planned on the young man waking up before morning. Now his brain was scrambling as he tried to think about what to tell the human. "The monster didn't do that much damage. It wasn't as bad as it looked."

"Did you tell me your name before?" Kismet asked suddenly. "I don't remember."

"Mal," the Horseman said.

"Okay then, Mal, don't lie to me. That thing ate right through me. I'm kind of more than banged up. That wasn't a wild dog." Every movement sent tingles of agony through Kismet's body. Gasping, he drew short breaths in through his teeth.

"Hold still. Let me see how your injuries look." Pulling up the other's shirt, Mal examined a stretch of redness on the young man's ribs, unsure if he should be happy or frustrated at the knitted skin. Most of the wounds were sealed, just a burr of raw flesh left open to the air.

"How's your head?" Mal asked. He had little experience with serious injuries, other than the occasional stab by a supposedly well-intentioned Ari during weapons practice. There was nothing that could be done about the bruises, Mal reasoned. They would just have to fade on their own.

"I can't see too well. I can see you okay but not behind you."

"Probably loss of blood. Vision likes blood and oxygen. I think it'll get better over time." Mal reached over to wave his fingers in front of Kismet's face, then spotted the needle marks on the inside of the other man's arms. Touching at them lightly, Mal drew back when Kismet shook him off. "Did he bite you there too?"

"Nope. I bit me there." Kismet fought with his body, trying to force himself off the couch, failing when his limbs refused to respond. He didn't feel the burn of the heroin in his system, but he knew it wouldn't be long before he started having the shakes. "Hang around a couple of hours. That monster scared the shit right out of me. I'm probably going to need to shoot again."

"A gun wouldn't have helped you," Mal said. "Nothing fired or thrown can hurt one. A weapon has to be anchored to someone Veiled for it to work on something like a wraith."

"Gun?" Kismet tried to focus on the face swimming just beyond his sight. He could make out a tousle of light blond hair and round glasses, the barest brush of stubble over a square jaw. "Wow, you're serious. Where the hell am I?"

"You're in my room." Mal noticed the tremors in the young man's fingers. They worried him. All of his experiences with humans inevitably led to them dying. Trembling wasn't a natural occurrence in most humans; he was sure of it. "You just need some sleep."

"*Where*? Narnia?" Kismet peered around, trying to make sense of the shapes and silence of the apartment. He strained to hear the whispering voices he knew lurked in the darkness. Nothing called to him, a slithering quiet that unnerved him. Resting back in the soft cushions of the couch, the silence became a comfort. Concentrating on the young man next to him, Kismet relaxed, letting the ache in his bones ease away. "And what the hell did you guys do to me? There's no way I should be as healed up as I am. That thing ate me."

"I told you, my room. At home," the Horseman replied. "In my home. Where the Four of us live."

"Four?" Kismet asked softly. "You've got a group thing going? Shit, I can't keep one person going, and you've got three others. Damn."

"A group thing?" Mal wasn't certain if the disconnect in his mind had to do with Kismet's speech patterns or his lack of knowledge of the human world. "The Four of us are a group, I suppose."

"Mal, no offense, but you're kind of dim. I don't think you're getting what I'm saying." Kismet tried to lift himself up, moaning in pain as his muscles protested. "Sweet and cute but dim. A group thing. Sex and love. Poly something or other? More than two people?"

"Oh!" The red started under Mal's skin and burned to the surface of his face. "No, it's not like that. We're… I'm not… we're not a group like that. There's nothing wrong with that… we're just not…."

"It's okay." Kismet grinned despite the ache in his face and neck, the tightness of his healing skin pulling with the motion. "You don't have to explain anything to me if you don't want to. Well no, I do want to know what you did to make me better."

"I just don't want you to get the wrong idea about…." Mal swore under his breath, finding words Ari used quite satisfying in this situation. "I'm not sure what kind of idea I want you to get. I should probably start over."

"Okay, start with why my guts aren't all over the sidewalk of the motel."

"I don't know," Mal admitted. "We just found you. Maybe someone took you to a hospital."

"Dude, you are the world's shittiest liar." Kismet plucked at the torn clothes stretched over his body. "There wasn't a hospital, and I'm still wearing what I had on when the monster attacked me."

"Okay, Ari and I took you home after the wraith bit you." The youngest Horseman worried at his lower lip with his teeth. "I don't know what else to tell you. Sit still for a moment. I need to see about something."

Mal took a deep breath, stretching his soul out. When he was around the others, he felt the press of their callings on his, linked together into a single strong unit. The other immortals avoided the Four, but the few times Mal had been around one, he felt their presence on the Veil, a soft beacon he could respond to. Despite the healing of Kismet's body, Mal felt none of that in the young man they'd rescued, a blankness where a calling should have been. Whatever Kismet was now, he certainly wasn't human anymore, but he wasn't an immortal like Mal.

"You're not one of us." Disappointed, Mal sat back. He'd wanted so much for Kismet to be a part of their world. "Shit."

"You okay?" Kismet reached for Mal's leg, his arm trembling with the effort. His body refused to respond quickly, each movement leaving him weak.

"I'm fine," Mal said. He felt the burn of a blush on his face again. Kismet's hand on his thigh disturbed what little calm he'd mustered up. Contact with someone other than the Four was rare. The last intimate touch he'd had was when Ari dragged him to Vegas and paid for a woman to show him pleasure. "I'm just not sure how much to tell you."

"You tell me as little or as much as you want to," he replied. "You don't have to explain anything. Hell, you dragged me out of that thing's mouth. I don't have any complaints about anything. I just don't understand what the hell is going on."

"I feel like I need to at least tell you what we are," Mal said. He touched the back of Kismet's arm, stroking at the warm flesh, marveling at the feel of a fine down on his fingertips. "You might not believe me. I don't know much about what people believe."

Looking down at his hands, Mal tried to decide what he should share. Other than the Four, Mal had never had someone to speak to before, someone open to the Veil and free of any preconceptions of the Horsemen. With the sloe-eyed young man nestled back into the couch's cushions listening intently, Mal found himself talking on about how the Horsemen lived, hidden from the world and saddled with the unenviable.

"So, you guys are kind of like angels?" Kismet asked after Mal finally wound down, his thoughts swimming. He'd often thought he was crazy, but the blond sitting next to him had him beat. "You want me to believe you're angels?"

"No, not angels. I'm not explaining this well." Mal knew he'd muddled things, going over what he'd said in his mind. "We're just the Four Horsemen, like in the Bible. Sort of."

"The Bible isn't on my summer reading list, man. The only thing I know about the Four Horsemen is what people bring in to get inked on their bodies," Kismet replied. "Maybe you are crazier than me."

"I'm not. This is real. I don't know what else I can do to convince you."

"So it's just the four of you, then. Here to save mankind."

"There are others like us, but they don't have much to do with us." Mal saw the doubt in Kismet's face. "No really, there are. Not just the Horsemen, people like Luck and even the Vices are real. Sort of real, anyway. And we're not here to save mankind, not really."

"Got to tell you, man," Kismet admitted. "You sound insane. Cute but really fucking nuts."

"Funny, that's what they keep saying about you." Mal laughed, a hearty, free sound. "Ari's sure you're crazy, and that's why you can see us."

"Oh, I'm definitely a bit on the crazy side. That's already been proven." Kismet groaned, his insides pounding to get out. He felt the back of his skull, mewling when his shoulder muscles screamed in torment. "God, that hurts. My head really hurts too."

"Maybe you need to get some sleep," Mal said, unsure of what to do for the young man stretched out on the couch.

"Do you have some aspirin?" Kismet beseeched him. The pain burned, hotter than the need ever had. It came in waves, ebbing at times, then flaring again, riding into his vision and nerves. His intestines twisted, a knotting pain chewing outward as the tangled cords attempted to right themselves. "Damn, I'll take anything right now."

"I'll go ask." Mal knew he didn't have any, but he knew the others sometimes took analgesics, usually after a long sparring round with Death. "Min might have something."

"Thanks." Kismet risked another movement of his arms, rubbing at his temple. The throbbing intensified, threatening to crack his head open. "My head hurts almost as much as my ribs do."

Mal left his room and knocked on Min's door. The sounds of a car chase barely whispered through the door, made louder when it suddenly opened. Mal stood there, nearly jumping back when faced with Min biting off the end of a peeled banana. Tires screeched loudly before she aimed a remote at the television she'd hung on the wall, condemning the action film to a temporary silence.

"Whatcha need?" she said around a mouthful of fruit. Her toes were separated by large wads of cotton balls, the smell of fresh polish fighting with the powdery tang of the banana. "Tell me he solved all of our problems by dying."

"Nope. He's awake, in fact," Mal replied. "I was hoping you had aspirin. He's asking for some."

"Aspirin I've got." Min waddled through her living space, walking around the wide-open staircase and into the upstairs bathroom. "Eternal life and still with the headaches. At least we don't get colds. I'd have to kick your ass if I caught a cold, because it would have been your fault."

"I didn't come up with the cold," Mal retorted. "You have to blame another Pestilence for that one."

"It's a legacy disease. All of you are responsible for it," Min shouted at Mal through the open door.

Unlike Mal's cluttered rooms, Min preferred clean lines and a nearly rabid neatness. The only sign of mess was a cracked-open nail polish bottle on a freeform glass table. The banana skin was nowhere to be seen. She made some sounds as she dug around in the medicine cabinet, bottles clattering against one another. Mal peered at her movie collection, mostly action flicks and Chinese epics, filed alphabetically. The shelf below held a few music CDs, also fanatically arranged by artist and release date.

"You're kind of odd," Mal said when Min came back in, checking an expiration date as she walked. "In an everything-in-a-line kind of way."

"You should talk." She handed over a bottle, a few small white pills jangling at the bottom. "You've got stuffed animals shaped like diseases."

"I thought they were ironic." He sniffed, slightly put off by her laughing tone. "It seemed ironic to me."

"Ironic would have been one of us buying them for you," Min pointed out. "Pathetic is when you buy them for yourself. Go dose the kid up. With any luck he'll survive the day, and we can return him to the wild. If you handle them too long, their mothers don't take them back into the nest."

"You think Death would mind if he stayed?" Mal was cut off by a shake of Min's head. "I don't think he's human anymore."

"Don't even think about it. If you want a pet, go get a cat." Min pushed Mal toward the open door. "Yeah, he's pretty. But he's not yours. He needs to go back where you found him. Some sad-faced girl is probably bawling her eyes out because the pretty little thing she cuddles with didn't come home last night."

"You're mean," Mal muttered, turning the bottle over to read the instructions.

"I'm Famine." Min leaned against the frame of her bedroom door. "You don't get to be Famine because you're all sweetness and light. Takes some balls to starve people to death. Go. I want to watch my movie."

Mal grabbed a glass of water from the kitchen, then returned to his suite. Holding a few of the pills in his hand, he slid between the table and the couch, staring down at the battered human. Kismet was fast asleep, the flicker of his eyelids faint beneath a blush of bruised skin. The morning light pinked the room, rays peeking up over the low mountains. Kismet shifted, mewling softly.

Turning onto his side, the young man flung one scar-dappled arm over his face, shutting out the dawn. The hem of his torn shirt rode up over his stomach, exposing a stretch of skin flushed with healed contusions.

"Probably better if you sleep it off." Mal set the water glass down, making sure the aspirin wouldn't roll off the table. Taking one final glance over at the young man, Mal turned off the lights and shut curtains. "Night, Kismet. Try to have only good dreams."

CHAPTER SEVEN

ARI STRETCHED out over Death's bed, luxuriating in the softness of fine cotton sheets and plump feather pillows. Of all the things mankind had created, Ari put bedding at the top of his list, possibly even above a powerful engine. The linens smelled of Death, pungent overtones of green tea with a delicate whisper of citrus floating just below. Turning his head, the immortal found a single black hair caught on the pillow. Ari grabbed one end and held it aloft, tickling the edges of his mouth.

The sheets were cold next to him, the linens dimpled from the weight of Death's body. A glance at the clock on the nightstand showed only a few hours had passed since he'd fallen asleep, much too soon for Death to be awake, in Ari's opinion. He slid from the bed, pulled on a pair of sweats, then went upstairs to search for the other Horseman.

Balboa Park glimmered below, expanses of trees punctuated by strings of white lights along the boulevards intersecting the greenery. The Museum of Man's ornate tower rose into the night, illuminated from within. In the daytime the long stretch of windows displayed a serene view of the park. At night it transformed into a dazzling panoramic pageant of lights, spots of white highlighting the museum's architecture. With morning just an hour or two away, the spire was dusted with the oncoming dawn's pink light.

Ari liked Death's study, a mishmash of old, comfortable furniture, soft couches set around low tables. A mug of cold tea kept company with stacks of old books and sheets of loose papers dotted with Death's scrawling handwriting. The deep red walls were lined with bookcases dotted with art pieces that Ari didn't understand and wasn't sure if he liked.

Death kept very little of his past around him, shutting artifacts into boxes before putting them away. The few things he kept were intimate, little tidbits of the life he shared with Ari. A tiny scrimshaw spinning wheel shone gold under the light, the worked ivory a gift Ari had left on Death's pillow when they lived in Shanghai.

Ari pushed aside the glossy leaves of a large dieffenbachia, studying the Asian sitting crouched over his books.

"What are you doing up?" Ari asked. "You should be asleep, not looking over dusty books."

"I never let books get dusty." Death barely looked up when Ari approached him, his attention fixed on the scattering of pages in front of him. "What are you doing up? And half-naked no less."

"I came looking for you. Maybe I was hoping I could entice you back into bed. You're tired, Shi." Ari sat down. He wanted to pull Death into his arms, telling the other man to shut up, let go, and sleep. It was an old argument, one Ari never tired of fighting, because once in a great while, it was one that he won. "I can see the bags beneath your eyes. They're not pretty."

"I feel like there's an answer here." A flip of a page waved the distinct fragrance of old paper into the air, a sweet, pungent smell Death loved. "I just needed to do something."

"Yeah, I get like that too. Neither one of us likes being helpless." A flicker of black ran across Death's notes, a single sentence moving slowly from right to left. Picking up the page, Ari attempted to make sense of the scribbles. "The infamous 'They' decided to speak up about something? What's it say?"

Death pursed his mouth, nearly a kissable pout to Ari's eyes. He turned the page around, then returned to his reading. "Try that."

"I still can't make this out." Ari returned Death's moue, mocking the other Horseman. "I learned to read after this crap became archaic, remember? Did someone behind the curtain actually cough up some information for a change? Do we look for a big neon arrow that flashes Stupid Magus Here?"

"Nothing that helpful."

"The moving text is a nice touch. Got to give them that." Ari touched the page, expecting to feel movement under his hand. The paper remained smooth, despite the shifting letters. "Might give you a headache if you stare at it long enough."

"I wish it would stop. I think I wrote something important there that I want to check against this," Death said, tracing a line of text in a book. "It only says that things will get worse for this world if we don't stop this thing, whatever it is."

"Oh yes," the blond shot back. "We didn't know that. Maybe we should just let them all die. I mean, sometimes, don't you just wish humans would clean up their own messes?"

Death glanced at his hijacked notes, hoping the moving text had stopped so he could reference a passage against what he wrote. "When did you of all people become judgmental?"

"Maybe I'm jealous. I like being the center of your attention." Ari stroked Death's bare arm, the back of his hand warmed by the contact. "Tell me you found something useful in the books at least. Or should I just drag you off to bed?"

"Only bits and pieces." Death's heavy sigh rattled in his chest. As he rubbed at his face, fatigue spread through his body, numbing him down to his bones. "I don't know what I thought I could find. I guess I hoped there was someone in the past who did the same thing and I could find something solid."

"And the wraiths that seemed to want to eat us?" Ari asked. "There's not a lot of accidental in that."

"No," Death admitted. "That definitely wasn't an accident. I don't think I have the right books or maybe even the proper translations. Reading through these is like trying to grab at a ghost. Just when I think I have something solid, it whispers out of my mind. The closest reference I can find is about a thirteenth-century sorcerer that disappeared into the shadows and never came out."

"If he never came out, how do they know it happened?"

"His apprentice was tasked with keeping track of his experiments." Death leaned into the curve of Ari's body, cradling a book between them. "This is a translation of the student's original journals. He says that his mentor worked on an elixir for decades, testing it on criminals."

"How did that go?"

"The text says most of the test subjects died. A few went insane." Turning a page, Death pointed to an illustration of a man parting a curtain. "He then wrote that the sorcerer took the potion himself and stepped through a lake of mercury. As far as the apprentice knew, no one ever saw the man again."

"So, the same things that happened then are happening now?" Ari reached for Death's cup of tea, making a face at the cold, bitter brew. "Walking through a lake of mercury. That sounds like the Veil."

"It does," Death agreed. "If the apprentice could see the Veil, he might have been a Seer and not have known it. The journals don't say much beyond that. I think Peace might have an original text. He gave me this one."

"Surprisingly generous of him." The next sip of tea was more palatable, Ari decided, the bitterness edged out by a light verdant taste behind it. "Let's get you back into bed. We can go talk to Peace about lending us what he's got. Maybe take a couple of goats and a basket of eggs in trade."

"He'll think you're offering him a dowry." Death allowed himself to be pulled from the couch, Ari's hand closed around his fingers. Ari turned the lights off, then led Death downstairs, back to the bed they'd shared. As Ari shed his sweats, Death shut the curtains, hiding the waking cityscape from view.

Joining Ari, the eldest Horseman tucked himself under the sheets War held up for him. They'd gotten no real guidance, and while Ari didn't expect any, Death hoped for at least a clue on where to start looking for the human.

They lay together often, sometimes for comfort, other times for warmth. Death slid into the hollow of Ari's body, easing against the other immortal's side. The blond's right shoulder cupped Death's cheek, Ari's hand sliding down to stroke at the Asian man's back, tracing the dip of his spine before following the bone line up to the winged jutting of blades beneath the brush of Death's black hair. The elder slid his arm over Ari's belly, the bend of his elbow just striking the edge of the other's hip bone.

Shifting, Death moved to free the loose ends of his drawstring pants, trapped between them.

Finding the edges of sleep just beyond his grasp, Death let his mind wander, his fingers finding the scar on Ari's rib cage and tracing the edges lightly. As the Horseman settled, Ari waited, naked and silent under Death's body, their breathing falling into sync.

"Mal will probably have to head to Hong Kong in a bit." Death spoke, his breath a whispering heat over War's chest. A lamp burned low on the table, giving him just enough light to see Ari's stomach muscles bunching under his touch. "I think there are things brewing for him in the burned remains of that slum I was called to."

"Let's leave work outside of this room for right now." Ari bent his head down, murmuring into Death's hair. "If you need to talk, I have things we can talk about."

"I'm too tired to revisit old arguments, Ari." Death knew he should remove himself from War's hold, but the seductive warmth of the other's body eased the weariness in his flesh.

"I have a new one, actually." Ari exhaled, finally releasing the knot of apprehension that grew in his belly. Death shifted as if to move away, but Ari stopped him with a firm hand against the rise of his backside, holding the Horseman against him. "Listen to me, Death."

There was no anger in War's voice, just a cold flatness edged sharp by the overwhelming fear he'd cut his throat on every time he swallowed. He was surprised to find a calmness in his soul. His emotions, which were normally at odds with his heart, were serenely in agreement with the decisions he'd made, a far cry from the chaos that ruled his mind. Death heard the change, staying quiet against Ari's body, his face still pressed on the ridge of the other man's collarbone.

"I need to ask you something." Ari spoke slowly, trying to find an anchor to his thoughts. "And I need you to tell me the truth, not avoid the question."

"I'll answer anything for you, Ari."

"Why Batu?"

"Why Batu?" Ari couldn't see Death's face, hidden by hair and shadow, but he heard the confusion in the elder's voice. "Why Batu what?"

Ari returned to stroking Death's bare back, not trusting himself to look down. "Why did you take Batu to your bed and not me?"

"Why are you bringing up Batu now?" Death whispered, his hand unmoving against the tuft of dark hair around the other's belly button. "He's gone from us. What good is this going to do, talking about this now?"

"Because I need to know if you loved him." Ari's fingers found Death's chin, lifting the other man's face up so he could see Death's expression. The thin silver scar ran cold across the Horseman's pale golden features, a hint of a violence from Death's previous life. "I need to know why you slept with one of my better friends and still turn me away."

"I don't want to talk about this." Death's words were cut off by Ari's thumb coursing over his lower lip.

"I think this is the best time to talk about this," Ari corrected. Turning over onto his side, Ari kept Death close to him, hooking one leg over the Horseman's long thigh. His cock stiffened, hot where he touched Death's skin, a needful warmth roiling over Ari's groin. "Because today, I waited for you, and let me tell you, there's nothing like terror to help clear your mind of all the bullshit that collects up there. So tell me, Death." Ari traced the scar along the man's face with the tip of his finger. "Why Batu?"

Time froze in the space between them despite the warmth of their combined bodies. Never patient, Ari held his tongue, letting the other gather his thoughts. Ari had held onto that question for years, a kernel of doubt in his heart that joined the many he'd already nurtured there.

"Because he was a friend." Death finally spoke, his eyes troubled and cloudy.

"And me?"

"Sometimes you're not a friend."

"Did you love him?" Ari prodded, his hand moving down over Death's shoulders, finding the curve of the other man's waist. Death's fingers picked at the sheet hems trapped under them, plucking at the thread edges. "Answer me, Death. Did you love him?"

"No." The eldest Horseman shook his head, unable to meet the other's eyes. "It wasn't… we were just…."

"Do you have any idea how hard it was to sit across of Batu and not want to smash his face in for touching you?" Ari asked. "And you both were so discreet, making sure you never flaunted what you were doing in front of me, but we all knew what was going on."

"He never meant to hurt you," Death replied. "It wasn't like that between us."

"I know," Ari admitted. "That's the hardest part. I couldn't hate Batu because I loved him like a brother, but there he was, with his mouth on you or his hands touching you and, worse yet, inside of you, where I should be. I wanted to kill him for it, and then at the same time, I wanted to beg to ask him how you tasted in his throat.”

“I sometimes think he left because of us, you and me,” the eldest murmured, his eyes closing in remembrance of the Pestilence they both loved. “I think he felt trapped between us. You were his brother. He loved your friendship so much. He just looked to me to ease himself and to be my friend. There never was any of what I feel for you between us. Batu knew that. He wasn’t looking for love.”

“It was just sex, then?” Ari didn’t know if he could comprehend the flood of passions filling his mind in that moment. Relief tangled horns with resentment, hatred for a Horseman now gone and the fondness he had for the easygoing Batu clashing in his heart.

“We both had needs. Sadly, parts of us are still human,” Death admitted, unsure of how he could explain to the other how the former Pestilence approached him, wanting only solace for his body, seeking companionship with a man he counted as a friend. There had been no love between them, a safe, comfortable easing of the tensions of their bodies but none of the hot passions that threatened Death’s heart when Ari was near. “It wasn’t just sex. We shared. We could talk about things. Sometimes that’s all we did. Other times when we did have sex, it was just nice.”

“Nice,” Ari repeated. “I can give you nice. Why don’t you let me give you nice?”

“There’s nothing nice about you.” Death tried to push away, stilled once more by Ari’s restraining grasp on his hip. “You want to push everything of yourself into me. There is no nice there.”

“No, probably not,” he conceded with a grunt. “But how it is between us has to change. I can’t do this back and forth dance that we’ve been practicing. Tonight it felt like forever until I could touch you. I’m not going to do that anymore. I sat there and made a decision about us.”

“Are you going to give up chasing me, then?” A part of Death broke, shattering beneath Ari’s surprisingly tender caresses.

“No.” Ari smiled, leaning forward to trace the other man’s facial scar with the tip of his tongue. “You, my Death, are the sin that tempts and burns me. I’d sooner cut my own throat than leave you be.”

Leaving a trail of moisture along Death's cheek, Ari blew to cool the heat he felt under his mouth. Pushing Death back, Ari lay prone over the other Horseman's body, scissoring his legs over Death's shins. With his greater weight, he trapped the slender Asian against the soft feather top, working his fingers into Death's hands and pulling the Horseman's arms up above his head. Holding Death's wrists easily with one of his hands, Ari shifted his hips to distribute his weight evenly, ignoring the man's mewls of protest at being handled.

"Get off. You're heavy." Death twisted, snarling as he tried to break free. Ari pinned him easily, the man's greater strength evident in the massive bunching of his shoulder muscles. "War, come on."

"No," Ari repeated. "I'm not giving up on you. And for once in our lives, Death, shut up and listen to me."

Subdued, Death turned his face away when Ari licked at his jaw, feeling the rough of the Horseman's tongue on his skin. His body responded hard to the feel of Ari on him, a thickening he often hid behind the cool dousing of his thoughts. Surprisingly, Ari didn't grin knowingly at the shaft stretching itself along Death's thigh, hidden by the thin cotton drawstring pants pulling down on Death's hips.

Instead the man continued finding spots of untouched flesh with his rough mouth, Ari's teeth nipping at the delicate softness at the edge of Death's lips.

"I've spent forever wanting you. I've always wanted you. I've wanted your body, and most of all, I've wanted to crack open your heart and see my name branded there." Ari shushed Death's protests with a firm kiss on his full mouth. "Shutting up means that your mouth isn't moving and you're not making sounds.

"You frustrate me, and I go running off, finding anything wet and warm to stick myself into until all of my aggravation is gone, and then what do I do? I go right back to hovering around you because you are my addiction." Ari's free hand played with the ends of Death's hair, pulling a strand down, feeling its smoothness between his fingers. "You've been telling me that we can't be together because losing me would be too much for you to bear. I've heard that. And I've listened to it. Gods know I've tried to stay away, but I can't. And then today, I finally figured something out."

"What?" Disgruntled, Death tilted his head away from Ari's hand, trying not to fall into the other man's warmth. It was harder than he expected. He'd been able to turn away the impetuous War's advances for as long as he could remember, but the slow seduction of words and touch wavered his resolve, his body traitorously reacting to Ari's caresses.

"I know you feel the same as I do. I know you, Death. I know your heart," Ari said, soft on Death's parted lips. "You think that by pushing me away, that means we're not together. But we both know, without question, that you're mine. Anyone who has touched you did so because you needed physical release, but not for love. Never for love."

"Is that why you asked about Batu? To see if you were right?"

"Yes," Ari admitted. "Of all of the people you've had in your bed, Batu was the only one I was worried about being in your heart. I will not compete with a dead man. Especially not one I loved. So I either had to make sure he was never there, or I would have to work to erase him." Ari listened to Death breathe, comforted by the simple sound. "When I watched that ghost crying for his family, I thought to myself, Death would do that for me. Then when you told me to shut up... again... I spent the time wondering if you have ever loved anyone besides me. And my gut told me no."

"And you automatically assumed that this means I'm yours?" Death's mouth quirked, bemused at Ari's arrogance.

"You are mine. You've never been anything but mine." Ari had thought long on how he felt and what was between them. "You worry that you're going to be left alone. And sometimes I wonder if there isn't a part of your mortal life lodged someplace in that busy head of yours that whispers betrayal and loss when you're not looking.

"We both know you came into being the first time some primitive genetic soup of a man thought to himself 'One day, I'll be no more.'" Ari's tone grew gentle. "In that moment when sentience reached through that little gray human brain and that first drooling idiot realized that he could die, you were born.

"And see, Shi," Ari continued. "We also both know that a second or maybe even a minute after that drooling idiot was bestowed with that miraculous awareness, he looked over to the man next to him chewing

on a piece of meat and thought, 'Hey, I can kill him and take that.' And then I was born.

"So, all things considered." Ari grinned at Death's shy smile. "We've always been together. You and I. Bound together by free will, a piece of meat, and the gift of awareness to a very short-lived species that can make fire."

"You reasoned all of that waiting for me to coax those ghosts through the Veil?" Death said.

"More than enough time to think on it, trust me. You spent enough time cajoling the damn soul, when I would have just shoved him in and been done with it," Ari said. "I also decided I wasn't going to sit back and let people drift in and out of your bed while I circled around you.

"So, Shi, from this moment on, you are only mine. No one else touches you. I'm willing to wait for you while you sort out whatever it is that holds you back from being with me, because I'm very good at doing just that, but I'm not going to watch anyone else's hands on you."

"You can't make decisions for me," Death insisted, his arms aching under War's grasp. "Not about this. Not between us."

"You've been making that decision for us day after day for as long as both of us have been alive. It's going to change," Ari said. "There's not going to be anyone who shares your breath besides me. No one. I mean it, Death. You're mine as much as I'm yours. I will lay waste to every living thing on this planet first, both behind and in front of the Veil, if you decide to test that."

"You're going to be celibate?" Death laughed, trying to steady the quivering in his throat. "You won't last a week."

"I can take care of myself." Ari grinned, white teeth flashing. "Hell, I'll even take care of you until you see reason. But I can't lose you." Ari released the Horseman's wrists, then cupped the other man's face.

Stealing a kiss, Ari filled his senses with Death's taste, swallowing the other man into his soul. "You drive me insane with want, Death. I'm never going to leave you. Admit that. Accept that."

"Not yet." Death shook his head, lowering his arms to wrap them around War's neck. "I'm not ready to risk myself that deeply. You can hurt me like no one else, War. Gods, I hate you for that."

"That's because you love me too." Ari bit at Death's chin. "You're too stubborn to say it."

"You're so sure I love you."

"Pretty sure about it," Ari agreed. "If you didn't, you would have gutted me four or five hundred times by now."

"True, I'd be too tired from killing you to do anything else."

Death lay against Ari, the other man's warmth lulling him into a sleepy peace. They'd fought too often to be just friends. Ari was argumentative and stubborn, but Death always reached for him when their lives seemed bleak. He always looked for Ari's cocky grin to bolster his spirits, even when the other man took advantage of Death's weakness to take a quick grope or steal a kiss.

"I'd be lost without you, Tyr." Death used an old name, shifting to lie at Ari's side, stroking the other man's right hand.

"I know that, Shi." He flexed his fingers under Death's touch. "Glad that hand grew back."

"I don't want to go back to those days." The world crawled with monsters then, the wall between their world and man's broken under the glut of mortal meddling. "I don't think either Mal or Min are strong enough for that."

"Agreed. As vicious as our Min is, she's not cold enough to kill a human being eaten alive," Ari replied. "Those days should be left behind us."

Ari wrapped his arms around Death's waist, drawing the other in. Lying against one another, they fell silent, appreciating the rare peace between them. Shifting his body up, Death propped himself on an elbow, gazing down into Ari's face.

"What?" The blond wrinkled his nose. "Something wrong?"

"No, nothing's wrong," Death whispered. It would be a risk, adding fuel to Ari's already inflamed ego, but Death was willing to take it. "Stay still. And say nothing."

Ari trembled when Death's mouth touched his. A spot of moisture formed against the roof of his mouth, trapped by his Death-ordered silent tongue. Turning his head, Ari angled for a deeper taste, ignoring Death's mewl of protest when he lifted his hands to work his fingers into Death's black mane. His lungs screamed for air, demanding oxygen, but Ari ignored the ache, savoring each sip he could take from Death's parted lips.

With his heart pounding hard, Death drew back, sliding his tongue against Ari's mouth to lave the moistness he'd left there. Ari's forehead rested on his temple, the other's heavy pants echoing the frenetic beat in his chest. Licking at his own lips, Death swallowed War's taste and lay back down against his friend.

"Say nothing, War." Death blindly placed his fingers on Ari's open mouth, stopping him from speaking. "I need some sleep. You do too."

"Night, Shi," Ari murmured, licking at Death's palm. "That's all I want to say. Good night."

KISMET WOKE up with screaming bruises under his skin. He felt at his neck, sure to find bandages, but encountered only the smoothness of his skin, the barest brush of downy hair along his jaw. For a moment he couldn't remember where he was. Then a rush of memories hit him, consisting mostly of a sweet-faced blond and an insane, ugly dog.

The next thing he noticed outside of the pain crackling through him was the silence. It was intense, deep, and without a shred of movement. He dreaded opening his eyes, fearing what lurked outside of his own mind and in the dark corners of an unfamiliar room. Yesterday seemed an echoing thrum against the back of his skull, something that happened to someone else.

The purity of the silence around him was heaven. There wasn't even a whisper of the outside world, nothing intruding into the softness cradling his sleep. Kismet let it wash over him. He couldn't remember the last time he'd heard nothing whispering in between his own breaths, soft little voices speaking just below what he could hear, an incessant whirring that rose and fell just beyond earshot. All of that was gone, whisked away by the blessed solitude.

Opening his eyes, he saw nothing stalking around him. The shadows remained inert, plastered to the flat walls where they lay. Nothing moved. Nothing crawled out of the corner of his eye, formless faces bending along the walls or hands reaching out from silvered mirrors. When he turned his head, nothing slithered out of his vision, just at the edge of sight. It was blissful and eerie. He'd never been someplace that quiet.

Pushing free of the velvety womb of the couch, Kismet gingerly put bare feet on a smooth woven rug. Still wobbly, he stood, grabbing at the coffee table for support. A glass of water rocked, nearly tipping over onto two aspirin tablets lying on their sides. Kismet eagerly swallowed them, letting the water wash down their bitter tang.

"Mal?" He looked around, whispering in case the shadows were drawn to him. When nothing came, he sighed, content to stand for a moment and drink it in. The amiable blond was nowhere to be found, but a set of stairs led down to another level below the messy den. "Probably asleep."

There was a shadow missing, a familiar darkness he often longed to be rid of, but now in the silence, Kismet turned, listening hard for the whispering to begin. A disquiet crept across him, a steady, gnawing unease in his belly.

"This is just weird." He laughed at himself. "Talking just to hear something. Hell."

Kismet peeked into the main room, wondering if anyone else was awake in the echoing emptiness of the apartment. The elegance of the ivory painted room shone in its simple furnishings, overstuffed couches made for lounging, covered in a burnished dark violet chenille.

The honeywood flooring appeared to run through the entire floor, disappearing down around the massive stone fireplace. He spotted three other doors off the main room, one left slightly ajar. Small touches of artwork were scattered about the room, placed to be set off by nearly invisible lights from the ceiling. A parade of freeform ebony pieces marched across the mantel, primal in shape.

An expanse of windows faced west, showcasing a view of San Diego Bay and the bridge that swept over to the island community across from downtown. A kitchen space took up most of the western area, long stretches of granite countertops and black lacquer low cabinets, keeping the space open and free of upper clutter. The only sign of human occupancy was a quirky cat-faced ceramic mug placed upside down on a gleaming stainless-steel dish drainer, its bright yellow face accented with a pair of black wire-rim glasses.

Kismet took a tentative step, forcing his body to move. The craving for heroin was biting at his blood, tiny centipede legs digging deep into his marrow. He'd have to get a fix soon, or the world would start to crack, letting all sorts of demons out and even more in. There was no clock in the main room, and he wandered toward the open door, stuck his head in, then softly called out a hello.

The paint colors changed, from muted jewel tones to golds and coppers, the walls washed with an exotic plaster, burred with a soft wax finish. Lurid masks leered at Kismet, boggle-eyed demonic faces with sharp red tongues and hammered-metal forms, interspersed between stacks of battered, worn ancient swords. One wall bulged with shelves, lines of books running from the door to a short wall built against the glass windows. The opposite wall supported glass shelves cluttered with tidbits.

Sliding out of the room, Kismet looked about for somewhere to wash the sourness of his sweat from his body and his mouth. The hallway led to an empty wooden-floored room and a laundry room. A quick glance in the dryer and Kismet pulled out a pair of jeans and a T-shirt. Liquid soap and hot water from the washroom's sink scrubbed most of the dirt and blood from his hair and body, a dish towel soaking up most of the moisture.

"Kiz, you need to get home, man." Leaving his soiled clothes balled up in a trash can, he pulled on what he found, stopping in the living room to find his sneakers, and headed to the elevator outside of the front door.

The elevator shot down. Then the doors slid open, and he stared out at a parking garage. After a breathless second, the doors began to shut, and he shoved his hand against the soft rubber stopper, holding them open long enough to step out. The blessed silence he'd wrapped around himself upstairs was gone, the pounding noises of the world creeping slowly back in. The shadows once more held voices, creeping into his hearing under the rumble of cars and the murmur of people walking on the sidewalk outside of the garage.

It felt like he'd come home.

The itching in his arms grew with his descent into the garage, driving him out of his black cocoon of numbness and into a jagged pain. The torment reached into the base of his brain, claws raking his concentration. Cravings inched along in his throat, parched dry and coated with sand. It was always the same, a slow ember smoldering in his stomach. He hated it, but he hated life without drugs more.

Shaking his head, Kismet tried to make sense of Mal's ramblings, of his memory, spotty from pain and fatigue. His body vividly recalled the blond's hands on him, easing him back onto the cushions and lingering on his face. Flushing red, Kismet pushed those thoughts aside as the addiction flared again, demanding to be fed.

"*Missed you, Kizzie.*" Chase slithered around to hug his leg. Kismet nearly wept at the sight of his brother's shade. His hand passed through the back of Chase's head as he cradled the ghost, his fingers touching his thigh. "*Time to go to school?*"

"Sorry, Chase," Kismet whispered, watching the shade disappear under his touch. Chase's spirit always fled when Kismet reached for it, always out of reach of the young man's touch. Speaking to the empty air, he nearly sobbed at the sight of the inky soot on his palm. "I'm sorry I left you."

The world was too much to take in. Even the smell of the poured blacktop filled his nose, a tarry stink fighting with the remnants of gas fumes. Reeling as he stepped from the lift, Kismet awkwardly maintained his balance. The world now pulsed with movement, noisy and screeching, with small scurrying nothings huddling behind every bump of asphalt and cement pylon. The air seemed full of motes, sparkling dust that winked when he staggered by. A single drop of water bowed and flexed, stretching out into a lake before snapping back into a dollop barely large enough to wet his little toe.

Several cars were parked along a short wall, the private parking area cordoned off by a steel mesh gate leading to an outer ramp. Kismet walked around a lean, sleek gray car, its front end rumpled and gnarled by long gashes. Torn metal dragged down over one side, an inky clawed handprint burned into the paint. Beside it, a new Mustang and pale SUV jockeyed for space, leaving room for a powerful, thick-bodied motorcycle.

A tendril of shadow broke off the mass, undulating across the garage. The world was back to its craziness, and while he missed the silence, there would be no going back to it. Mal, with his sweet prettiness, lived in a world Kismet just didn't understand.

The form snaked closer, a triangular head weaving about. It left no trace of its progress, not on the ground or cast by the faint daylight finding its way down through the short walls blocking out the city. Made of air and grease, it wrapped around his ankle, leaving a smear of gritty oil behind.

Shivering, he wished he'd grabbed a jacket as well as the shirt and jeans. The cold air was obviously making him dizzy after being in the warm confines of the penthouse for too long. Either that, or the drugs he'd shot up yesterday were coming back in flashes, leaving echoes of madness behind. The day's unseasonable chill seemed to be seething up from the ground, working through the stolen clothes and under his skin.

The mesh gate rose easily on rollers, propelled with a simple push of a yellow button marked Open. It rolled down behind him when he passed through. There was no button on the other side. He wouldn't be returning to the penthouse any time soon. There simply was no need for a button on the other side.

Two guards manned a gatehouse by a wooden arm blocking off public traffic. Other levels of the garage were filled with cars, diagonal slashes of white filled with money and steel. He stopped, wondering what story he would tell the guards or if they would even care.

"That gate's acting up again." The smaller of the guards, his thin face twitching, peered through the open window of the covered structure, the gray flicker of monitors casting a pallor on his sunburned skin. "It just opened and closed by itself."

"It's a problem sometimes. I think there's a glitch in the system." The other man barely glanced up, his eyes watching the video rolling past. "I'll call maintenance again, but they don't ever find anything wrong with it."

Kismet slipped past them, ducking his head as he hurried past the guardhouse, unable to believe they didn't notice him walk up the short ramp and onto the sidewalk. Not one to push his luck, he broke into a fast trot, disappearing between streams of people leaving a downtown building and heading to a trolley stop. Figuring it would be easy to get back to the College Area by catching one of the red trolley cars, Kismet tried to get his bearings, looking for a familiar route on the map tucked behind a weathered, milky Plexiglas case.

A man brushed past him, jostling him roughly. The hit was hard enough to turn Kismet, his shoulders twisting. The artist swore at the man's back, but he continued on his way, oblivious to Kismet as his feet moved quickly over the cooling sidewalk. Another, a woman, struck his arm, jerking Kismet to the side with a spin. Her eyes continued to track the movements of the traffic, playing dodge with the lights as she scurried across the street. All around him people flew past, intent on their own business, not noticing the lithe young man struggling to maintain his balance amid the stream.

Without warning, a burn arched through him. He'd never had his cravings take him over so quickly. Everything hurt, the torment suddenly searing him open. Kismet gasped, clutching his rolling stomach. Sour bile hitched up into the back of his mouth, an oily green taste that would stick to his tongue. Blinking, Kismet looked up, hair tangled with sweat, and stared into the sinking sun.

Kismet shivered. He was colder than before, the wet on his skin smelling bitter, the drugs pushing out of his blood and into the water he shed. Somehow he'd lost himself, crouched on the side of the street, unseeing eyes looking right through him. His hands dove into the pocket of his stolen jeans, finding the crispness of the bills he'd left there warm from his leg. Clutching his fingers into his shirt, Kismet gasped as his body cramped, bending over his abdomen as the drug cravings shook him apart.

"It's like I'm invisible." Kismet peered into the reflective window of a hair salon, catching a rare glimpse of barely familiar pretty features staring back at him. "It's like no one sees me."

The mirrored surface held all manner of faces, not just his own. Elongated eyes blinking in rounded heads, noses and mouths mere suggestions for many, pronounced in others, but all staring back at him. One of the creatures licked its lips, tongue forked as it left a slimy trail on its dry reptilian skin.

A woman stood among them, her arms flailing as she tried to get the wraiths off her, a slip of a ghost trapped between panes of glass. The tips of the woman's fingers pierced the soft surface, frozen blue as they briefly touched the warm San Diego air. Her arm went limp, sliding back down into the glass, consumed by the serpentine shadows writhing over her limbs. Her face surfaced from the black, the end of her nose gnawed off, a pale shredded mess working to draw air through the enlarged hole. Her mouth formed a black *O* as rot swept under her skin, webbing branched veins together until nearly solid patches covered her cheeks.

Rumbling, an ancient school bus choked the street with fumes, smoke billowing from its exhaust system. Shrieking teenagers called out from the window, a trio of girls whistling at a young man passing by Kismet, laughing when he waved and shouted back at them. Startled by the noise, Kismet's attention fell away from the window, returning in a split second and discovering nothing but his own reflection staring back at him.

"Shit, suppose I'm dead?" His chest tightened, choking the breath from his lungs. Kismet tried not to stare at the windows, keeping his head down and eyes on the sidewalk. "I definitely don't feel dead. If I was dead, wouldn't I have been able to touch Chase?

"Come on, Kiz." Shoving the face of the woman from his thoughts, he tried to shake off the dread. "You've seen crap like this all of your life. Dead people don't take showers or steal clothes out of a dryer. Get real. Just get home and fix yourself up."

He found his way to the C Street trolley stop, looking out for any transit cops that might have noticed he didn't have a ticket. Not paying much attention to the people around him, he jerked when an old man bumped into him.

Pungent, the old man's scent wafted from his clothes, a chemical rot of cologne and skin oils. He reached out and grabbed handfuls of Kismet's T-shirt, pulling the collar nearly down to the young man's chest. His yellowed teeth poked up sporadically from his pale gums, a bottom stump jiggled by his moving tongue.

The man was a talker, mouth moving and unrecognizable bits of conversation tumbling past his rotted teeth. Stepping to the side, Kismet avoided eye contact for a moment, and then the man grabbed at his wrist. The man turned, caught still and firm as he stood fast against Kismet's struggles. Kismet tried harder to get free, twisting away from the man's grip.

"Let go." Grabbing at the man's wrist, Kismet pulled, unable to work loose. The man's flesh gave slightly under Kismet's fingers, spongy and yielding. Glancing down, he gulped at the shadowy forearm emerging from the man's sleeve. "Holy fucking shit!"

A gnarled stump connected to the ethereal appendage poked out of the end of the shirt's sleeve, its cuff folded up above the man's elbow. A dirty, yellowed slipover sock covered the appendage, violent pink flesh showing through the gaping holes on the wrapping's end. The smoke arm was attached to the stump, voracious tendrils chewing on the tender skin, weeping drops of pink water dripping onto the cement sidewalk. Crooked teeth poked out of the shadowed end, pushing and gnawing farther up the man's flesh arm, the shadowy appendage scraping down in an uncontrollable slide with each gulping bite of the maw as it tried to consume more of the homeless man than it could hold on to.

"Just take it off. Someone, please." The man's bleary eyes were sticky with pain, tears running around the raw pink edges of his lids. "They cut it off, but it just doesn't go away. Please. Help me. Stop the pain. It just hurts so much."

"God, I'm sorry. No, I can't help you." Kismet staggered, suddenly released when the man's arm spasmed, the shadow struggling upward to regain ground it lost during its slide down the tortured flesh.

Catching himself before the blue line trolley edged to a stop, Kismet hopped away from the yellow warning curb. His itchiness flared, shoulder blades aching, his bones weeping with the pain. A trolley slid around the curb, brakes jerking the line of bright red cars to a stop. Kismet yanked himself away from the old man, leaping up the stairs of the car behind another passenger.

By the time Kismet reached the corner of University and College, he was shaking from the addiction demanding to be fed, his stomach churning. Wrapping his clammy hands over his abdomen, Kismet retched, heaving up several mouthfuls of water mingled with bile. Burning, he swallowed, trying to get rid of the taste of his guts. Stumbling, he ducked into the coolness of the alleyway he'd scored at before. The space was empty, a lingering scent of piss clinging to the graffiti-sprayed walls.

An ache traveled from his chest down to his groin, kicking him hard when he tried to step up onto the curb. Thighs cramping, he tumbled down onto his knees, tearing a rip in the leg of his jeans. Palms hurting, Kismet crouched on all fours, head down. Panting, his vision blurred, the sidewalk bending up toward his face. The motel's pale blue roof was just beyond the stone wall blocking off the alleyway.

Rolling off the street, Kismet stood, using the wall to hold himself up.

"Shit, not even a couple of blocks." He inhaled, smelling the exhaust of passing cars. "Just around the wall.

"God, this fucking hurts." Pins poked up through his hair, rubbing over his scalp. Scratching at his temples, Kismet tried to convince his body to hold out just a little while longer, not to shut down until he was able to get inside. He turned into the alley and made it down the walkway, heading to the front of the motel, to his room. "Just a bit more. Hold it together, man. It'll be there. It's going to be where you left it. Enough to get this off you."

Kismet heard Carl before he saw him, the man's loud voice carrying through the courtyard.

Yellow police tape hung from the chain-link fence lining the end of the parking lot next to the alley, a futile attempt to keep people from driving through the back way and cutting through the motel's property to reach the street.

Sections of the grimy links were scalloped where drivers tried to cut the corner and struck the low curb, careening into the barely visible barrier. A slip of the bright, sunny ribbon flapped, black letters warning bystanders off, its end jagged.

The door next to Kismet's room was still splattered with a spray of dried blood, dark brown blooms crackled over the worn paint. Someone had already tried to wash the wall clean. Deep crevices in the plaster were thick with gore, faint whiffs of fatty oils and organ meats covered with the sharpness of bleach.

Carl was berating someone on his cell phone. From the sounds of things, the conversation wasn't going well for Carl, his voice straining with the effort of shouting. Kismet approached cautiously, realizing he had no way of getting into his place. In his stupor, he'd left his keys inside, probably still on the dresser next to his wallet.

The manager's face turned to him, eyes watching the traffic bundled up near the intersection. Kismet nodded at the man, astonished when Carl turned away, continuing his conversation without acknowledging Kismet standing not more than a few feet away from him.

"Carl." Kismet strolled closer, barely ducking Carl's fist as the man gestured, making a point to whomever he was talking to on the phone. "Shit, man. You almost hit me!"

Carl moved toward the end of the walkway, brushing up against Kismet's shoulder. Irritated, Kismet opened his mouth, anger rising. The world bubbled, tightening around him. Time dragged down on his body, a plastic-wrapping sensation elongating his words. The feeling made him sick, tugging at the back of his head and threatening to snap him back a few steps. Forcing out his words, Kismet tried to shake off the creeping tingle.

"Carl, I need to get in. I left my key." It hurt to speak. Air spiked in his lungs, and Carl jumped in surprise, whirling about to stare at Kismet. The effort to keep his mouth working tired him, and Kismet shivered, the familiar cold chewing into his guts and thighs. "Can I get you to open my door?"

"Hey." The manager drawled out the word, shock turning to a wide smile. "How you doing, kid? Where'd you go last night?"

"Just needed to get away from what happened, I guess." Kismet's hands instinctively reached for his forearms, rubbing at the insistent buzzing on his skin. He didn't want to talk to Carl, however decent he was being at the moment.

"Can you let me in?" Kismet stilled his arms, keeping his voice calm.

"Sure, not a problem." Carl grabbed at the huge ring of keys dangling from his belt loop. Normally he would have played at fitting every key into the lock. Kismet was surprised when he opened the door on the first turn, the knob twisting. "Here."

"Thanks." Kismet slid into the welcoming darkness, shutting the door behind him. Resting his head back, he took a deep breath to calm himself, trying to tamp the shivers down long enough to reach the kit lying in full view on the floor. Chest heaving with every breath, Kismet fell to the carpet, reaching for the small packet of latex tucked into the pocket of his kit, each movement painfully precise in case he dropped a grain of heroin.

Outside, Carl hung up on who he'd been talking to, a deafening quiet smile curved over his florid face. He pulled out the linen card he'd tucked into his shirt pocket, then dialed the number on it.

"Hello? This is Carl down at Casa de Mar." He turned the rectangle over in his fingers, playing at the rumpled corner. Tucking the end into the space between his front teeth, he picked at the remnants of his lunch, then sucked at the paper left behind. "Your boy just came back. ... Uh-huh, I let him in. ... Nope." Carl paced down to the end of the walk, stepping around the dark splotches on the artificial turf. "I didn't tell him nothing. That druggie doesn't know I talked to anyone. I can tell you this, give him a couple of minutes, and he'll be flying. Take your time. He ain't going anywhere for a while."

CHAPTER EIGHT

MAL WOKE to the sound of a pounding fist on his bedroom door. Blinking in the darkness, he pulled a discarded towel off his alarm clock, its dull red numbers telling him he'd only been asleep for six hours. Stumbling out of his bed, he caught his foot on something hard, hand groping for something to put on his naked body. After shouting at the knocker at the door to wait, he found a pair of sweatpants with its legs too knotted to pull on and tightly held them in front of his waist.

"What?" He opened the door, then stared down at the watery image of a pale face and a shock of black hair. "Min?" Everything swam out of focus, partly from the sleep still clinging to his eyes but mostly from his poor vision. His glasses were back on his nightstand, probably buried between stacks of books by now. He could barely make out a bobbing black hedgehog perched on sheets of hard plaster, the dimple of a nose among the blur.

"Go grab some clothes." She wrinkled her nose. "But get a bath first. You reek. Your human's run off, and he's pissed."

"He's what?" Mal tasted his breath on his teeth. "Kismet's pissed?"

"Death is pissed. As in mad… not drunk," Min repeated slowly, knocking on Mal's bare chest. "Kismet? Are you talking about that damned thief you dragged in here half-dead then raided the dryer for my clothes? Who the hell names their kid Kismet?"

"He took your clothes?" Mal stammered, trying to sort through the fuzz in his brain. "Why did he take your clothes?"

"Probably wouldn't have if you didn't wear the same size clothes as a little boy. In fact, if it weren't for those pebbles you tuck under your shirt, Min, I would swear you were a boy most of the time," Ari said. Tugging on the fringe of hair near her ear, Ari grinned. "Maybe if you grew your hair out, people wouldn't be making that mistake."

Mal blinked. All he could see was a slight jerk of the tall man's head and the possibility of Min's finger waving in Ari's face. The gesture was followed by a thump of a fist hitting Ari's shoulder, his laughter soon joined by hers.

The two Horsemen wrestled with one another verbally, Min finally crying off when Ari hooked one arm around her neck and twisted her against him, holding her tight.

"Let go." Her teeth flashed, grabbing at a piece of his chest, his shirt wet from her mouth. Ari released her, rubbing dramatically at the spot, Min rolling her eyes at him. "Please. I know you. You're more excited than hurt."

"Meh." Ari poked at her nose, tweaking the end with a twist of his fingers. "My heart beats for only one Horseman."

"Definitely not me." Min poked back, finding the ticklish spot between his ribs. "Speaking of Death, he'll have our heads if we don't head back upstairs. He's in a foul mood. Well, for him, it's a foul mood. It's hard to tell."

"Not hard to tell at all. He's a bit pissed off," Ari replied. "Get upstairs as soon as you can, Pest. We're going to have to go find that pet of yours."

"Yesterday all you guys wanted to do was get rid of him," Mal reminded them, grumpily rubbing at his tousled hair. The news of Kismet's flight bothered him, making his chest ache. "Now he's gone, and you want him back?"

"Death wants the kid back. He thinks the boy might have something to do with the Veil thinning." Ari grinned at Mal's nearly nude body, a salacious smile plastered on his face. "When I told him about the wraith this morning, he got very quiet. His mood got worse by the time I got to the kid. Then he went straight to inferno when he started sniffing around the boy's clothes. He says something big happened to the kid. We'll talk about it upstairs."

"You should have told him about this crap last night, Ari," Min scolded lightly. "He would have done something about the kid then, and we wouldn't have to be playing needle in a haystack today."

"Shi was dead on his feet," Ari responded sharply, his voice hard. "I wasn't going to do that to him. I figured the kid and the wraith could wait until he got some sleep. How the hell was I supposed to know the boy was going to leave? He couldn't even stay conscious for longer than a minute. All of a sudden he can cut and run?"

"I'm surprised we still have silverware. Probably jacked some of the electronics in the living room. I think everything else was locked behind closed doors. Ari, it would serve you right if you go in your room and it's stripped. Probably called his friends on your cell phone, and they cleaned the place out while you were trying to spoon Death in his sleep," Min scoffed, turning her back on Mal and heading upstairs to the main floor. "I'm going to check if there's anything else missing besides my clothes."

"She's furious. He probably took her favorite shroud," Ari said, watching Min bound up the stairs. "I checked my room. I don't see anything missing. My wallet's sitting out with money in it. That's all there."

"I'm sorry. I didn't know he would leave." Mal sagged against the frame, rubbing at his forehead.

"What?" Ari asked. "You expected the street rat you brought in half-dead and nursed back to health was going to stick around in the morning? Come on, Cooties, you can't be that naïve. He's practically feral."

"He seemed nice," Mal struggled to explain. "I talked to him before he fell asleep last night."

"Gods, you are an idiot," Ari said, ruffling Mal's tousled hair. "I don't think I was ever that innocent. Don't worry about it. That kid was pretty rough around the edges. I'm surprised we still have a TV."

Mal felt around for the light switch, fingers fumbling. The room flared brightly, making his eyes water. "I need a shower. I'll be right up."

"Better hurry," Ari said. "Or there'll be hell to pay. If there was a hell. And if it cost to get in."

"War." Mal's voice was low, making Ari pause. "Is Death really mad at me?"

Ari heard the insecurity rooted there. They'd all been hard on the youngest, deriding his efforts to reach out to the other Horsemen.

It wasn't just that he missed Batu. Ari didn't understand Mal or what drove their youngest to do the things he did. Ari's world was simpler. Mankind's growth was a game. He moved certain pieces to draw mortal attention to or away from things, not interfering with either its wars against injustice or wars against itself. Mal saw the Horsemen as a way for Mankind to better itself. Humans would either condemn themselves to extinction or avoid it, without any help or deliberate hindrance of any immortal. Mal had walked too close to that line more than once, always pulled back from the brink of disaster by Death's steady hand.

"No, Death's not mad at you. Besides, there wasn't much left to what the boy was wearing. Min can afford to lose a few things. Hell, he might even return them." Ari's voice gentled, a reassuring rumble. "I think Death's more worried about the kid. That wraith shouldn't have formed here. Shi thinks someone called it up. We've got to figure out first what happened to the kid and then find out who wants to hurt him."

Ari patted Mal's shoulder. "Go take your shower. I've got some coffee going. It'll be done by the time you come up."

"Thanks, Ari." Mal located his glasses, surprised to find a sheen of tears still burning his eyes when he put them on. "He just looked lost. I know what that feels like, being that lost."

"Not a problem, Cooties." Ari took the stairs two at a time, calling down them when he reached the top. "And by the way, whatever you were holding up to your waist doesn't cover a damned thing. You might want to consider wearing it next time we go trolling for sex. Could get you laid."

MICHAEL BECKETT walked the length of the hallway from his bedroom to the main room in his La Jolla home, his eyes blind to the seascape just outside. Perched high on a sea cliff, the house gleamed with stretches of polished glass and chrome, set high enough on the rocky crag to be safe from the crashing waves spraying foam into the air. Shadows avoided the place, the splotches of nonlight clean of any living darkness. The house loomed over the bluffs, eerily silent despite the nearby ocean and the two-lane road winding just beyond the main gates.

Standing in the middle of the living room, Frazier waited patiently for Beckett, his broad shoulders straightening to attention as the other man approached. Dressed in matte gray slacks and a matching long-sleeved cotton shirt, his tanned skin shone bronze from years of being out in the sun. A brush of silver-shot brown hair bristled over his head, cropped nearly to the skin above his ears. Nodding a brusque welcome when his employer entered, Frazier sipped from a bottle of water, his fingers picking at its plastic label.

When Beckett first approached the older man, Frazier thought it would be easy money guarding the insane man who offered him immortality. When the shadows became creatures around him and slips of half-people caught the corners of Frazier's eyes, he no longer doubted the man's sanity. Although at times, he admitted to questioning his own.

The taste of the water was bitter on his tongue, the liquid clouded from the powdery substance both he and Beckett consumed on a regular basis. With the boy's probable successful crossing into the unseen, Beckett suggested increasing the dosages, something Frazier initially resisted until the blackened, oily corpse of Beckett's wraith lay outlined against the motel's stained concrete. Then Frazier realized it was better to see everything around him, even the things that couldn't quite touch him.

Beckett had his own reasons for wanting the substance to work, intensely personal reasons, but Frazier wanted something different. Being able to see and manipulate what was unseen had potential. If forever came with it, then it became all the more attractive.

"The manager of the motel called me. Left a message," Frazier said casually. "The boy's back."

"So soon?" Beckett smiled at the news. "Humans are ever creatures of habit. I take it you'll be heading back there shortly."

"I just wanted to give you an update," the man said. "I told the manager to stall the boy if it looks like he's going to leave."

"Good." Beckett took an iced bottle from the wet bar, then tapped a crystalline mixture into the cold water. "Were you able to find out anything from the creature's corpse?"

Dehydrated lime added a pleasant tang to the water, an astringent flavor Beckett quite enjoyed.

Shaking the bottle until the lime dissolved, he smiled at the man he'd tricked into consuming the untested elixir, wondering how long it would be until the insanity ate at Frazier's brain. Sipping at the water, he joined Frazier in the living room, motioning for Frazier to take a seat.

"I couldn't touch it, but I'm not sure if that's because it was almost gone or if I've just not got enough of the elixir in me yet." Frazier rubbed at the tips of his fingers, showing Beckett the inky stains of the wraith's fluids. The gore burned at first, then turned numbing. The feeling was finally returning, a tingle spreading up to his palm. "The boy definitely was bitten. His blood was all over the sidewalk, but none of the cops could see it."

"Bitten is good. But what happened to the wraith?"

"The creature was killed by a blade," Frazier said. "Something very sharp. Clean cuts and precise. Someone who knew how to kill, and I'm guessing by the cuts, it was something bigger than a knife."

"Really?" Beckett ran his fingers along his lower lip, contemplating the puzzle before him. "Think our boy killed it?"

"Doubtful," Frazier said, digging a small notebook from his pocket. He found the scribbled notes he'd made while talking to the residents of the motel. "Kismet Andreas. He's lived at the motel for a year or so, fairly quiet and sticks to himself. Mostly does drugs and paints, from what I can tell. He works part-time at a tattoo parlor one of the suppliers owns. That's how he came into contact with the batch you released."

"Curious how we all are connected." Beckett sipped at his lime water, swishing it around in his mouth. "Does he prostitute? He'd need to know how to handle someone threatening him if he works the streets. He could have been armed."

"The neighbor across of him says no, but then the boy probably doesn't bring anyone home." Frazier shrugged. "But he could do business somewhere else. Plenty of alleys around the area or even down by the park. But honestly, he doesn't sound like someone disciplined enough to have that kind of skill. Whoever carved up your creature knew what he was doing."

"So probably not our druggie," Beckett said. "There are others behind the Veil that could have helped him. One of the Sidhe perhaps. It could get complicated if he has someone to help him."

"Complicated I can handle, as long as I can see it." Frazier handed his employer one of the folders he'd left on the table. "Here, I thought you might want to take a look at these. They were all over the boy's room. The manager let me in after a bit of persuasion."

"Dear God." Beckett nearly grinned at the photographs Frazier had taken of Kismet's room. The man had carefully placed canvases against the wall, recording as many paintings as he could in each photo. "Our Mr. Andreas definitely has the Sight."

Horrors crawled through paint, stretched tight over the canvas and reaching out to the unaware. Wraiths curved around lampposts, snagging at the skulls of passersby. A picture of a homeless woman, filth and despair dominating her battered face, writhed with the tiniest of shadowy tadpoles, a few bulbous heads already buried under her dirt-splattered skin. Each photo grew grimmer with each pass, until the magus reached the bottom of the packet, his hands trembling with the images of darkfae and slender, lithesome forms of hidden Sidhe.

"So he's like you, predisposed to see things?" Frazier asked softly. "But probably unable to touch anything. Until now."

"Until now," Beckett agreed, trying to keep the excitement from his voice. "God, these are beautiful."

"We're assuming the drugs worked." Frazier leaned forward, taking another sip of the bitters. "We just need to snag him and confirm it. Then we'll be able to use the new mixture without worrying about any side effects."

"That's what I'm hoping for," the magus murmured, tracing his fingers along one of the red lines of Kismet's paintings. Looking up, he saw the calculation in Frazier's eyes, a hunger lurking just below the surface. Beckett welcomed that hunger, hoping to exploit Frazier's greed and manipulate it. "We're so close."

"Here. I want you to take this now." Beckett passed Frazier a packet of brown powder, minute flecks glistening amid the dull tan. "This should help you hold on to the boy if he's passed fully through. Once you get him secured, come back here immediately. The effects of this will wear off in about four hours, so you'll need to get him locked down before then."

"I'll have him here by tonight." Frazier stood, taking the packet from Beckett's table. "I'll see you in a few hours."

Beckett waited until he was certain the man was gone, then smiled at the immortal standing by the counter. Charity had slid out of the Veil nearly as soon as the door closed behind Frazier's back, greeting his sister's lover with a wave.

"I think he believes every word you say. You've gotten him to agree to take what you gave the boy without even a whisper of suspicion." Charity walked out of the shadows, his bare feet barely leaving a trace on the carpet. "We're on our way, then. My sister chose well in you."

"Thank you. I try," Beckett replied.

"I'm kind of worried that we lost the boy."

"Frazier will find him. Nothing motivates like greed."

Charity turned, leaning his back against a pane of glass. "So the boy killed your wraith? That seems a bit unlikely."

"I think someone else helped kill the creature." A frown crinkled Beckett's forehead. "I'm worried that whoever killed the wraith will try to prevent Frazier from grabbing the boy."

"I don't like someone sniffing around the boy. We're just so close." Tapping his fingers on the window, Charity made a face. "It worries me too. He shouldn't have any allies. Humans and immortals don't mingle. And none of the Veiled would have the strength to fight off a wraith. They'd sooner avoid that kind of trouble."

"Can you think of anyone who might have stepped in?" Beckett asked.

"I can't imagine one of the Sidhe Courts helping a human," Charity said. "The same can be said of the darkfae. No one just walked by and helped the boy out of the kindness of his heart. Darkfae don't do anything unless profit or family glory is involved."

"Someone helped him." Beckett drained the water in the bottle. "Something that exists in the shadows."

"The Horsemen are in this area." Charity fretted, thinking of Death and his crew. "But they aren't known to get involved in human matters. Their hands are dirty enough as it is. I can't see them lifting a finger to help a single human."

"Would it be possible to ask anyone about them? Poke around and see if they're interested in the boy?"

"It would look suspicious. They're not something brought up in casual conversation." Charity shrugged at his sister's lover. "None of us have anything to do with them. Ari wouldn't think twice about someone asking after them. If word even got to him, it would just stroke his ego, but Death, he would hone in on me."

"I thought you were immune to Death."

"No one is immune to Death." Charity mulled over the scar-faced immortal interfering with the young man they needed. "He's more of a hunter than Ari is. I don't want Death's notice. If I start asking after the Horsemen, there would be more questions than answers."

"There's got to be someone who pays attention to what they're doing. Maybe not an immortal but one of the other Veiled?" Beckett asked.

"I'll see what I can do. I've already told you too much about the others. Speaking about them sends ripples. That's one of the ways we know we are needed. I have to be careful." He canted his head to one side, feeling the summons of a calling. The man felt at the edges of the request, worrying at the threads reaching out to him. He would have to respond to this one. It was too big to ignore. "I have to leave."

"I'll try to get this resolved," Beckett promised. "You can't live your life being dragged from place to place. I don't want that for Faith. She deserves more."

Charity's bitterness rode high in his throat, burning and sour. "None of us have lives. There is no privacy, no days when I can say I am not responding to a call. Humans are always mewling and whining about their existence, not realizing that on this muddy spit of a world, they have everything right at their fingertips. I would give anything to just say no, I'm not going to go, but none of us have that luxury."

"This will bring me over." Beckett held his hand out to the immortal. His eyes burned with fervor. "And then we'll know for sure that it will help you."

"Do what you can, and no matter what, remember we're doing this for her." The immortal faded, drawn along the line of his call. "I don't care about me, but she deserves to be free of this prison."

"WAS MAL awake?" Death's husky voice greeted Ari as he entered the living area. Min was nowhere to be seen, probably counting boxes of cereal in the pantry off the laundry room.

"We woke him." Ari watched the long-legged Horseman fixing himself a cup of tea. "Mal said he'll be up once he gets showered and dressed. Poor kid was sleeping hard."

Death didn't respond, swirling the tea ball around in the hot water. His thoughts were half on the boy who fled the Horsemen's home and also on the blond hovering close. Waiting for the water to darken, Death tensed when Ari drew near. The other man's strong hands rested on Death's hips, Ari's touch intimate. Pressed up against the counter, Death considered shoving Ari back, sending him away, but the delicious tingle of their bodies barely brushing against one another comforted him, as well as startled the kernel of secrets Death kept deep inside of himself.

"Leave off," Death said, nearly whispering. Ari smiled at the wavering in Death's words. Ari's hands slowed but remained on Death's hips.

"You and I both know that you don't want me to leave off." Resting his chin on Death's shoulder, Ari inhaled the spicy green tea cologne Death preferred. The soft cotton of his chambray shirt pillowed under a scar on Ari's chin, nearly as sensuous as the tickle of black hair along his cheek. "I don't know why you push me away when I know you want nothing more than to hold me closer."

"We can't," Death murmured, closing his eyes. He allowed himself the moment, just that single touch of Ari on him. His mind screamed a mute defiance, his body rebelliously luxuriating in the skimming of Ari's hands over his stomach, resting there before dropping back down to his waist. "We have things we have to do. This complicates everything."

"I think you're wrong," Ari whispered into the shell of Death's ear. "I think it would simplify things. I'm not sure what you're afraid of more. What you think I'll do to you or what you think you'll do to me. I'm not going anywhere. Neither are you."

"You might." Twisting away from the other Horseman, Death reached for the sugar, hands shaking with the effort. "We don't know. I can't."

"No, we don't know anything. We never know anything," Ari responded. "I'm willing to take any chance I can get. I've always been the risk taker. Sometimes I wish you would just say to hell with it and for once take a chance. What do you have to lose?"

Death tilted his head back, saved from answering as Min strolled into the main part of the penthouse. Looking from one to the other, she sighed, fixing a baleful glare at the blond Horseman. "What the hell have you done now? Wasn't he pissed off enough?"

"I'm not mad," Death insisted, waving off Min's protests. "Ari and I were discussing a few things."

"I know how he discusses things," Min retorted. "Everything's all hands and tongue."

"How about if we just go back to worrying about Mal's little pet? Sad to say, that's a safe topic." Ari's smile was cold, icy with fury. Pushing past Min, he strode over to Mal's rooms, shouting at the Horseman to hurry up.

"Are you okay?" Min asked quietly, drawing near to Death's side.

"I'm fine," he assured her, the words sounding hollow in his ears. "Really, we're both fine. It's just something that we need to work out between us."

"You've had eons," Min reminded him offhandedly, running her fingers through her hair, spiking the ends up more. "If you two haven't worked it out by now, you're never going to work it out."

"We'll be fine," Death insisted. "I just frustrate him a bit."

"Well, try not to do that much." Min looked worried, a furrow across her brow. "Last time you frustrated him more than that, we had World War II. I'm busy enough as it is. I don't need any more work, thank you both very much."

"Promise." Death's angelic face creased with a smile. The silver line across the bridge of his nose caught the light, kissing a white streak over his cheek. "It won't get to that."

"Better not." Min wagged her finger at the eldest Horseman. "You all ran me ragged, and it just made me grumpy. Grumpy leaves lines. Makes wrinkles. I'm too pretty to get wrinkles."

Ari returned, wordlessly helping himself to a cup of coffee, brushing against Death's leg while reaching for a spoon. Their eyes met, and Ari's gaze softened, his mouth forming a curse against the power Death had over him.

The dark-haired Horseman gave him a soft smile before heading into the living area with his tea. Ari poured another mug of coffee, adding sugar, then a hefty dollop of cream before handing the steaming cup to Mal. Mal gratefully accepted the creamy coffee, deeply inhaling the steam and letting the aroma creep into his tiredness, chasing it away.

"What do we know about this boy?" Death waited for Mal to sit down. Ari straddled the arm of the couch near Death. Min slid down into an armchair, swinging her leg up and tucking it beneath her.

"Other than the fact that he's a thief?" Min snorted.

"And the same scrawny size as our Famine?" Ari grinned as Min bared her teeth at him.

"I know his name is Kismet Andreas. And that he uses drugs." Mal struggled to remember more, something other than the pout of the artist's lower lip and the cinnamon heat of his eyes. "Heroin, I think he said. I thought his arms were damaged by the wraith, but later I realized that they were needle marks."

"Well, now that message from beyond makes more sense. Kismet. And he really is a druggie. I was just guessing." Ari sipped at his coffee, ruminating over the information. "I'm surprised he didn't take the cash to get more drugs. An opportunist but not disrespectful to the people who helped him out. Got to admire that in a street kid."

"The drug use makes sense." Death nodded. "I think he was seeing the Veil before whatever happened to him to force him through to the other side, to our side. I found slips of drawings in the pocket of his jeans. It looked like he sketched wraiths and other Veiled."

"What makes you say that?" Min cocked her head, swinging her foot back and forth. "You think he's one of us?"

"The blood on his shirt smells like ours," Death said. "But from what Mal says, Kismet knows who he is. He's been human all this time, and now he's an immortal."

"So no calling?" Min whistled under her breath. "An immortal human. Guess they were right about us bringing on the Apocalypse."

"That wraith had him full around the throat. I thought when it happened it was because the thing was that strong. Like one of the old wraiths from Eire," Ari replied. "That monster just didn't fall out of the shadows without someone yanking its chain."

"Kismet probably broke the Veil open, but that wouldn't have called a wraith," Death remarked, stroking the scar across his face. He leaned forward, a pale stretch of skin showing along his back as his shirt rode up. "Did he call up the wraith? Could this boy have gained that kind of knowledge?"

"Shi, from what I saw of the kid, I'd be surprised if he could get his own shadow to follow him." Ari shook his head. "The kid barely had enough strength to scream in pain."

"What about the wraith that jumped us in the garage?" Mal asked. "That thing was plenty strong. Did that fall out of the Veil too?"

"That thing was old. It ate its way up the food chain." Ari shot the blond a dirty look. Giving Death a cocky grin, he dismissed it outright. "Nothing really to worry about. I took care of it."

"You didn't say anything about an attack in the garage." Death looked up at Ari. Shifting uncomfortably, Ari waved him off, clearing his throat when the black-eyed Horseman prodded him with an index finger to the small of his back.

"It attacked us." Ari shrugged. "I figured it was because we just walked into its hunting. You know how some of them are. I think it strayed out of its normal hunting grounds and figured it could feed on us."

"They aren't that bold. Think it's connected to the boy?" Death said, shaking his head in disbelief.

"Some of them are pretty cocky. Especially if it finds itself someplace without a lot of emotion to feed on. After a while they get desperate. Anything behind the Veil becomes food," Ari replied. "It was hungry and went after Mal. I took care of it."

"It tossed me into one of the columns." Mal nodded, sipping at his coffee. "I was surprised it could do that much damage to your car, but then that wraith today took a hydrant apart. And that was much smaller than a car."

"How much damage?" Death tilted his head, staring up at Ari's innocent-seeming face. "You let it damage my car and attack Mal? Is it still drivable, or is it dead like my horse?"

"Told you." Ari pointed at Mal. "Shoot his horse once and that's it. Everything is blamed on you for the rest of eternity. That horse would have been long dead by now, Death, with or without the arrow in it."

"It's not that bad. The car, I mean. You won't be able to drive it because the fender's dented down over the wheel, but it can be fixed," Mal protested, slapping away Ari's hand. "And it wasn't his fault. The wraith attacked me out of nowhere. Ari got it off of me before I got seriously hurt."

"Uh-huh." Death pursed his mouth. "Anything else you left out, Ari?"

"Can we get back to the kid and forget about the car for a bit?" Min asked. "You can scream at Ari later."

"Yes, let's yell at Ari later." Ari reached over, playfully slapping at Mal's head. "The kid will probably head back to the place we found him. I'm guessing he lives there."

"If he's using drugs, he'll need something soon. He might have more stashed there. Or we can hope he has more there. I don't want to spend hours hunting for him on the streets," Death said. "I also want to know what brought him over. That's not happened for centuries. I wonder if someone in the Courts pulled him over and he got loose somehow."

"Tam Lin. Johnson. Pousão." Ari ticked a few off on his fingers. "The Courts do like their artists."

"But not lately. Not like they used to. They haven't grabbed anyone in decades." Shifting forward, Min rested her chin on the mound of her palm.

"No Fae would be able to make him immortal. He'd have remained human. Just unseen. This is different," Death said thoughtfully.

Ari stood, absently reaching for Death's empty cup of tea. Ari grunted when the other Horseman nodded and murmured his thanks. His attention followed Ari's progress to the kitchen, dragging reluctantly back to the others.

"Someone had to pull him across the Veil. Someone with power and probably wanting to do it again."

"Did he say anything about someone else?" Ari asked from the kitchen.

"I didn't talk to him," Min remarked. "Pest did."

"He doesn't have anyone else." Mal turned his mug in his hands. "I think he's alone, but I can't see him letting someone do something to him. He's pretty strong willed."

"Cooties, you don't get out enough to know about humans," Min muttered.

"How strong could his will be if he's using drugs to run away from the shadows that can't even hurt him?" Ari padded back, handing Death a refilled mug.

Death turned the cat's face around until its nose rested against the crook of his thumb, then spoke. "Sometimes, humans use drugs or alcohol to numb themselves so they don't see the Veil. It doesn't mean he's weak."

"The wraith attacked him directly. It was standing over him and ignoring the other human." Ari reconstructed what he saw when he pulled the Mustang up to the motel. "It saw me, but it didn't even blink. It wasn't going to let him go."

"A summoned creature usually goes for a prey that someone's cast for. So there's someone who held its leash," Death mused aloud. The boy was definitely prey for someone. "An immortal showing up should have drawn it away. You'd be a threat. At the very least, it would try to protect its prey, thinking you were the greater predator. It could be someone in the Courts wants him."

"Or human," Min pointed out. "There's always a few out there that meddle in things they shouldn't."

"It was trying to drag the kid someplace." Ari tried to reconstruct what he'd seen, the incident clouded from the adrenaline in his blood during the fight. "The wraith was hunkered down over him. Its feet were dug in and pulling on him. I think it was trying to take him elsewhere."

"And since they're not that smart, it would have to be given a simple command." Death sipped at his tea, feeling the heat sink into the chill in his body. "It would have to take the boy someplace close. The wraith wouldn't be able to drag the boy by jumping through the Veil. It wouldn't have the strength."

"I don't know," Ari said. "It was dragging him off, but it was having problems. Something powerful enough to affect the outside world should have been able to pick up the kid and fling him around like he was a rag doll."

"So perhaps it couldn't get a good hold on him? Maybe right then, the boy was between worlds?" Death set his mug down. "Whatever it was changing him could have finished the job by the time you two brought him here. You said he wasn't conscious while you drove. Was he disoriented?"

"I'm guessing yes and with a big headache," Min said, motioning toward Mal. "He woke up and asked Pest for some aspirin. I don't think Mal pushed himself out of the Veil to talk to him."

"No. I didn't." Mal realized he'd just sat down and started talking to the young man sprawled out on the couch. He hadn't had to take the time or energy to pull himself into Kismet's reality, using his will to force himself into view. "I didn't even think about it at the time. I mean, I never do that at home."

"You wouldn't have thought of it," Death assured him. "This is our home. Remember? The Veil doesn't extend inside our home."

"He said something to Mal after I got the wraith off of him." The others looked at Ari, sliding off the arm and nestling into the space next to Death. "Spoke right to him. I didn't think anything about that at all either. A lot of the crazies talk to us. Doesn't mean they're one of us. It just means they can see us."

"But you carried him here," Min pointed out.

"I'd pushed the Veil aside." Ari shrugged. "Since I had to drive here, I kept it down until I came upstairs. Cops tend to want to pull over cars if it looks like no one is driving."

"The question is, what do we do now?" Min asked, moving off the chair and next to Mal. "Do we go after him? And what do we do with him once we find him?"

"We have to find out what made him immortal," Death said. "Someone did this on purpose, and I don't think it was the boy. Whoever changed him probably wants him back to make sure it worked."

"You think this someone will change more people?" Mal asked.

"Bet on it," Min replied. "Damn. If the Veil snapped apart from one human, imagine what will happen with more."

"I don't want to spend the next century hunting down spooks and wraiths. It was bad enough when those damned priests kept bringing them over." Ari shook his head. "I thought we left those days behind."

"That's what's going to happen if we don't stop this," Death pointed out. "As for what to do with him, we bring him here."

"Bring him here? What the hell are we going to do with a human here?" Ari turned sideways, amazed. "It's not like he can live here."

"Where else are we going to take him?" Mal moved to the edge of the couch, the cushions crimpling with his weight.

"This isn't the Four Horsemen and their Little Pony." Fuming, Ari gritted his teeth, Death cutting him off with a wave of his hand. "Come on! You can't be serious."

"I am serious. The discussion is over." Death stood, ignoring Ari's huff of anger. "We'll split up. Two of us can start with the motel and the other two work inward from a few blocks out. If he's out looking for drugs, we can hope he'll probably go to someone close to where he lives."

"It's down by College," Mal offered, gathering up the cups and heading into the kitchen, avoiding Ari's hot stare. "I know where the motel is."

"Lots of dealers down that way. It's like a Chinese buffet." Min stepped over Ari's long legs, grabbing at the jacket she'd tossed over the back of the couch. "It might take us a long time to find him."

"Should be easy enough. Find one drugged-out kid amid all the other drugged-out kids in the area." Ari straightened up, resigned to Death's plan. "Just thought I'd say this now, I think this is a bad idea."

"It's our only option," Death replied. "Now who's driving? I certainly can't. Ari let a wraith eat my car."

CHAPTER NINE

A WOODEN bookcase hid the staircase leading down to the basement. The swinging shelves were installed after a housekeeper stumbled on his workroom. She'd been the first person who died after coming into contact with the things he summoned from the Veil but by no means the last. The stairs were wide, accommodating for some of the larger arcane pieces he had collected over the years.

The downstairs space initially served as a fallout shelter in the paranoia of the midcentury. Over the years it served as a pantry or a wine cellar until Beckett purchased the oceanfront property. He'd immediately seen the windowless space downstairs as a place to conduct his experiments, which depended heavily on the presence of pitch-black shadows.

Divided into two chambers by a long wall, the shelter now boasted a comfortable library on one side of the landing's opening. Beckett left the other chamber relatively unaltered except for wide surgical sinks and long tables against the wall. He'd paid for a stonemason to groove a permanent circle in the middle of the poured cement floor, its radius wide enough to hold the largest of shadow creatures.

Glass boxes holding his most prized possessions lined the shared wall, curiosities he'd gleaned from his travels. Small dollops of mewling black dots climbed around behind one pane, their small maws biting and chewing off pieces of weaker wraithlings. A misshapen skull stared out into the room from another, its gummy, yellowing eyes darting about with frenetic movement. Beckett admired the frothy collection of minute glossy wings he'd gathered into a glass square, tiny drops of inky black blood splattered around the ripped ends of the spines.

Each box held something taken from the Veiled, anchored in the visible world by a whisper of power. Some he'd gathered himself, the cruder pieces that he could grab and pull over. Others he'd paid dearly for or sometimes stumbled upon without the owner knowing the article's true worth. Just last year he'd come upon a man who was interested in selling off pieces his uncle left in a basement. Beckett nearly wet himself when he discovered the preserved skins of Veiled kept in a flat museum case, nearly perfect after years of storage in the dry darkness of a root cellar.

Taking a sharp scalpel from a table, he touched a length of muddied green skin he'd left out on the low countertop beneath the grisly collection. Beckett at first was horrified at the idea of cutting into the darkfae hide, but its precious flesh was key to summoning a powerful wraith.

"No matter." Beckett stilled his fingers, slicing into the buttery soft flesh. "After I drain the boy of his blood, getting more components will be simple."

The magus who had taken the skin awed Beckett with his mastery of preservation. As the blade cut into each layer of epidermis, a redolent stink rose as the fat was exposed to the air, the odor released from the darkfae's musk glands. Using a pair of metal tongs, he plucked up a wide swath of skin, then placed the flesh in the middle of the lopsided star he'd poured out earlier. After filling the groove with coarse salt and gold filings, Beckett dusted off his hands and stood back, taking a deep breath into his lungs to steady his nerves.

Spitting directly on the piece of hide, Beckett invoked the first stage of the summoning, binding the creature to his will. He preferred Italian for his dealings with the arcane, feeling the language lent a smooth elegance to the arts, but the summoning language was clear in its demand for the harsh nonsensical words scribbled in the various books he'd found on the subject. It left his throat scratchy as he finished the incantation, the flesh nearly raked raw and bleeding from the strain of pronouncing the spell correctly.

The shadows along the groove thickened, gathering until the ring filled in and spilled over into the cement circle. Stretched too tightly, the Veil burst apart at the center of the circle, minute wraithlings drawn by the smell of darkfae flesh and Beckett's spit. Falling upon their feast, they chewed off nibbles, growing larger with each bite. Soon the dried meat was gone, and the wraiths intertwined, beginning to form a larger creature, a dark, malevolent intelligence dimly flickering in their round crimson eyes.

Beckett ruefully sliced off more of the darkfae flesh, feeding the developing mass as the Veil's edges buckled under the pressure of staying open. Struggling to reform, the shadowy curtain stretched to right the natural balance between the visible and the arcane worlds, held apart by the strength of Beckett's will. Switching to Italian, Beckett laid down the groundwork for the summoned creature, letting it form from his thoughts.

Very few of the tadpole creatures remained, all of the others absorbed by the larger creature beginning to dominate the circle. Gaining power, the shapeless creature stretched and formed a head, then wings along its elliptical body, a sleek, glistening beak snapping at Beckett's head. He jerked back, not at all reassured by the circle's strength in holding the creature at bay until he finished the spell.

Beckett regarded his creation with satisfaction. Nearly the height of a tall man and heavy bodied, the creature's enormous wings, sweeping leathery stretches, would carry it along the shadows of clouds and over buildings as it hunted. His texts warned of creating implausible creatures. Fanciful imaging would cripple any creation if certain laws of physics weren't observed. The birdlike creature he formed fit those rules, its powerful body supported by two muscled legs bristling with talons and a raking spike along the back joint.

"Now, let's see if I can get you on a leash." Beckett walked around the circle, noting the sharpness of the creature's gaze as it followed him. It was always a risk pushing a summoned creature into development. He could never be sure of its hunger and temperament until the final words of the binding spell and the creature submitted under him.

"Simple words, layered," Beckett reminded himself. He started with the simplest of commands, his mastery over the creature. Tossing another sliver of flesh into the circle, the man wove the protections over the creature, invoking its hunger to protect Beckett's prey and a clear missive to kill any who would defend the young man from being brought to Beckett's side.

When he was done spinning his will around the summoned bird's mind, Beckett sighed with fatigue, his clothes drenched through with sweat. A trickle of blood escaped from a popped cluster of cells in his sinuses, his concentration nearly breaking under the creature's rush to free itself from the constraining spell. Beckett touched the splotch with his fingers, wiped the blood on a tissue, then tossed it at the creature's snapping beak.

The blood seared the wraith's tongue, burning along the length of its throat as it gulped the paper. Beckett pronounced his final invocation, calling the bird back to its creation point following the completion of its task. If successful, the creature would return to the circle, another tool in Beckett's growing arsenal. While he regretted losing the darkfae skin, his creation would be quite useful in the future.

"There." Beckett released the creature back into the Veil, watching the curtain seal up behind the slither of its wings. Turning the lights off behind him, Beckett climbed the stairs back up to the main floor, his stomach rumbling with hunger. "First a shower and some lunch. Then we wait for Frazier to return with our prize."

"MAL LIKES this kid. That could be a problem." Ari broke the silence in the Mustang, his eyes flickering off the road and onto Death's chiseled moody face. The Horseman clammed up immediately after seeing the ruined Vanquish, a sure sign he had a temper brewing behind his hooded sooty eyes.

Not getting a response, Ari grumbled under his breath, then spoke. "You ever going to talk to me again?"

"Probably not," Death muttered. "You're a danger to anything I ride in or on."

"The damned horse died centuries ago," Ari pointed out. "And the car wasn't my fault. I'd think you would be happy that I didn't let Mal get killed. He seems to think that he can die."

"Many of the Veiled can die. They're just hidden from humans but still mortal," Death clarified. "You seem determined to prove that we can as well."

"Yeah, there are a couple of those others I'd like to kill," Ari muttered, swearing at a car that swerved too close to his beloved Mustang. "These people drive like shit."

Leaning over, Death punched on the stereo, switching the channel until he found a station he liked, a heavy bass thumping through the speakers. Ari sucked at his teeth, annoyed at the fiddling with his car stereo, but knew better than to press Death when he was in a mood. Ari debated leaving the argument alone for a moment. Then the niggling push of his irritation barbed his tongue.

"You telling me next time I should just let the wraith eat him?" Ari pulled the Mustang to a stop, catching sight of Mal and Min behind them in the SUV. "I'll be sure to tell him that next time he's screaming for help. Or maybe that's your plan to toughen him up. Let him fight his own battles when we both know he can barely wield a knife to cut butter?"

"No." Death reluctantly dragged the word out, sliding down in the leather seat. Slouching, he hooked his foot up over the dashboard, resting one arm on the door. Twisting, Death watched while Ari maneuvered around a slow-moving minivan. "I'm glad you protected him, and no, I don't know why he won't defend himself."

"You keep telling me Mal is different and that we need different. But we need him to be able to defend himself," Ari reminded him. "Maybe he just needs to understand how damned serious this is."

"The boy might help with that," Death said. "Mal might need someone he feels responsible for."

"Then we get Mal a turtle or something. Taking the boy on is a very bad idea." Lines of cars slowly flowed around them, feeding into the concrete veins of the valley's various freeways. Ari let a car into the stream, puffing his cheeks in frustration at the delay. "There must be a game or something. I've got to get off of the freeway, or you'll be sifting through the people I'm going to kill. Hope they can keep up in that piece of crap Mal likes to drive."

The freeway sliced through the city, striated concrete tunnels interspersed between tracts of greenbelt. Death missed the cobbled-together community gardens that once covered the stretch of street, a neighborhood casualty to the growing needs of the city's traffic. While he preferred the quiet green of the Northwest, the high desert city certainly had attraction, at the very least, its nearly perfect weather and the preponderance of good, cheap Mexican food.

Mal's SUV took the ramp right behind them, keeping a few cars' distance. Ari resisted the urge to gun his engine and pull away, the Mustang growling under him. Pulling out of the off-ramp, Ari spotted the strip mall where they encountered the wraith, the decimated fire hydrant already removed and its empty space covered with sheets of plywood and traffic cones. Ari came to a rolling stop near the fire zone's curb. A flickering Open sign hung in a Chinese buffet's window, the red-and-blue neon reflection running along the chrome of a steaming food line.

"That wraith did a lot of damage," Death remarked upon the torn-up concrete sidewalk and the gouges in the asphalt left by flying metal. Death unhooked his seat belt, ignoring Ari's snort of derision at its use, then slid out of the Mustang, taking his katana from the car's backseat. "Someone must have poured a lot of power into it. Look at this."

"Think we'll need to bring weapons?" Ari grabbed his own blades, sliding the harness carelessly over his shoulder.

"Considering what happened here the last time, yes," Death said. "It might come in handy defending your car in case another wraith attacks you."

"You are never going to let that go," Ari muttered softly. "And no, I'm not reparking the car."

Mal parked nearby, and the other two got out as Death swore at Ari. Min trotted across the parking lot, falling into step next to the tall Horseman.

"You just like being difficult, huh?" She poked at his ribs, finding the center of the scarred sunburst on his torso. "You know how OCD he gets."

"Yep," Ari agreed, grinning broadly at Death's mock disgust at his petty challenge. "Keeps him on his toes. He'll never know when I'll disobey him."

"If you're done being a child, walk me through what happened here." Death paced around the gash, noting where splashes of blood dried on the curb's rounded edge. Mal jogged over, dodging a motorcycle zooming by. Min watched the sleek machine weave through the parking lot, listening to its motor. "And the wraith was unveiled? Did anyone get hurt?"

"It definitely broke free from the Veil but went back in when it left," Ari admitted. "To be honest, we didn't stick around to check for any casualties. The wraith took off down the street toward the motel."

"I'm surprised it didn't stay to feed on its carnage," Death mused, crouching down to sniff at the remains of the hydrant, a shorn piece of metal poking up under the edge of a sheet of plywood. "If it was powerful enough to get outside of the Veil, why wouldn't it stay to eat what it hunted?"

"It had places to go, other kids to eat." Ari stepped close, bending down beside Death. "I have no idea what you're smelling."

"Mostly, Chinese food right now." Death glanced over his shoulder, inhaling the scent of burned sweet and sour sauce on the breeze. "I was trying to see if I could follow the power back to its origin, but it's too old."

"That makes a difference?" Min asked. "Here I thought you were like a bloodhound. Able to snatch the slightest of scents out of the air."

"Age makes a huge difference with impressions," Death replied. "If Ari was more skilled at this, he could have found out who was at the bottom of this when it happened."

"Just can't seem to learn it." Ari spotted the security guard's golf cart parked askew in front of the doughnut shop at the end of the rambling strip mall. The Mustang was safe from being ticketed for a while. "Maybe you haven't tried hard enough to teach me, Shi. I'm thinking some wine, a bit of splashing in a tub, and then I'd be more amenable to learning those kinds of things."

"You're not a dog to be taught by treats." Death stood, dusting the grit from his hands. "You don't seem to have the patience or the palate."

"I keep offering for you to taste my palate, but you keep turning me down." Ari ignored Death's pointedly exasperated sigh. "I'm telling you, Mal and I didn't stick around—"

"What is that?" Mal pointed to the sky as a fluttering whirl of dust broke free from a bank of low-lying clouds.

The swarm grew, forming shapes in the malleable darkness. Death and Ari glanced up, a single fluid motion between them. The elder Horsemen reached behind their backs, the snick of blades leaving oiled sheaths.

Ari whistled out loud. "Fuck me. Looks like we've got company."

"Well, at least we know the wraith wasn't chance." Death wove in, tilting his lean body sideways, shoulders squared against Ari's. "That's always comforting."

"This is going to be nice." Ari grinned wildly, the adrenaline pumping in his veins. "It's been a long time since we've been together in a fight. Those are always fun."

"Min, take up behind us. Keep Mal between."

Death stepped into the space to Ari's left. Ari spun a long dagger in his hand, settling the hilt comfortably in his palm. Another wicked-looking dagger slid free from its sheath, a sheen on its razor edge. Death's katana hummed when its tip was struck by the barest kiss of Ari's left blade. Back to back, they waited, feeling the Veil stretching thin around them.

In the distance, a single shrieking caw belled, rattling the Horsemen's eardrums. The cacophony rose, small ripples of sound driving a piercing throb into their temples. Around them, pedestrians strolled by, unaware of the hideous rent in the space above them. A little girl, barely out of diapers, ran toward the Horsemen, her brown pigtails bouncing about her head. Giggling, her sweet voice screeching when her mother chased after her, the girl nearly ran into Ari's leg. Flailing, her fist passed through his thigh.

Min pushed at Mal's back, shoving him between them. She tugged her mace free, its silvered handle nearly black with the oils from her body, worn smooth in places from her hands. The woman's fingers tightened, flexing until she found her grip. Boots shuffling on broken gravel, Min tensed, body coiled tight.

"Can you see what's forming?" Ari turned, following the arc of the swarm. The shapes shifted again, becoming one mass as it caught a thermal rising off the street.

"Looks like a bird." Death followed Ari's worried look, falling on the wide-eyed Mal, his fingers nerveless around a knife, holding the weapon too tightly and at a bad angle. The creature's wings were coalescing, stretching out pinfeathers from the shadowy nothingness.

"Birds are good." Min fought to keep the volume of her voice down, excitement rising in her throat. "Right? A bird is good?"

"Nah, one of the squat things would be better," Ari said. "It would be stuck to the ground. Something with wings has an up option. That makes it a bitch to fight."

"Think whoever is after Kismet summoned this too?" Mal asked, concentrating on the movement of the dust cloud. The air around the shape was clearing, the shadows solidifying in the center of the mass.

"Has to be. He probably called them up to hunt the boy down or stop someone from getting to Kismet first." Death weighed their options, wondering if it would be possible to reach Kismet before the wraith formed. "We can't assume that the magus doesn't know we're here. If he's got enough power to summon something this big, he might know more about the Veil than he should. A simple command, retrieve the boy or take up where the wraith left off."

"If he has this much power, why does he want Kismet?" Mal asked. "What can Kismet give him if he can do this?"

"Why do you think it's a he?" Frowning, Min poked at Mal's ribs. "It could be a woman. Maybe it's a she."

"Don't think that really matters right now," Ari replied, the anticipation gnawing at his patience. "It all comes back to humans being crazy and thinking they can be all-powerful. They never learn."

"Min, you and Mal might be able to get over to where the boy is." Death stilled, feeling the air grow cold around them. "Ari and I should be powerful enough to draw the bird's attention. It might be fooled into thinking that the strongest thing it senses down here is the boy and not manifestations."

"I don't know if we should leave you," she protested.

"We'll be fine." Ari tossed her the keys to his Mustang, briefly sliding a dagger under his arm to tug the ring free. "See if you can get the kid and come back. We'll be fine. We've fought more with less."

"Go on," Death urged them. "Before it comes down and you won't be able to get free without drawing it to Kismet's side."

Folding the mace away, Min dragged at Mal's waistband, pulling him with her toward the red Ford. Slamming the door behind her, she pulled the Mustang from the curb, tires screaming a black rubber trail on the lot. Torn between swearing after her and the flock, Ari sensed a gentle nudge against his ribs, Death's elbow turning him. Tucked under his left arm, the dark-haired Horseman *felt* right positioned there, a comforting harbinger of destruction that matched his own bloodthirsty nature.

"Been a long time," Ari said, the rumble of his deep voice rich with laughter. "Since we've been like this, I mean."

"You like this." Death moved, his shoulder briefly rubbing Ari's shoulder blades. The wraith spotted them and dived. Talons stretched out, it spiraled down, cutting through the air with a whistling sound, piercingly loud. Balancing himself, Death settled into a ready stance, katana poised over his arm, edge up.

"Damned right I do," Ari responded. "Lets me know I'm alive."

FRAZIER PEERED out from behind the dirty muslin curtains in the manager's apartment, the thin material stiff with grease and dirt. Even through the thin latex gloves, his fingers felt grimy, a film of cigarette smoke and fried foods sticking to his skin. Carl's body held court in an ancient white box freezer in the small dining room, rust spots and dings marking up its thick metal walls. The myriad of TV dinners the manager had stored there lay defrosting in the kitchen sink, a small pile of plastic food Frazier wouldn't dream of putting into his body. He'd pocketed the stacks of cash he'd found wrapped in newspaper and ziplock bags.

A hastily scribbled note, barely legible, fluttered on the motel office's door, notifying anyone stopping by that the manager would be out until Monday. It would be days before the tenants of the building noticed the man's absence. Perhaps even weeks before the cops were called. Frazier planned to have the boy extracted from the premises before the hour was up.

Frazier's need for a cigarette gnawed at him. He fought off the urge, knowing that he couldn't risk leaving even the slightest speck of his spit or skin in the manager's apartment. A skullcap pulled over his short hair would serve to prevent any accidental root discoveries, and he'd been careful to wear long sleeves to prevent any scraping of skin against sharp edges. The longer he stayed in the man's apartment, the greater the chance of discovery before they could get the boy back to Beckett's house.

He hadn't planned on killing the manager, not at first, but as he listened to the man wheedle for more money, Frazier saw the uselessness of the situation unfold. Carl would become a loose end, and those were better left tied up before they unraveled and people starting asking questions. Besides, it gave Frazier great pleasure to stop the man's whining voice.

Something flickered in the corner of the room. Turning, Frazier frowned, staring at the emptiness there. The living area was sparsely furnished, a broken-down couch with threadbare cushions taking up most of the wall beneath the window looking out onto the parking lot. A battered television perched precariously on a pressboard table, a length of cable running from the set to a splitter in the wall.

While rank and tight on space, the manager's apartment was a prime spot to watch the boy's place until Frazier decided to make his move. The motion pulled at him again, Frazier whipping his head around. He'd already looked through the small space for any sign of a pet, finding only stacks of porn and dirty laundry piles in the tiny bedroom.

Rats scratched in the crawlspace above the ceiling, or at least Frazier hoped the endless scrapings were from small rodents. He'd heard a story of a family of skunks suddenly startled by the smell of blood from a particularly violent murder, their oily scent spraying through the air-conditioning system. He certainly didn't want to be found out about Carl's death by an odor. His pride would never withstand the indignity of it. Staring back out of the window, Frazier ignored the scrabbling and concentrated on the boy's closed door.

Since Frazier began squatting in the apartment, only a few of the motel's residents had walked by, giving the boy's door a wide berth. Dark splotches wrinkled the building's stucco wall, shadows moving back and forth with the lights from passing cars. Frazier reached for the pack of cigarettes in his pocket, the crinkle of its wrapper flaring his nostrils. Tongue swollen with moist want, the bodyguard tensed. A pair of young men were approaching his target's home.

Glancing back toward the locked freezer, Frazier swore at Carl's metal coffin. "Shit. If I could kill you again, I would. You told me he never had any visitors."

Carl remained mute in his frozen prison, eyes iced shut against the cold blackness. Moisture leaking from his dead body crystallized against his slack skin, sticking the pair of brown polyester pants to his thighs. With the remainder of his warmth leeching from his corpse, Carl was slowly turned into a long slab of meat among frozen microwave burritos.

"Screw it. Time to grab the boy and leave." The fog must have moved in, Frazier thought, as the two young men appeared to float in and out of his vision. Twisting his head, he tried to focus, blinking to shake off the watery tears filming over his eyes. Broken shards of darkness fought battles behind him, sucking on the tendrils of madness emanating from Frazier's head.

"I think there's a mortal watching this place from across the parking lot." The rounder of the two men scratched at the thin smattering of hair on his chin.

Tucking his fingers into the fold of stomach hanging over the waistband of his sweatpants, Gluttony tried to make out the mortal's aura, searching for a shred of vice in Frazier's psyche. He found nothing emanating from the mortal, at least nothing connected to him. His fingers found his chin again, the under flap of his dusky thick arms wiggling as he scratched.

"I can feel him. But I can't touch him. He's not one of mine," Gluttony remarked.

His companion was tempted to wave at the mortal, wondering how thin the Veil had become around the motel. Lanky, his body held a youthful gracefulness, flowing movements at odds with the jerky, bloated fumbling of his brother's footsteps. Lust ducked his head, nearly nose-to-nose with Gluttony.

"Maybe he's free of vice," Gluttony deadpanned, his round face serious until Lust's luminous green eyes glinted with humor. They burst out laughing, cheeks aching from the effort and then falling apart to small hiccupping gasps. Pounding his taller brother's back, the rotund Sin caught his own breath, heaving a sigh and coughing out the air in his lungs. "He feels kind of normal. I'm still surprised he can see us."

"I'm not," Lust remarked, tilting his head back to watch a stream of shadows overhead. "Look at how thin the Veil is. Things are going to start crawling out really soon. I don't want to be here when that happens."

All around him, Lust felt the pull of humans on his calling, their covetous nature hooking into him and yanking small pieces of his control back and forth. He ignored them all, concentrating on the need trapped behind the thin painted door to Kismet's private hell.

"Can't you feel the tightness of the mortal world on you? That sticky wrapping on your face when you walk? I've never felt it so thin. Not like this. It's incredible." Lust fought the pull of a couple walking down the street, their hands intertwined. Their fingers winked gold, the rings' matching bands wrapped around other fingers far from their mates. "Someone's done something that he shouldn't have. There's something wrong with this one."

Kismet's soul literally wept with need, and Lust's cock twitched in response, nipples tingling beneath the rub of his shirt. Kismet's wants were nearly overpowering, energizing Lust down to his bones. "I want to know what's going on. Use it if we have to."

"Use it how?" Gluttony's eyebrow crooked, a thick golden stud waggling in his nearly ebony skin. "It's not like we can auction him off."

Squat bodied and rounded, his face naturally creased in a smile, dimpled and merry. Never lacking company, he often shadowed Lust, moving through the world of the humans with a practiced ease. Chasing after the thinning Veil and the mortal at the center of it didn't make much sense to Gluttony, but he was willing to see it through, more out of loyalty to his brother than anything else.

"I don't know," Lust admitted with a casual shrug. "And maybe auctioning him off isn't a bad idea."

The other Vice prodded at the bony remains of a wraith. In a few days, under the glare of harsh sunlight, it would disperse, leaving nothing behind. The creature's skull bore the marks of several blows. Gluttony poked his fat fingers through its eye sockets, nearly jumping back when a tendril slithered out of the hole.

"Why are you doing this?" Gluttony looked up from the wraith's bones. "Why are you dragging me into this with you?"

"Why do I have to explain everything to you?" Lust hissed between his teeth, exasperated at his brother's apathy. "This kid is important. I don't know why, but I can feel him pulling at me, and it's like kissing a star."

"And you think this kid will do what for you?" the Vice asked, poking at a lingering tendril of inky blackness lying on the broken cement walk. It dissipated under the touch, unable to hold it cohesion when struck with flesh.

"Think on it. We're more vital than any of the immortals, but we're relegated to the back of the bus, sucking on the scraps of fame they might toss to us, like dried chicken bones leftover from a stew," Lust said. "This kid is worth something. If we have control over him, who knows what we can do?"

"If we're so important—" Gluttony leaned against the wall of the building, sniffing at the remnants of carnage caught along the Veil's stickiness—"then why are we hiding here in the shadows sniffing around a human that probably will be more trouble than he's worth?"

Lust replied, "Shut up and help me do this."

Kismet, lost in the scent of acrylics and the images unfolding in his head, continued to paint, dipping brush strokes into his nightmares, then onto the canvas. Lust inhaled deeply, filling his body with the scent of the artist's pain, cut sweet with the powerful drive of hidden passions. So much lay beneath the surface, pushed down deep below Kismet's conscious thoughts, nailed down into a coffin of denial. The loss of family hung a shroud over the young man's eyes, a loneliness haunting him. Narrow shoulder blades worked furiously beneath Kismet's thin T-shirt, arcing motions dipping bony wings beneath the cotton.

The Vice jiggled the knob, hearing it rattle in his hand. His temptation to just walk in was strong, but Lust wanted to draw this moment out, savor something instead of consuming it whole. If he played the boy's emotions right, Lust could have the artist eating out of his hand, willing to do anything to satisfy him. "I just want for us."

"You should have been Envy." His brother shook off Lust's jealousy with a wave of his fat hand. "Why aren't you satisfied with what we have? You'd never get any peace, always bobbing about to deal with bigger things."

"Don't even talk to me about Peace." The Vice stroked at the door separating him from the artist. "What a weak piece of shit."

"Everyone has their use, even Peace," Gluttony reminded him. "You don't have any idea what this kid can be used for, do you?"

"No, not yet." A patter echoed under Lust's fingertips, drumming a pattern along the doorjamb. "But I have to get ahold of him before any of the others do. Someone wants him bad. Bad enough to change the world."

"He probably did it to himself. A Ouija board and chicken blood. That's what we'll find inside." Gluttony worried at his lip, pulling at it with his teeth. "Someone's going to end up paying for that. Probably him."

"No, he's not," the Vice disagreed. "He's human. Free will, remember? Every damned thing they do is their choice. Chances are someone's been sent to stop him from being, and something wrong happened."

"That kid inside isn't worth anything more than any of the other specks of meat on this Earth." Gluttony edged past Lust, peering through the crack in the curtains. "He doesn't look like much. Pretty but just another mortal."

"Look around you, brother. There's a wraith carcass at our feet. Battles are going to be fought over this one. We'd be stupid not to take advantage of that." Lust looked up at the sky again, seeing the cloud breaking apart and reforming into a larger stormy horror. "If we don't move, we're going to be caught in the middle of a war that neither one of us can win."

"Better hurry, then," Gluttony fretted. He was ill suited for ambition, preferring a quiet life spent among mortals who knew how to indulge. Lust's need for recognition from the others perplexed him, something Gluttony secretly felt would be his brother's downfall.

"Want to keep an eye out for our peeping Tom across the courtyard? If he comes in after the boy, we'll have to do something about him." Lust's knuckles dragged along the rough surface of the stucco, barking the skin. The pain felt good, a familiar sour bite on his tongue. Pressing his moist mouth on the dirty windowpane, Lust breathed, a smoky mist clouding the glass. "Open the door, pretty boy. Open the door for me."

Kismet's face caught the light as he turned, hearing the call whispering under the door. Fingers trailing over the fold of his elbow, he stumbled back from the half-imagined dream, acrylics muddied from colors run together. Lust stepped in, slithering away from the noise of the street, sliding his hand around the door's edge and pulling it shut. There was a snick of the bolt mechanism hitting the strike plate, hanging before sliding into the hole gouged out by a screwdriver.

"*Someone's come knocking, Kiz.*" Chase's silvery voice worked into the curve of Kismet's eardrum, rattling around with a steel ring pitch. The young artist winced, screwing down his teeth over his bottom lip until he could taste the sharpness of his own blood.

"Shut up. God, can't you just shut the fuck up?" Kismet's fingernails scraped at his own cheeks. Savagely opening up his flesh, Kismet tried to bury his brother's voice in pain, shoving Chase's digging whispers behind the sting.

"*You want me to shut up? Like that night?*" Chase drew closer, his form wavering and nearly lost in the waves of agony burning through Kismet. "*I shut up then, Kizzie. And you didn't even wake up to watch me die.*"

"That wasn't my fault." Kismet stepped away from the canvas he'd painted, catching his foot on a lump in the carpet. "God, I was a kid. We both were kids. You're not even real. Fuck, why the hell am I talking to myself?"

When the door cracked open, he turned, seeing the two men in the doorway. His blood screamed as it sucked the last few grains of heroin from its reserves, burning through the drugged peace, leaving nothing behind.

Lust stood for a moment, letting his essence enrapture the young man, reaching out with trembling fingertips. Sliding his hand into Kismet's shaggy mane, he leaned in close, catching the last hot breath from the young man's mouth, drawing it into his own. The Vice reveled in Kismet's chemical craving, the sharp sourness of his blood run thin with tarry powders. The boy no longer felt human. He'd be forever caught behind the Veil. That excited Lust to no end.

The floor lay scattered with discarded clothes and several pizza boxes, white cardboard hardened from dried moisture. A locker's lid held evidence of Kismet's addiction, the burned bottom of a cut-off aluminum can scorched from use, its crease smoky from heated liquids. Lust grabbed the boy's arm, then turned Kismet around as Gluttony came through the door, his eye still fixed on the mortal watching through the curtains across the way.

"Who are you?" Kismet shook off Lust's hands, distancing himself from the Vice.

"Baby, you've known me all of your life." The Vice slid his arms around the young man's waist, fitting his body against the slender curve of Kismet's hips. "I'm pretty sure if I were a god, you'd be one of my priests."

"Get out." There was something about the man that was confusing. His thoughts were muddied, even more so than with the heroin lingering in his system.

Lust wrapped his influence around the young man, tilting the world onto its side. "You don't want me to leave, baby."

"What the hell is this?" The large black man skidded, brought short by the paintings leaning haphazardly against the far wall. "Lust, what have you pulled us into?"

Screaming mouths emerged from bloody skies, wings feathered with slender scales arcing over crumbled bodies, arms wrapped tight around broken heads. Skulls floated free of undefined limbs, soaked through with tears, sorrow dripping from fingers bent back in pain. Wraiths howled in glee, reaching out to the spectator just behind the painter. The entire world of the Veiled lay thick on canvas, captured in the fluid horror of a young man's madness, held at bay just outside of his control.

"He's just insane," Gluttony whispered, voice muted at the collection of his world in simple strong strokes. "He's just like those other humans."

"No, he's not," Lust insisted. "He's immortal but without a calling. Feel him. How fucking cool is that?"

"You're the one that's insane, Lust. Look at this stuff. He's gone over the edge. There's nothing human left in him. The shadows have eaten it all," Gluttony said, stepping farther into the room.

He approached Kismet's newest creation. Long sheaves of wheat blotted harsh with boiled pinks and browns, dots of cornflower fighting against the strong hues of a diseased mauve. The hint of gold circles surrounded the dots, a floating sheen below clouds of squirming worms dripping from a rotted sky. "I know that face. I've seen that face before."

"You know, I can hear you." Kismet wove, nearly tumbling off his feet. "I'm right here, bastards. I'm just a little stoned."

"Baby, I need you to be quiet." Lust stroked the young man's face, wrapping his influence around Kismet's soul. "I need to think."

Kismet resisted, dragging his feet on the floor. The heroin he injected numbed his body, but his mind was racing. Kismet felt Lust's manipulations, knew the man was doing something to him but didn't have the strength to fight it off. Erotic tendrils set his blood on fire, and Kismet purred under Lust's wandering hands. As the Vice's influence grew, it reached deep inside of the young man, breaking him down.

"Like giving candy to a baby." Lust ran his lips over Kismet's mouth, tasting the other man's sweet breath. "Gods, you are so one of mine."

"I think it's supposed to be the new Pestilence."

Lust gave a quick glance at the painting, shoving at Kismet's back, trying to get the young man out of the door. "He must have seen them, the Horsemen. That's probably who tore apart that wraith outside."

"Well, that's it, then. Time to go. I'm not facing one of the Four. And I sure as hell am not going to stick around to see if those shadows are coming after him." Gluttony pulled on his brother's shirt, ignoring the young man. "Let's find a calling far from here and just get there."

"He can't follow us." Lust's green eyes gleamed. "Feel around inside of him. He's one of us but not one of us."

"Then forget him. He's the last thing you need on you right now." The Vice gripped his brother's shirt, hauling Lust close. "I'm not going to cross the Horsemen just because you want something you shouldn't have."

"We'll make a run for it." Lust shook Gluttony off. "We can hide among mortals until I can get us someplace safe."

"We really don't have a place to hide," Kismet rasped, husky voice velvet and dark. Fervor gleamed in his eye, the altered heroin working through his blood. The addiction fed, he nearly collapsed in Lust's arms, his limbs refusing to cooperate. "Can't stand well. And the shadows keep coming at me. They shouldn't. I'm stoned. They should leave me alone."

"Yes, I'm going with crazy." Gluttony threw open the door, reaching out with his mind for a human's call, looking for something far away from the motel's cramped courtyard. "I'll see you later, brother. Well, either you or whoever takes your place when the Four are done with you."

"Fucking bastard. Come back here!" Lust swore, grabbing at empty space when Gluttony rushed on to the call he found, his round body easing into the Veil's folds, disappearing to someplace else. "Who helped you when you fell into that mess with the Virtues? I'll keep the boy hidden."

"I really need to stay. I have my stuff here." Kismet shook his head, steadying himself on Lust's shoulders. "Someone will take my stuff."

"We are not hidden here, pretty." Lust curled up close into Kismet's body, feeling down the length of his thighs. The Vice grinned broadly at the thickening between his fingers, mouth hovering near Kismet's parted lips. "I'll just keep you drowned in me. That'll hide you from any of others. Chances are you're not going to call one of the Horsemen."

Kismet reached out, his hand jostling the lid of his footlocker. "Can't leave it."

"I can get you more of that too." Lust slid his arm around Kismet's waist, shoving him toward the open door. His options were limited in San Diego, tied mostly to nighttime activities that had yet to start. With the falling sun, his power grew as people's desires increased. "Come on. I've got someplace we can go and get you a really nice fix."

The Vice heard sounds coming from the courtyard, a screeching of tires and slamming of doors, as well as the grating accented voice of Famine shouting at another of the Horsemen. Peering out through the crack of the door, Lust craned his neck to see which of the Four were outside, holding his breath in hopes that it would be one of the younger ones. He didn't want to face Death. Lust had no desire to find out if Death could kill him just by wanting him dead.

Cupping Kismet's face, Lust lay into the other's mouth, savoring the edges of sour hanging at the corners of the boy's lips. Gluttony was right. There were taints of insanity in the boy's soul, a childlike specter drawn into him and anchored by guilt. The boy's lust-ridden eyes darkened, his pupils gulping at the color of his eyes, leeching the last shreds of Kismet's will. Drowning in the seductive pull of Lust's influence, Kismet broke away, dazed with the struggle to fill his lungs with cool air.

"Come on, pretty." Lust yanked on Kismet's arm, dragging the young man out onto the walkway. "We can probably cut around to the back and out the alleyway before anyone notices us. With Luck, we'll be gone soon, and then I'll find out exactly how much you're worth."

Chapter Ten

Death being near was comforting, Ari decided. In the beginning, when they first fought wraiths, Ari lost all sense of what was around him, thrilled at the taste of blood in his mouth. Neither of them had any defensive skills, and when the battle ended, Ari discovered he'd caused most of Death's injuries.

Over time, they learned to fight alongside the other, more out of survival at first, then habit, until it became second nature. Ari's side felt empty without Death there, aching in the dark of the night when his bed lay cold. During a fight, Ari could touch freely. Once weapons were forged, they established where they were standing with the touch of their blades. It became a sound Ari loved to hear.

"What's taking it so long?" Ari chafed with the waiting, looking around him with a practiced, assessing eye.

Death grinned beside him, a slanting flirtation marred by the run of silver scarring over his pretty face. The child inside of Ari amused Death, a feral innocence simplified in Ari's glee.

Stretching his arm out, Ari yanked at the Veil, trying to pull it closer as a woman stared at him and Death, her chin dropped nearly to her chest. Ari risked taking his eyes off the bird, noticing that their presence was drawing more than a little attention from the humans around them. The security guard they'd spotted earlier spoke urgently into his radio, a squawking rattle in his voice as he called for assistance.

"Shit. We're visible. Damned *human* can see us." Ari felt a lurch in his belly when the Veil broke around him. Desperate to fold it back, Ari reached out with his mind, finding nothing to hold on to. "Fuck, Death. We're in trouble here."

Death pushed at the Veil, trying to shove it closed as it tore, its edges unraveling from around Ari and then pulling free of them both. Exerting his will, Death reached deep into the well of power, his ability to manipulate the shadows greater than Ari's, but the Veil buckled and slipped away from Death's grasp.

"Damn it, it's not closing." Death tried again, the shadowy curtain sliding away from their bodies.

A woman watched them as she passed, her grocery cart laden with bags. Creasing her forehead, she hurried past, giving the armed men a wide berth.

"Try a bit harder." The blond swallowed the bile burning his throat, the fluctuations making his stomach turn.

"I can't close it, Ari." Death bit back his anger, feeling naked stripped clean of the shadows. "The Veil's trying to close, but it's too thin. It keeps breaking apart."

The wraith circled again, trying to reach its prey below. Death stared up at the sky, seeing the stark ice blue without the filmy taint of the Veil. Ari followed Death's gaze, taking in the expanse of brilliant cerulean with a shrug.

"Death, we've got other things to do besides stare up at the sky." Ari nudged him. "Yeah, it's a pretty blue, but it's just blue."

"Stop for a second and pay attention for a change." Death pushed at Ari's hand, the elder Horseman scanning the sweeping shadow overhead. "It's heading away from us. We should be pulling it in just by being here."

"Shit, okay I see it. What the hell is going on?" Ari asked. The bird hovered, searching for something on the ground. The immortal was spoiling for a fight. The temper he'd been carrying over the past few days needed to be worked out of his system. The wraith would be a fine distraction from his want for Death.

"I don't think it's interested in us," Death murmured, pointing up at the trail of a talon as it struck downward, leaving a smear of charcoal along the rim of the Veil's tear. "It's heading away."

"Son of a bitch." Ari gnashed his teeth. "It's probably got the boy's scent."

"How far is that motel? Do you remember?" Death asked. A small crowd was gathering at the end of the sidewalk, intrigued by the two men wielding weapons in the middle of a San Diego strip mall. The cluster of mortals made him uneasy, their too short lives shining out of their curious eyes. "If we're closer to the boy, it might get confused by our presence. We could mask him."

"It's not far, maybe a block away, but I think Mal took his keys with him. The place is pretty easy to find. It's got a bright blue roof." Ari jerked his chin toward the east, pointing out an alleyway past the grocery store. "We can just cut through the crowd there. Probably make it on foot."

"No killing the humans. Come on, then," Death said, breaking into a sprint toward the alley.

Ari sighed, running after his friend, avoiding the people gathering at the grocery store entrance.

"Gods, we need to work on your English," Ari muttered, easing his shoulders through a gap in a chain-link fence, Death a few feet ahead of him. "And if that was a joke, then we also have to work on your sense of humor."

Sirens sounded off in the distance, a complication neither of the Horsemen wanted to deal with. The air shuddered as the mortal world shook around them. The outlying shadows buckled, trying to seal its ends together. Death debated their options. Heading into the Veil would draw the wraith toward Kismet, but standing out in the open would lead to trouble. Decision made, he pulled Ari toward the break in the buildings.

The wail grew louder, and Death's elbow into his ribs urged Ari to break out of a steady run toward the motel. A lingering shadow clotted the alley entrance, promising a thicker cover of shadows just beyond the side street. The Horsemen sprinted, disappearing into the ebbing curtain.

"We must have made someone nervous." Ari watched the shadowy creature dive down, circling tighter around the area. "Guess cops don't like people showing up at grocery stores with weapons."

Ari grunted when the Veil swallowed them, the shadows bursting into his chest, welling into his blood. Standing exposed in the middle of the sidewalk had been soul wrenching, an experience he never wanted to have again. Death pulled the curtain close, corralling it until the shadowy camouflage hid them from sight. Echoes of their bodies cast long, dark shapes against the nearby walls, the cracked Veil unable to fully envelop them.

"There!" Death pointed as the bird broke off its arc, drawn by the ripple of the two Horsemen entering the thin shadows.

"Still kind of open here." As he crossed into the comfort of the darkness, Ari's lungs filled with the sweetness of the Veil, flowing through his ancient body. Glancing around, Ari edged into a side street, assessing the space for a fight. A nearby pair of dark green Dumpsters would provide cover to cut down the wraith's angles of attack. "Over there, Shi. We need to minimize its options."

"I think killing it will minimize its options," Death remarked, following close behind Ari.

Stepping clear of the garbage spilling over onto the ground, Death lifted his gaze, searching the sky for the summoned creature. A sooty trail arced over behind them, the wraith's wings leaving an echo of gray as it struck the Veil. Screaming with renewed strength, its cry rattled down onto the pair, Death firmly planting his feet in anticipation of its attack.

As the wraith came closer, its stink rankled Ari's nostrils, overloading his senses. The shadow's odor overwhelmed the sickly sweet rot of human refuse, and Ari cleared the stench from his nose with a snort. Death raised his weapon, the scar on his face turning silver in the light when he turned his shoulders toward Ari's back.

"Why are we doing this?" Ari gagged on the creature's smell, scraping his tongue under his front teeth. "Why aren't we just letting it eat the kid?"

"This is just the beginning of it, Ari," Death said. "It'll grow bigger and break out of the Veil."

"And eat more humans." The blond Horseman sighed, balancing his weight to be ready for the bird. "Yeah, got to save the humans. Can't let them get eaten by shadows."

"Do you really think we should let this one get the boy and walk away?"

"No," Ari growled. "This damned thing isn't getting as far as the boy. Hell, it's not getting down the street. Don't put words in my mouth."

There was no worry in Ari's voice. The lack of concern wasn't surprising to Death. He was accustomed to Ari's faith in winning any argument or battle he set his mind to. To lose something he wanted was inconceivable to the blond Horseman. He would continue to hammer at a problem until the person or thing surrendered. As far as he was concerned, Ari would lay siege for all eternity to get what he wanted. As far as Death knew, this wraith had no chance.

Before humans concentrated on hating one another, a break in the Veil meant relatively easy hunting, slithering demonic creatures clustered in a small area, the holes punched into the shadowy curtain pulled back together and held by an immortal's will. The Veil healed itself, knitting threads back together, then strengthening the bond. As mankind spread and paranoia began to taint innate hatreds, blood and curses called forth wraiths, summoned unknowingly through small magics and ill wishes.

Then the humans began to learn how to summon the shadows, and the Horsemen found themselves in a battle against the Veiled creatures.

Death and Ari lived through the centuries of hunting large shadow wraiths feeding off entire villages, the creatures often leaving nothing behind but smoking bones. The Horsemen spent hours in the cold of a winter river washing the ashen powder from their bodies, the pale dust from walking through fields littered with dried, crackling skeletons. Their lives were a blur then, often falling down exhausted to sleep where they could, only to be up an hour or so later to hunt again.

They would have to find the human responsible for calling up this latest wraith, or the Four Horsemen would return to those long days, smoky, depressing months searching for things that fed on human flesh with a delighted, ravenous glee. The other immortals would hopefully help close the Veil's breaches, but Death had little faith in that.

What help they got these days seemed to be grudgingly given, usually ignored until Death begged for support. He had no confidence that any help would be forthcoming if wraiths broke through the Veil.

Standing ankle-deep in the runny, spoiled garbage behind a convenience store, Death was sorry he'd forgotten Ari's dedication. A fierceness ran strong in Ari's character, devoted to the Horsemen and, more importantly, to their leader. He'd wondered if Ari would always be there beside him, a constant companion until time burned down. Now Death began to have doubts that Ari would ever leave. The thought both scared and thrilled the eldest Horseman.

"Paying attention here, Shi?" Ari asked, noticing the distracted look in Death's eyes. "I'm about to save you from getting your ass kicked. I'd like you to at least notice."

The wraith's talons stretched outward, its thick body barreling down through the air. Wings tucked behind its fabricated shoulder blades, it sliced at Ari's head, nearly catching the tip of its diamond-hard claw on his cheek. Jerking his head away, Ari twisted, letting the momentum carry him around and leaving room for Death's attack.

The dark-haired Horseman stabbed at the space where Ari's head had been moments ago, carving a chunk of shadowed meat from the wraith's outstretched limb. Its thick blood spurted from the wound, Death wincing and gritting his teeth in pain when the acidic fluid splashed over his bare forearm. Rolling his shoulder under the strike, Death continued the motion through, curling around Ari's hips as he moved past.

Ari surged forward, one of his long daggers a flash, biting into the wraith's back before it turned away from them. Nearly losing his balance on the slippery asphalt, the blond swore, stepping back to avoid Death's legs. Ari's face bled feral with delight, hands clenched tight around the hilts of his weapons, and he urged the wraith to circle around again.

It arced, its crimson eyes narrowing in wicked malevolence. Screaming with pain, the wraith wobbled in midflight. Its right leg hung useless from its body, the joint severed by Death's katana. The elongating shadows clustered in the alley shivered under the dripping fluids of the bird's wound, faint smoke rings puffing into the air when the drops struck, tadpole-like wraiths feeding voraciously on the mewling, injured bodies of their dying swarm-mates. The ground at Ari's feet emptied of ambient darkness, a hungry tide flowing toward the carnage.

"You okay?" Ari didn't dare take his eyes off the bird, its wings beating a gale wind through the narrow street, the carrion smell nearly choking the blond as he inhaled.

"I'm fine." Death steadied himself, the ground dangerously slick beneath the soles of his shoes. "It's softer, fleshier than I thought it would be."

"Seems pretty hard to me," Ari growled. The wraith beat its wings, trying to get enough altitude for another dive. "Times like this make me wish I had a really long spear. Other than the one I already have, you know."

Death waited a heartbeat before glancing under his lashes at Ari's grinning face. Winking, the blond showed a wide swath of white teeth, his smile tinted lascivious with wicked promise. Disgusted, Death returned to staring at the winged wraith.

"That was funny," Ari grunted, nudging his friend with his elbow. "You need to laugh sometimes, or I'm going to start taking it personally."

Death refused to answer, turning to face the wraith's attack. Its sharp beak snapped, a crackling boom cutting off its piercing cries. Tucking its body into a tight arrow, the bird plunged, its crippled leg flapping behind it, its maw wide open.

The bird could be powerful enough to slice one of them in two, Death realized, focusing on the angle of the bird's attack. This wasn't something that crawled up the food chain, battle-scarred and wary of engaging another predator. This wraith emerged from the darkness with no fear of conflict, not knowing of its own mortality and driven by the will of its creator. These were the most dangerous of creatures, summoned with enough power to cripple or kill with no thought to its own survival.

He and Ari would have to take care not to leave even the tiniest of openings for the bird to exploit. It was too strong and big for a single Horseman to fight. They couldn't afford for either one of them to be crippled before the wraith could be killed.

With the screaming wraith fast approaching, he drew his blade up over his shoulder, feeling Ari close to him, the blond's body searing a line of heat on Death's side. Habit made Ari edge one step in front of Death, offering the breadth of his chest as a target to draw the bird from noticing the lean, rangy man next to him.

"Watch the beak," Death warned Ari.

"Yeah, I think I've done this before, Shi." The blond laughed at Death's answering grumble.

"I am trying to watch out for you."

Ari's heart surrendered to Death, seduced by the softness in his friend's tone. These kinds of moments, caught in a fight with the sloe-eyed Asian by his side, were what made immortality with all of its flaws worth it for Ari. Nudging the other man with his shoulder, Ari murmured, "Thanks."

Seething, the wraith bit at the air, catching the edge of Ari's forearm, spinning the immortal around. Jabbing his dagger up into its chest, Ari gritted his teeth when its blood poured over his bare hand, peels of skin lifting under rising blisters. Metal rattled, the thunderous sound of the bird hitting the Dumpster ringing in the Horsemen's ears. A man jogging by glanced down the side street, perplexed by the echoing gong. The slap of his sneakers was lost to the immortals, their hearing momentarily deafened.

Turning tight on its one good leg, the bird lunged forward for a bite of Ari's shoulder, leaving its neck open for Death's blade. The eldest's katana sliced into the shadowy flesh, breaking off chunks of solid muscle, peeling back the bird's leathery skin to expose the burgundy meat below. Death's katana smoked, the tempered steel dipping repeatedly in the creature's acidic blood, his blows arcing away from Ari.

Pulling back into the corralled trash bins, the wraith stumbled, blood pouring from its wounds.

Beating at the air, the tip of its wing struck Death across the face, opening up a small cut over his cheek. Stepping away from the bird's floundering blows, Ari dug the tip of his dagger into the bird's throat, cutting down deep into the long stretch of muscle under its beak.

The bird's head popped loose from its spine, elongated tendons snapping apart under the edge of Ari's sharp blade. Its beak cracked where it hit a stretch of asphalt, the severed head bouncing in uneven hops along the side street's gutter. The bird's body thrashed about, one of its wings slamming Death against a Dumpster, the Horseman unable to get away from the dying wraith's spasms.

Ari drove his daggers into the wraith's muscled body, then grabbed the bird's wing, cracking the delicate spines as he wrenched at a shoulder joint. After dragging the wraith's weight off Death's trapped body, Ari pulled his friend away from the dented Dumpster and ran his hands down Death's arms to check for broken bones.

"You okay, Shi?" Ari asked, concern adding velvet to his rough whiskey voice. "Shit, that thing was strong."

"I'm good." Death nodded, opening his mouth wide and listening to his jaw pop back into place, the loud crack reverberating off his eardrums. "Ache a little, but I'm good."

"Told you I'd kick its ass for you." Ari grinned. "Damn, that was fun!"

Cupping the eldest's face, Ari ran his thumbs over the rise of Death's lower lip before leaning in close. Exuberant, his nerves hyped on adrenaline, Ari stole his mouth over Death's, taking the older Horseman by surprise.

Death tasted of green tea and orange marmalade, sweetness mingled with the erotic spice of the darkness that spotted his friend's soul. Ari murmured contentedly, taking in Death's gasp of breath, drawing the air into his lungs to hold for a moment before reluctantly allowing it to whisper away. Nipping at the bow of Death's upper lip, Ari stole a final brushing butterfly of a kiss, lingering against Death's mouth with the heat of his own.

"You...." Death was unable to breathe, his thoughts scattered into flight, hematite pigeons fleeing under the attentions of a tawny hunting cat. "You never let up."

"You already knew that about me, Shi." Ari's cocky grin mocked Death's halfhearted protest, the older Horseman not pulling away from Ari's grasp. "I was happy to save your ass. I have plans for it, you know. Let's find the others and head home. I need some lunch. Killing makes me hungry."

MAL GLANCED behind him, his thoughts on the two Horsemen they'd left behind. The Mustang's tires hit the curb hard, jostling Mal into the car door. He bit his tongue, tasting his own blood in the back of his throat. The coppery taint made him sick, a roil of metallic disgust filtering up to his nose.

The walls of a bank rippled with shadow as they passed. Scenting the presence of the Horsemen, a large wraith broke free to hunt its prey, its forming head searching the streets for the pull on the Veil.

The creature swooped around a squat building, snarling while it chased the car.

Min spotted the glimmer of red in its visible eye, swearing, then hitting the gas pedal, hoping to distance the Mustang from the hunting shadow. She wasn't deluded into thinking they could outpace the powerful creature, despite Ari's choice in cars. The siren call of the two Horsemen would draw it in, the ripples of their moving through the Veil nearly impossible to hide from something created out of chaos.

"Min, there's a wraith hunting us." Mal grabbed at the dashboard, trying to keep his seat as he watched the creature gain ground on them.

"Mal, shut up and tell me where I'm going." Min hooked the car into another lane, avoiding a lumbering red Caltrans bus. The Mustang screamed in response, the tires catching on the street's slick, plastic white lines. "I know there's something hunting us."

"Sorry." Mal turned back around. The streets poured past him, a liquid flow of asphalt and green street signs. A familiar steeple-framed office whipped past, its bright blue roof faded from the harsh desert sun. Set closely against the small building, the motel faded into the background, the Mustang gunning by without a whispering hope of slowing down. "It's behind us. Kismet's place is back behind us."

"I should kick your ass," Min growled, gritting her teeth. She hit the Mustang's brakes, its heavier rear end careening and fishtailing, tires hitting a patch of gravel. Kicking up a stream of rocks, the car slid into an alleyway, Min working to avoid a green Dumpster set diagonally against the back of a taco shop. "How far back do I have to go?"

"Just a block." Mal counted off the streets in his head. "I think there's two alleys and then the motel."

"Bastard better be there. I don't want to have to fight that wraith off ourselves." Min winced, working the wheel hard to the left.

A concrete block hung loose from the back alley wall, unseen until she was upon it. Mortar flew up, a powdery puff hitting the side mirror, a heartbreaking gnashing sound when the car's quarter panel tore under the block's jagged edge. The peeling tear curled back paint, plastic, and steel, a long, undulating ripple on the Mustang's once pristine body.

Min winced. "Fuck. Ari's going to make my life miserable."

"There!" Mal pointed, a gap between the buildings visible before they were upon it. The hilt of the long dagger he practiced with felt foreign and alien. Despite the long hours of training with a very patient Death, Mal knew he was no closer to being able to defend himself any better than a newborn baby.

Mal held tight to the seat, the car bucking over the cement hillocks in the pavement. "Go down there. I think it opens up to the front parking lot."

"Think? You think it opens up?" Min cracked the steering wheel with her fist, the leather covering buckling beneath the blow.

The stretch of buildings seemed endless; then the break was suddenly upon them. Barely taking the time to slow down, the woman tapped at the parking brake, using the car's sideways momentum to hook into the narrow space. Min yanked at the car's steering wheel, slamming the Mustang between the wall and the back of the motel, striking a load of wooden pallets left behind a liquor store.

The hood absorbed much of the impact, a plank gouging the flat surface and rolling up over the windshield, shattering a spiderweb fracture in the glass. The creased glass splintered, folding inward as the edges of the break began to crumble. Min debated telling Mal to kick the glass out with his foot, but one glance at Mal told her he had other things on his mind. The Horseman's stormy eyes tracked the darkness clotting the sky above them, concern for the two they'd left behind clear on his face.

Mal gripped the armrest, trying not to bite his lip. His worry had grown. The summoned bird was fully formed, an enormous airborne shape dropping from the sky, its long tail streaking up behind spread wings. *Death will be okay*, Mal told himself. Ari was there. No one could beat Ari at his own game.

Nearly hidden from view, a black tar pylon jutted up from the asphalt. The Mustang's axel struck it, jerking the car into the air. Min swore when the Mustang's subframe rocked wildly underneath them. Narrowly missing a chain-link fence, she swerved to avoid being struck by passing vehicles. Ignoring the shuddering coming from the undercarriage, Min gunned the car forward, sliding into the parking lot of the motel. She popped the driver's side door open, then moved quickly out of the Mustang, casting a quick glance at the winged shadow circling over the next block.

"Find the kid and let's go." Min pulled her mace out of the car, stepping clear of the door. A twitch of movement caught her eye, a curtain flicker from an apartment near the lot. Male, she gathered from the squared-off fingertips she could see, a strong profile hinted at behind the soiled curtains.

The thinned Veil struck her when Min crossed out of the parking lot's main slab, a cloying honey-like feeling over her face. It stuck to her, making it hard for her to move forward until she shed the Veil, pulling free of the shadows. Gagging at the taste of the darkness in her throat, Min shook off the sensation, the popping of her ears throwing her off balance.

Mal suffered through the shift more than she did, still new to manipulating the shadows. His body rippled with the sensation of prickly tendrils wrapping through his pores, and his lungs felt full of quicksand, a burbling mass of silica filtered through his nose and clogging his veins. The drawn thumping of his heart halted his steps, a pressure building up along his chest bone.

He'd fallen into the ocean once, discovering that the body he'd taken with him from the mortal world knew nothing about swimming. Water flooded into his throat, cutting off any airflow from his nose and mouth. Mal learned several things that day. He couldn't drown, but water still choked him into senselessness. The drowning paled next to having the Veil pulled tight around him. As his head swam with the threat of blacking out, Mal wondered if his lungs were being ripped clean from his body and if it could hurt much more than what he felt at that moment.

"Mal," Min said, slapping at his face. "Stay with me, brat. Step clear of it. That wraith is coming, and someone is stealing your boy."

Blinking, Mal followed Min's pointing finger, spotting a slinking young man leading Kismet out of his front door and back toward the rear of the building. Opening his mouth to shout at the man, Mal wasn't prepared for the burst of activity from the apartment across the tiny courtyard.

Mal knew craziness plagued mortals, a creeping disease of the mind that seemed to leak into their features, stretching the elasticity of normal out of their faces. But the broad man coming toward them had left his sanity somewhere in the darkened, cramped room Mal could see through the open door.

The man's uneven screaming sharpened when he hit the pavement running. Powerful legs carried the human closer, his hand clenched tightly around wicked-looking black steel. It was obvious he saw the Horsemen from his insanity, or the Veil had thinned so much that they were visible to the casual passerby. The foaming spit across his open mouth lent weight to the former.

"Gun." Min identified and dismissed the threat. Unless the madman came at them with a blade or even the butt of the weapon, neither Horsemen had to worry about him. Min quickly located their prey, along with the overly familiar face of one of the Vices creeping around the walkway, hoping to reach the back exit and escape into the alleyway.

"Fucking Lust." Min jerked her chin toward the young men, ignoring the raving man careening toward the Horsemen. "You grab the kid. I'll take care of the Vice. If we hurry, we can make it back to help Death and War."

It seemed like a simple plan, at least to Mal's ears. He'd taken three long strides toward the apartment building when his world suddenly exploded into a shifting slide of time and pain. The madman was so near and easily disregarded when he raised his hand no more than a few feet from Mal's chest. The pop of a gun report didn't slow his run. He'd been a Horseman long enough to know he was invulnerable to that threat.

Mal's body jerked and turned, his chest cracking open under the torment of a bullet ripping through his skin, burrowing into his muscled flesh. Mal knew what it was like to be knifed, a stray blade sliding into his rib cage during one of his forays into a war zone with Ari, but the pain in his chest was agony. His heart stuttered, his torso ripped apart by the small metal fragment, and blood bubbled up from his throat to fill his mouth. He fell, his knee striking the hard pavement where the wraith's carcass rotted, a cracked mass of bones bleached gray from being sucked clean from smaller shadows.

His immediate thought was that he had been shot, an amazing thing that should never happen to a Horseman. His second was that he would finally prove Ari wrong. Something could kill one of them. And he would be the first one to lay claim to that dubious honor.

Blood spurted over Min's face, blinding her until she blinked it away. The gunshot still echoed in her ears, her balance thrown off-kilter by the piercing ring bouncing inside of her head. For a brief moment she wondered who had been shot. Min had seen no other human around them besides the boy, and he appeared unhurt, drawn quicker toward the exit by a hurrying Lust. Then the shock of Mal toppling hit her.

The Veil had ripped apart, leaving Min open and vulnerable to the madman's weapon. She cried out for Mal as he fell, his throat working to pull in air, mouth contorted in anguish. With a hand clawing at the darkened hole in his chest, Mal's blood spurted from the wound, leaking out from between his clenched fingers.

"Sorry, Death." She clenched her teeth, lifting the mace up above her head as Frazier took aim again, the barrel of the gun pointed at Mal's temple. The human's hands shook, his mind unable to get a fix on the Horseman amid the shifting, closing curtain. "I'm going to kill this one."

Instincts took over, her fierceness wrenching a battle cry from her shocked throat. Shoulders bunched, she took aim at the human's head and swung, the mace's spikes cutting into the mortal's tender skin. Frazier barely seemed to feel the blow, turning around to aim his gun at the diminutive woman. Min raised her mace for another blow, squaring her shoulders to strike at the man's jaw.

Frazier's eyes rolled back. The sound of his skull cracking was louder than the gunshot echo burning through Min's eardrums. The give of the man's skull and its meaty burst of brains over Min's face gave her little comfort, a sluice of gray and pink ichor running down her neck and filling in the creases of her fingers when she raised her hand to block the splatter. Disgusted by the mess, Min stepped aside to avoid the dead man's falling weight, his sightless eyes turned upward to stare at the sky.

She stared at Kismet. The boy stood on the bloodstained sidewalk, mute and in shock, his nerveless fingers dropping the hefty chunk of concrete he'd used to bash Frazier's skull in. It broke into smaller pieces as it struck the asphalt, powdery white bits dusting over the spilled gore. Kismet's brown eyes were clouded from the drugs in his system. The young man whispered Mal's name as he fought to retain his balance, his desperate anger drilling down into Min's guts.

"Mal. God, the bastard shot Mal." Spitting on Frazier's prone body, Kismet lurched forward. He was about to head toward the fallen

Horseman when Lust grabbed his arm, drawing the human back. "Get off of me. He needs help."

"Screw that, baby." Lust yanked harder, dragging the reluctant Kismet back a foot, the boy's sneakers skidding along the sidewalk with a loud shriek of rubber on cement. "The Horsemen can take care of their own."

"Damned human," Min spat. "This should be you on the damned ground, not Mal."

Mal's soft groan jerked her around, a hiss of breath pushed out of his clenched teeth. Lust took advantage of her distraction and pulled Kismet back, wrapping his calling to cloud the human's mind. Pulled by his desires, Kismet followed the other man, his thoughts drawn shallow and instinctive.

Reaching the end of the sidewalk, he stopped, protesting with a mewl about leaving Mal behind.

"Come on, pretty," Lust urged. He was made to coax humans into doing what they felt they wanted deep inside of their souls. The young man could put up a resistance, but Lust knew he'd eventually win. "Come along. We need to get you safe."

"No." Kismet jerked back, his face fierce with passion. "I'm not leaving Mal behind. Not when he came for me."

Darkness pressed in on the immortals, tendrils of shadow knitting together, reforming the curtain that concealed them from the human world. Behind them, it shoved into Frazier's body and pushed at his soul, urging it back into the void. The man's soul tore from his corpse, a puppet of darkness and flat features. It hovered there, a soundless specter. Min glanced at the ghost, merely a minor annoyance compared to the stress of putting pressure on Mal's wound.

The spirit tried to reach Min with shapeless hands, passing through her. The ghost folded, unable to hold together under the weight of the Veil, then reformed, struggling to retain some form of existence and continue its work.

Casting what little power she had over the dead, Min snagged the soul with her mind, holding it away from Mal. Unsure of what to do, Min turned back to face her younger brother, crouching closer with fingers trembling in shock. She applied more pressure, wondering how much longer he would bleed and when his body would begin to heal over the wound.

"So much blood." Mal gaped, pulling his hands up to stare at the redness dripping from his fingers. "I didn't know we had so much blood. Not inside of us, I guess. And I've seen so much before. Why is this a surprise?"

"Don't talk." Min looked for the entrance wound, ripping apart Mal's shirt. The skin struggled to reform, working to free itself from the chunk of mortality shoved in alongside the bullet. "I think we need to get that thing out of you. Why isn't it pushing out? It's supposed to just come out."

"You shouldn't hover over me." Mal strained to look behind him. "Kismet. We need to go get him."

"Don't worry about Kismet." Min glanced back at Lust.

"I can't let him go." The wounded immortal hissed from the pain. His mind started to shut down, the blood loss making him swoon. "He's my friend. Okay, he's my only friend, but still, mine."

The Vice froze, his hand curled around Kismet's arm. Blood trickled down to Kismet's wrist, the puncture from his injection site leaking around bruised skin. The young man stood still, set firm and fierce. Stubbornness remained behind as Kismet's lust faded, his addiction leeched off by his anger.

Cocking his head, Kismet challenged Lust's hold, unsteadily rocking as his legs threatened to give way. "Let go. I'm going to him."

"Fine, screw this." Lust spat on the ground, the moisture nearly striking Mal's face. Shoving Kismet to the ground, Lust fled, heading back to the relative safety of the motel's walkway. "Keep the damned boy. I hope you all choke on him."

"You need to go find him." Mal bit down on his lower lip, fighting off another wave of pain. He wanted to throw up, his body cramping and a coldness working through his guts. Min dismissed his pleas with a shake of her head, wondering if she could lift his weight into the Mustang.

"He didn't go anywhere, Mal." Min worked her arm under Mal, pushing up with her legs to get under him. The sounds of Kismet vomiting turned her stomach, the foul stench of his purge a sickening wetness in Min's ears. "Your bitch is tossing his cookies on the lawn behind us."

The cooling body of the insane man lay next to them, mortal flies finding his corpse and burying long appendages into the flesh, laying eggs that would probably never hatch. Other wraiths had yet to gather, probably held off by the presence of the Horsemen. The sky above them was empty. Min was glad for it. Mal was more important at the moment.

"Worried about him." Mal's eyes rolled back, the pain nearly taking his consciousness. "I'm tired of being lonely, Famine."

The young man was slowly giving in to the shivers, his blood drinking in the final grains of heroin. Mouth trembling, Kismet batted away at the shadows clustering over his face. From the corner of his eye, Mal spotted a slender form huddling just inside of the Veil's thinning curtain, the ghost of a little boy wearing features similar to the young man he held firmly.

Frazier's soul twisted under Min's hold, pinioned in midair as she focused, straining for the strength she needed. Breathing a sigh of relief, Min reached for the hope she had in her heart and whispered into Mal's ear, "Stay still. I think I know what to do."

CHAPTER ELEVEN

SWEAT BEADED on Death's face, leaving a wash of dew on his pale skin. Ari slid his blades away, then reached up with a free hand, wiping at the moisture along Death's cheekbone.

"Don't." Death warned him off with an unsteady hand. "You break my concentration. I don't know how long I can hold the Veil together here. It's like trying to weave together broken threads."

"Well, at least that's a good reason to push me off." Exasperated, he hid his bitterness behind a tight smile. "I can accept that as an excuse."

"War." Death was too weary from holding the shadows around them. He brushed his shoulder against Ari's, the last of his strength seeping from his body. The struggle with the Veil was draining him quickly, but holding the darkness together would give them some cover until they found Mal's human.

"I know. I'm sorry." Ari ached to touch the other's face, his hands skimming the air just above Death's cheek and mouth, longing to trace the paleness of the scar on the other's nose.

Death paused, feeling a tendril of panic cross through the remnants of the curtain around them. A calling, strong despite the Veil's weakness. Ari's head came up, his eyes dark and searching to pinpoint the pulling on them.

"That's Min. It feels like her." Ari turned back to Death. "What the hell is she doing?"

"Someone's dying. Or trying to die," Death replied. "She's holding onto a soul. Damn, suppose it's the boy."

"Shit. Come on." Ari nodded toward the back alley. "The motel is over that way."

Running, Ari kept up with Death's long strides, the leaner Horseman's legs eating up the distance. Broader, Ari ducked to the side between the tight spaces Death easily passed through. On open ground,

Ari pulled away, circling around the corner to head to the front of the building.

"Damned hells." Ari skidded to a stop, shouting back at Death when they approached the motel's side entrance, a long stain of red paint fresh on the concrete divider. "Look at what just crawled out from under a rock, Death."

"Shit." Lust stared up at the blond Horseman, the taller man towering over him. "This is screwed."

"Lust. It is so good to see you here." Death's face stilled, wiped clean of emotion. The shadows clustered quickly, drawn by the elder Horseman's power. "War, go find Famine and Pestilence. I'll take care of this one."

Ari halfway turned as he ran down the alley, shooting Death a wink. The Vice backpedaled, sending himself spinning toward the wall. His hands scraped against the rough concrete, a shocked hiss lost amid his surprised stutter.

"I could say that I was going to deliver him to you." Lust went for bravado, hoping to bluff his way out of trouble. The Veil was clouded with Death's call, making it difficult for the Vice to find his own bearings on the world. "But we both know that would be a lie."

Death frightened him, plain and simple. Dark crow eyes piercing down into his soul and a mysterious, scarred pretty face that held more than a hint of menace. Slighter than War, Death held his own in the terror department, the end of eternity at the brush of his fingertips. The Veil hungered around the Horseman, visible to the Vice as he pushed at the curtain of shadows around himself.

"Is there any reason you're here, Lust?" Death asked. The boy was nearby. Death could smell something odd on Lust, an almost human presence, an overlying taint over the Vice's sweat.

Lust grinned at Death's surprise, astonishment clear on the Horseman's pretty face. Shocked, Death's suspicions were confirmed. The human Mal found was definitely immortal.

"Yeah, it shocked the shit out of me too. I thought he was one of us… well, one of you. He's definitely an immortal but not enough of one." Lust's chilled fear returned when Death brought his dark gaze back to the Vice. "There's nothing there. No calling to draw on. Nothing at all."

"Did you have something to do with this? With what happened to him?" Death gripped the Vice's arm.

"I found him like that. I had nothing to do with what he's become." Lust shook his head. "I swear to it."

A pair of women a few doors over began to kiss behind closed curtains, their arousal clear and clean in Lust's mind. Grinning, he took the chance of breaking free from Death's attention as Ari popped his head around the corner, shouting for Death. Distracted by Ari's urgent cry, Death felt the rush of Lust folding the Veil around himself, tapping into a call nearby, sliding free from the alleyway and out of Death's reach.

"Death!" Ari shouted again, his booming voice demanding attention. "Leave off and get over here. Mal's been shot!"

DEATH BENT down over Mal's gasping body, blood oozing from the Horseman's chest. Death explored the edges of the wound, carefully holding the Veil around the youngest of them. A sliver of reality, torn from the world, had embedded itself deep into Mal's heart, disrupting his body's natural flow. Min paced, a slender dervish around the other Horsemen, her eyes hot on the shivering crouched young man sitting at the edge of the walkway. Frazier's body lay unnoticed near a pile of trash. Ari hastily dragged the man's corpse off to the side, then hid it behind a dumpster.

"It was good thinking to hold the human's soul here," Death reassured Min, her face bunched with worry. "I could feel it."

"It was the only thing I could think of, and I couldn't hold it for very long. I screwed up. I told him he had nothing to worry about." Min's helplessness rose, her anger fighting to overcome her fears. The hardest of the Four, she struggled with her emotions, angry at herself for dismissing the threat of the gun and then for the helplessness that took her over as she held Mal's blood in her hands. "I let Mal down, Death. I'm sorry, but I let you down too."

"No, you didn't," the eldest replied. "You did what you could. It was more than enough."

Mal drifted in and out of consciousness, waking long enough to ask after Kismet. He floated back away when Death reassured the youngest Horseman that they'd found the young man safe. The eldest was much more worried about Mal than the shivering, angry young man Ari stood near. The blond Horseman shifted on his feet, his version of pacing off lengths, his back to the concrete block wall of the building and his eyes scanning the streets around them for trouble.

"We have to get out of here, Death. We have to hide the boy too. I think he's coming down from something." Ari checked on Kismet, watching him shiver as the drugs faded from the young man's veins. "There's blood all over the pavement, and it's a matter of time before the cops move down from the grocery store and spread out to find us."

"I'm not a chair. You guys seem to think I can't hear you," Kismet spat. The release of anger made his head throb. The unfamiliar man glanced his way, and Kismet wrapped his arms tight around his waist, trying not to shake his teeth loose. "Can we move Mal? Take him home? Well, where you guys live? Can you help him there?"

"He's been shot, you piece of shit." Lunging forward, Min balled her fist and aimed for the human's head. "He got hurt because of you. The stupid shit came looking for you, and this is what he got for it."

Ari nudged her away from Kismet's side, easily turning the petite woman away with a hard shove. "Back off of him, Min. This isn't his fault."

"No, he's not to blame," Death said softly. "Neither are you."

They'd had to pull Min off the young man when Death arrived. The shock of Mal's injury fueled her anger as she drove her fists into the young man's belly. Kismet tucked himself into a ball to escape the blows, unable to do anything more than protect his head from the woman's furious assault. Ari grabbed her mace, tugging it free from Min's clenched hands before she struck Kismet with it. She'd continued to go after the human with her bare hands, the other Horsemen unable to stop her in time. A bruise bloomed on his cheekbone, red welts left from her knuckles.

As the heroin left him, a lethargy wormed through Kismet. Sweat dewed over his chilled skin, soaking into his thin shirt. Kismet's mind boiled behind dazed eyes. Even breathing was a tortured exercise in movement. Small things were returning to him, his tongue able to moisten his lips, and the aching pain of torn skin on his hands made him want to weep, but no tears fell from his nearly unblinking lids.

The smell of the young man's body was vaguely familiar to Ari, and he tried to place where he'd first smelled the odor of burned flesh mingled with salt and metals. He could see the boy slowly numbing before his eyes, his body stilling in an attempt to hold on to every grain of drug he'd injected.

"I think we're going to have to find Auntie Kay." Death chewed at his lip. "I think that bullet pushed a piece of something from the outside world into him. It's too much for his body to work out."

"Damn it." Ari stared down at their youngest. "Just like that Wisdom."

"Hopefully, not like that Wisdom," Death corrected. "She died, remember?"

"Mal can die?" Kismet stuttered, a chill curling his insides. The shakes were impossible to control, and he struggled to make himself understood. "I thought you guys can't die. What the hell?"

Death lifted Mal's shoulders, easing the immortal up, concerned over their youngest family member. The wound worried him. While the bleeding stopped, his skin knitted over the bullet, sealing a slice of reality inside of his body. It would continue to work through Mal's tissues, possibly driving him insane or, worse, making him want to leave them behind.

"You sure about Auntie Kay?" Ari sighed, rubbing at his face for a brief moment, his keen gaze falling back on the young artist shivering at his feet. "She's not always helpful. We might get to where she is, and she slams the door in our face."

"I don't think we have a choice," Death said, stretching out a kink in his shoulder. Cradling Mal in his lap, the eldest Horseman felt the younger man's heartbeat falter and then strengthen. "She likes Mal. She'll help him."

"Do you know where she is?" Ari asked.

"She's in San Francisco, last time I checked." Death tested the curtain's strength around them, the breaks subsiding as the drugs left the boy's blood. "I'm guessing she's still there. Kay's not one to give up some place she feels comfortable in unless she's pushed out."

"I'm going with you." Min turned on her heel, rubbing at her arms. Cold seemed to dig into her bones, the sight of Mal lying against

Death's leg chilling her deep. "I got him into this mess. I have to see this through."

"You're too tired to take more than one. Just take Mal with you," Ari said.

Death gazed up at his friend's face, seeing worry etched along the Horseman's strong features. Min's hackles rose, challenging Ari with a tilt of her chin.

"Think for once, Min. Death's done too much this afternoon…."

"You're going," she countered.

"I'm old enough that I don't need a calling to get there. I just can't carry your sorry ass with me." Ari pushed in close to her, staring her down. "You can watch the boy."

"Fuck the boy," Min snarled.

"I don't want this to become crossing the river in too small of a boat," Death responded. "A bag of grain, a goose, and a fox. I can't leave Min alone with Kismet. We can't leave him alone. And I know you too well, Ari. You wouldn't want to leave me there if I'm too weak, and someone has to talk to Auntie Kay. She won't have anything to do with me.

"I'll take Min with me." Death adjusted his hold on Mal, trying to lift as much of the younger man off the ground as possible. "And we have to take the boy. You know that."

"There are times when I hate you as much as I want you." Ari gritted his teeth, leaning his head back in frustration. "Yeah, we can't leave the boy. Lust can't be the only one hunting him down. Whoever called up that bird will be hot on his trail."

"We can knock him on the head, tie him up, and leave him in the penthouse. He's probably stolen everything he could already," Min offered. She threw her hands up in surrender at the glares both men gave her. "It was a suggestion."

"A bad one, Min. Last thing I want on top of his injuries and withdrawal is a concussion." Death nodded toward the young man sitting down. "Bring Kismet over to me, Ari. It'll help if he's nearby when I do this. I won't have to stretch as far outward to include both of them."

"I'll wait for you there. If you're too tired, we're staying in the city." Ari gave one final sorrowful look at his ruined Mustang. "Bye, baby. It was good having you."

"You can kiss the car farewell later, Ari. I'll see you in San Francisco, then," Death admonished Ari, urging the blond to help him get Mal up off the ground. "Min, hold on to Kismet, and don't choke him. I'm going to have to have you very near."

"Don't get lost." Ari touched Death's shoulder with a brush of his fingers. "Please."

"I won't," Death said, seeing the concern in his oldest friend's face. "I'll see you there, Ari. I promise."

SAN FRANCISCO was a city used to death. The streets held more than their share of tears and pain beneath the gaily wrapped package of buildings and trolley cars. Buried under tons of dirt and asphalt lay the ruins of lives, specters continuing their endless, eternal searching for family lost in rubble or fires, sometimes floating to the hilltops and screaming their agony into the fog. Faces swirled in the mists, the Veil over the city nearly as clotted with memories as it was with shadows. It was an easy city for Death to find and one of the hardest for him to walk through.

Chinatown was the simplest place for Death to find in the city. Small nooks and crannies made it easy for him to slide through the ether and locate a presence about to leave the mortal world. It was harder to shake off the area's ghosts, each weighted with the belief that Death held the answer to end their misery. Death avoided those specters if he could. If he didn't, then he would waste too much of Mal's time speaking to the unwilling dead.

Death's hold on the Veil broke nearly as soon as he located the calling he needed. Carrying others through the curtain was something he rarely did, the drain on his strength too great for it to be a common occurrence. He'd only tried to carry, at the most, himself and the other Horsemen, only discovering he was able to take other immortals when an injured Peace stumbled into a battle between darkfae forces. Now Death regretted ever learning he could take others with him through the

Veil, especially since his innards began quarreling as soon as San Diego disappeared around them.

Clouds greeted them in the folds of the Veil, a simple step into the shadows that split open to envelop them. Maneuvering within the ether took little skill, but finding a mortal location in the chaos was often problematic, especially when ghosts screamed and cried for him as he passed.

Carrying extra sentient weight with him made moving difficult, something Death anticipated, but it wasn't until he fully fell into the Veil that he realized that carrying a catatonic Kismet and an unconscious Mal would render him nearly immobile. Min's assistance in moving forward nearly unseated them from his calling, her own purpose dragging them in a different direction, aiming for parts of the world that she seemed to rule with an iron fist.

Pushing his stronger will against hers, Death careened them back on track, all the while hoping they would reach the bridged city without any further harm to Mal's damaged body. Kismet was nearly dead weight, neither a hindrance nor a help, drawn by nothing and empty of any calling.

Amid the darkness, a bright, familiar soul flared along the trail. Ari's call to Death held frustration, worry, and usually affection in Death's weary mind. Holding tight to the spot of Ari shining through the Veil's darkness, Death focused and pulled the others along, leaving a large wake in the rippling shadows.

Death almost dropped Mal when they hit the street, Ari rescuing the youngest Horseman before they tumbled to the hard ground. Death fell to one knee, his stomach emptying into the gutter filled with cast-off takeout containers and rotted vegetables. Bile clung to the back of his teeth, a bitter yellow taste burning the roof of his mouth.

The city was cast in night and streetlights, a half-hidden moon winking out from behind clouds. It had been just at the crest of sunset when they'd left San Diego, the sun riding the horizon in preparation for a long night. For the darkness to have fallen, hours would have had to pass, Death reasoned through the nausea, the fight through the Veil draining the last of his reserves.

They'd lost too much time in the fold, Death realized when he felt Ari's hands on his back, the other Horseman easing him onto his haunches, cupping his chin, and running fingers over the circles under Death's eyes. Death glanced up at the sky, then at the other Horsemen, troubled by what he saw around him.

The moon shouldn't have been up, and Min's blue-lipped shivers were no comfort. Mal's body moved softly with his breathing, a comforting sight for Death. Kismet stumbled as well, his lanky body rolling and striking an outcropping on the nearby building. The young man's fall had been an ungraceful tangle of arms and legs, barking his elbows and knees on the stone surround of the alley. Kismet's instinctual mewl of pain as he moved his leg was sharp, eyes focused and aware, a far cry from the walking slumber he'd been in prior to their fold in the Veil.

"Gods, Shi." Ari hitched the slender man up, wrapping strong arms around the elder Horseman's shoulders. Ignoring Mal and shivering Min, Ari breathed hard into Death's ebony hair, Ari holding the other tight against him. "What the fuck happened in there? You took so long. I nearly thought I'd lost you."

"I'm okay. Are they okay? I just need to know that the others made it through." Death patted at Ari's bulging arm, barely able to breathe under the stronger man's crushing grip. "It was just harder to move than I would have liked. I could feel you against the Veil. You're what I pulled on to get us here. Next time we do this—"

"There's not going to be a next time." Ari held Death's face in the cup of his palm, lightly tasting the other's mouth with his own, refusing to let him go. Death savored the sweet heat he found there, regretfully pulling away before he fell into it. Ari didn't fight the retreat, knowing Death was too raw from the day's trials to have another row about their dancing around one another.

"I've been sick." Death turned his head when Ari released him. "That can't be a good taste. Where are the others?"

"Min's helping the kid and his pet. They look fine," Ari said, his voice rough with emotion. "And you taste just fine to me."

"How long were we gone?" Death gladly accepted Ari's assistance in getting to his feet. Aches echoed in his body, shoulders knitted tight from the tension of riding through the Veil. "Are you all right?"

"It's nearly midnight. See? The bird bites are all healed," Ari said with relief. Death was back to plotting their path, his focused mind honed in on what they'd come for. "The woman's just a bit away. You nearly landed on her doorstep."

"Good." Death shuddered at the thought of having to hunt for the Seer in San Francisco's neighborhoods. Warrens of buildings barely leaning against one another hid doorways that the woman might hide behind. He'd wasted too much time as it was. The Veil might have sustained Mal, enveloping the reality inside of him.

Min had dropped Kismet as soon as they arrived, her thoughts only on the youngest of the Four. Min's teeth stopped chattering, her cheeks flushed red with the blood rushing back under her skin, relief washing over her tight face.

Now awake, Mal nodded reassuringly when she lifted his head to check on him. He swallowed hard, trying to get air into his tortured lungs. His vision blurred from the pain, but he searched for Kismet, trying to peer around Min.

Kismet stood, although his body seemed ill equipped to do so. He gave his bruised hands a quick inspection, confirming other fears. Bits of gravel and dirt filled the raw scrapes on his palms, watery blood oozing from a deep gash along the inside of his arm. His legs hadn't fared any better, his beat-up jeans torn anew around his knees, the edges matted with dried blood. His skin tore beneath the denim as he moved, and Kismet hissed at the slight burn.

A bit of conversation jerked Kismet around, his knee giving out under him. Catching his already damaged hand on a nearby wall, he grunted with the pain, trying to determine where he was. The air around him felt heavier than San Diego's, a ripeness to it that he couldn't place. It held the promise of a hard rain, none of the parched brown scent of the high desert. Tight buildings around the dead-end side street echoed, a foreign bounce of fluid tones and round vowels, very different from the Latino dialects he'd grown up with. Kismet shook off the last bit of fog hanging on his brain, his thoughts fuzzy and distant.

The other end of the alley was closed off by a meshed puzzle of structures, wooden lean-tos cobbled together in a dizzying architectural array. The woman glared at him from her vigil over Mal, her face hard with distaste. He recognized the blond, barely. The man talking to the Asian man stared at him from a short distance away, their conversation too low for Kismet to hear.

"Have you spoken to Auntie Kay yet?" Death asked, his watchful gaze following Kismet's slow, painful movements. So far the boy didn't look like he was going to bolt, but the human had run before. Neither he nor Ari had the time to chase Kismet up and down Stockton Street.

"I told her Mal was hurt. She's willing to heal him if she can." Ari jerked his head toward a ramble of walls, planks of wood set at odd angles and decorated with gold-painted wood medallions. "She's older than I remembered. I don't think she's going to be alive much longer. I didn't realize it had been that long since we'd seen her last."

The back-alley shop Ari pointed at was bright, despite the darkness. Tattered red tassels hung from green plastic beads, carved to simulate precious jade figurines, mold seams bled white from San Francisco's harsh weather. Faded navy fabric hung halfway down beside the main doorway's frame, split into four panels and loosely hemmed. Drops of white paint dribbled through Chinese calligraphy, marring the already indistinct pale yellow characters. A curtain of bamboo beads rattled, a wrinkled liver-spotted hand sliding them aside.

A stooped-over Chinese woman hobbled out from the dark interior of the ramshackle cramped storefront, folds of loose skin flapping under her pointed chin. Splotches of bright pink scalp shone from under her thinning white hair, tufts standing straight up from her fingers pulling nervously at the sparse strands. Peering out from under a drooping brow, she narrowed her already thinned eyes nearly shut, spotting the tall, slender Horseman standing midway down the alley.

"Death is not welcome here," the woman shrieked at the Four, her high-pitched voice carrying over onto the main street.

Pointing a bony finger shakily at the eldest of the Horseman, her lips cracked in the cold of the shadow-drenched alley. A black dribble of long-steeped hallucinogenic herbal tea slipped from the corner of her mouth, her tongue darting out quickly to lap up the trickle. The drugs in the costly leaves kept the shadows from her mind, her consciousness bolstered by the chemical walls she'd erected around it. The tea stained the furrows of her flesh, the chapped patches of her lips nearly ebon from years of sipping at the brew.

Hobbling a few steps forward, Kay glared up at Death, her chin trembling at the sight of the dreaded Horseman. "You are not welcome in my home or my shop. I will not have Death walking near me. Not now. Not ever."

"We are here for Pestilence's sake," Death replied smoothly, falling into a formal Wu, his words rounded with an archaic tone. "I will not cross your threshold."

"I want to bargain for healing him," she responded, her eyes shifting to the youngest Horseman.

Mal stood with Min's assistance, his legs shaky beneath him.

"I want more time here, a longer life."

"I can't give you that, Auntie," Death said. Shades often bargained with him, hoping he could somehow return them to their expired flesh shells and they could continue their living. It had been a long time since a living human attempted to deal with their truncated mortality. "I can't do anything to fix your soul into a dying body."

"There has to be a way." The ancient woman stared around Death's slender form at the young artist Min kept herded in front of them. "Who is he, then? You've given him more life. He's one of you. There should only be four, but there's five. I can see that. Death is not known for his lies."

"I don't know what happened to make him how he is," Death said, his hands spread wide, palms raised. "Who he is isn't as important as Pestilence's life. War asked you to help, and you agreed. Can it be said that Shen On-Sang doesn't keep her word when given?"

"No! You do not speak my name!" Her hiss rattled the cough lodged in her chest. "Never my true name. Not from your lips. I always keep my word when given. And I've given it."

Muscles contracting with stress, the old woman fell into a fit, trying to dislodge the irritation in her lungs. Sienna-flecked spittle hit the cement surround of her door stoop, the wraithlings clinging to the porch finials craning to reach the moisture while avoiding Death's advance. The eldest Horseman nearly touched the woman before she jerked clear of his outstretched hand, her crinkled eyes wide with terror.

"No! You will not touch me before it is my time to go!" Her voice rose with her fear, a siren call that lured the shadows even closer. Hands shaking, the woman pressed at her chest, trying to calm the rattle lodged deep in her lungs. "War, bring the boy in with you. I'll look at him away from Death's prying eyes."

"I can walk, Auntie," Mal grunted when Min's arm came up around his waist, the small Horseman carrying his weight on her shoulder. Her stubborn face was set firm, daring Mal to refuse her help.

Smiling at the gesture, Mal bent over and whispered into her ear, "Thanks, Min."

"I'll stay out here with the boy," Death whispered to Ari when the blond Horseman came up behind him, a wide palm on the small of Death's back. The elderly woman hobbled into her shop, turning her back on the Four. "He doesn't look like he's in any shape to run. I know I'm certainly in no shape to chase him."

"If he does run, just shout. I'll chase him down for you," Ari said. "Maybe even stab him to keep him in one place."

Ari's fingers curved over Death's jaw, the ball of Ari's thumb smoothing over the silvered line running down the other's nose and cheek. Leaning in, he dared a tiny sip of Death's mouth, laving at the corner where their lips met. The elder Horseman leaned into the affectionate touch, allowing himself the barest of comforts from Ari's kiss. Pulling away before he lost himself in Death's taste, Ari allowed himself a small smile, touching foreheads with the other as he turned.

"I'll definitely yell for you," Death agreed easily. "Go on. She will want to take care of Mal quickly and get us off of her doorstep. We're bad for her business. Even the most obtuse of humans will avoid this alley while we're here."

"We're always bad for anyone's business," Ari teased, stepping clear of the other Horseman. Glancing at the young man they'd fought to secure, Ari pointed at Kismet's chest, stabbing at the air with a firm menace. "Stay put, little boy. If I have to find you, I swear on Death's head that I will take a very long time tearing you apart."

Crossing through the open threshold, Ari wrinkled his nose at the acrid scents inside the woman's cramped shop. The old woman's apothecary had too much of the Veil lying in its clusters of muddied potions and sawed-off animal paws dangling from low ceiling beams. The plump black pads of a monkey's fingers brushed against Ari's cheek, the feel too close to a corpse's emaciated touch for the Horseman's liking.

"Don't start without me. I've waited a long time to carve Mal up like a goose," Ari called out, finding no one in the main room. A heavy powdery odor worked into his nostrils, and he fought not to sneeze, wondering if anyone would notice if he blew his nose and left a trail of snot on the counter. Min yelled for him, a thin sound filtering through the debris that cluttered near a doorframe at the back of the shop. Stepping over boxes, clearing a wider path with his feet, Ari entered the woman's living space behind the counter.

Mal lay back on a futon, its thick padding covered with a plastic tarp and towels. Bare to the waist, the young Horseman's chest bore evidence of the reality caught beneath his skin. Long streaks of purpled red angrily pulsed along the ridges of his rib cage, the edge of one pectoral muscle blackened from poisoned blood running through his veins. A cicatrix scarred over the bullet hole, the rounded smooth scar nearly watery in appearance.

Kay pressed at the edges of the wound, watching the skin slowly bounce back. Clucking at the Horseman, she leaned over to grab at her teacup, sloshing the pitch-oil brew over her fingers. Gulping the cup nearly dry, the woman swallowed hard, focusing on the Veiled gathered in her presence. Ari crossed over to the woman's side, taking the cup from her shaking hands.

"Don't drink too much of that, Auntie," Ari warned her. "We need you at least able to see for this."

"I'm fine," she snapped back, her blackened teeth peeking up from her moistened lips. "I have to be able to see him clearly. The tea helps with that. Keeps all of the other things away. And don't you tell me how to do this, pox on humanity that you are. I've been doing this sort of thing since…."

"If you were going to say since before I was born"—Ari cocked one eyebrow, a smug smile over his wide mouth—"then I'd have to argue that point. Just do what you have to do, old woman, and we'll leave you be."

"I get to keep anything I take out of him, right?"

Auntie Kay's cunning eyes roamed over the injured Horseman's body, Mal's startled look toward Ari getting him nothing more than a reassuring grimace from Ari.

"Blood and the bullet," Min replied. "And whatever reality you can find inside of him."

"That will dissipate as soon as it finds a path outside of his body." Auntie Kay spat in disgust, a wet splotch on the dirty floor. "It's only solid inside of him. Won't do me any good unless I carve it out with chunks of his meat and blood around it."

"How about if we just stick to the blood and bullet?" Ari said. "I'm not going to let you go around digging for spare kidneys. The kid needs them to pee."

"The kid happens to like peeing," Mal remarked, still slightly unnerved at the woman's eagerness to cut him open. A wave of pain rocketed through his lungs, leaving him gasping for air. Min's hands clenched down on his bare shoulders, her fingers biting into his tanned skin. "Min, you're hurting me as much as the bullet is. Let go a bit."

"Did you take a long time killing the son of a bitch that shot Mal?" Ari asked Min.

"I didn't do it." She shook her head, chewing on her lower lip. To her eyes, it looked as if Mal was bleeding out, his life soaking through his clothes. "The boy did it. With a piece of cement or something."

"No shit? The kid?" Ari whistled under his breath. "Well damn, sounds like the kid's got some balls. So if Mal dies, we can just use him as our new Pestilence."

"Go to hell, Ari." Mal winced as the pain traveled through his abdomen.

"We should get started." The old woman cleared her throat, swallowing a mouthful of drug-laden spit.

Ari made a face at the selection of knives and probing instruments Kay arranged on a low table near the futon, the edges shimmering dully in the scant glow tossed off by the exposed light bulbs dangling from the ceiling. "I have a small whetstone on me. I can sharpen those for you, Auntie."

"Pain is good for him. It will cleanse the wound better." Kay shrank beneath Ari's piercing stare. "Fine, if his cut festers because the pain didn't wash it clean, then it will be on your head."

"Thanks, Ari," Mal muttered, riding out another gut-wrenching wave of pain. "It'll be ironic if I die of infection, right?"

"No, still pathetic," Min snorted, brushing the hair from the younger man's forehead.

The elder Horseman made short work of the dull-edged scalpels, the gritty stone wet with his spit to lubricate the sharpening. As the old woman finished her preparations, Ari set the knives back down on the cloth, then wiped the blades clean on Min's shirt.

"There. Now all you need is for Death to kiss the boo-boo when this crazy old woman is done with you, and all of us will have helped you get out of the mess you got yourself into." Ari crouched down next to Mal's head, the youngest Horseman's face paling beneath the growing anguish working into his limbs. Reaching over, Ari grabbed Mal's hand, crushing the younger Horseman's fingers with his own. "Feel me here, Cooties. Death would be here too if she would let him."

"He has to take care of Kismet." Mal gritted his teeth, trying to shove aside the prickling needles creeping into his brain. Sweat darkened the hair at his temples, his glasses steaming from the heat of his skin. Panting between tight lips, Mal let a small, painful breath escape, hoping he could keep his wits about him.

"Yeah, when this is all over, you're going to be responsible for that little ferret. If you think I'm going to take care of his feeding and walking him when he needs to go, you're as nuts as the old woman here." Ari grinned at the short laugh he pulled from Mal's grimace. "There, see? All better. We don't even need this crazy woman to cut into you."

"The crazy woman is ready." Kay shuffled over and patted Mal's bare chest. Switching back to her native tongue, she continued, "Can you understand me?"

"I don't speak Chinese well," Mal replied in the same language, his eyes glazing over. "Oh, wait… shit. Where is my head at? I guess… yes."

"Ah, he's so young and stupid. Why don't any of you come over with some sort of sense of what you can do?" The elderly woman removed Mal's glasses, then dropped the spectacles to Min's waiting hands. "What have you been doing with this one? Letting him roam free like a water buffalo?"

"We've been a bit busy over these past couple of decades." Ari shrugged off the woman's criticisms. "And water buffaloes have more sense."

"Hold him, please." Auntie Kay picked up her first knife, the thin blade wicked and gleaming. "I don't have anything that I can give you to sleep."

"Oh, I can bet that won't last long." Mal's breath shortened, his hands clenched tight around each of the other Horseman's fingers. "I'm pretty certain I faint at the sight of my own blood."

Ari's free hand cradled the side of the younger man's head, Mal's damp pale hair wrapped around Ari's long fingers. The warmth and strength of the older Horseman was a comforting reassurance of the bond the Four shared. Leaning over, Ari pressed a gentle kiss on Mal's forehead, wishing Death was here to help them hold their youngest together.

"Don't worry, brat," Ari whispered. "We're all here for you."

Chapter Twelve

Red and blue lights flashed across Beckett's face as he stepped out of the backseat of his town car, his driver closing the door behind his employer. Nodding for the man to wait by the vehicle, the magus approached the motel, noting the barriers of Do Not Pass tape around the covered form of a dead man. The black bag was left partially unzipped, and a pale strong hand flopped outside of the gap.

Pushing his way through a crowd of onlookers, Beckett strode to the crime scene.

He'd purposely chosen an expensively cut suit when he dressed for the excursion, wearing his wealth in fine fabrics and the black town car he had his driver take him in. When the police rang him to tell him of the man's death, the magus sighed heavily, more disgusted at the failure to secure one addict than losing Frazier's services. Once again, the motel was a flashpoint for disappointment.

A uniformed police officer pointed Beckett toward the detective in charge, a slightly built, potbellied man bent over a splash of blood on the building's wall. The detective scribbled a few notes in the brown notebook he held tightly, flipping the pages back and forth as he referred to something he'd written previously. Another barrier of tape roped off one of the apartments, another swarm of serious-faced people standing in the open doorway, their mumbles lost in the noise of the evening.

"Detective Brown?" He schooled his face into a look of careful concern.

Beckett suppressed a smile at the ease the detective accepted the man's offered hand, a brusque shake and then noises of condolences for the loss of a valuable employee. In Beckett's mind, there would be no connection with the ruinous fallout of Frazier's killing. When the detective first called him, he'd panicked that Frazier had killed the boy instead and the now dead man was looking for bail.

"Were there any another victims?" He worked on forcing more disquiet into his low tones, rolling the waves of distress under his words. "I would hate to think that someone else lost their life in this."

"The manager of the motel." Detective Brown scratched at the itch creeping across his cheek, his skin rippling with an irritation. "Was there any reason for Mr. Frazier to be down here? Did he make any mention of meeting someone down here?"

"No, none at all," Beckett replied. It was hard not to stare past the man's shoulder to the spot where Faith stood. She moved cautiously through the crowd, trying to avoid contact where she could. "I can't imagine what Frazier was doing down here. It's very far from where he lives, and I certainly didn't send him out here on any of my business."

Smiling flirtatiously at her lover, Faith winked before sliding out from behind the detective, pushing the darkness around her into a trace of lacy black shadows. The minute grains of the drug mixture in Beckett's system filtered her into a misty echoed image. He had trouble focusing on where she truly was, a halo of her face appearing and disappearing as she moved about.

"What capacity did you employ Mr. Frazier in?" The detective returned to his notes. "Did he normally carry a weapon on him?"

"Yes." Beckett brushed at a speck on his trousers, touching the fractured shapes of his lover's fingers where her hand rested on his hip. "He… is… was my bodyguard and a friend. Really, Frazier and my secretary keep me on a tight leash. I'm very rarely late for anything."

"We need to find out more," the immortal whispered in Beckett's ear. "I'll push to influence him. You'll just need to ask the right questions. Go slowly. Make it appear as if you are interested, and he'll be more than willing to be helpful."

It was so incredibly easy. The whisper of power Faith wove over the human helped pull information from the detective. In a few minutes, the magus learned the manager had been shot, possibly by Frazier's weapon, and that there was a bullet left unaccounted for, possibly taken with the body of another victim whose blood was splattered over the parking lot's asphalt and cement sidewalk.

Thanking the detective, Beckett agreed to wait on the side of the scene, insisting that the police officer inform him of anything else he might find in the next half hour or so. Flipping open his cell phone would hide his conversation with the Veiled hovering next to him, Beckett covertly sneaking looks at her face as it floated in and out of his sight.

"So we've lost the boy again." Anger filled him, nearly burning away any reason he might have left. Every step forward he made in securing the addict seemed thwarted, and the bird he'd created was gone. "We can't risk having anything else happen here at this godforsaken dump. The last thing I need is for them to find the boy stoned out of his mind and haul him off to jail."

"I don't think that will happen." She stared out at the parking lot at one of the police officers who'd glanced in Beckett's direction. The man rubbed at his eyes, his attention returning to where she stood and not on the man standing near her. "We need to move away from here. The Veil is still too thin. It's shifting around me, and people might begin to notice."

He hurried toward the car, allowing the woman to slide in first. Ordering his driver to wait for the police detective to return with any information, Beckett closed the door behind himself, the tinted windows keeping out prying eyes. She pushed out from the shadows and leaned into Beckett's kiss, her mouth passionate against his forcefulness.

"I hate having stolen moments with you. Not being able to touch you is making me die inside," Beckett whispered against her neck, feeling her skin slip away under his touch. "I can't wait until we find that boy and see if the drug worked like it was supposed to. I can't take much more of this."

"I hate this too." The woman pouted, her brow creased with worry at his distress. "But concentrate on what we have to do. The blood out there smells immortal. I wonder if the Veil was so far gone that Frazier actually shot an immortal. Or do you think he shot the boy before he fully crossed over?"

"I hope not." Beckett sat back against the leather seats, chewing on the edge of his fingernail. "The cops are going to take blood samples from the area. If they run it for any narcotics, they'll find the heroin if it was the boy that was shot."

"He'd have to find medical assistance, yes?" She leaned forward, rubbing at Beckett's leg with a brush of her fingers. "Perhaps that's something that you can trace down? If he has to go to a hospital or clinic, won't they have to report the bullet wound to the police? Isn't that how this works?"

"Yes," Beckett agreed, his mind scattered with the possibilities. "That's definitely something that I can follow up on."

The addict was the answer to their prayers, human turned immortal. He'd spent countless hours trying to perfect the rituals over ground herbs and scorched bones. It had been an accidental trapping of a brownie crossing over one of his tapped ley lines that led to Beckett's greatest discovery, the existence of immortals and other creatures that drew their power from the shadows embedded in the between space of his world. He owed everything to that chance discovery. It led him to his Faith, and now a means to spend a life with her.

"Let me finish up here." Beckett spotted his driver heading back across the parking lot, pushing past the crowd to the car.

"You go on." She pressed a chaste kiss on his cheek, worming her will into his soul. "I'll just complicate matters. Besides, I don't know how long I can stay on your side of the Veil. It's too erratic."

"Okay." Beckett's upraised hand passed through her face, and he watched as she ghosted away from him. Resting his forehead on his fist, the magus composed himself before the driver knocked on the car window. "Faith. I promise we'll be together. Even if I have to cut the boy open myself and see if it worked. I will get to you."

FAITH STOOD on the sidewalk, watching as the car slipped away from the curb. Her heart ached, missing Beckett's gentle touch. When hands closed on her waist, she jumped, nearly swallowing her tongue.

"How are you, sis?" Charity kissed Faith on the cheek, resting his chin on her shoulder.

They'd spent nearly a century together, their lives increasingly hampered by their callings and the general state of humanity. Over time, Faith grew sour about her role, slowly convincing Charity that things could be different. When she fell in love with Beckett, they'd both taken it as a sign that their dreams weren't outside of their reach.

"I'm fine." Faith sighed, leaning into her brother's arms. "I hate humans. Well, not Michael, but I just want to be free of them and live my own life."

"Careful, love. The more you think about not wanting to be Faith, the greater risk you have of leaving." Charity pressed a finger to her lips. "The very last thing we want is to lose you. Michael and I both need you to be Faith for just a little while longer."

"I know." Turning to slide her shoulders against Charity's chest, Faith wrapped her brother's arms around her, cradling his forearms and rocking slightly. The police lights played over the motel's outer walls, turning their faces red and then blue.

"We're going to miss having Frazier around. Beckett needs to have a puppet," Charity said.

"Michael doesn't need a puppet," Faith replied with a frown.

"Puppets are good for doing things for you," Charity reminded her, rubbing his thumb on her pout. "And if you're going to make faces at me, I won't tell you what I found out."

"The police know where the boy is, and we can go get him ourselves as a present for Michael?" Faith mimicked Charity's grimace back at him. "I knew it couldn't be that easy."

"No, although that would be sweet. It's even better," the Third of their grouping reassured her, holding Faith tighter. "The blood on the ground isn't our boy's but one of the Horsemen. And, I think, the result of our clumsy human's bodyguard and his gun."

"Are you sure?" She pulled away, shock registering on her face. "How?"

"I think the boy's alteration rippled the Veil so much that when the gun went off, it actually struck one of the Four," Charity said. "I could smell the remains of Hope's calling and followed it down, a prayer that someone wouldn't die.

"I'm guessing it was the boy who was calling Hope. Even immortal, he's still got a soul. I think he still counts as human," Charity continued, holding up his hand for Faith to see the specks of blood caught under his fingernails. "I was surprised to taste one of us on my fingertips. I'm guessing it was one of the younger Four. I think Death and War would have burned my tongue black with their age."

When Charity had lifted his fingers to his lips, he'd been rocked back with the power held in that dab of blood on his tongue, far greater than any other immortal he'd encountered. He'd tasted Faith's blood before, a small puncture wound made by a crazy woman's fingernails on his sister's face. Nothing prepared him for the taste of a Horseman. Nothing ever could.

"But that's impossible." Faith's hushed whisper held her heart, wondering at the implications of what they'd done. "Do you think the Veil will thicken and go back to how it used to be? We can't risk wraiths finding a doorway into this world."

"I don't know." Charity shook his head. "We knew this was going to change things. What we're doing is going to shake the Veiled world. Once we use this drug to step away, there will be no going back to what we were. We'll be fully human again with free will and still immortal, if Michael does his job right. That's what we planned on. You have to keep that in front of your mind."

"I know." She breathed in deep, trying to calm her fears. "I am scared that we'll come so very close and it will all disappear from our grasp."

"What crossed the boy over will free us," he reminded her. "It's nearly been done before. We'll be the first to succeed. You know once we shake off the calling, nothing can touch us, not even Death."

"We need to find the boy quickly, then," Faith asserted. "If the Horsemen are so close to him, they might already have him, and we don't know what they'll do to him. They probably were the ones who killed Frazier. War wouldn't blink at killing the boy if he thought it would mean that it kept the world intact. Not even Death could argue against that."

"Death would hesitate to kill the boy in cold blood. Besides, he might be immortal by now. Without a calling but still one of us," Charity replied. "We did learn something from this."

"What?"

"With the Veil that thin, one of us can probably be killed. We can use that to our advantage."

"If the boy slid fully behind the Veil, it won't thin near him anymore." Faith shook her head, feeling a call run down the shadows to her. She tested its strength, seeing if it needed her immediate attention or if it was something she could ignore. With every day, Faith found herself responding less and less to smaller devotions, only attending to things she felt would be noticed if she didn't appear. As their goal neared fruition, her slavery to humans chafed at her.

"You're forgetting the one place where we exist fully outside of the Veil." Charity tapped her on the nose. "We are exposed where we live, sis. And if the Horsemen have the boy, they probably have taken him to where they now reside. It would be simple to go to where they live and take him from them. A very easy and distracting thing. Something they wouldn't expect."

"There is no way either of us can fight off Death or War," Faith argued.

"We won't have to. I'm guessing that if a gun works on us when the Veil is very thin, then it would also work where we live."

"I'm not risking Michael." She watched the darkness churn, her mind working at their problems. The shadows were clustering again, small tidbits of wraiths creeping out of the Veil's torn edges, lapping at the spilled Horseman blood on the pavement. "I'm not risking you either."

"You can't make these decisions for us, sis," Charity said. "I know Michael would agree with me. Give me some time, and I'm sure we can bring death to the Horsemen's doorstep."

KISMET SHIVERED in the cold wind whipping down the alley, his thin T-shirt and torn jeans more suitable for the high-desert climate of San Diego's hills than the rolling fog of San Francisco. He tried to imagine how they'd gotten to the Bay Area, but his brain began hurting when he probed too hard at the memory of traveling. Instead, he sat huddled in the curve of a nearby building, hoping to minimize the cutting breeze before it chilled him down to the bone.

The man everyone else called Death sat on a curb nearby, his long legs stretched out into the street, hands tucked into his jeans pockets. The young man shivered again when the wind picked up, the chatter of Kismet's teeth catching Death's attention.

"Come here." Death patted the space next to him. "Use my body to block the wind. You're sitting right in its path."

Rubbing at his arms, Kismet warily stood up, moving slowly over to where the other man sat, his gaze suspicious. The aching in his blood had yet to reach critical mass, his addiction still lulled into a slumber by his recent hit. Kismet figured he would have at least half a day before he would start craving more heroin, a long enough time to shake the Four. Settling down near Death, Kismet made sure he was at least an arm's length away, figuring he was no match for the other man's strength and speed.

"Better?" Death asked, his eyes returning to the door of the apothecary.

"Thanks." Kismet relaxed in the relative warmth of the spot. A heating unit for the restaurant at the front of the street pumped out warm air over them, washing the cold from Kismet's skin. He felt sensation coming back to the spot between his shoulder blades and the chill work free from the stainless-steel barbell piercing his left nipple. Goose bumps rippled over his pale skin, a taint of blue creeping out of his lips.

Working up his courage, the young man asked, "What are you guys going to do with me?"

"Truthfully, I don't know," Death responded, his eyes fixed on the shop's door. "How much do you know about what's going on around you?"

"Just what Mal told me from before," Kismet said. "I didn't believe him, and now it looks like he wasn't fucking with my mind. He was telling me the truth."

Death winced at the sound of the youngest Horseman's name on the boy's lips. The others took names to establish an identity outside of their callings. Those names were never shared outside of the Veil or even with other immortals. Yet Mal broke that rule easily, trusting his name to the complication now thrust into their lives.

"You don't know Mal. He's very honest." Ari's words came back to Death. It sounded to him like their youngest member had practically handed every immortal secret to the young man sitting next to him. "I'm surprised that his being hurt is bothering you."

"I'm worried about him." Kismet's voice was strained, emotional and thick. "He's a nice guy. I don't meet a lot of nice guys. I don't want him to die."

"He won't die from this," Death said. "He's strong enough to want to stay with us. Mal won't leave now. He's got too much to be curious about."

"Guess if Death tells me someone's not going to die, I should believe him." Kismet's mind stretched at the sheer breadth of what he was supposed to accept as truth. "Are we really in San Francisco? Or is my mind just all screwed up?"

"No, I think your mind is doing just fine." Death heard the young man snort under his breath. "Yes, we're in San Francisco. I carried you through the Veil. That woman can help Mal. She can take the bullet out of him."

"Well, then, it's the first time in my damned life that my mind is doing just fine," Kismet retorted.

"If you have any answers to what happened to you, I'd like to hear them," Death said.

"Shit, I don't even know what really happened," Kismet replied, leaning back on his palms.

Realizing they no longer hurt, Kismet sat back up, staring down at his hands. "This is crazy. If I heal like this, why isn't Mal?"

"More than likely, a piece of reality was torn by the bullet entering him and is lodged in the wound. It's happened before." Death touched his bicep. He wasn't going to mention the Wisdom that died, but she'd refused help. Hopefully they'd gotten Mal to the Seer in time. "I had that happen to me once with a spear. When the Veil is thin, reality and the shadows are mingled. We run the risk of getting a piece of the real world inside of us."

"So someone's got to take it out?" Kismet slanted a look at the man sitting next to him. "Why can't one of you?"

"Because none of us would be able to grab at the reality, no matter what instrument we used," Death explained. "The Four, and other immortals, are too connected to the Veil. Only someone who exists in the real world would be able to cut down into the wound and release it. Once she touches the space, she connects that slice of reality to the real world, like an electrical circuit."

"This is still insane." Kismet rubbed at his forehead, an aching tangle of thoughts clustered behind his eyes. "And I'm supposed to be one of you? Be like you?"

"How much did he tell you about us? About who we are?" The eldest Horseman turned to face the newly created immortal.

"That there's a world outside or inside of the real one. I'm not really sure about that part of it." Kismet wrapped his arms around his belly, wondering when the chill on his soul would subside. "I really thought he was fucking with me. Or the smack was just making everything make sense. It does that sometimes. Makes everything right, and then the world goes back to how it was before I shot up."

"Not so much outside as wrapped around. I'm guessing the drugs helped you manage how you saw the Veil. It happens that way for others like you," Death corrected, his words soft and without reproach. "We live behind what we call the Veil. Did he tell you why we live here?"

"He said you were called the Four Horsemen, even though one of you is a chick." The young man's stomach growled, empty and needy. From the looks of things, food was a far off idea better left unspoken. "I've got to admit, I was a bit stoned, and well, it sounded like he was crazy."

"Mal is probably the most sane one of the Four of us," Death admitted with a smile. "You don't know who the Four Horsemen are?"

"I've done it as a tattoo. But it was copied from a piece of art. And I know it's a song." Kismet tried to remember the lyrics. "Um, Time, Pestilence, Famine, and Death. Right?"

"Close, and Ari really hates that song," Death said. "War, not Time. Time doesn't exist as an immortal. It's a linear construct, not a manifestation. And by the look on your face, I think I've lost you."

"Public school kid." Kismet shrugged. "And that's when I bothered to go."

"It's a biblical reference, although we predate the written text. One of the insane slid us in near the end of the writings for some reason. We've been called by other names in different cultures, but the Four Horsemen reference comes the closest to what we do and are." Death saw the disbelief on the boy's face, Kismet's world bending under the weight of the Veil's reality. "There are four of us, Death, myself, War, the tall blond arrogant one, Pestilence, whom you know as Mal, and Min—well, Famine."

"The girl," Kismet interjected.

"Yes, the girl, but I wouldn't call her that to her face." Death nodded. "The Horsemen and others like us exist to provide humanity with the concepts of existence. I'm not sure why you came into being. None of us have ever crossed over the Veil and retained our identity. So I have to conclude that something unnatural happened to you."

"You're telling me walking around as Death is natural?" Kismet heaved a shuddering sigh.

"Well for me, it is. It's all I've ever been." The man leaned forward, hearing a cry coming from the shop. Mal's torment had begun, worry for their youngest eating away at Death's will. With a focused effort, he canted his head and faced the young man next to him, Kismet's face paling at the sound of pain from inside of the shop. "Who we are is all we've ever known."

A squat form scurried out from behind a dumpster. From a distance, the boy thought it was a dog, but the horns curled back from its sloped head and its wide curve of a mouth set into an oblong face quickly changed his mind. Pearly greenish-gray skin stretched over its rotund, misshapen body, slender arms hanging from the barest hints of shoulders. Strong haunches moved the creature forward, sometimes shuffling on all four legs, reaching up on powerful back limbs to crane into mounds of discards.

"What the fuck is that?" Kismet followed the creature's progress, its furtive shuffling circling it around the clusters of shadows clinging to the alley's brick walls. Dropping down to sniff at a grate, the creature glanced at Death, its eyes rolling back before it flattened to minimize itself as a perceived threat.

"That is a troll," Death said. From the broken end of one horn and the slack skin around the creature's neck, he put its age near the end of its life if the limp in its back leg got much worse. "It's one of the creatures that live behind the Veil. Very distantly related to the darkfae. Like a monkey is related to a human."

"What the hell is a darkfae?"

"They're sentient Veiled, usually living in clans that are attached to the UnSidhe Court. The Fae consider darkfae to be lesser beings, but they are intelligent but brutish even by Ari's standards," Death explained. "There are a lot of people, for lack of a better term, that live behind the

Veil. Most don't deal with humans, living in unpopulated areas, but there are a few Fae and darkfae that interact or even live outside of the Veil."

"So that's like a Veiled monkey." Kismet grunted at Death's nod. "What is he doing?"

The young man leaned forward. The movement froze the troll in its tracks, still exposed by the light from a nearby window but staying quite clear of the wall's relative shelter. When nothing feinted toward it, it snuffled back into the garbage, rooting out a bag from the bottom of the pile.

"It's probably looking for something to eat. And they're an it, really. They switch genders depending on what other sex is near them." The Horseman glanced at the rapt attention on the boy's face. "Trolls aren't very intelligent. More animal, really."

Looking at the troll, Death tried to imagine how the creature would look to someone who'd never seen one before, a curious cross of reptile and capybara. Its pink tongue darted out past its thin blue lips, its loose wattle jiggling as it shambled to the next garbage bag that caught its interest. One of its horns was broken off a hand span from its root, its uneven end probably a result of a territory battle or failed mating ritual. Dried blood crusted over a wound on one of its back legs, a black bubble of decaying flesh along its hind.

"It can't just eat those shadow things we've seen?"

"No, it's not like a wraith. Those are evolved from the Veil, born from very strong emotion, and usually can only eat other shadows. This is… flesh, like us."

"That damned dog thing ate at me just fine," Kismet pointed out.

"That's because it was big enough to eat flesh. A wraith can be summoned or evolve to that point if it eats enough small wraiths. If left unchecked, a wraith that large can decimate an entire community," Death said. "Trolls are flesh, like something from the Courts. It needs food to survive.

"See how it stays clear of the wraiths clustered away from the light?" Death pointed out the slithering masses on the walls. "It's old. If it strays too near, it probably isn't strong enough to fight off the wraithlings. They would overpower it just in sheer numbers and take the troll down. Wraiths prefer to eat flesh because it makes them stronger, but it isn't often that wraithlings find something too weak to fight them off."

"Kind of unfair that he can't eat them but they can eat him."

"Life was never meant to be fair."

"Those wraith things are like rats." Kismet made a face. "If you slept outside, sometimes you'd wake up and find rats chewing on your legs or fingers if you weren't covered up all the way. I have a friend that had those things all over her face when she didn't take her meds. I used to think they were just things I saw because I was sober."

"They'll do that," Death agreed. "If someone's weak and injured, they'll swarm on them to feed."

"There's food behind us, probably." Kismet twisted around, looking at the restaurant's Dumpster. The latch on the lid fed over a hook. "If I open it up, will he come and look around? Can they jump that high? Could he eat that food?"

"It should be able to eat, but I don't think it can jump that high. It looks too injured." Death nodded. "I doubt it will come near us. We're larger Veiled, predators. We're more of a threat than the wraithlings. The reason the shadows aren't afraid of us is because they're too young to recognize anything larger. They're more like a primordial ooze."

"Screw them." The young man stood, brushing at the dirt on the back of his pants. "Fucking black maggots."

Standing, Kismet shoved at the Dumpster's heavy black plastic lid. Balancing on the Dumpster's rigid lip, he reached inside, wrinkling his nose at the smell. Several white garbage bags gaped open, the tied ends easily ripped apart under Kismet's strong fingers. Discarded to-go containers filled with noodles and fragrant deep-fried chicken were within the artist's reach, and he grabbed at the boxes' thin metal handles.

Yanking several free, he dug out what he could, sliding unsteadily back onto his feet. Still light-headed, Kismet nearly stumbled off the curb. Death rose swiftly, catching at the boy's hips to steady him. Stubborn, Kismet shook the bemused Horseman off. Carefully approaching the apprehensive troll, Kismet padded farther into the softly lit alley.

"I'm not going to get too close, boy." Kismet kept his tone low, soothing the troll's nerves. Spilling the food outward, Kismet tried to keep most of the containers as far away from the writhing walls as he could. Kismet backed away slowly, then returned to sit by Death's side.

"It's not going to do any good in the long run," Death commented softly. "It's too weak to survive much longer."

The troll moved slowly over to the food, trying to sense a trap. Its small hands dug into the noodles, shoving long lengths of *chow fun* into its gaping maw. Slurping up the strands, it closed its eyes into narrow slits of pleasure before chewing, stopping only long enough to shovel more food into its gullet.

"Doesn't matter." Kismet kept his eyes on the feeding troll. "If he dies with a full belly, then he's better off than a lot of people I've known. Shit, it would be all I want."

Another cry shattered the night, the sound caught behind the Veil. The troll bolted back into the safety of a hole in the wall, dodging the outstretched tangles of shadows reaching for its decrepit body. Mal's scream of pain brought tears to Kismet's eyes, his worry nearly overwhelming him.

Death swallowed at the lump in his throat, holding in his concern for Mal. The young man beside him obviously shared his pain. Kismet hunkered down, arms wrapped tight around his shins. The air went silent again, and still no one came from the shop to give them any news, good or bad.

Death touched Kismet's leg when the young man leaned toward him. At least he would have company in staring at the door, Death thought. Perhaps with both of them hoping Mal was in good hands, Faith would see fit to help the youngest of his Four.

Chapter Thirteen

"You. Get out of the way. You're too big." Kay shoved Ari aside with a poke of her sharp elbow.

Powders flew into the bowl she'd tucked into the crook of her arm, a hefty splash of hot rice vinegar serving as liquid for the thickening brew.

Ari shot Mal a grin when the younger immortal blanched at the smell. Muttering at the older Horseman, Mal wrinkled his nose. "She's going to make me into a *nori maki* roll."

In the close confines of the back room, Min was the only one of the Horsemen who could move freely under the hanging labyrinth of dangling sacks and pots. Ari's temple bore more than one mark on it, his head a target for anything heavy hoisted up onto a hook on the beams above.

Enormous glass jars lined shelves on the long side of the room, a flattened snout floating in and out of view through one canister's milky liquid. Another held dried beetles, dark hematite carapaces broken open to reveal the delicate beige lacy wings folded against the insects' wide bodies. The old woman shuffled past the containers, occasionally peering at the contents until she found the one she was looking for. A pus-hued fine grain joined the bowl's contents, frothing the mixture with an oatmeal texture.

Sincerely wishing the woman would allow Death to come inside, the blond patted at the youngest Horseman's arm, a pained expression flitting across Ari's face. He wasn't good at comfort. Between the two of them, Death nurtured the Horsemen, guiding them with a gentle hand and kind word, a mentor that expected discipline and commanded respect. Ari much preferred his own role as the ne'er-do-well. Immortality was much easier that way.

"Don't move, Pest. She's got to finish mixing this crap up first," Ari said. "I'm sure you'll be puking before she even digs down past your rib bones."

"You ever do something like this before?" Min sniffed at the bowl, wrinkling her nose when the steam burned her nostrils. "Pull something out of one of us, I mean."

"All the time on the Courts' people." Kay paused, thinking before continuing. "On immortals, three times in my past life. None in this one so far, but that doesn't matter. You never lose these kinds of skills."

"Wait! Hold on a minute." Mal's eyes grew wild as he started to rise up. Ari shoved him back down, the hard shock of hitting the futon's frame sending pangs through Mal's chest. "Go easy, Ari. That hurts more than the bullet."

"Lie back, kid." Ari's tone left no room for argument. "You have to trust us on this."

The woman hovered near Mal's side, her fingers dipped into the slimy concoction. Trailing her hand upward, she dribbled the potion over the bullet wound, mumbling under her breath. With a hissing splash, the mixture burrowed into Mal's skin, festering at the edges of the healed-over hole. As Mal fought unconsciousness, the upper layers of his skin began to bubble, pockets of blisters that jiggled before popping under the pressure of the water beneath.

"What can you do to make the shadows stay off him?" Kay asked, her arms nearly a blur as she returned to beating the powders into the vinegar, smoothing out the last of the grainy pockets. "Or are all of you so strong that they will leave him alone?"

The wraiths in question slithered around the edges of the back room, catching in the rough grain of the wood planks the woman had used to build shelves to hold loose supplies. The inkiness of the shadows grew deeper as more gathered just outside of the light, drawn by the scent of Mal's flesh opening up beneath the acrid potion. Hungry, the wraiths clawed from the Veil, sensing an easy meal.

"I can keep the Veil down," Ari said. "That should keep the bloodsuckers out."

"Well, except the one cutting into him," Min muttered, watching the woman set down the bowl and begin to unravel lengths of silk to soak up Mal's blood with. "I can't believe we're letting her keep his blood."

"Small price to pay to keep him with us." Ari winked at Mal's awestruck look. "Well, that's what Death said. Don't give me that puppy-dog expression, Pest. You know how much hell I gave you for that redcap? You think I'd let her have that much from one of us unless Death said so?"

Mal was about to answer when he choked on his words, his lungs unable to catch at the air. The pain returned full force, unyielding in its quest to break him apart. Concentrating, Mal reminded himself of wanting his existence, fighting the rise of depression each push of anguish shoved farther into his brain. Nearly shattering under the onslaught, Mal pushed back, keeping the other Horsemen in his thoughts.

Clinging to anything to anchor him to the Veil, Mal found his mind wandering over to the image of the sloe-eyed artist smiling at him, talking in hushed tones while lying back on a couch. For those few minutes, he'd held a sense of normalcy in his world, a connection he never quite understood existed until Kismet sat there and listened to what he had to say.

There was something between them. More than the protectiveness Mal felt in his heart when Kismet was around. A heady potential was just within reach, a future Mal wondered if he could possess. The pain of the bullet didn't seem as overwhelming as the fear of losing out at the chance for something. Even a friendship would be better than the lonely existence the Horsemen led.

Min held onto Mal's ankles as the youngest Horseman fought the pain riding through him. An unearthly howl tore from his throat, raspy and anguished. Ari leaned forward, grabbing Mal's hands, holding tight to the younger Horseman. After moving to the other side of the futon, away from where the old woman stood, Ari got down to his knees on the padding.

"You have to hold your other arm down, Mal." Ari slid his belt free from his jeans, looping the leather under the edge of the bed frame. He buckled the strap closed, then held the circled end out for Mal to grab onto. "You either have to hold on to that, or I have to tie your wrist down. Can you do that, kid?"

"I can do that." Mal panted, the poultice boiling down into the soft unhealed flesh under the wound.

He swore he smelled himself cooking, the burning, acrid stink of human fat wiping out the foul stench of the potion. Another kick of torment left a metallic oily taste along Mal's gums, nerve endings raw with pain. His teeth now ached, the bones in his head shifting under the pounding of his abused nervous system. Grabbing at the belt, Mal wrapped his hand into the loop, feeling the buckle bite into the soft mound of his palm.

"You sure you can't give him something to knock him out?" Min hissed at the woman, a hot flow of Wu crackling with anger.

"No." Kay shook her head, the hair on her temple bobbing with sweat. "It's better if he's awake. He'll feel more pain the closer I get to the space where the festering is. That's the only way I'll be able to tell if I am reaching it. Your kind heals up too quickly. There's no wound to follow."

"Great. More pain." Mal bit down on his lip, tasting blood on his tongue.

Ari gripped the younger Horseman's free hand with both of his own, holding tight. Mal knew one of Ari's hands was for the Horseman they'd left outside. Death was in Ari's touch, as if he were there beside them. The elder Horsemen shared a connection Mal could feel in Ari's comforting strength.

Despite all of the troubles and arguments between them, the close-knit pair sustained one another, lending that compassion and vitality to Mal when he needed it the most.

"Don't fool yourself into thinking I'm going to like you more once this is done," Ari whispered, hot in Mal's ear. "You're still going to be a pain in the ass until you get your shit together, Cooties."

"I'd think I was dying if you treated me any different, asshole," Mal responded, hearing Ari chuckle low in his throat.

"Maybe having that kid around is a good thing for you." The older Horseman kept Mal's attention on him, the edge of a newly sharpened knife glittering in Kay's hand. "You're finally growing some spine there."

The first slice into Mal's chest seared, a serpentine curve downward as his nerve endings curled back from the blade's intrusion.

Hooking the knife into the cut, the woman pushed aside muscle, probing for any hint of lingering darkness that would guide her in. Dipping her fingers back into the bowl she set on the floor, Kay scooped another handful of the caustic mixture, then let it dribble down into the cut.

Blackness overtook Mal's vision, a faint droning buzz echoing in his ears for nearly five seconds before he realized it was his own scream echoing in his throat. Fighting to keep the pain at bay, Mal heard Ari's whispering entreaties, finding a focus in the Horseman's voice.

Probing farther in, Kay found a thread of silver wrapped tight around one of Mal's blood vessels.

Before she could poke at the strand, it wisped upward, a dusty tendril catching on the fresh air of the outside world. With his body breached, the Horseman's flesh easily gave up the tormenting slice of reality caught within him. The sliced muscles were already knitting together, edges of skins sealing up around the blade's steel. Cursing, Kay cut into Mal again, hoping to open the gap wider and reach deeper inside.

"Gods, Ari," Mal hissed, his stomach falling into spasms with the pain. "I can't...."

"She's probably close to the bullet," Ari reassured their youngest, fixing a glare on Kay. "You are close, right?"

"He's healing too quickly." The knife dripped with blood, any sheen lost beneath the slick red fluid.

Kay wiped at her forehead with her arm. She dropped the thin scalpel onto a tray then reached for a wider blade, hoping the larger intrusion would seal slower. "I can't keep it open long enough to dig in."

"Here. Sorry, Mal, but I have to do this to you." Reaching over, Ari shoved his fingers into the incision. "You cut down, and I'll use my hand to hold it open. He won't be able to heal over me."

"Fuck," Min swore, biting her tongue as she was nearly thrown by Mal's twisting legs. Lying down fully across the Horseman's knees, Min wrapped her arms around Mal's hips, hoping she could keep him still.

"Just hurry this up." Mal's vision swam, his focus lost in the screaming pain of his body's rejection of Ari's fingers. "Damn. This hurts so damned much."

"Just don't wiggle your fingers," the woman warned Ari. "If I cut anything off, it's going to stay in there until I'm done."

"Honey, my dick's not anywhere near your knives, and that's the only part of my body that I'm ever worried about," Ari shot back. "Almost there, Mal. Just hang on a bit more."

Losing consciousness, Mal let the numbness envelop him. Free of the pain, he sighed, his mind drifting along the comfort of sleep. The euphoria proved to be brief. A sharp, harsh burn on his torso woke him and filled the back of his skull with new agony.

Coughing at the odor pouring into his sinuses, Mal choked, his lungs screaming for clean air. The dank perfume of the stock room returned, fresh compared to the contents of the cotton-stopper vial Kay pulled out from under his nose. Mal's chest ached, the intrusion of Ari's hand a steady push against his skin, the older Horseman's spread fingers keeping the incision from sealing closed. Min rested nearly on Mal's abdomen, her triangular face pale from the exertion of holding the youngest Horseman down.

"Sorry, Mal." Ari bent closer, shoving his fingers in deeper to fill in the excavated space Kay made. "We need you here with us, kid. She really can't tell where this thing is unless you can scream hot or cold."

"Can't tell the difference between your damned fingers and the bullet," Mal gasped, panting to gain some control over his agonized breathing.

"I'm not going to move for a bit." Ari met Min's eyes. The woman slid back down to grip at Mal's hips, holding the youngest steady. "You figure out what hurts more and where."

Mal lay there, two of his companions on his body while another, two others, remained outside. At that moment, he wanted just a shred of the eldest's self-control. His mind clouded with what would happen to Kismet if he pulled away from his calling, falling back into the Universe's embrace. Going away didn't terrify him, not as much as he thought it would, but regrets suddenly filled Mal's thoughts. He'd never know what it was like to be kissed by a mouth not paid for by Ari's charms or money. Or even sharing a quiet meal with someone who didn't spend most of their existence elbow-deep in humans' shit.

A pang echoed in his chest, and his heart twisted with pain. Besides the ache of his wound, Mal could feel the foreign slice of reality embedded in his muscle, Kay's metal knife a few centimeters away.

"To the left. My left." Mal closed his eyes. Fear remained in his thoughts, reminding Mal to focus hard on staying. A single devout wish to be gone from the pain would send him under, his body whisked off to wherever immortals disappeared to after they'd given up. "It's under Ari's hand. Right near the third finger down."

"There it is." The blade hit metal, a fragment of a whirlwind spinning up from around the bullet's misshapen form. Kay exchanged her knife for a pair of long tweezers, then slid them carefully past Ari's fingertips. Shards of metal clung to the reality caught inside of Mal's body, wrapping tight around the injury. "You have to hold still now. I don't know how deep this is. It's going to hurt when I dig around. I don't want to stab your heart while I'm doing this."

"Is it that close?" Ari sounded worried to Mal's ears, faint and distant. "Death needs to be here."

"He stays outside, or I cut your fingers off and let him heal up around them." Kay's voice bounced off Mal's hearing, a tinny, high-pitched sound.

The shadows crept closer, a different sort of darkness that Mal couldn't get a focus on. Acting mostly on instinct, Mal strained to hold the Veil down, hoping it would ease the shadows back into the corners of the room. Frustrated at the lack of response, Mal pulled on his control over the Veil, slapping back at the wraiths hovering close. The darkness lingered, graying out slowly until nothing remained but a powdery dusting of ash that eventually faded away.

Ari's face blurred back into a familiar bad focus, a wavering blond curtain filled with a tan balloon. His vision watering his surroundings, Mal snorted, delirious under the pain's influence. Min said something to him, the words barely out of her mouth when the loud sound of the bullet hitting something hard pinged in Mal's left ear. Ari slid his hand free of the gash in Mal's chest, his fingers covered in blood. Although still out of focus, Ari's smile was clear to the youngest, Ari's face pressing in tight.

"She's got it, brat." Ari's contagious jubilance nearly deafened Mal, his eardrum ringing. "There you go."

Min patted Mal's stomach, a hard blow on his abdomen, her hearty slap nearly rocking the air from his body. "How do you feel, Mal?"

"Like shit." Mal groaned, his chest aching. "But much better. Thanks."

"Not a problem, Pest." Ari patted Mal's shoulders with both hands. "Just remember, I could have had your heart in my hand, and I left it right there."

"You know something." Mal coughed, his body closing the incision swiftly. The excruciating pain of his nerves stitching together brought the ache back to his teeth. "The next time you tell me that something isn't going to hurt me, it might take me a few centuries to do it, but I am going to kick your ass."

"You keep thinking that, Cooties." Ari laughed. "Finish patching him up, Kay. I'm going to tell Death our Pestilence is okay."

DEATH LISTENED to the still world around him. The morning was far from breaking, and the sounds of traffic had slowed down from the main street. The aroma of cooking oil and heavy spices from the restaurant they sat behind prodded a rumble from Kismet's empty belly. The boy's lean frame worried Death. Seeing the immortal look his way, Kismet gave Death an unapologetic shrug when his stomach growled again.

Except for a brief bout of Min's swearing, they'd heard nothing from the shop for a few minutes.

Death knew if Mal had taken a turn for the worse, Ari would have insisted he join them, defying the woman's demand that Death remain outside. The eldest Horseman wouldn't abandon Mal in his pain. Only the promise of much-needed help kept him out, a vow he would easily break to be at Mal's side.

"Is what happened to me normal?" Glancing at the man's emotionless face, Kismet broke their silence, chewing on his lower lip. "How often does this stuff happen?"

Death had almost forgotten about the boy sitting next to him, a stone-quiet sentinel. The ground around them was thick with shadows, wraiths drawn in by Kismet's apparent newness to the Veil. To the larger slithering creatures, the boy would appear to be a weak, tasty meal, an easy piece of pretty meat they could chew off in small bits. Death's steady strength had kept them a few feet away, but with his focus on the shop, the wraiths crawled in tight.

As the Horseman watched, a stray pseudopod sometimes craned into the clearing, hoping to snag the tiniest shred of Kismet's blood or flesh. Pushing against the Veil, Death forced the shadows back. Unwilling to attach itself to a greater predator, the wraith pulled in, slinking back into the darkness.

Sighing, Death resigned himself to handling Kismet like the Courts guarded their young, keeping the children safe until they grew strong enough to peel back the outer layer of the Veil themselves.

"No," Death replied, wondering if the boy realized he'd been stalked by the minute shadows. "Do you have any idea?"

"Not really," Kismet said. "It wasn't like there was a cake sitting on the table saying Eat Me."

"You know *Alice in Wonderland* but not the Bible?" Death contemplated the gaps in Kismet's knowledge. "Society has changed. There was a time when people only knew religious texts. It's funny how things turn over."

"*Alice in Wonderland* was much more interesting." The young man shrugged. "Try reading the Bible stoned. All you do is fall asleep, then dream about snakes and animals marching onto a boat. And remember, public schools. No mixing God and school."

"You never went to church?"

Kismet's laugher bounced against the walls around them. "Dude, church is where you go to find soup, not God."

"Well, I'm guessing someone did this to you. I don't think this is something that you did to yourself," Death surmised. "Mortals don't become Veiled. Even people who dabble in the Veil don't ever fully cross over. They're anchored to the world they're born into. It's troubling, but we'll have to learn how to deal with it."

"Shit, I can't even deal with living in the world I knew," Kismet scoffed. "How the hell am I supposed to live between it?"

"I don't know," the Horseman admitted. "I've looked for a calling in you. There's nothing there...."

"I don't know what that is. A calling, I mean." Kismet shrugged. "Is that what Mal was talking about when he said you got pulled into doing things? Or is my mind just cracked?"

Death leaned back, resting his hands on the curb. The cement was cold on his bare skin, the graveled grit harsh against his hands. A short, ironic laugh broke through his contemplation. He'd never had to explain who he was before. He was Death. His calling always came with a shudder of fear from other immortals, and any human who could see beyond the Veil fled long before he could approach.

"No, your mind isn't playing tricks on you. Something happened to bring your body over to where your mind could see," Death replied. "There are humans who can naturally see past the Veil and into the shadows. A lot of times, these people are insane, or at least right on the very lip of sanity. Some of them are what we call Seers, people who can manipulate the shadows around them or see the creatures who live behind the Veil."

"Like ghosts?" Kismet turned his head, pulling his knees up. "I keep seeing ghosts. Well, I call them ghosts. People that I never knew, but then, well, Chase."

"The little boy that follows you? Is that Chase?" Death grunted at Kismet's astonished nod. "I've seen him behind you. Don't look so surprised.

"Ghosts are souls that are trapped inside of the Veil. It's like a curtain that we can peel back so we can be seen, but it's usually always there," Death said. "When the dead resist leaving, they can get tangled in between the real world and the Veil, trapping themselves here."

"Does he know he's dead? Chase, I mean."

"A lot of the time, they don't know they are dead, or they walk over a familiar path over and over, just reliving that echo of their lives. Or sometimes, a soul attaches to a single person," Death continued. "I'm gathering he's attached to you. Does he follow you where you go?"

"He's my brother. Was my brother." Kismet swallowed.

He could still taste the juice their mother made that night, ordering them to drink it all. It had been cloying, a familiar heavy taste that always meant she would have company that evening. He'd refused to drain the glass, letting his younger brother drink the remainder of the too sweet concoction.

"My mother… I was six or seven… and she liked to have men over but didn't want us to be awake for it. I think she used to give us something to make us sleep, but one night, Chase didn't wake up. And then, all that was left of him was that shadow."

Kismet's heart clenched. He could still smell the sour odor of his brother's cold form lying on the bed's blood-soaked covers. Coughing, he'd turned over onto his stomach, crying from the pain and shaking Chase awake. His brother's eyes were open, a dull staring blue rolling around scarlet-yellowed whites. When he slept, Kismet dreamed the spider webbing of red vessels along Chase's eyes, the mattress soaked through with bodily fluids.

"Ah, classic tragedy of infanticide." The immortal caught the odd look Kismet gave him. "What is it?"

"Most people, when they hear about something sad, say I'm sorry or something." He smirked.

"I'm not people."

"True." Kismet said. "It's kind of ironic I'm sitting here talking about shit that bothers me with Death. So my brother's a ghost?"

"Yes." Death wondered how long it would take the other three to come out. "And yes again, it's ironic."

He'd never been good at talking to humans. He usually left such things to Ari. The boy's questions took his mind off Mal's pain, but Death's mind whispered hot thoughts. He should have protected their youngest member more or given him better skills to defend himself. If Mal survived this, Death promised himself to take better care of Mal.

"Is he ever going to go away?" the young man asked. With Chase gone, Kismet could stand the other shadows that reached out for him. His guilt at wishing his brother would leave closed up Kismet's throat, tightening it with unshed tears and unspoken emotion. "Chase. Not Mal."

"No. Maybe not." Continuing gently, Death tried to break the artist's heart carefully. "He has to find his own way out."

"Is that what's going to happen to Mal if he dies?" Kismet's eyes watered at the thought of the amiable blond Mal becoming a shadow.

He'd tried not to get attached to anyone. Friends were fine to have, but they faded off, mostly without saying good-bye before they drifted away. Relationships were dangerous, an opening up to someone who could reach in and shred his heart with careless abandon. That was a lesson Kismet didn't want to relearn at this point in his life. Kismet's mind whispered that with Mal, it would be different. The Horseman was as lonely as he was, maybe more so, but the artist's heart shrank back in terror, erecting hard barriers before hope could lodge into the chinks.

"No," Death said. "When an immortal dies, we simply aren't here anymore. Our bodies and our souls rejoin the Universe. No one really knows. I can't even tell you where any souls go. All of that is beyond our knowledge. We have a calling to attend to here, but anything past the death, we can't see."

"So you help everyone die, then?" Kismet rubbed at his forehead, lack of food and the ebbing of heroin in his system giving him a headache. "Wouldn't that make you like Santa Claus? Everywhere at once?"

"I don't have to be there. Just by being, I'm helping people die," Death said. The boy's presence was a comfort, a shared worry over Mal. "I'm sure a lot of people don't see it that way, but it is an assistance.

"Natural or human disasters kill thousands in a few moments. The souls of violent deaths usually don't know they're dead and remain here." The Horseman contemplated what he did for a brief moment.

"I have to be at those mass deaths to get them to cross over before they become too entangled in the Veil and are trapped here on this side of it," Death explained. "If there are too many in one spot, then the Veil breaks, and well, you've seen what happens when the Veil breaks. It's easier for wraiths to cross. It becomes very dangerous for humans then."

"Sounds like a shitty job." His stomach growled again. Kismet couldn't remember the last time he'd eaten. Worrying over Mal killed his appetite, but the word hadn't yet gotten to his innards.

"It's the shittiest job we have," Ari said, stepping clear of the doorway.

Death stood, advancing on the Horseman. Ari caught at his friend's waist, hugging the lanky man tightly against his body. Death returned the embrace before pulling away, unspoken questions on his tongue.

"It's okay. He'll be fine. Kay's just letting him heal up a bit and forcing some tea down his throat."

"I want to see him," Death said.

"Me too." Kismet started to rise, shoved back down to the cement by Ari's hand on his shoulder.

"You stay there, kid. He'll be out soon, Shi." Ari glanced down at the shivering young man at his feet. "She's bathing Mal down with some smelly potions and soap to help with the healing or prevent him from ever being laid. I'm not sure which.

"Min thinks she can get Mal home. I don't want you to strain yourself any more than you have to. She'll be able to do it going home. You know home is the easiest place for us to find." Ari touched Death's open mouth with his fingertips, brushing over the man's lips to hush him. "Don't argue, Shi. I'll take the boy with me. I can carry him there."

"Kismet. My name's Kismet," the young man said, eyes narrowed. "Not boy. Not kid. Kismet."

"Yeah, gods save me from Californians who name their children stupid things," Ari commented.

"I'm glad Mal is okay." Death's relief shone through his fatigue, warming Ari's belly. "Maybe he brought Mal luck. Luck is more contrary than you are. Who knows?"

"Maybe I did." The young man strained to see around the immortal's legs. "I probably owe him more karma than he owes me."

"Let's get one thing straight. There's nothing predestined. Not about you or anyone else." Ari shook off Death's warning hand on his chest. "Let me finish, Shi. I didn't let Min tear him apart because you asked me to, but I've got to admit, she's right about him being the reason Mal's in the shape he is in right now."

"War." Death's soft reproach stopped Ari in midrant. "Kismet isn't the cause of Mal's injuries. Whoever did this to him is responsible. The boy's just a vessel for that."

"I'm just saying. There's no Fate, no Karma… none of that shit. You and I know that, Death. This kid should know it too in case he thinks that being around here is somehow predestined." Ari hooked his hand under Kismet's arm and yanked the boy to his feet. "There aren't three women standing around spinning thread. Drinking coffee and cutting off lives isn't real. You shouldn't be here, boy. You're a mistake. A really bad mistake that we're stuck with."

Death caught at Ari's shoulder, turning the blond Horseman toward him. "Leave off. It's not his fault."

"I just want things to be clear between all of us," Ari replied, meeting Death's gaze. "Something like this happens again, then I'm not going to be as forgiving. We could have lost Mal because of this little piece of shit."

"Yeah, you were right," Kismet said, yanking his arm free. "He is an arrogant fucker."

Mal gingerly made his way down the short steps, Min's hands hovering near his waist in case he fell. Kismet approached cautiously, unsure of what to make of the young Horseman's broad smile.

Mal caught Kismet in a hug, crushing the artist to him.

Squeaking with surprise, Kismet took a moment, then returned the embrace, glad to see a friendly face in the shadowy world he'd been thrust into. Min glowered at the human, Kismet ignoring her as he made over Mal's healed wound, peering under the oversized Year of the Rat T-shirt Auntie Kay gave Mal to wear.

"Great. Mal's got a crush on the asshole." Ari heaved a disgusted sigh. "That's all we need."

"Mal?" Death said with a shake of his head. "You think Mal…? No."

"Trust me, I know that look on Mal's face. I see it on mine all the time." Ari crossed his arms over his chest, the day's events sneaking up on him. With their youngest healed, he wanted to crawl into his own bed and sleep. "Let's get home, and we can deal with this in the morning. With any luck, the kid will escape again and get hit by a ghost garbage truck. It'll solve all of our worries."

"And our problems are never solved that easily," Death reminded him, reaching out for the jubilant Mal heading toward him.

"Can't blame a guy for wishing," Ari muttered at his friend's back. He allowed himself to be jostled by Min's enthusiastic pounding on his shoulder, the diminutive Horseman's hard fists bruising the meat on his bones. Grabbing at Kismet's arm, Ari wrestled with the boy until

Mal reassured the human they would just be heading back home where it would be safe. Reluctantly, Kismet let himself be pulled along as Ari gathered what little energy he had to pull himself and the young human along the Veil.

"I'll see you at home, War." Death's face softened, the icy porcelain mask he normally wore outside of their home set aside for the moment.

"You owe me, Death. Big time." Ari grinned broadly. "Tell you what, you sleep with me when we get home, and we'll call it even."

"We can share a bed, but just for sleeping, War. Thank you for keeping me company, Kismet. You helped me worry less." Death slid into the folds of the Veil, drawing on the strength of their home to guide him along. The whisper of his parting words worked into Ari's gut before the shadows claimed the eldest Horseman. "I'm tired, Ari. Let's go home."

"You know, kid, I think I might hate your guts." Ari glanced down at the human right before he yanked them both through the shadowy curtain. "But if you put him in that good of a mood all the time, I probably won't kill you."

CHAPTER FOURTEEN

THE DARKFAE came along in the middle of the night, sliding out from under the cover of the Veil and onto Beckett's stoop. They dragged the shadows with them, streamers of gray mist clinging to their broad shoulders. When Charity opened the door to let the first one in, Beckett exhaled sharply.

Stepping into the main room, the creature loomed over him, wide bodied and menacing. He moved gracefully, unhindered by his enormous girth. Tusks sprouted on either side of his flat mouth, his jaw jutting forward to make room for the bony spikes. The hair on the darkfae's head stuck up along his skull in tails, pulled tight from his forehead down to the base of his neck, the root of each tuft caught together with brass bands. A light blue tint marbled his face and arms, darker splotches appearing along the folds of his skin. Seeing the patterns in living flesh, the magus understood why some of the insane swore they saw gargoyles moving about a city's streets.

Over the years, Beckett had collected artifacts of the Veiled, but those were dead, lifeless things that he reluctantly carved into bits and slivers to use in his spells. Standing before him was a wealth of power, shade-infused flesh that would allow him to raise armies of wraiths, servants to his will. That thought died nearly as soon as it surfaced, seared from his brain when the darkfae pinned Beckett in place with his milky red gaze.

"Charity." The darkfae acknowledged the immortal, an accent roughing the edges of his speech.

"Aegus," Charity replied with a nod. "I'd offer you a seat, but this isn't going to be a long conversation."

"You're bold doing this in front of a human. Is he tainted enough to see our kind? Or are you wanting to drive him mad by hearing voices?" Circling Beckett, the creature snorted, foamy specks ringing his nostrils.

"I'm very sane," Beckett answered for himself, meeting the amused immortal's smile with one of his own. "And I see you quite fine, thank you."

"Seer or magus?" The creature leaned forward, sniffing at the air around the human. His breath was hot on Beckett's face, ruffling his collar when the darkfae snorted in derision. "I'm guessing magus. He doesn't have the smell of poison in his blood."

"Poison?" Beckett repeated, questioning the word.

"Humans that can see past the shadows usually stink of drugs to calm their nerves." The creature smiled, showing the pointed long teeth hiding behind his lips. "Chickenshit creatures, humans. Hard to believe they're the reason we all exist."

"This chickenshit creature is going to be your boss," the magus pointed out.

"Charity is the one who sent out word that he wanted assistance with something," Aegus replied dryly, staring down at the human from his greater height. "I'm being rented. No one is my boss, human or otherwise. What's the job?"

"We need to secure a human boy." Charity stepped into the conversation before it could dissolve any further.

"Secure?" A turn of his sloped head bobbed the tails into a cascading wave. "Do you mean bring back to you alive or in pieces?"

"Alive," Beckett responded. "I need him alive."

"Hardly worth the amount of money that you're offering and not much chance of a trophy from it." The darkfae narrowed his eyes, sizing Charity up. "What's the catch?"

"The catch is that the Four have him." Charity let that tidbit sink in, watching the creature's expression change from cocky arrogance to a guarded wariness.

"I've never heard of an immortal going insane." Mumbling, the creature shifted. His leathers creaked as he moved, his bowed legs pacing off sections of the floor. "It's impossible."

"Nothing is impossible, Aegus," Charity said in return. "I'll need to know if you're in on the job before I go any further."

"Now, the money you offer is hardly worth dying for," the darkfae mulled. "If Death and War have the boy, then let them keep him. There are plenty of humans around. Just pick another one."

"We've got too much invested in this one," Beckett said. "It has to be this one."

"You'll be getting more than money for this." Charity leaned against the back of a couch. "There are boasting rights beyond what you can imagine. Perhaps even a clan trophy if you play it right."

He knew how the darkfae social structure worked. The lower ranked in an individual clan spent most of their lives searching for ways to raise their bloodlines' status. Trophies brought back from raids far outweighed any monetary gain a darkfae might bring to the families' coffers. Money was spent, but bones and boasts were eternal. He was depending on this ambition to forward his plan, but it would require some level of commitment before he would offer up the potential prize.

Charity saw the lure catch his prey. He'd chosen carefully among the brutish darkfae. Their success would depend not just on the killing skill of the individual but also on personal motivation. It would take something nearly irresistible dangled in front of the creatures to assure their loyalty. Money wasn't going to be enough to keep them from abandoning the fight if it turned.

"I know your ranking in your clan, Aegus." Charity caught on the darkfae's ambition, playing to his status. "What you can get from this would be enough for your family to acquire a lot of influence, possibly even leadership of some sort."

"There's nothing that can offer us that." Aegus stepped away from the conversation, turning his back on the men. Tempted to walk away, leaving Charity to his own devices, his clan status and his position in his family chafed at him. If he could raise his bloodline's ranking high enough, it would be possible to kill his father, and he would become the head of the family without any political fallout. His clan wouldn't mind losing a popular leader if their status was raised high enough.

"There is," Charity disagreed. "And I have the means to give it to you. Curious enough?"

"I am curious, so I'm in. I give you my word on that." The darkfae nodded once, his gaze moving to rake over the magus. "But if there's any funny business, I'm killing your pet human first."

"Understood." The immortal shook his hand behind his back, shushing Beckett before he could say anything. "But there won't be. I promise."

"I think the pet human might have something to say about it," Beckett mumbled at his lover's brother, keeping his voice low. Charity turned his head to the side, giving the man a quick smile.

"So how are you going to get him away from the Four?" the darkfae asked, shifting on his feet. "And how many others are you intending to hire?"

"I think we could use five others, perhaps," Charity replied. "And getting the boy away from the Four isn't going to be as hard as you might think."

"I still think you're crazy in thinking you can just walk up to them and take something they have." Aegus grimaced, his mouth working around his tusks.

"Let us worry about that," Beckett reassured the darkfae. "We'll talk further once we decide on the others."

"This better be good, immortal," Aegus warned Charity. "Where can I wait until you two wade through the rabble waiting to talk to you? And I'll need something to drink. It's going to take you a long time to pick through the trash I walked through."

EVENTUALLY CHARITY decided on five, choosing from the dozen or so that answered his initial summons. For the most part, the darkfae he hired knew one another, either by reputation or from prior jobs together. The creatures broke off, talking low and sizing up the next. They'd each been promised the same thing, money and a chance to lift their personal and clan status. Achieving the latter would more than likely depend on the failure of another, and the darkfae were calculating which among them would be that loser.

"Is this all of us?" One of the smaller darkfae slurred, his shoulders wide and thick with muscle. His mouth was ill equipped to speak, rows of blunt broad teeth folding his lower lip out. Genetic evolution and the low status of his clan had led to his bowlegged stance and hunched back, bred into his line for mining work that was no longer being done in the modern world the Veiled now found themselves in.

"The cavefish's counting how many boots he's going to have to polish." A deep laugh echoed through the darkfae. Hearing the derogatory clan nickname angered the shorter darkfae, his face hardening as he looked at the others.

"Look, I'm not going to expect all of you to get along." Charity looked out into the room, watching the creatures jostle for position. "I do expect you to at least work with one another. You can kill each other later if you like. For now, any killing that you do is done for me, and is directed by me. Do you have any questions before we start?"

"What about the human?" The male who taunted the shorter darkfae spoke up. "Are we expected to answer to two of you or just one?"

"The human is named Beckett." Charity motioned for the magus to step forward. Beckett dropped an ice cube into a glass of water before joining the immortal, standing shoulder to shoulder with him.

"How crazy is he?" The darkfae they'd first interviewed grinned widely at the harsh laugher his question brought out in the others. "He can see us clearly and doesn't look drugged."

"I'm not insane," Beckett offered. "Well, not in the true sense of the word."

"Beckett is a magus," Charity said. "And has some means to help him see into the Veil."

"Those means include carving up one of us and cooking the flesh into a potion?" One of the gray-skinned darkfae spoke up, the slant of his ears and the almond shape of his pitch-black eyes evidence of UnSidhe blood somewhere recent in his lineage. "Isn't that what magi do? Collect bits and pieces of the Veiled to use for their experiments?"

A rumble of anger echoed through the creatures, disquiet forming among them. Beckett sighed with disgust. The shortsightedness of his own species irritated him. Coming face-to-face with more closed-mindedness annoyed him more. Clearing his throat, he kept his temper in check.

"Yes, that is what a magus does, and I'll make no apologies for what I do. And as Charity pointed out, I'm paying the bills. Do you really want to walk away from this opportunity because you have some misplaced outrage or disgust? Can any of you eat off your pride? No?" Beckett scanned the group, looking for any further dissent. "Good, then I'll let Charity explain what we need you to do."

"You said we're looking for a boy, a human," Aegus said from the back of the group. "And that the Four have him. What's your plan?"

"My plan's simple." Charity passed around sheets of paper, a sketched-out schematic of a floor from a high-rise. "We'll be taking this fight to the Horsemen's doorstep. What I'm handing you is the layout for where the Four live in San Diego."

"So the human's the sane one and you're crazy." There were murmurs of assent from the darkfae at the shortest creature's words. "What you're asking is impossible. They'll slaughter us."

"Beckett will be providing a distraction," the immortal continued. "What I need the five of you to do is keep the Four occupied long enough for him to finish what he needs to do. Then we can grab the boy and leave."

"And when the Four hunt us down?" Aegus asked thoughtfully. "What then?"

"They won't be coming after you," Charity assured the wary darkfae. "They're going to be too busy mourning to be concerned about one of you."

"Mourning?" Another cocked his head, tilting his chin up.

"One of you is going to kill Death, maybe even War." Charity grinned at the stunned silence that struck the darkfae. He pulled a slim automatic out of his jacket and held it up for the creatures to see. "And this is how you're going to do it."

MAL MOVED gingerly down the stairs to the lower level, a nearly disastrous descent when his foot caught on the edge of the top step. Kismet caught the brunt of Mal's weight before the taller man toppled over and before Min pushed the human out of the way to support Mal with her own body, grumbling on his lack of common sense. Mal wanted his own bed and the quiet of his room, curtains drawn over the impending sun and the noise of San Diego's downtown district.

After they'd all come through the Veil, Death locked the door behind them, removing the key from the deadbolt for the first time in Mal's memory. With a single click, the penthouse became a silent prison, keeping Kismet within its walls. The young man fought his resentment, jaw muscles working around his anger as he swallowed bitter words.

"Fucking son of a bitches. Why don't you guys just microchip me?" Kismet glared back at Min when she pushed at his shoulder. After challenging Min with a frustrated hiss, he slid his arm around Mal's waist, helping the immortal down the stairs to his bedroom below the main floor.

Reaching the bed, Mal sat down heavily, wondering why the bathroom was so far away.

Another shuffling walk to the toilet exhausted him. Pulling the final strained remnants of his strength, Mal returned to the bed, sweat running down his back.

"Okay, I'm done," the exhausted immortal gasped, clutching at his side. "I'm just going to fall over and try to heal the rest of the way."

"Call me if you need something," Min said before she reluctantly left the two men behind, her final backward glance at the young man sitting next to Mal filled with menace. Kismet silently snarled back.

Kismet's addiction was beginning to test him, probing at his nerves to see if he would break. It was a fight he was used to. More often than not, he gave in to the seductive pull of nothingness heroin gave him, anything to peel the feel of shadows off his soul. Inside of the Horsemen's home, Kismet found the pressure lessened in the invasive, disturbing silence. If he could ignore the want for a few minutes, Kismet knew he could fall asleep, providing he could get his mind to stop crawling with thought. Breathing deeply, he concentrated on more important things, like getting Mal's shoes off.

"Here, let me help." Kismet leaned down near Mal's feet after watching him struggle with his shoelaces. The last person he remembered helping with their shoes was Chase; his younger brother's laces often tangled into tight knots that were nearly impossible to undo. Mal lifted his feet, kicking at the heels of his shoes to work them fully clear. "I'll head upstairs to sleep. That sofa you got up there already has my drool on it."

"You can sleep down here." Mal felt a burn of bashfulness on his cheeks. The stretch of mattress was a cool invitation to the Horseman's healing body, but the thought of Kismet sleeping in the room above him left a curious tendril of unease in his belly. "The bed's large enough for five people. Ari ordered it. I think he hoped I would have orgies down here or something."

"Orgies?"

"I think he had high hopes to corrupt me." Blushing again, Mal adjusted the pair of glasses he'd found upstairs. "But yeah, I'd like to know you're safe."

"Sure. If it's okay. I'll take a bed over a couch any day." Kismet shrugged, not seeing the red blush on Mal's face. "Let me go pee first and turn off the lights. Can you get your clothes off, or do you need help doing that too?"

"No, I'm fine." Mal pressed the heel of his hand against his forehead after Kismet disappeared into the bathroom, wondering why his tongue suddenly seemed too large for his mouth. "If you need to shower, there's some T-shirts and sweats in the closet you can borrow."

"Thanks. I think I reek," Kismet called out. "Hot water without rust would be great. Sometimes my room's shower is so red with it, it's like pouring blood over me."

Mal peeked out through hooded eyes, glad his glasses emerged unscathed. Catching sight of Kismet's pale body reflected in the bathroom's wide mirrors, Mal watched as the young man stripped off his shirt with an unconscious grace, free in a way he could only envy.

Kismet hooked a finger around a broken belt loop, absently pulling the waistband of his jeans down over the dip of his navel. Mal watched surreptitiously as the other rubbed the pad of his thumb over the small bump on his nose. The break hardened the too pretty femininity of Kismet's face, and Mal wondered if it was from a fight.

Long veins throbbed under the skin of Kismet's arms, faint punctures fading along the inside of his elbows. A single keloid burst an ugly purple over a red dollop of healing flesh. His fingers trembled, nails caked with the stain of oil paint he could never completely scrub off in the shower.

When Kismet's tattered jeans shifted down over his legs, Mal spotted the tattoo stretching over his hipbone and rolling around his thigh. Brilliantly orange, an inked koi fin peeked up out of the waistband of his boxers. The fish swam down the young man's skin, the rise of Kismet's ass a spray of ocean mist, curves lightly inked with white and teal foam. Mal swallowed as the carp moved when the artist tested the shower spray with his hand. Then Kismet disappeared from view, lost in the water stream.

Looking away, Mal hated the hardness in his groin, breathing in deeply to wash the cold air into his lungs. He hastily shed his dirty jeans and the borrowed shirt he was fairly certain he would never return. Lying back on his bed, Mal drifted off, letting the sounds of the water lull him, trying to tell his body to stop reacting to the erotic images playing through his mind.

The sound of quiet footsteps shocked him into wakefulness. Kismet shut the bathroom light off behind him. A pair of Mal's sweatpants was rolled up to his ankles, and a worn T-shirt hung on Kismet's narrow chest, the hem brushing the rise of his rear as he sat down.

"Hope you don't mind, but I found a package of toothbrushes and stole one." Kismet rubbed at his wet hair with a towel, hoping to soak up most of the water. "If you've got a hair dryer, I can dry my hair and not get your sheets wet."

"It's okay." Mal swallowed. His chest felt too tight, and he wondered if he was having lingering effects from being shot. "I go to sleep with wet hair all the time. Unless you want to dry it. Then I can find it for you."

"Nah, too tired. If you don't care, then I'm not going to." He returned the towel to the bathroom, then flopped down on the bed, nearly rolling into Mal's prone body. Sighing, Kismet lifted his arms over his head, the past few days' events catching up with him.

"Did you want to take a shower?" Kismet sat up, fatigue running dark slashes under his wide eyes. "I can help you to the bathroom if you need it."

"Do I stink?" Mal lifted his head, rolling over onto his side. The sheet he'd hastily pulled up over his body slid from his bare chest, the purpling mark from the extracted bullet vivid against the light tan of his skin.

Wincing at the healed-over wound, Kismet swallowed and lay back to rest on one elbow, staring at the immortal.

"Auntie Kay sponged me down, but the soap smelled weird. I'm kind of afraid to wash it off after she told me it was to help the healing process. For all I know, it's just burned cat hair and chicken bones she ground up."

"You're good. You smell a bit like spices." Kismet reached forward, about to touch the mark on Mal's chest. With his fingers barely skimming above the slick, shiny skin, he sighed at the sight of the puckered flesh. "I think you getting shot is my fault. Actually, pretty sure about it."

"Don't think like that," Mal said, covering Kismet's hand with his own. The young man was slender, his long fingers almost frail in Mal's mind. "Believe it or not, I think getting shot was good for me. Maybe next time I'll take time to think. Death's always telling me to do that. I have to train myself to think before reacting."

"Hell of a rolled-up newspaper." The young man slid over the sheets, laying his cheek on his forearms.

"Besides, Min's really jealous. None of the other Four have ever been shot with a bullet." Mal wondered why Kismet had pulled free from his hand. He debated asking, but he wasn't sure how to bring it up. How did someone ask if their touch was repugnant? "She's always wanted to be the first in something, and here I went and took that away from her."

"Good, so long as Min's pissy about it." Kismet pulled himself up onto his elbows, then rested his chin on Mal's chest, carefully avoiding the healed-over wound.

Something in the young man's eyes made Mal ache. There was pain there, a questioning unknown that Mal wanted to soothe away. Touching Kismet's cheek with the tips of his fingers, the immortal traced along the smooth skin over the other's cheek before poking at the corner of Kismet's mouth to pull it upward.

"Are you okay?" Mal asked.

"Yeah. No." The young man couldn't shake the memory of the man he struck sliding down onto the pavement, the back of his head caved in and his brains splattered on the cinder block. Tremors ghosted over his limbs, a shaky cold touching his shattered nerves. "I've never hurt someone like that before. Hell, I've never really hurt anyone that wasn't hurting me first, but today I really killed someone."

"I'm glad you killed him." Mal reached for the other man's shoulders, pulling Kismet closer. He wanted to offer comfort, hoping to erase the distant pain that lurked in the young man's eyes. The human came along without complaint, resting against the immortal's side. "I've never had someone outside of the Four do something like that for me."

"Dude, that guy's dead." He resisted being dragged closer, then surrendered, looping one arm over Mal's stomach. The immortal's breath stopped for a moment, held tight in his chest. Then he exhaled before moving his hand down Kismet's spine, letting his fingers brush along the small of the other man's back. Sighing at the small comfort, Kismet said, "There's no coming back from that, Mal. I killed him. Shit, the cops are going to know I did it."

"If that happens, we'll take care of it," Mal reassured him. "Death is good at that sort of thing. You think you're the first one to leave a crime scene? Ari is a master of screwups. Death's always pulling him out of one mess or another. But really, that man, he didn't seem all there. Crazy people with guns are okay to kill. I'm pretty sure of it."

"Remind me not to stand next to you holding a gun," Kismet replied.

"You've got to remember, you're not crazy." Shifting, he finally relaxed. The strange feeling of another person against his body was turning into a pleasurable one. Having someone as close as Kismet was at that moment seemed odd, but it was something Mal was sure he could get used to. Cradling the other man felt good, even comforting. "Everything that you saw in the shadows was real. Or rather, is real. I know that no one probably understood, but you've got to believe that."

"Mal, crazy is pretty much what normal people think about other people seeing shit move around in shadows." Kismet's laugh was bitter, poisoned from every whisper he'd ever overheard. "People avoid crazy. It's hard to chant to yourself that you're not insane when people give you the eye on the bus and keep their kids away."

"That sounds sad," Mal said, brushing at Kismet's hair. "Lonely too."

"We're all lonely. Humans, anyway." Pursing his lips, Kismet reached under himself to scratch an itch on his stomach. "I think it's why we all have sex. So we can be lonely together for a few minutes and pretend like we're getting some sort of connection, but it's not real."

"Do you really believe that?" The thought concerned Mal. Lying in the bed with the young man beside him, a warmth filled him, lifting his fatigue away. "That you're alone?"

"Most of the time," Kismet admitted. "When I hit that guy today, I didn't feel like that. It pissed me off that he hurt you, and I wanted to hurt him back. Maybe you're alone until you give enough of a shit to feel something. I don't know. Mostly I know how much it hurts when someone I like splits because they can't handle the nuts part. Crazy brings the alone. It just does."

"I'm sorry. It shouldn't be like that." The hitch in Kismet's voice pained Mal. "I've always had the other three, even if sometimes I feel like I don't fit. But I know I belong. Even if sometimes I feel like I've more in common with humans than the Four, I still feel like I'm one of them."

Kismet slanted a look toward Mal. "You're human, right? Or were?"

"Death says we are. Human, I mean. Or close to it," Mal said. "And I feel human. There's a difference between what a human feels like against the Veil compared to someone who lives behind it. It's like a silvery tint on the black. It's hard to explain. I'm pretty good at telling when someone's human, but I can't identify a lot of the other immortals. Min's better at it, but she's been a Horseman for a lot longer."

"When all of this started happening, I wondered if I was still human. Or if I was dead. That hit me too." Kismet's hand moved up until he felt Mal's heartbeat below his palm. "There's been so much shit inside of my head, just gnawing on me. I sometimes just wanted to crack open my skull like an egg and scoop everything out. Anything to make it go away. Then today, after I realized you were hurt, it all became real. It scared the hell out of me."

"Maybe it'll go away now that you're here with us?" Mal suggested.

Kismet snorted. "Nope, still scared shitless. Guess that's going to take a while to go away."

"You'll be fine." Mal hoped he would be. Something in his guts trembled at the thought of the change to his world, and he wasn't sure if it was a good thing or bad, but it was welcome, regardless. He felt like he needed a change, something to embolden him. "Don't worry. We'll take care of you. Death won't let anything happen to you if he has any control over it. I'll help. I promise."

"Maybe I'm just caught in a bad retelling of *I Am the Cheese*, and I'm cycling around some loony bin looking for my dead brother?" The young man curved his body tight around Mal's stomach, feeling each second of his years. "This is insane, you know, hoping that things will be okay. You can't just wish the crap in the world to go away."

"Not from what I can see," Mal reminded him, hitching his hips closer to the nearly fetal young man lying next to him. "You're safe in here. Nothing can touch you here. It's one of the sacrosanct things in our lives. Once through the door of an immortal, you're safe from harm."

"Even from Ari?"

"Especially from Ari." Mal hesitantly slid his arm around Kismet's waist when he nestled in close, his body curling against the immortal. The other man's casual touch and warm length made his nerves tingle. Shutting away the excitement riding over his body, Mal continued, "You told him where to get off earlier. The only person I know who does that is Min, and she's rarely on my side. It's usually the two of them against me. It was kind of nice."

"He's a dick." Shivering, Kismet wondered if the cold along his spine was the return of his addiction or the terror in his belly finally catching up with him. "Are he and Death a thing?"

"A thing? Oh, lovers. Sometimes it's hard to understand you."

"Lovers." The young man nodded. "Yeah."

"Not now, but they have been. Probably should be," Mal said. "Sometimes I think the world is spinning out of control because both of them fight about how they feel. But I know that's not true."

"Can I ask a weird question?" Kismet blinked, trying to stay awake long enough to see if the addiction would crawl back into his blood or if he would be able to get a full night's rest. The burn came and went with an unpredictability that often infuriated him. Mal was easy to talk to, far less awe-inspiring than Death. Tucked into Mal's hold, sleep whispered seductively into Kismet's ear.

"Sure."

"Did you pick Mal, or did the others name you?"

"That's kind of—" The immortal searched for the word he wanted. "—an odd change of subject."

"It just hit me," Kismet replied. "Did you come with it? Did you know it was your name? Do you know who you were before you became one of these guys?"

"I chose it. It took me a while to find one I liked," Mal said. "I liked the way it sounded. Ari's been called Ari for a while. Min wanted something that was shortened from Famine. And no, none of us know who we were before we become immortal."

"And Death is just Death?" the young man asked. "He doesn't have another name?"

"No. Ari calls him Shi sometimes." Mal remembered the first time he heard Death speak his own name, somber and cold. "Ari is the only one who calls Death something else. He doesn't have another name. I think he doesn't take another name because he never wants to forget he's Death."

"Glad you didn't decide to be Len. That's a suck-ass name."

"That one never even occurred to me." He contemplated the sound in his head, then said it aloud. "Len from Pestilence. No, I don't think it fits. Ari calls me Pest sometimes."

"Once again proving Ari is an asshole. When you go out to be Pestilence—" Kismet yawned, his eyes heavy. The soap on Mal's skin didn't smell unpleasant, more like an oolong tea left too long to steep. "—do the others go with you?"

"Not often. We don't really go out as a group. Sometimes Ari and Death do. I do a lot of things alone," Mal said.

The young man's lashes flickered, drawing long shadows over Kismet's face.

Fascinated, the Horseman studied the other's face in the dim light, watching awareness fade in Kismet's sleepy gaze.

"And you thought I was sad," the young man murmured, his words husky. "I mean, you all are supposed to be together. What's the point of being a group of something if you're having to go off to do things by yourself?"

"It's just the way I'm called. Pestilence really doesn't interact with the others. Min is the same way. We do sometimes follow where Ari's been," Mal clarified. "A lot of times what we do helps mankind to change for the better, even if it doesn't seem like it. I try to help people along, make the species as a whole stronger. That doesn't happen as often as I'd like it to. But mostly I go out and come home before anyone notices I'm gone. It's not so bad."

"If you have to go tonight, will you wake me up at least?" Kismet's eyes watered with another yawn, his teeth glittering sharp in the dark. "I wouldn't want you to come back and no one was waiting up for you. Ari said he waited up for Death. Least someone could do is wait for you."

Stunned, Mal barely breathed as Kismet tucked under his arm and nuzzled down into the linens covering them both. Kismet drifted off, eyes closed against the day's light creeping in around the curtains, rolling into Mal's embrace. Kismet's steady breathing lulled Mal's nerves, the fragile trust between them firm for the moment.

Wrapping his arms tighter about Kismet's shoulder and waist, Mal lay back. Temptation warred with a cautious trepidation in Mal's mind, the other's face a few inches away. Mal bent his head to brush his lips against Kismet's cheek, tasting the young man in his mouth.

"Sure," Mal promised the sleeping young man. "I'll let you know if I have to leave."

A musky sweetness caught in the back of his throat, heavy with a need Mal didn't know how to act upon. Burrowing his cheek into Kismet's drying hair, the immortal surrendered to the sleep that nagged at him. He'd deal with how he felt in the morning, Mal promised himself, letting the small sip of Kismet's skin run over his tongue.

CHAPTER FIFTEEN

MAL WOKE hungry, his body craving to restore some of the energy he'd spent healing. The warm form tucked against his ribs gave him a start until he remembered falling asleep to Kismet's soft whispers. Awash in the sunlight from the penthouse windows, Kismet lay bare of any covers, his feet tangled in a quilt. The purple scarring on his arm had faded to a blush pink, a raw anger raging below pale skin.

The shaggy strands of Kismet's hair covered one of his eyes, touches of a deep red hidden under a coffee brown. Slender, nearly too thin, the young man's belly was firm, Mal's too large T-shirt riding up nearly to his chest. To Mal's eyes, there was a feral quality to the human's face, a feline wildness that both invited and repelled. Kismet looked like he would bite as soon as he would welcome a touch, something Mal certainly respected.

Paint clouded the skin under Kismet's fingernails, midnight rainbow stains caught in chewed-on cuticles. Seafoam ink peeked out from under the young man's sweats, the orange and reds of the tattooed koi swimming up over his body brilliantly vivid. Mal wondered if the ink could still be felt, the smooth skin alluring and begging to be touched. He'd heard Ari mention once that a tattoo took a while before it sank all the way down. The fish was a lure, vivid and bright, but Mal kept his hands to himself and quietly slipped from the bed.

Turning on the shower, Mal let it warm, waiting until steam poured from the glass enclosure then stepped in. The hot water felt wonderful on his tender skin, the hole in his chest healed over and smooth. He was reluctant to leave the warm water, but his stomach was growling loudly, stabbing sharp pangs under his diaphragm. Dressed in a pair of jeans and a shirt, Mal wandered upstairs to see if any of the others were awake.

Min's door was open, a Post-it Note scrawled with her illegible handwriting saying she either was in Thailand or, as far as Mal could make out, had been eaten by squirrels. Death's door was shut, keeping a silent guard against what sometimes raged inside that suite.

A quick check of the pantry yielded nothing he would eat, mostly a collection of fungi and canned foods that were too salty to be palatable. A paper bag on the kitchen counter held soft jeans and T-shirts, a pinned note from Min informing Mal that this would be all she would donate to clothe their pet human, warning Kismet off any further pilfering of her wardrobe.

"Hey." Kismet's husky voice rubbed velvet tingles over Mal's stomach, awakening the butterflies Mal thought had gone into hibernation. Rubbing at his face, the young man yawned, a fleck of toothpaste on his face. Kismet stretched his arms over his head, working the sleep out of his body.

"Morning. Or what's left of it." Mal took a quick glance at the clock. After handing the bag over to Kismet, he opened the fridge, making a face at the barren wasteland he found there. "Min left some clothes for you."

"Thanks." Kismet tugged Mal's shirt up over his shoulders, then dug into the bag until he found something he liked. The stripping continued, Kismet standing bare to the morning before dragging on worn denim and a sage green T-shirt from an indie bookstore in Clairemont Mesa. Shoving Mal's sweats and shirt into the bag, Kismet straightened, finding the immortal staring at him.

"What?" Eyes slightly narrowed, Kismet cocked his head at the other man. "There's only us here. Does it bother you?"

"No, it's okay. I'm just not used to having someone else around." Mal swallowed, trying to erase the image of ink splashed over long stretches of the young man's body. "We probably should head out and grab some bagels or something. The only things to eat in here are things Min hauled home."

"You guys go shopping?" Kismet whistled under his breath. "I can't imagine you guys down at the grocery store."

"There isn't a cornucopia that we shake out to get food," Mal said, teasing lightly. "Shopping is usually something we do only when we finally can't stand eating takeout anymore. Or if one of us remembers to order groceries."

"You're telling me that you're immortal and none of you cook?"

"Death cooks," Mal commented, thinking on some of the dishes the other man prepared. "Sort of. He likes a lot of raw things. Ari likes meat chunks that are black on the outside and dripping blood on the inside."

"Remind me to teach you how to use a microwave." Kismet shook his head. "Or hell, mac and cheese. You can't go wrong with instant food."

"We'll have to walk. I think Death's car is in the shop for repairs, and well, Ari's Mustang has probably been towed to a graveyard by now, and my SUV is still down near the motel." He hoped his car was still there. From what he remembered of the area, it was an iffy thing at best.

"I have to head back home anyway," Kismet replied, looking for socks under the clothes. "If you want, you can come with and pick it up. The trolley isn't too bad this time of day."

"Shit." Surprise struck Mal, and an odd pressure filled his chest. "I never thought about you going back there. You're immortal now."

"Hey, it's not like I'm leaving for Europe or something. I'm just down University." Seeing the stricken look on Mal's face, Kismet bent across the counter. The young man asked, holding tight to the sock ball he'd found, "Where'd you think I was going to live?"

"I guess I thought you'd be with us." Mal swallowed his disappointment. Of course Kismet couldn't stay with them. Ari made his opinion on the subject crystal clear, and Death had yet to be heard, but it appeared that the young man had decided for them. Back out into the world he would go, open to the dangers that now lurked in wait for him.

"Yeah, I can see that happening." Kismet laughed. "Besides, I'm going to start twitching in a few hours, and somehow I don't think your roommates are going to want me around then. But breakfast would be good. I think I've got a couple of dollars in my jeans."

"Don't worry about the money. I have more than enough," Mal said. "There's a bagel shop a block away. We can bring some back. Min will be starving when she comes back. She always is."

The foyer outside of the penthouse jogged into a short-legged L, the elevator designed to be aesthetically hidden from the door's view. Wide-leafed plants fought for space amid planters filled with thin spires of bamboo. On the far wall, a thin sheet of water flowed from the ceiling to the floor, its delicate splashing trapped between a clear pane of glass and a rippled granite backdrop. Kismet stood for a moment at the apartment's threshold, marveling at the edges of the Veil pooling against the walls.

A gray film coated the lower baseboards of the foyer's clean white birch walls, its edges a crumbled velvet. Clean of movement, it lay inert, pulled back by the sheer force of the Horsemen's abode. Mal stopped when he noticed Kismet wasn't behind him, turning to shoot a curious look at the young man.

"What's the matter?" Mal returned to Kismet's side, wondering what he was staring at.

"I can see those edges." Kismet stepped closer to the wall, his sneakers nearly touching the rough stone trough under the waterfall. "That Veil of yours, I can see the edges of it. And there still isn't any of that humming noise. That's the one thing I noticed the last time. Nothing buzzed in my ear when I was inside. It was so quiet. I'd never heard that kind of quiet before."

"I guess I'm just used to it by now," Mal said. "There's nothing like coming home to this. If I had to live in the shadows all the time, well, it's no wonder humans go insane."

"Yeah," Kismet agreed, his voice nearly as soft as a rush of water over stone. "I'm still not convinced that I'm not nuts."

"We'll have a lot of time to convince you." Mal grinned. He hooked an arm over Kismet's shoulders, hoping the gesture seemed as casual as he intended. "Come on. Let's get some breakfast."

THE STAIRWELL stank with the press of bodies, the darkfae gathering tight against the fire door. Tusks sprouted from one of the darkfae's wide mouth, his thick-lipped face nearly flat. Two slits fluttered between wide-set eyes, their whites nearly goldenrod in hue. Another male stood to the side, a three-fingered hand scratching his face, a splintered nub of a horn curled down from his forehead to the middle of his cheek. There were five darkfae besides the immortals and Beckett, mute, glowering men whose thick skin shone, with small scales and soft hair covering their visible forearms.

"It's so cold in here." Faith rubbed at her bare arms, trying to pull the shadows closer to her body. "Are the others in the stairwell ready?"

"Everyone's primed. They're listening for the signal to attack once we're on the top floor." Beckett reassured her. "The other darkfae have those exits covered just in case."

"Good. We'll need them if we're going to kill Death." The Veil crackled thin, and Faith's influence thinned. She could feel Death in the air, the burden of the eldest immortal's power pushing back all the layers of the curtain. "Everything here smells like the Horsemen. Even with the Veil peeled back, it smells like them."

"I'm hoping that in a little bit, the only thing you'll smell is blood," Charity replied. The immortal picked through the shadows, hoping to find a pool of untainted darkness to pull on, dipping his hands into the inky curtain and drawing what strength he could muster from its thinness. "Do you have everything you need, Beckett?"

"Yes." The magus held up a small duffel bag. "Once we enter the foyer, there's nothing to keep them hidden, right? I don't want them hiding the boy where we can't get to him."

"No, they won't be able to get into the shadows," Faith replied. "We have to go outside of our sanctuaries to travel through the Veil."

"Just remember, don't raise a hand to the Four," Charity warned Beckett. "No matter what is happening, they can't touch you unless you move against them."

"One of them killed Frazier. Forgive me if I don't believe you," the magus said.

"Your lap dog was an idiot for shooting Pestilence," the immortal remarked. "As soon as you attack one of them, they are free to defend themselves against humans. Death keeps them on a short leash, but there's only so much the Four will stand for."

"Immortal," one of the men grunted at his employer, his wide finger holding the fire door open a crack. "There are two in the foyer. One is Pestilence. I'm guessing the other is the boy."

"This is just too easy." Charity nodded at the darkfae. "Keep the boy whole. Or as much as you can. Kill the others. It doesn't matter how. Just kill them. Might do the world some good to be free of the Four for a few hours."

KISMET STARTED at the raucous sound, feet stomping over steel stairs, heavy and authoritative. Mal jerked around when the stairwell door blew open, a rush of bodies pouring free. A fist to Mal's face stunned him, his surprise cut short by a wave of pain. Struggling to see through the blood flying over his face, the Horseman yelled at Kismet to stay behind him.

With his vision cleared, Mal lashed out with an elbow, hearing a grunt as he made contact with someone's face. His attacker stood nearly a foot taller than him, a jutting square chin furred black with a soft pelt. Spitting out what leaked into his mouth, the immortal blinked, unsure of what was happening around him.

Darkfae were ascending into the foyer from the stairwell, forcing through the doorway and into the Horsemen's home. Popping sounds bounced off the walls as the darkfae broke through the Veil's resistance, their thick bodies pushing past the shadowy barrier. Turning to shove Kismet back toward the front door, Mal slammed into a darkfae that appeared between them.

An arm hooked around Kismet's throat, jerking him back against solid meat, nearly taking the breath from his lungs. He twisted, turning his attacker sideways. The creature responded by slamming the boy forward, using the wall to stun the human into submission. Amid the stars across his eyes, Kismet's anger took over.

Hit fast. Hit hard. Run. Kismet knew the formula well. Repeat if necessary. If he did it right the first time, it was rarely necessary. With his slender frame and delicate, pretty face, more than one person had believed he could be easily victimized. Kismet learned at an early age that heavy objects and quick reflexes could often win over brute strength, especially when he attacked hard and repeatedly.

Trying to get a good look at the area around him, Kismet cursed the lack of anything within reach. With his air slowly being choked out of him, the human knew he wouldn't have long before he passed out. A terra-cotta pot filled with a tall shaped evergreen would be his best bet if he could get a hand on it. Stretching his arm out, the top of the tree skimmed his fingertips, just out of grabbing range. The creature bashed him forward, again snapping his temple against the foyer's hard wall. Black spots appeared in his vision, the edges of his sight starting to gray out. Gritting his teeth, Kismet took the next course of action left to him.

Kismet tasted blood from his bitten tongue, red smearing on the penthouse lobby's birch paneling. Leaving a crimson path along the wood grain, the young man jerked back, slamming his head into the soft ridge of his attacker's nose. The satisfying crunch of cartilage breaking coupled with suddenly being released pushed his adrenaline into overdrive.

Spinning about, Kismet doubled down, pushing his weight up behind his fist, jabbing upward into the meaty softness just within reach, an anguished oomph washing hot air over his face as he made contact with the flat of his attacker's midsection. Stepping back to be clear of the man's bent-over body, Kismet stopped suddenly, stilled to a stunned silence as he saw the small group of people coming toward him.

Four creatures towered over him, the top of his head barely at eye level. Their yelling rose, a harsh, guttural crescendo unintelligible to Kismet's ears.

A woman, delicate and ethereal, stood near a tall shaven-pate man and another man who looked to be her twin. She turned her face from the fray, as if reluctant to watch.

The shaven man had no such qualms. His gaze was fully fixed on the circling darkfae, and his hands twitched at his sides, as if it took every bit of effort not to wade into the fray and bash his clenched fists against unwary skulls. Meeting the man's eyes, Kismet took a step back when the man's face curled with a cold smile.

The blond man shouted at the two creatures in front, sending them lumbering toward Mal and Kismet. The bottleneck against the foyer walls opened up, spilling the creatures forward. Screaming in rage, the one-horned darkfae raised his arms above his head, bringing a long-handled machete down toward Mal's shoulder.

Mal was rarely thankful for Death's training. Too often he spent hours trying to recover from the beatings he received when the elder Horseman tried to teach him how to defend himself. As the blade whistled in the air, Mal dodged, sliding his body to the side, nearly stumbling over Kismet's leg. Rolling into a crouch, Mal steadied himself with his fingertips against the wooden floor, trying blindly to gauge the distance to the front door behind them.

"Kismet!" Mal shoved the young human toward the wall, his hand connecting hard on the young man's hip. "Get to the door. Get back inside! Don't let the darkfae get between you and the door."

Mal's voice penetrated Kismet's brain, startling him into action. He slammed a fist to one creature's stomach, succeeding only in hurting his own knuckles, as thick clothing absorbed most of the impact of his blow. His teeth worked better, sharp and tearing through the short pelt furring an arm that tried to wrap around Kismet's throat.

Kismet expected the creature's blood to taste the same as his. It should have been the same copper tang he was used to. He'd been struck many times in the face, fallen or bitten the inside of his cheek, even once stupidly licking his mother's shooting track when it pooled on the inside of her elbow, the bittersweet taste of undiluted heroin a sharp contrast to the thick heaviness of her body's life. Blood was a familiar taste, so he wasn't prepared for the acrid sour orange flavor spurting from the creature's open wound, a choking rush that burned the back of his throat. Spitting out the foul mouthful, Kismet backpedaled quickly when the arm pulled away, and he stepped over Mal's outstretched leg. His skin was slick with sweat, the bookstore's logo clinging to his back as his borrowed T-shirt soaked up his nervousness.

"Faith!" Mal spotted the blond woman, shock closing over his stomach. Suddenly the arrival of the darkfae was a much more sinister taint. They'd been delivered by another immortal, someone the Horsemen should be able to trust. The violation of their home had been brought on by one of their own, his thoughts shoving aside the danger of the darkfae in front of him. "Shit, Charity! What the hell?"

"Mal, I can't get the damned door open!" Kismet had reached the front door, fighting with the knob.

The latch had closed tight behind them, locking the world out. His hands were shaking too hard, his addiction beginning to leech energy from his body.

"Fuck, not now." Kismet pleaded with his trembling body. The spiders of his addiction were stirring beneath his skin, lengthening their barbed legs into the soft meat of his arms. Taking a deep breath, he grabbed the latch and shoved hard against the thick door with his shoulder. "Just for once, hold off."

Kismet winced when a fist crashed into Mal's temple, the Horseman failing to see the attack in time to duck. His glasses were askew on his face, skittering down his cheekbone. With their denser bodies, the darkfae had a distinct advantage over the Horseman. Mal instinctively kicked out, striking the creature's knee. The weak joint cracked, bending back with ease. Pain crawled across the creature's face, his body in agony as the shattered bones popped out of the back of his leg.

"Keep the door closed! Don't let him get inside!" Charity shouted to the darkfae. He was trying to edge through the massive bodies to reach the new immortal. Beckett stood behind him, bending over the duffel he'd brought with them.

A darkfae barreled closer, a large crowbar coming down at Kismet's head. Ducking, the young man tried to roll out of the way, the air pushed from his lungs when the creature kicked at his ribs. The darkfae swung at the door's latch, the iron shearing off the turning mechanism. The darkfae's enormous hand closed over his face, nearly cutting off his air supply.

Biting at the fingers shoved into his mouth, Kismet balked at the taste. Jerking his head around, Kismet yelled for Mal. "They broke the door. We can't get back inside!"

Kismet twisted against the creature's hands and fear turned his blood. The darkfae moved apart, leaving a corridor through their bodies. Caught between the desire to escape and the need to help Mal, he struggled, kicking against his captor's shins.

He was being worked through the corridor, duck-walked past another of the creatures. The hole between them closed, tightening up behind him. Kismet fought harder, making the creature work to keep him contained. Gnawing on the darkfae's skin, he choked when the creature forced his hand farther into Kismet's mouth. His jaw ached, pushed wide apart by the muscled arm. Gagging, he pulled back, his chest spasming with dry heaves.

"Bring him here." The man who'd made eye contact with Kismet earlier approached him, motioning toward the wall. "Keep the other away. Don't try to kill him yet. Charity, help me, please. I need his shirt off."

A metal object glinted in the man's hand, unfamiliar and menacing. Cylindrical and sharp on one end, it resembled a tube of some sort, with a thick-mouthed spigot at its top. He drew closer to Kismet, a thin smile on his face. There was a lust in the man's expression, a simmer bubbling in his cold eyes. It chilled Kismet's guts. The metal tube looked ominous. His fear grew when the blond man came over and dug his hands into Kismet's shirt, ripping it apart to expose his chest.

"Beckett, you're going to have to hurry up with what you're doing. The others will be here soon. I'm sure of it." Balling up his fist, Charity backhanded Kismet across the face, splitting his lip. "What is that thing?"

"It's an oil can punch. I've used it before. It gives a steady flow of blood." The magus lifted the cylinder above Kismet's body. "Hold him still. I need to do this right the first time. We don't have time for seconds with this."

"What the hell are you doing?" Kismet gasped, then screamed in pain. His tortured voice sliced above the sounds of the darkfae crowding against Mal, awakening a deep fear in the immortal's heart. Begging, he cried out, "God, no! Please, stop."

"Don't worry, boy." Beckett positioned his hands. "It's just like when you poke your veins with a needle. Just bigger."

The sharp cylinder end cut into Kismet's chest, pushing the skin into the muscles beneath.

Beckett shoved down harder, reveling in the crunch of bones giving way beneath the hard steel. Blood started to seep from the spigot end, a slow, steady stream that grew as the punch dug deeper into the young man's body.

Kismet strained to get loose from the darkfae's hold. The anguish was incredible, a tightening across his chest, then finally a release when his nerves shorted out. It rose to fill his chest, a scrambling fear. The numb feeling spread up from his torso, crawling over his face. His legs grew heavy, and he slumped over, unconscious and trapped against the wall.

"Kismet!" Mal flailed at the darkfae around him. One cut at his face, a knife edge coming very close to his eyebrow. The blade bent the wire rim of his glasses, a nick appearing in the hard metal. Unable to get around the massive wall of flesh keeping him back, he yelled, hoping to knock some sense into the other immortals. Mal's heart stopped, his mind numbed at the sight of Kismet held against the wall. Blood poured from the device shoved into the human's chest, a slowing fountain of dark, foamy red. Panic hit Mal hard, closing his throat with fear. "Faith, what are you doing? Let him go!"

"I can't, Pestilence." She turned to face Mal, her eyes saddened at the immortal's anguish. "We need to do this. I'm sorry. So sorry."

Beckett's face gleamed with the success of their plan. As the young man's blood poured from the top of the spigot, he cupped his hand, catching a mouthful in his palm. The liquid tingled on his tongue, a sharp, coppery wine that poured down his throat. Something definitely had changed in the young man's body. He could taste it in the blood as he licked his hand clean.

Charity nudged the magus with a not-so-gentle shove. Beckett looked up from his adulation of his work and wiped at the crimson splatters on his mouth.

"Hand me the container from my bag." Beckett nodded with his chin toward the duffel. "We'll need at least three cups' worth. That'll keep him down long enough for us to move it."

Mal heard the human clearly, almost as if the shifting tread of the darkfae fell away. He could feel their hands on him, shoving him back, jostling him away from the prone young man and his assailants, but none of it mattered to the immortal. Nothing except for Kismet's too still body and drained white skin.

Panic battered at his throat, rising to feed his fear. He was the weakest of the Four, useless in a fight, according to Ari and Min. But the young man lying nearly broken apart from another immortal's doing was owed more than that, Mal thought. Kismet had killed for him. He deserved the same in return.

Death taught him, Mal scolded the mewling human remains living in his mind. The quivering needed to stop; it served no purpose. Ari often pounded that into Mal's head, usually while standing over his body after a sound beating in the practice room. Death could reach them, the immortal thought. Their eldest could use the thinnest of shadows. He would be able to get to the foyer somehow.

Mal struck, hard and quick, hoping to gain some advantage by surprise. His foot hit the leg of the creature in front of him, and the darkfae crumbled, landing hard on his hip. Rolling over, the creature howled in pain and clutched at his damaged knee. A sheathed dagger buckled to the creature's shin was the immortal's ultimate target, evening the playing field in Mal's mind.

Taking advantage of the confusion of the downed creature, the Horseman reached for the weapon, then slid it free from its leather sleeve. The hilt felt large in his hand, carved from green bone and made for a wider grip. Mal didn't stop to check the sharpness of its blade, hoping the darkfae took care of his tools of trade.

His world shrunk down until it focused on the creature's crimson iris, the black pupil square and wide as bodies ducked through the foyer's steaming light. Crouched on the floor, Mal readied himself, watching the darkfae's eyes widen to track the Horseman's right hand. The dagger's tip slid easily into the darkfae's right eye, its pulpy orb popping around the thick metal blade. Coming up onto one knee, Mal shoved the weapon down, using his weight for added force. The first layers easily gave beneath the sharp tip, an explosion of clear fluids running pink with blood. A tangle of nerves unraveled quickly as Mal leaned into the hilt, feeling the blade hit the edge of the orbital socket.

His thoughts focused solely on one thing, taking the darkfae to the brink of Death's touch. A soft cracking sound murmured through the steel, reverberating in the dagger's hilt. Crushing the hand guard into the darkfae's skull, Mal barely blinked as the creature's brains spurted over his face, the bilious fluids catching the corner of his open mouth. Pulling the dagger free from the male's torso, he snatched at the slithering soul as it escaped from its fleshy prison. Mal called upon the bond he shared with the others, pushing his will along the edges of the shadowy curtain woven into every aspect of their lives. They existed in a world folded into the space between realities. He would make use of that world and its hold on the Four.

The darkfae were outside of Death's immediate influence, but he'd hoped that the act of dying could somehow be enough. Tilting his head back, the Fourth Horseman mentally screamed across the Veil for the First, calling Death to his side to take the soul hovering just inside of his clenched hand.

Gasping with the effort, Mal slid down across the dying darkfae's body, exhausted and refusing to cry. He would be damned if he went down without a fight. And even more damned if he let Kismet die alongside him.

A word whispered through the darkness, a single plea. Strident. Nearly commanding the eldest to come.

Death.

"Come on, Death," Mal pleaded aloud. With the door no longer an option, it was all he could do to save them. He could only hope it would be enough and in time. "I need you."

CHAPTER SIXTEEN

WHEN DEATH came to the call, Mal felt it down in his guts. The press of the air in his lungs flattened, and the Veil buckled under the ominous weight of the First Horseman arriving for a soul. Even in the thin shadows, Death had enough strength to walk through the Veil, and he arrived, a whisper of power flowing from the eldest's lean form. The foyer's diffused light picked out the scar over Death's serious features, his hard, dark gaze raking over the gather of darkfae standing on his doorstep.

Death's presence touched off a deeply held dread in the creatures clustered in the tight space around the front door. The darkfae cowered as the air went thick with terror. Living in the shadows, they saw its inhabitants for what they truly were, and Death wore the Veil in his bones, a cloak of shadows and sorrow woven from each soul he sent into the beyond, threads stitched too tight by those he lost amid the specters wading back into the ghostly memory of their lives. What the darkfae saw was a nightmare come alive.

Darkfae living below the UnSidhe lands whispered stories about the Horsemen, a brutal Four that had no mercy. Suddenly faced with their own demon, the darkfae stilled. Humans spoke of the terror in seeing the First Horseman skulking at the edges of battle, often stopping to reap the last remaining breath from a stricken soldier's body, but the darkfae knew from personal experience the intimacy of his touch.

The darkfae never forgot stories embedded into their clan memory. Death's grip was felt through the shifting of the darkness, a trembling shiver running hot over any shadow-hidden creature born behind the gray curtain. There were faded Courts still licking their wounds and counting the pieces of their dead from battles they raged against mankind, only to be nearly extinguished from existence when the Horsemen arrived to even the odds. From behind the Veil, the

Horsemen responded swiftly to defend humans the Sidhe wanted out of their lands. The skirmishes never lasted long but left the Fae and the darkfae with a healthy fear of the Four.

Death's dark eyes burned, and his katana shone as it slid free of its wooden sheath. He reached inside of himself for the thread that connected him to Ari, calling for him to come to his side. A moment later, he felt the other man arrive, the Veil shuddering from the Horseman shoving his way into the space, drawn by the resonance of Death on the shadowy trails in the curtain. For Death, Ari was as constant as the sun. He never worried about being alone as long as Ari was alive.

One of the darkfae staggered back, trying to distance himself from the blond lowering his head, War's eyes black with anticipation. Cowardice was spat upon by the lower Courts, but the darkfae were silent as their comrade retreated, the crowd stepping back nearly as one.

"Hello, Death," Mal murmured, wiping the blood from his face. Streaks of red burned along Mal's skin, his glasses clotted with darkfae blood. He'd found them after searching with trembling fingers, the spectacles falling off when he'd killed the creature. With the world now in focus, Mal started to move toward Kismet.

"Faith, get back." Ari quickly glanced around him, assessing the situation. He'd appeared nearly over Kismet's prone body, almost straddling the young man's legs. "How the hell did darkfae get up here, Pest?"

"We brought them to you, War. To help us do this," Charity said, drawing his arm back. He shoved upward, hooking a sharp-edged knife into Ari's side.

The blade speared through the sunburst scar on the immortal's torso, slicing apart his T-shirt. A rib deflected the cut, sending the weapon astray. Charity lost his grip on the hilt as Ari jerked away, shocked at the other immortal's betrayal. Nearly losing one of his blades, Ari bent over, holding his arm to his side. Shoving his shoulder into Charity's chest, he pushed the younger immortal, sending him to the floor.

"Son of a bitch." Ari kicked out, keeping his arm pressed tight against the wound. His foot connected solidly against the other immortal's face, the strike making a sickening crunch when he hit Charity's cheek.

Charity sprawled back, sliding over the slick floor. Faith gasped, reaching for her brother, unable to get ahold of his flailing limbs as he passed her. Beckett grabbed the plastic container he'd filled with Kismet's blood, red splashing over its edge, and snapped a clear blue lid over the lip. Rolling aside, he pulled on Faith's upper arm, yanking her out of Ari's reach. Charity followed, getting to his feet with a quick roll. The darkfae closed in around Faith and Charity, protecting Beckett with raised weapons, long knives forming a wall of menacing points.

Beckett hadn't known what he would see when confronted with Death. He'd not expected a nearly pretty-faced man, lean-bodied and scarred across his nose. Death's calm unsettled him. It seemed as if he were invisible, a speck of dirt floating in the air. War suited his image, broad shouldered and muscled, a distinct rage fueling his powerful movements.

A few feet separated Death and Ari, the area emptied of darkfae and other immortals. Mal scrambled across the tile, his hands slipping out from under him as he got near Kismet. The older Horsemen flanked him, blades ready for the darkfae to attack.

"You okay, Ari?" Death didn't dare glance at his friend's side. Taking his eyes off the creatures in front of them would be dangerous, and dropping his guard would definitely bring on an assault. "Do you need help?"

"Nah, I'm fine, Shi." The knife made a small sucking sound as Ari pulled it from his side. Death moved in, giving Ari some protection as he tucked one of his long daggers under his arm, still within easy reach should any of the darkfae move toward them. The length of the blade made him laugh, a few inches of bent steel. "Gods, he's got to be kidding. I wouldn't even fuck someone if he had something this tiny."

"You're horrible." With Ari's side healing quickly, Death took a moment to look down at Mal, the youngest Horseman's hands hovering around the oil punch sticking out of Kismet's body. "You're going to have to take that out of him, Mal. He can't heal with it in him."

"I can't do it." Staring down at his friend's still form, Mal bit his lip, uncertain and afraid. "Suppose I hurt him more?"

"Cooties, we really don't have time to talk about this." Ari nudged Mal's leg with his foot. "The more he bleeds, the more you're going to have to clean up after we kill these guys. Better start now. Death and I are going to be busy in a few."

They stood staring at one another, quiet and stiff. Tension was high, with the darkfae wavering between their instinctual fear of the Four and the promise of glory to their clan while the immortals glared at one another with varying degrees of anger and disgust. Faith moved in front of them, keeping an eye on Death and Ari in case they moved. For a long moment, Kismet's gasps of pain filled the air, his tortured breathing mingled with piercing groans.

"Take it out, Mal," Death ordered. "Now."

The blood was nearly too much for Mal. It seeped around the metal cone sticking out of Kismet's chest and spurted up the flexible metal spigot bobbing near his face. Kismet's face was white, the blue of his veins vivid under his pale skin. His chest barely moved now, his lungs struggling to provide oxygen to a body shutting down around them. Mal gripped the oil punch, then tugged, hoping to pull it free.

Its edge caught on a bone, and Mal lost his hold on the cone, his wet fingers sliding up its length.

Resting on one knee, he wrapped both of his hands around the cylindrical spout and yanked. He fell back, tumbling onto his rear.

"Put pressure on it, Pest. It's not that bad." Ari bristled when Beckett took a step forward. "Stay back, bitch. You come any closer, and I'm going to rethink what we consider acting against us."

Pressing his hands over the torn flesh, Mal pushed down, hoping the skin would seal over. Strands from the shirt's torn fabric were caught under his palms, and he worried whether or not he should pull them out before the threads were sealed under Kismet's skin.

"Keep the pressure steady." Carefully avoiding the spilled blood, Ari moved until he stood on a patch of unblemished floor. "I'd say pray, but the bastards responsible for all that crap are standing in front of us with our blood on their hands."

"Why'd you bring this to our door, Faith?" Death asked, his calm voice carrying over the darkfae's heavy breathing.

"We just need the boy, Death. Give him to us, and we'll walk away. You don't need to be involved in this." Faith stepped forward.

Stopped by Beckett's hand on her wrist, the immortal comforted the magus with a murmur. "Let me do this. We can end this without any more trouble."

"Your human did this to the boy, then?" Death slanted a look at Kismet, the young man's shivering body pressed up against the wall. Faith's glance at the magus confirmed his suspicions. "He has to be the one who crossed the boy over. Any immortal smart enough to do it wouldn't have."

"So we kill the human first?" Ari grinned, a lupine smile that pushed the darkfae back another step. "Save Charity and his bitch sister for later?"

"You can't kill a human," Faith reminded them. "Not unless he raises a hand to you. He changed a *human* with his potions. Not an immortal. You cannot touch Beckett, Death. Not for *anything*."

"Nice of him to bring someone who knows the rules," Ari muttered under his breath to Death. "Fucking whores betrayed us, Shi."

"We didn't do anything to you that you couldn't have avoided, War," Charity slurred, working his jaw back into place. Ari's hit broke his cheekbone, shifting the bone in and shattering his orbit. The swell against his eye bothered him, his vision blurry and unpredictable. It would take a few hours before he'd be able to see clearly. "All you needed to do was mind your own business for a change."

"Do you have any idea what he's done, Faith? This threatens us. Threatens our existence," Death said. "You weren't around for the days when we lived in blood, fighting off wraiths coming through a broken Veil. Doing this, helping this man bring that about, will take mankind back centuries. They'll lose everything they've accomplished, and for what?"

"Maybe it's what mankind needs right now, Death," she responded, conscious of the shifting darkfae around her and the men standing next to her. They were getting impatient and, in the presence of the Horsemen, were quickly losing their nerve.

"You're supposed to be helping them, whore." Ari paced out a step before returning to Death's side. "Trust me. They don't need wraiths chewing on their asses."

"What would you care?" Charity sneered. "You only exist to torment mankind. You'll be in your glory if what Death says is true.

And if not, then it's just more of the Four manipulating things to keep the rest of us in line."

"Kick his teeth in for me, Ari," Mal growled. Kismet's blood was cooling on his hands, and his fingers were going numb. The young man's skin was slowly knitting, not quick enough for Mal's liking, but it was moving together. The feel of the tear undulating to join back together made his stomach twist, and he looked away, glaring up at the immortals behind their wall of darkfae. "He talks too much."

"I agree with the brat, Death." Ari winked at his partner, his confident arrogance filling his face. Canting his shoulder down, War affectionately bumped Death's hip. "Too much talking. Not enough killing."

"Keep your head down and protect Kismet. See if you can keep him behind you, Mal," Death said, his voice low. "If not, then at least keep him down."

The fight exploded before Mal blinked. One moment the air bristled with violence, and then it spilled over them, a wave of bodies and grunting shouts.

Hot liquid splashed from the severing blow of Death's katana across the attacking Veiled's forearm, a wave of foul acidic blood cresting into his open mouth. War's shirt was already nearly black with blood, his hands sticky with offal and shreds of intestines, a malevolent grin breaking through the gore across his mouth. Death's mouth slid into a half smile at the look of childish glee on his oldest friend's face.

A motion caught Death's attention, pulling him back into the fray, the katana arcing bright with a trail of silver threading through a darkfae's throat. They would have to provide protection for the boy until Mal could remove him from the foyer. After that, he and War could move into the middle of the fight, depending on their youngest to take care of their charge.

Sputtering, Kismet coughed, hidden by the relative safety of Mal's body, trying to clear the taste of his own blood from his tongue. Kismet's trembling limbs seized under his body's demands, his nervous system contracting him into a fetal ball. Panting hard, Kismet opened his eyes and bolted nearly upright. Mal pushed him back down, keeping him clear of the fight.

"Shit," Kismet gasped, a shuddering roll starting in his blood. "I need a hit."

Ari growled, "Think it was mingled in with drugs?"

"Easiest way to get it into him," Death agreed, blocking a blade coming at his ribs. The darkfae were coming slower, more wary now that blood had been spilled. After a few jabs, the creatures pulled back, trying to circle in and test the Horsemen's abilities. "Mal, try to keep Kismet calm."

"That's going to be a bit hard," Mal sighed. Kismet was fighting him as he regained consciousness in spurts, his body painfully knitting together. "I can't keep myself calm."

"Do your best, Mal," Death replied.

"Just knock him over the head," Ari suggested with a sneer. "Hell, do us all a favor and knock yourself out too."

"Watch your side, War." Death nudged his friend. "They're coming back in."

Rising from his knees, Mal ducked around War's upswing, trying to keep out of the older Horseman's way. He felt the Veil ripple again, a call flowing from Death along the shadows straining to close in on the foyer. Death was reaching out for the other in their Four. A resonance built up in the darkness, spilling out with an echoing need. Min would be certain to feel the call, Mal was sure of it. If he hadn't already been there, he knew he would have been pulled to the fight.

"Beckett!" Faith's head jerked up, her eyes wild as she clutched at Beckett's arm.

The magus turned, his mouth wide as he watched the walls convulse, disgorging the petite Min, armed with a long blade and a fierce temper.

"Famine's here! We won't be able to fight off all of them. We should leave now!"

Swinging wildly, Min fought viciously, dropping down under the taller creatures' arms, stabbing up into their rib cages. The meat and bone in the darkfae's torso halted some of her thrusts, but as she found her rhythm, Min angled her attack better, feeling for the ripe softness of an organ giving way. She stopped short, in shock, at the sight of Faith and Charity standing by the attacking force.

"Faith! Charity!" Min moved quickly, trying to slash her way to the immortals. "I'll get to you!"

"Don't go in, Min," Death warned her. The steel in the eldest's voice pinned Min to the ground.

"They brought the darkfae...."

"What?" The woman dove to the side, bending her torso back to avoid a blow. "Why?"

"Why later," Ari argued back. "Kill now. Whys and hows are for later."

"Damn it, he's trying to get the door open." Beckett spotted Mal working at the door latch, the heavy body of a fallen darkfae blocking his way. "We shouldn't have let go of the boy."

"I'll see if I can get to him. Mal's not a threat," Charity said. "Keep Faith safe."

"We'll never reach him." Faith gasped when Beckett grabbed her arm, yanking the immortal around. "There's no way to him! Charity, just leave him."

"There's no way we'll ever get this chance again." Beckett drew a short-barrel gun from the holster at his waist. "Let's even the odds."

Aiming for Death, the magus lifted the muzzle of the gun and pulled the trigger. The gunshot boomed, rebounding and bouncing back in waves of sound through the crowded foyer.

Min's heart raced, then stopped dead, her eyes finding the dark-haired Horseman at the head of the darkfae pack. Ari jerked around, his mouth peeled back into a growl, viciously stabbing at the creature closest to him to clear the way to his friend.

Death stood firm, pulling the scant Veil tight around him. The shock of a projectile weapon passed through him. He was taking a chance, gambling on the age of his body and how long he'd been immersed in the shadows. The bullet shimmered through his flesh, then flew into the wood behind him. A sunburst of gunpowder bloomed on his shirt, minute fragments caught around the hole punctured by the bullet.

"You said this would work!" Beckett brandished the gun under Charity's nose, the heat from the muzzle leaving a blister near his lip. "Why the hell didn't it work?"

"Maybe he's too old," Faith shouted, panic filling her heart. "He has too much of the Veil in him. That's got to be it."

"Damn it." Charity gritted his teeth. He needed to draw the Horsemen away from the boy. The darkfae were going to be slaughtered, and more importantly, they would lose any chance of securing the human from the Horsemen. He spotted Mal trying to work the door open, the younger immortal nearly sprawling over a fallen body.

Mal dug his fingers into the broken metal pieces of the door latch. He wished he had more curses in his arsenal, swearing ineffectually when a screw tore at his finger. The darkfae's blows had made a tangled mess of the mechanism, and he strained to work the whole plate loose.

"Trust them to protect your back, Mal," he muttered to himself. "The Four will never let you down."

A few more fumblings of the latch, and the whole piece tumbled to the floor, a clattering sound that sang sweet music in Mal's ears. Hooking his fingers into the empty space, Mal pulled hard on the door, astonished when it refused to open more than an inch. Yanking harder, he felt a softness give under his struggles, then looked down at his feet, the heavy, broad body of a darkfae keeping the door shut.

"Shit." Mal crouched, shoving at the corpse. "Didn't I move you enough?"

"If Death's too old, then one of the others. One of the younger ones." Beckett tried to get a good sighting on Min, but the slender woman was nearly lost behind the darkfae's thick bodies. Pestilence would have to be his target, hoping Death and War would be drawn off by seeing their youngest's brains splattered on the wall.

Shouting for the others to give him a clear shot, Beckett strained to get a good angle on the youngest Horseman. Mal ducked down under the fight, working to remove the darkfae blocking the door. War moved to the right, swearing loudly at the slipperiness underfoot. The foyer's slick floor wasn't the best for a fight, something he would mention to Death once they were done.

Kismet jerked when Mal touched him, his chest heaving with the strain keeping his body under control. Something strange crawled in his blood, licking at his nerves until they ran raw and hot. Craning to get around the Horsemen's influence, he could see wraithlings drifting along the walls, an inky tide dashing up against the darkfae's backs. Shivering, Kismet turned over, trying to squeeze the cold out of his bones, his limbs nearly frozen and locked.

"I can get up," Kismet reassured Mal, unsteadily trying to get to his knees. "It's healed up enough. I'm okay."

"No, you're not okay. Stay down," Mal begged. "Please, Kiz, just stay down."

"Can you get the door open?" War shouted at the youngest, kicking at Mal's thigh with a bloodied foot. "See if you can get the kid inside!"

"I got the lock part out," Mal yelled back, panic rising in his chest. "There's a dead body in the way."

Kismet was shutting down beside him, the young man closing up against the addiction tearing his body apart. The denser mass of the dead darkfae were difficult to move, stumps slimy from leaking wounds. Mal heaved the last meaty piece he could manage, then grabbed at Kismet's waist, hoisting the human to his feet. Grabbing at the edge of the door, Mal pulled at the handle, swinging the portal open just enough to slide through.

Beckett took aim and shot, grim and determined to hit at least one of the Horsemen. The spout of blood splattering War's face sent a wicked grin over the magus's face, the man thinking he'd hit the blond.

Turning, Ari shouted something Beckett couldn't hear over the rush of the dying screams of the darkfae. His victory turned to horror when Faith grabbed at his arm, the immortal's horrified words a piercing scream in his ear.

"You shot the boy!" Faith clutched the stained folds of her dress. "You've killed him!"

Kismet screamed when the bullet struck him, intense pain dancing black stars over his eyes.

Struggling to stay alert, he stumbled and caught at Mal's arm, sobbing from the torment working into his flesh. His muscles shook with a rolling spasm, unable to respond to the simple command to move forward, the dubious safety of the partially open door nearly in reach. Kismet's knee struck the wooden floor as he fell, his kneecap cracking hard under his weight.

Min hacked at a nearby head, splitting open the creature's temple with a sharp blow. As the darkfae stumbled, she planted her foot in the center of his shoulder blades and vaulted to get closer to the other Horsemen. Spotting the woman, Death slid around to War's right, covering Ari's side as the blond ducked to avoid a blow. With no slack in his stride, Death grabbed one of Ari's shorter blades, then jabbed upward into the underside of a darkfae's jaw, cracking open the creature's chin.

"Kismet!" Mal held the young man's body up from the floor, not wanting the ocean of darkfae blood to enter the wound. Mal felt War at his side, the older Horseman's steady hand on the youngest's shoulder. "Ari, I can't tell how badly he's hurt."

The fabric of Kismet's torn shirt was too sodden to absorb any more blood. His wound dripped, a trickling flow forming near the still healing gash on his chest. The edges of the gunshot were frayed from the bullet's impact. Coughing, Kismet gasped, unable to process the pain in his side. Clearing the gore with spit and his fingers, Mal found the wound along the boy's upper rib cage, now barely seeping. The hole had already begun closing, the bruised skin around the entrance wound a violent purple.

"God, this fucking hurts," Kismet gasped, his breath shortened with the effort to pull air into his lungs. His addiction ran under the breadth of the pain, hidden below his screaming nerves. An icy cold spread over his chest, his ribs aching with each slight shift he made in an effort to ease his anguish. "Shit."

"That kid is cursed," War muttered to Death. "Just so you know."

Min's opponent feinted in, trying to draw the woman out with a rounded fist. Min dodged the blow, bending almost in half as Death's blade sliced across the creature's face. Nearly losing her balance, Min backpedaled, easing onto her heels to recover. Slamming his elbow up into the Veiled's soft throat, Death pushed the creature back to give Min room to fight. The other remaining darkfae pressed in, their flat-faced leader berating them.

"Charity's yours, War," Death replied. "Faith's mine."

"Death, what do I do?" Mal called out.

"Cut it out of him, Mal." Death kicked over one of the darkfae's dropped knives. "Use this. Don't nick his heart."

Ari grumbled under his breath, barely loud enough for Mal to hear, "Try to keep him alive long enough for me to kill him. He's the reason for all of this mess."

"I can't believe you got shot." Mal crouched over Kismet, wondering if he could keep his hands steady enough to carve into the young man. "Damn them. I can't believe they shot you."

"You have to stop!" Faith grabbed at Beckett's hand, pulling at the gun. "We can't do this. They'll kill you."

Min jerked at the sound of another gunshot ringing out, nearly losing her grip on her weapon. The incident at the motel had rattled her more than she cared to admit, the heat of Mal's blood on her hands still a thing of her nightmares. A small pain in her side panicked Min until she realized it was a slice of a blade over her skin, the cutting wound soothing despite the stinging of her severed nerves. Looking around, she scanned her own people before looking toward Faith, the speckle of gunpowder mottling her breast.

Faith stared down at the blood on her chest, her fingers finding the edges of the hole in her body.

Strangely, the wound didn't hurt as much as she thought it would. Rather, it spiraled out into tentacles, sucking and releasing sharp pangs along her limbs. The world became taller all of a sudden, her mind slow to realize that she'd fallen to her knees. It was then that the pain began, screaming wretches clawing into the back of her skull. Her heart strained, trying to fill the vacuum left by the blood pouring from the breach in her chest.

With the agony of her body being violated by a small piece of metal, Faith surrendered to the terror in her heart, allowing it to take her. She fell, and her lungs exhaled hard from the impact. The floor felt so hard beneath her, her fingers digging to gain some grip on the slick surface. Faith's breath came in little pants, panic cold in her lungs. With the Veil pushed thin into the building's perimeter, the immortal strained to reach the tiniest shred of shadow.

"Faith!" Charity caught at the woman, supporting the back of her head. Numb, the magus stood, holding the gun in his limp fingers. "What the hell did you do?"

"I don't know." Beckett fell forward, casting the weapon to the ground. "She grabbed at the gun. It just went off."

"We need to get you out of here." Gripping Faith's waist, he lifted her up, straining to find a thick enough shadow to push her through. "If we can get you to Peace, he can help. See if you can find a call, anything to help you."

Faith heard only an echoing nothingness in the shadows that tasted of the Horsemen. The Veil retreated around her, a wasteland of ghosts. She tried to reach at least the youngest of their Three. Hope was the easiest immortal to call, an ethereal hold on the Veil, but she couldn't feel even the faintest whisper of the little girl.

In pain, Faith choked on the bitterness in her throat. She felt her lover's hand on her face, the same hand that shot her. Charity's desperate voice sounded like a distant echo, drowned out by the anger she could feel rolling through the darkness from Death. War shouted at Mal to help the boy, a buzzing echo fading into a soft hum. The Second Horseman would sooner help a human than another immortal, Faith realized, the burring noise of voices now a rushing ocean of sound.

"Charity, I'm so sorry. Take care of Michael for me. Please," the woman cried, her eyes weeping hot fire. Faith let herself slide away, ashamed she'd strayed so far from why she'd manifested. Whispering a final apology to her absent lover, the woman released her will and wished herself gone.

The last face Faith saw before returning to the Veil was Beckett's, his expression fixed with shock. Without the phantom world between them, the magus watched the woman who lured him into love disappear from his arms, leaving nothing behind but the searing anger in his heart.

IN A house on a grassy hill, Hope lifted her head from her play, petite hands stilling over the long blonde hair of her doll. Peace watched the smallest of the immortals, the eternal child, tilt her head and close her eyes, sunbursts of blue hidden behind a pale wash of café au lait skin. Sitting on a long stretch of mahogany carpet, Hope checked the attendees to her tea party, a collection of dolls and plush animals arranged in a semicircle near the sweep of windows overlooking a lake.

Solemn and near the end of her term as Hope, the little girl pondered speaking for a moment, her words lost in the tumbling shadows whispering through the Veil. The murmuring increased, a gossiping sibilance weaving across the miles. A flicker of thought crossed her mind, a still statue of quiet amid the rush of sound carved from far-off screams.

Hope's lashes flitting open, she found the tiny pink plastic brush she'd set down and began brushing another length of doll hair, her fingers wrapped around golden strands. The Veil shook again, a shuddering tremor attuned to the Three Gifts. Hope caught the edge of it on her thoughts, the stilled scream of a woman's voice tinting the dark curtain's flutter.

Hope turned her face toward the man who once made their Three a Four, staring with all-seeing eyes at Peace's shock, his nerveless fingers gripping the edge of the kitchen counter. A teapot whistled shrill for his attention, the steam rising in an angry column toward the high ceiling.

"Oh, Faith." Peace's anguish broke into his voice, shattering his heart. "What are you and Charity doing?"

"I hope this next Faith likes kids, Penelope." Hope undid the buckle of one shoe, then slid it onto her doll's unwieldy foot. "It would be nice if there was someone who would play with us."

Debating if she should retire to her room, Hope decided the fog-drenched lake would make a better backdrop for her gathering, a spray of roses just under the windowsill lending an English tea touch to the festivities.

Besides, the immortal thought to herself, she would want to be presentable when their new Faith arrived. Charity would be in no right mind to deal with anyone, and someone would have to be strong.

Gathering up the Veil in her mind, Hope pinched off the trembling call from Faith, slicing the woman off from the Three and banishing her to the shadows that fed off the weak.

"There," Hope said to herself. "That's better. It'll be better now, Penelope."

Penelope's second shoe took longer to wrestle on, Hope's small fingers struggling with the minute buckle. Sighing hard, she bent to the task, working the leather over the doll's foot. Satisfied, she gave one last pull on the doll's filmy socks before returning her to her place at the gathering. The tea would have to be brewed from air, Hope decided, the sounds of Peace's sorrow continuing behind her. No matter, the little girl shrugged as she poured a ghostly chai into a dainty porcelain cup. The view was more than enough to make up for the lack of tea, and the dolls certainly weren't going to complain.

CHAPTER SEVENTEEN

BECKETT FELL to his knees, eyes wet with pain. He raged and wept, his heart speeding with intense agony. Charity's hands were on his shoulders, the immortal's fingers clenching hard enough to bruise down to the bone. He couldn't see past the tears, but he could hear the whispers for revenge in the back of his mind.

"They need to die."

Charity nodded at Beckett's words, his face wrinkled into an anguished mask. "You can do that," the immortal reminded him. "Call something. There's enough of what you need inside of me. Pull it out. Make them hurt, Beckett. Let them watch each other die."

Gathering the power Beckett kept simmering in the well of his soul, he lashed out, pulling at the tiny shadowed edges around him. Enough of the Veil pulsed in the darkness, giving the man a channel outward to where inky wraiths thrived. Hitting a thread leading out of the penthouse exterior, Beckett poured his energy outward, his ire and pain at Faith's loss hot with fierce emotion.

Mal eased Kismet over, his hands gentle on the boy's shoulders. The young man's face gleamed ivory, the blood bleached out of his skin. Kismet grabbed at Mal's hands with cold fingers, holding the Horseman's arms tight across his upper chest. Bending his head down, Mal rubbed his cheek against the human's, hoping to warm the chill in Kismet's flesh.

"Kiz, you've got to stay still," Mal pleaded. Kismet blinked, hoping to hold on to his consciousness just long enough to curse at Mal for jostling him. "You're making me more nervous."

"What are you doing?" Gasping, Kismet hissed. Harsh pains jabbed his stomach, the muscles battling convulsive waves. Fighting Mal's hold, he turned before nearly blacking out from the agony of his body ratcheting and failing. "God, fuck. That hurts more."

"Just do it, Mal." Death ducked behind Ari, trying to keep his attention on the fight while glancing at the bleeding human. The paleness of Kismet's face didn't bode well. Mal's palpable fear did little to help the situation. "His body isn't strong enough to push the bullet out."

"Please, trust me," Mal said, his voice soft in Kismet's ear. The scent of his own shampoo blended with the erotic sweet musk he'd come to identify with the feral human he'd taken in. "I'm not trying to hurt you, not on purpose. But I think Death's right. That's got to come out of you before it kills you."

"Trust you to carve me apart?" Kismet closed his eyes tight, swallowing at the thick spit on his tongue. "Shit."

"Yeah," Mal admitted. "But it's either me, or you wait for Ari."

"Screw that." Kismet laughed, a sharp pang in his chest. "Hell, use a chopstick if you have to."

Behind them, Mal heard Death telling Min to move in closer, tightening up the space between them. Fingers shaking, Mal cut into the human's tender skin. Kismet hissed, loosing a torrent of swear words, the profanity mingled on the blood of his bitten tongue. Gritting his teeth, Mal dug the blade in deeper to widen the opening.

Kismet's belly clenched, hot bile rushing to his throat. Mal turned the young man's face, hoping the rush of warm fluids would pass freely onto the floor. He couldn't risk him choking. The tremors would drive the bullet in deeper, making it impossible for Mal to reach without slicing Kismet nearly apart.

"I'm sorry, Kiz." Mal winced when he hit one of the boy's ribs with the blade. Kismet gurgled and arched before going slack in Mal's embrace. "Kismet!"

The boy's chest rose and fell, unsteady but constant. Sighing with relief that Kismet had merely passed out, Mal continued to explore the wound, trying to find something metal in the soft tissues. Gritting his teeth, Mal cursed as the blade slid around the opened wound. "I can't tell what's bone or metal."

"Reach in and feel around," Ari shouted behind him. "Bone is grittier than metal."

"Right. Sure, I should know that, because I do this all the time." Bracing himself, Mal whispered into the young man's ear. "I'm sorry. This is going to hurt."

Mal placed the knife within easy reach on Kismet's stomach, took a deep breath, and tore into the young man's wound with his fingers, scissoring the hole apart with brute force. More blood poured over Kismet's side, soaking through the shirt fabric and into the thick denim of his jeans. Mal dug through Kismet's side, his eyes closed as he worked around the spokes of bone until he found a metal pellet barely round enough to be held on a fingertip.

"Got it." Mal twisted the tiny bullet between his fingers and yanked it free. Pulling the slender man into his arms, Mal cradled Kismet against his chest, willing the tear in Kismet's side to heal. "Stay with me here. Don't let go."

Death cut upward, his shoulders tiring under the strain of slicing through the denser mass of a darkfae's body. Min's strength was lagging, her shoulder dropping as she fought. He stepped in to block a knife blade aimed into her chest. Smiling her thanks, Min shook her arms, trying to get the feeling back in her tingling muscles.

Behind him, Kismet gasped and choked, Mal's murmuring encouragements a soft, calming brush of sound over the boy's pain. The air beside Death shifted, growing warm and sensual. Ari reappeared to balance his calm. The bump of a shoulder against his felt as erotic as stolen kisses they'd taken from one another over the centuries. He turned, grabbing the merest of glimpses at the blond Horseman at his side, and caught Ari's wink, disarming Death's wariness with a cocky grin. Shoving Min aside, Ari stabbed outward, working his blade past the last darkfae's defenses.

"Go sit down, Min." Death nodded, tipping his head back to avoid getting a wash of blood in his face. "We'll take care of whatever they're planning."

Min thankfully collapsed onto the ground beside Mal and Kismet. Her body ached, and she worked to slow her breathing, catching huge gasps of air into her chest. She rubbed at the hot burn crawling in her arms, her legs shaking. Min's face ran brown with clotted blood, cuts across her jaw and temple drying under the hot lights of the lobby, and her side ached where a blade got past her defenses, the skin knitting together through the weave of her shirt fabric. She'd have to cut it out later or get Ari to yank the cloth out of her stomach.

"How's he doing?" Min reached over to grab at Mal's leg, using the Horseman's heavier weight to pull her across the slick floor.

Mal swallowed, fear closing his throat. Patting at the youngest's chest, Min shook her head and mumbled, resting her head on the fluffy doormat Mal had purchased for their home, an object of derision at the time but now a soft comfort to her aching head. "He'll be fine, Mal. Just give him some time to heal. Hell, he took on a wraith. He can survive one bullet. Even you survived that, and you suck."

THIS WHOLE mess started with a book, Beckett thought. A woman and a book.

Before he'd found Faith staring back at him from the shadows, he'd nearly given up ever truly understanding the world behind the curtain placed over his own. The Veil was a magician's trick, the ultimate smoke and mirrors of illusion and sleight of hand. She'd shown him the truth of her world. Now the woman who held his heart and hand as she led him through the final corridors of comprehension was gone, a wisp of nothingness caught on his breath.

It was a small, unassuming book, but it held so much. The words nearly glowed off the page, written in a gold-tinted ink beside spidery black print scrawled over thin sheets of pulp paper. Faith told him the text had been dismissed as the ramblings of a madman, but Beckett found the words fascinating.

She was gone, leaving the book she'd given him behind. The pages would be a small comfort to him. Faith's betrayal laid ashes on his tongue and heart. His heart ached, refusing to give up his love for the immortal.

Wild with grief, the magus ran his hands deep into the pools of blood on the floor, smearing the drying liquid around him. Carving waves of circles with his trembling fingers, Beckett reached inside of himself, tapping into the electrical spark of his power. Already on the brink of madness, his grief pushed him further into the abyss, tapping the unending well of dark every human possessed. The shadows shivering against the corners of the foyer trembled with the forceful emotions crawling out of Beckett's soul. Steeped in the Horsemen's essence, they swarmed, called to the magus's summoning.

"You are going to die." Beckett raised his bloodied hands.

Tilting his head back, the magus gathered the threads of the summoning spell, drawing the shadows together into a single entity. The darkness shuddered, a hushed murmuring as the animalistic wraiths were forced together, a hive mind growing under the magus's purposeful intent.

Charity knew the feel of the Veil. Intimate with the shadows' movements, he felt the stirrings of the magus's summons pull at his body. Giving in to the human's power, Charity let his grief bolster him. A slow agony crawled along his marrow, his bones twisting under Beckett's magic.

"Hurry, Beckett," Charity urged him. "The darkfae are either dead or run off. Death and War will be coming for us."

"They'll never reach us." Concentrating, Beckett scraped at the darkness, trying to build the shadows around him. Charity's strength fueled his efforts. The immortal's skin dripped black, drops of inky blood striking the floor. The liquid shimmered, vibrating, then slithered, flattening out into a film over the floor. "Go wait by the elevator, Charity. We'll need a quick escape once the summoning is done."

"I am still here." A darkfae stepped out from the shadows, closing the stairwell door behind him. His armor shone dully as he stepped into the light, worn and ancient ill-fitting pieces dented from past battles, but his sword threw off a wicked gleam, its sharpened edge glinting dangerously. A silver ring swung from the tip of his ear, swaying back and forth with each step he took toward the Horsemen. "I will be the one to take home a Horseman's head for my clan's hall. The dead shall weep in their hell when I send the Four's souls to their side, and they will mourn leaving me behind to guard their sorry backsides when I could have been the one to take them to glory."

Driven by bloodlust, the last darkfae roared in defiance at War. Bringing his head down, the male charged, leading with the long tusks jutting out from the corners of his flat mouth. Ari waited for him, drawing him back with a side step, careful not to leave an opening for the creature to slip through. The younger Horsemen and the human lay nearly unmoving a few feet beyond, Min worn down to the bone.

He wouldn't risk them. As far as he was concerned, the creature wouldn't make it a footstep past him. As the darkfae brought his blade around, Ari grinned at the feel of meat giving way under his plunging strike, gleeful with the bliss he felt in the hot gush of fluids spurting over his forearm. In the thick of a fight, he reveled in the carnage, drops of blood burning his eyesight. He felt alive with Death beside him and death around him.

Aiming deep into the darkfae's body, Death twisted the blade up into the creature's chest. The edge nicked a rib, splintering the bone into the lung sac below. A gurgling froth pinked over his opponent's mouth, foaming around his tusk roots. Gasping, the darkfae struggled to pull air into his chest when Death pulled the blade back and stabbed again. The tip of the weapon found the soft meat of the creature's heart, buried deep in its broad chest. Death's bicep ached with the effort of shoving through the heavy muscle, the close-in work leeching his stamina. Repeatedly, the immortal worked the same opening, obscenely splaying the wound apart with a detached viciousness.

Ari winked at his oldest friend and sliced deep into the darkfae's side, severing his spine. Licking at the drops around his mouth, his soul hummed, rolling in the dusting of Veil settling over them. Imbued with his calling, the minor wraiths fed heartily on the fallen at the Horsemen's feet, anticipating the other creature to join in the littering of corpses on the foyer floor.

Leaning his head back, Ari spread his arms out wide, letting the shower of fluids wash over his face and chest. Clenching the blade in his fist, he opened his hand, splaying his fingers apart to catch the final dash of drops on his palm. Mouth slightly parted, he filled his lungs with the scent of sweat and blood, letting the perfume pour into his being. A final thrust, and the darkfae lay still, a crumbled pile of meat at Ari's heels.

"Gods, that was fun!" Ari turned to look at Death, his face nearly masked with drying and fresh blood. Long shanks of blond hair matted dark on the man's jaw, clinging to the strong column of his neck. Shaking the loose drops free, he splattered Death's face.

"War," Death reproached, running his thumb over his lips, trying to clean his mouth off.

Reaching out, Ari wiped at Death's face with the back of his hand, a quirky smile on his face. "There. You're all pretty again."

"Guys, when you two are done congratulating yourselves." Min propped herself up on her elbows, her breath still coming in short pants. Jerking her head toward the magus, the woman pointed to the clustered shadows feeding on the darkfae remains around Beckett's bent body. "I think we've got another problem."

"What's going on?" Mal strained to see around the Horsemen's legs. The rise and fall of Kismet's chest evened out, a reassuring slow intake of air. His face flushed with color, the artist murmured with discomfort when Mal slid his hands under Kismet's armpits. With Beckett drawing on the thin curtain of the Veil, Kismet was left naked and raw, vulnerable to the intrusive, ravenous wraiths attracted by the intense fighting.

"Hey." Kismet stirred in the crook of Mal's arm. The pain stole his breath, razored pangs jabbing through his chest and ribs. His voice husky and groggy, the artist attempted a smile, his eyes sharp with agony. Driven back from blood loss, the craving for drugs crawled on broken knees through his body. Kismet swallowed, rasping carefully around the dryness on his tongue. "Did you guys win?"

"Shit, we should move them if you're thinking about keeping them alive, Shi," Ari grumbled.

"We haven't won yet, Kismet," Death said. "It would be better if they stayed where they are, Ari. We can't defend multiple locations. The wraith will be able to get through the walls to get to them."

"Defend against what?" Mal heard the human in the foyer mumbling, long strings of disconnected words blended harsh with guttural pleadings. "What is he doing?"

"He's calling a wraith or something, Pest," Ari said. Shifting his grip around the hilt of his dagger, he shook the blood from his arm. "Like he hasn't caused enough trouble."

The Veil convulsed around the magus, jerking the last wave of burgeoning wraiths into the growing bundle of darkness welling up near his clenched hands. The darkfae's blood dried pitch on his palms, cracking as he made fists to slam into the floor. Pouring the last of his rage into his creation, Beckett summoned the creature from the darkness, its mind focused on a single thought—killing everyone in its sight.

"Didn't we just have a wraith thing?" Kismet asked. His head pounded in an unsteady rhythm, an insistent knocking on the inside of his skull. His skin itched where Mal's fingers had probed at the bullet, the entrance stretched wide by the Horseman's invasion. Nothing remained of the hole, his body healing over the wound. "How many of these things can he make?"

"As many as he wants." Death pursed his mouth. "There's enough blood and Veiled flesh here for him to call something big."

"Okay." Kismet coughed, a clot throwing inside of his lung. He choked on the obstruction, spitting his airway clear. Swallowing the metallic taste, Kismet rubbed the flat of his tongue against his teeth. "A wraith like the one that chewed on me? And we're going to sit here and let him kill us?"

"We're immortals, Kismet, not human. We have to obey different rules." Death's face was a sheet of poured ice, slashed dark with his grimly set mouth and narrowed eyes. "We can't move against any human unless we're attacked directly. Summoning isn't a direct attack. We can't touch him."

Beckett no longer saw the Horsemen or the carnage around him, his focus tight on the growing mass of shadows writhing to take form. The sheet of water behind the magus splashed free of its stone basin, a fallen darkfae's arm partially blocking the drain. Tinted red with blood, the liquid wove into slow-moving rivulets, working around the mountains of shorn flesh in its path. Ari shifted his feet, testing the slickness of the polished wood floor.

"Hold on to this, Mal. You've probably dulled your knife on your human, and it's got a better reach." Min put a long blade into Mal's hand, stolen from under a darkfae's torn apart body. "Use it to protect yourself, just in case."

Mal nodded mutely, the large weapon an unfamiliar heft in his palm. The wider hilt was difficult to encompass in his hand, forged for the dead darkfae draining onto the foyer floor. Long strings of shadows poured from the cool stairwell, drawn by Beckett's call. The promise of a feeding lured miniscule wraiths from their protective swarms, the magus's pain cast as bait into the still air.

Out in the middle of the floor, Beckett squatted alone, his clothes slowly soaking up fluids. Power poured into the dragged circle around him, pulling every tendril of darkness infused with an inkling of will into the forming creature before him. The magus's eyes rolled into the back of his head, the whites nearly red with bloodshot veins.

Charity stepped back from the human, giving him room to work his magics. His eyes burned with tears, and the emptiness in his heart slowly filled with revenge. No matter what happened, he would make the Four pay for Faith's death. If he tore apart the young man that caused the chaos around them, even better.

Kismet's stomach twisted with fear, long barbs stabbing intestines. He was tired, beyond tired if he was to believe his worn-smooth brain. He felt the enormity of the past few days strike him. The effort to stay sane amid the shadows grabbing at his every thought wore down the threadbare blanket of sanity he'd gathered up to warm himself. Sitting amid the carved-up bodies and the dying, Kismet shook with the press of his blood's need for drugs, his eyes downcast and unseeing.

This man crawling through the blood had made his nightmares whole. Everything that fed on the sides of his head while he slept now had teeth. Beckett had to have doctored the heroin he'd been getting from Nick. It was the only way he'd have gotten it into his body. The drugs were to keep away the creatures lurking just out of the corner of his eye. Now his vision was full of them, and they were looking right back at him.

The rims of Kismet's eyes smarted with the sting of tears. He'd wanted to hate the magus or tear him apart to make him feel the overwhelming fear that clouded his mind. The finality of slitting someone's life from their body lodged a glacier in Kismet's soul, but he couldn't find the energy to scrape together to care.

Kismet looked up at the waiting Horsemen, a motley range of emotions on their faces. Death stood, a pillar of snow and soot, starkly silent in his patience. Ari shifted back and forth, readying for the thing the magus would spring on them. The blond man's rawboned face and set mouth kissed the edge of amusement, fed fully on the fight. Min merely seemed weary and resigned, her lithe, petite form struggling to remain standing.

Pestilence. Mal, he would forever be Mal in Kismet's mind. Mal wore his passions on his face, wet blue eyes gleaming in a silent plea for the young man to stay at his side. The look wasn't unfamiliar to Kismet, merely odd that something that powerfully caring would be directed at him. It left a stain of regret in his soul, a dapple of tea spilled over soiled linen. He looked away, unable to look at Mal's raw emotions any longer.

Dropping the blade, Mal reached him, hooking one arm around the young man's waist. Kismet felt Mal's hands on him and turned, wanting to pull the fear from Mal's face. Warmth enveloped Kismet's body, Mal's bear hug pulling him free from his muted shock. Kismet pressed his forehead against Mal's chest.

"So, a canine?" Ari tossed off toward Death, who shrugged. Bound by their leader's decision, Ari spent the passing seconds wondering what form Beckett would shape the shadows into. Speculating, Ari said, "It would be nice if it were something different. It's always a canine or bird. For once I wish someone would do something inventive, like a bear or, hell, even an octopus."

"You want the oddest things, Ari," Death replied with a shake of his head. Tossing Ari's borrowed blade back to him, Death worked the fatigue from his fingers with a shake before retrieving his long blade.

"Min, can you stand to help?" Death didn't look back, not wanting to meet her eyes if she refused. The woman grunted, pushing free from the wall to grab at her discarded blades. Nodding at her decision, Death glanced at their youngest.

"I'll do what I can, Death." Mal reluctantly dropped his arms from Kismet's waist, stopping when the older Horseman shook his head. "I can help."

"Just keep Kismet behind us, Mal," Death said. "If the creature gets past us, you have to get him to safety. We can't risk someone else grabbing him. Take him to Peace if you have to. He won't refuse you sanctuary."

"Shit, if the kid's got to run to Peace for protection, then this world is fucked." Ari made a face when Death gave him a disparaging look. "Hey, I'm just telling the truth here."

"Listen to me, Mal." A warm smile reached the cold coffee ice of his eyes, a reassuring presence from the eldest Horseman. "I trust you to do this. If we can't fight this thing off, you have to promise to take

Kismet away. We can't afford to have the magus get ahold of him. Agreed?"

"Okay." Mal nodded, pushing his fears back down to their haven in his belly.

"Death, the best thing we could do is kill that kid." Ari turned, muttering under his breath. "And the magus too."

The creature's broad head turned toward the Horsemen, bloodred steel eyes nictitating as it blinked. Death would have loosely called it a canine, its four appendages ending in long sharp talons that tore up the floor as it walked. The summoned wraith stepped free from the pool of blood Beckett used to shape his rage into the shadowed form.

Min swallowed loudly beside War, gulping down her trembling shock at the size of the creature.

It tasted the air, a long flick of a serpentine tongue licking the space under its flat muzzle. Horns stabbed up unevenly from the crown of its skull, the mottled shadows of its body writhing into continuously moving spirals.

"Gods, it's huge," Mal whispered to no one in particular. The hard wood floor surrendered curls of lacquer and peeled grain under its claws, leaving shreds of honey-beige shavings in its path. The creature's barely formed lips peeled back from its mouth, long, jagged points lining its uneven jawbone.

"Looks like a Rottweiler and a triceratops fucked each other silly and left that at the back door of some whorehouse." Ari grimaced. "Gonna be a bitch to kill. Have to probably saw through that neck."

"Probably," Death agreed. "It might be hard to pierce the eye socket into the skull. I'd be afraid to break the katana on its bone. Are you ready, Min?"

Min nodded silently, her nerves taut and near to the breaking point. The aches along her thighs and upper arms twitched when she moved with the faintest effort. Despite her weakness, she stood shoulder to shoulder with War, wondering how much good she would be able to do against a wraith forged from grief and revenge. The wraith's muscular legs bunched as it crouched, preparing to attack.

Beckett sat back on his haunches, becoming aware of his surroundings. The beast's breath ruffled his clothes, running hot over his shaved pate. Drawn by the power of his largest creation, the magus touched the slavering string of drool hanging from the wraith's gaping maw, tangling his fingers into the viscous stream. Beckett's flesh smoked as he came into contact with the creature's acidic saliva.

Howling in pain, the magus shook his arm, trying to free his skin from the burning fluid. The spit splattered wide, separating into dots that curved in the air, striking the human's tender body. Drawn by the screams, the monster stepped closer to the magus, his nose nearly touching Beckett's face.

Scrubbing at his arm with the edge of his shirt, Beckett howled when he realized he'd only driven the acid farther into the sheets of skin peeling back from his arm. The open meat below cooked with a low sizzle, the foyer filling with the sweet sickly odor of crackling, decaying flesh.

"Beckett!" Charity shouted, starting across the floor. The wraith raged at the immortal, splattering spittle as it shook its head. Startled, he reared back, his common sense warring with his desire to protect Faith's lover.

Rot dripped into Beckett's body from the wraith's mouth, eating through the fabric of his clothes and ripping through the skin below. Burrowing down into the magus's stomach, dots of shadows migrated toward the tender promise of ropy intestines, offal swelling from the heat of Beckett's cooking body.

Another bite, and a chunk of the magus's cheek disappeared into the creature's ravenous mouth. Barely stopping to chew, the wraith placed a heavy paw on its creator, its claws digging deep into the man's chest. Holding Beckett down with its massive weight, the wraith continued to assault the man's squirming body. A piece of arm vanished, the joint ripped from Beckett's shoulder with a wrenching twist of the wraith's head.

Mal started forward, instinctively reacting to the man's pain. Death's steady hand on his shoulder stopped Mal short, the magus's dying cries rising and falling under the wraith's vicious bites. Fighting to break free, Mal tore loose, just in time for Ari to envelop him from behind, firmly holding Mal in place. Angry, Mal turned on Death, his face red with frustration. Ari released the youngest Horseman at a nod from Death, Mal pushing away the other blond's arms.

"No, Mal," Death said quietly. "Leave the magus be. You won't help him."

"He's going to die, Death." Mal glanced at War, the blond Horseman shrugging off his concern. "We have to help him."

"Free will, Pestilence." Death's coldness shocked Mal's soul, the younger man stunned to silence. "Our noninterference works both ways. We're not here to save mankind from itself."

"That's wrong," Mal insisted, yanking his arm away from Death's touch. "We can do more than that. Hell, we just can't let that thing eat him alive."

"Nope, Cooties, that's exactly what we're going to do," Ari said, his eyes firm on the wraith. At the first sign of the creature moving toward them, he would attack, the spot between his shoulder blades itching in anticipation. "It's not wrong. Humans make their own choices and live or die by them."

"You two are so fucked-up," Kismet replied, fighting with the helpless rage consuming him. Tears streaked his pale face, his long lashes clotted with dried salt. He shivered, a wave of dizziness swaddling his senses. The world spun on a pinprick, trails of colors following the Horsemen as they moved.

Charity broke free from his shock. He slid through a pool of blood, nearly spilling him onto his belly. Kicking at the wraith's chest, he fought to get his hands under Beckett's flailing arm. The creature struggled to regain a hold on the magus, its jaws snapping at the man's head.

Desperate, the immortal pulled, wrenching his shoulders. A thin sheet of darkness welled behind him, pulsating through the seams around the elevator door. Pushing the Veil apart, Charity reached into its darkness, finding a thread resonating of Peace. The portal buckled around the edges, unstable and rippling.

"Bastard's going to take him in." Ari whistled low, stopping when the sound jerked the wraith's head around. "Great, now I'm helping them go."

"Let them go," Death replied. "Charity's not strong enough to carry a human through the Veil. If they survive, it won't matter anymore."

"If they don't survive, then I won't have the pleasure of killing that son of a bitch." Complaining, Ari rolled his eyes at Death's exasperated sigh. "Let me have my kicks, Shi. You keep dusty books. I kill people. Win-win."

A silver thread rose from the darkness, pouring light into the lobby. Undulating, the ribbon sent a siren call, keening for the human soul in Beckett's body. The magus went limp in Charity's hands, overwhelmed by the draw of the unknown beyond the Veil. Holding onto Beckett, the immortal tumbled into the portal, burdened by the mortal's extra weight.

Screaming, the wraith lurched after the men as the portal swirled closed. The dark sealed up, leaving the scent of singed flesh and metal behind. Angry at losing its prey, the wraith bit into a darkfae's body, standing over its kill and growling at the Horsemen. Its head canted with each movement the Four made, protecting its meal against the other predators. Chewing, the creature gulped enormous bites out of the twitching bag of flesh and nerves, eating as quickly as it could fit the meat into its mouth.

"Damn, that thing's going to eat us." Kismet's blood ran to ice, slowing him down. The young man tumbled forward, Mal reaching for him before he fell on his face. Shivering, he grabbed at the Horseman's shirt, searching for warmth. "Shit, Mal, I'm so fricking cold."

"He's probably lost too much blood and needs a fix." Ari looked over his shoulder. "Lay him back down before he passes out."

Mal moved quickly, cradling Kismet as his legs gave out from under him. Easing against the wall, the youngest Horseman set him into the curve of his lap, an arm wrapped around Kismet to keep him in place. Kismet's eyes fluttered closed, his body rocking with a shuddering wave of spasms. "I'm here, Kiz. I'm not leaving."

"Why are we standing around waiting for that thing to start on us? Let's just kill it," Ari grumbled by Death's side. He eagerly stepped forward, keeping his blades down.

Death followed closely, keeping a watchful eye on the summoned creature. His feet stuck to the floor, a sticky clinging mess trailing from under his heels, and his shoulder ached, a healing muscle torn from wrenching his sword free of a darkfae's knee. With his fingers moistened with sweat, Death sighed again, circling around Ari in his approach to the wraith.

The creature growled, smoky trails rising from the floor where its spit dripped onto the wood. Digging its talons in, the wraith set its shoulders, craning its head to the side. Ari paced to the right, waiting for Death to mirror him. Pointed horns gave Ari pause, their tips hooked back toward the wraith's narrow eyes. Coming in tight, Ari studied the creature's squat body, looking for weaknesses in its structure.

"Shit, this thing is big." Ari whistled under his breath. "Hell, it would take decades for one of these to grow this big naturally."

"There's nothing natural about this thing, Ari. Even for us." Death nodded at the creature's slight shift, its attention drawn by Min's stealthy approach. The katana reflected the wraith's body amid the splotches of drying blood, the sword's edge scalloped and sharp.

Ari circled in tighter, stepping as loudly as he could, trying to draw the wraith to flinch and attack. The creature's shoulders dipped slightly toward Death, its haunches bunching underneath its wide body. Diving in, Ari plunged a knife blade into the wraith's side, hooking the tip into the creature's ribs. The bone gave under War's thrust as the creature twisted to lunge at Death.

Ari caught the wraith off guard, and it yelped, its maw closing over empty air. Death skidded out of the way, his bare feet slipping on the floor. Min echoed the wraith's high-pitched screech, the wraith's elongated fangs a whisper away from Death's bare arm. Min cursed, berating herself silently for reacting, wincing an apology at the men.

"Need you to shut up, Min," Ari grumbled, shaking the remains from his foot. "Making a noise like that means you're being attacked."

"Min, don't draw it to you. Step in behind Ari. Use his body to shield yourself." Death moved away, the wraith curling back to worry at the man's long limbs. "Keep your attention on this thing, Ari."

"Rather be on you," Ari growled, stabbing down into the wraith's neck. The creature's thick muscles deflected his blow, sliding the blade across its neck. Dropping in close, he recoiled at the smell of the wraith's breath in his nostrils. Snapping at Ari's arm, the wraith caught a piece of the Horseman's skin, peeling back curls of flesh with its sharp teeth.

Grunting at the sting from the wraith's acidic spit, Ari smelled himself cooking, his skin bubbling black. "Oh, you are going to be kissing that and making it better, Shi."

Ari twisted away, nearly turning his shoulders parallel to his hips as he ghosted past the wraith, pricking at the creature's hocks. The summoned creature followed, trailing splotches of blood from its side, rearing, leaving its throat open for Death's blade.

As the creature's head turned, Death sliced out, letting his arc guide the blade into the softness of the creature's gullet. The hit hammered a shock wave up his arms, a thick layering of scales biting back the attack. The wraith kept moving, segmented scales providing triangular armor over its throat, nearly hidden by the folds of muscle and stout fat around its neck.

"I can't cut through its throat. It's too protected," Death shouted over the wraith's growls. Ari stepped around, putting Death directly to his left. Death feinted a blow to the creature's shoulder, hoping to draw its head up and bring a glistening eye within War's reach.

Ari plunged in, a sharp jab at the fiery red target.

He nicked the edge of the creature's eye, ribbons of rancid steam bursting out of the round orb. Screaming, the creature jerked free of the blade, snapping blindly at the Horsemen in front of it. Min saw a chance when the wraith raised a paw, hooking talons into Death's leg. Stabbing at the creature's head, she cursed at the thickness of its skull, her thrust deflected by the bony ridge above its eye.

The wraith turned, tracking Min's follow-through, her shoulders twisting away from its snapping jaws. Her foot caught on a corpse, the darkfae's wrist snagging at her balance. Tumbling, Min rolled, shifting her fall. She hit the floor hard, her lungs shocked into releasing her breath into the twitching muscles of her throat. Gasping, she fought for air, her empty hands frantically searching for the blade she'd dropped when she struck the unforgiving wood.

Leaping, the creature growled, spittle flying as it pounced at the woman. Its teeth closed on her leg, ripping apart her thigh muscle with a savage twist of its head. Shreds of skin crisped, her flesh poaching white from the caustic saliva. Unable to keep her screams down, Min grabbed at a darkfae's broken blade, its handle lost in the fighting. Its keen edge cut into her bare hand, hot blood running down her slender arm. A hiss of curses was all Min allowed herself as she shoved the blade under the creature's jaw, hoping to hit a soft spot in its gullet.

The fractured steel bit into its mark, sliding up through the creature's chin and lodging in the striated roof of its mouth. Shaking its head, the wraith fell back, clawing at the embedded metal thorn. Raking its paw on the sharp metal, it bled streams over Min's prone body, the woman struggling to get clear of the frantic seizures working through the creature's limbs.

Ari straddled the wraith's hips, his blades poised. The creature's neck arched, bending its chin up and exposing the flat of its head to War's weapons. Plunging the daggers down, Ari felt the soft pop of the wraith's eyes as he found his mark. Smoke rose from War's bare forearms, long blistered tracks peeling up layers of skin where the spurting fluids of the creature's rupturing brain hit him.

"Get her free, Shi." Ari jerked his chin at Min, her limbs twitching as she tried to pull loose from the tangle of corpses. He clutched the hilts of his blades, hooking the edges under the creature's brow ridges. Taking a deep breath, Ari met Death's eyes, the oldest Horseman cradling Min's shoulders. Winking, Ari pinned the wraith between his clenched thighs and twisted its head about.

Its neck broke under Ari's hands, the shadows torn loose out of its skin. The skull came free, throwing Ari back, clear of the blood pouring from its shorn throat. A splash caught Ari across his face, cheek taking most of the damage. White bone shone along his cheek, the meat pulled back from under his hot gaze. Bitter curses spilled from the remains of War's mouth, the edges of his lips sealed tight from the searing acid.

Min pushed Death from behind, urging him toward Ari. Crawling over the littered corpses, Death approached Ari, his pants matted to his skin with Min's blood. Ordering Mal to help Min and Kismet inside, the Horseman kneeled beside his oldest friend, fear chilling Death's blood. Sliding an arm under the blond's shoulders, he strained to lift Ari, the other man's greater weight pushing a sharp ache into Death's tired body.

"Hey." Ari hooked an arm under Death's ribs. The creature's gyrations had broken his hip, the cracked bones rubbing raw as he walked. Speaking loosened the seal on his burned lips, tearing the chap and starting a fresh bleed. "Think I can get you to kiss and make it better?"

"That's you," Death snorted, picking through the bodies. "Always looking for a way to turn a perfectly good battle into sex."

Death licked at the tear on Ari's lips, then sucked the air from the other's man mouth. Coppery and masculine, Ari tasted of conflict and comfort, someone willing to take on the impossible to protect the ones he loved. The kiss was a small one by Ari's standards, but it stung down into his soul.

Death stepped back, his mouth momentarily stained red with Ari's blood until he turned, his tongue wiping away evidence of their kiss.

"Yep. Always happy to turn anything into sex." Ari licked at drops on his face, the sting of acid hidden in the taste. It burned down into his throat, his spit carrying the wraith's poisons into his stomach. He'd survive as he always had, healing behind the rancid touch of the Veil's creatures. For now, he enjoyed the killing and the tender care of Death's long body on his.

"We do have one problem, Shi."

"Other than the boy or including him?" Death turned as he approached the door, easing Ari through the opening.

"Ah, didn't even think about him." The blond shook his head, banging his blown knee on the wall. Stars bled light into his vision, a red curtain of pain washing anew over his nerves. "We can deal with the boy later. I was wondering how we were ever going to get all of those bodies out of the foyer. That kind of shit is why you never have battles at your front door. You're left with all the crap to clean up afterward."

HOPE DANCED along the hills below Peace's cabin, the sky lit pink with a dying sun. Her shoes were left on the gravel driveway, socks cast aside a few feet away. Her tiny form dipped and weaved among the white daisies blooming along the trail, an unruly bouquet balanced in her slender arms.

Peace's jaded gaze followed the young immortal's path, her unrestrained joy as bright as the flowers she gathered.

The painfully thin man shifted his weight, leaning against the broad beam supporting the deck he'd built around the broad-sided cabin. In the distance, a mountain range groaned under the weight of an unexpected snow, the Rockies nearly blue against the graying sky. Charity watched Hope as well, a flat expression on his bitter-etched face.

"How's the human?" Peace asked, staring out at the seemingly endless stretch of unspoiled landscape around him.

"Drugged," Charity replied. "He's in too much pain right now. I'm hoping the boy's blood will help him heal enough to watch me kill the Four. He might not make it, but I need to try. I owe Faith that."

"The Four didn't bring this trouble to your door, Chare."

"They killed her." He stared at Peace, the other immortal as silent as the stones poking in the field.

"The Horsemen don't kill their own." Peace let the words slip free, cast on the breeze, where they tossed and tumbled. "Death would never let them take an immortal life, even if it were possible."

"It's possible. You and I both know it is," Charity muttered darkly.

The haggard-faced immortal beside him ignored the comment, his attention still on the tiny girl playing on the hills below.

"I need you to watch her."

"Until the new Faith arrives?" The elder immortal struck a match, cupping his hand around the flame as he lit a hand-rolled cigarette, the flare of coarse tobacco bright red under the fire. A few hard puffs started the cigarette's slow burn, a wave of his wrist extinguishing the blaze. Carefully tossing the burnt match into a coffee can filled with sand, Peace drew in a lungful of smoke, holding it in until he nearly burst from lack of air.

"No." Charity shook his head. "Until she leaves us. Hope's not long for this world. I give it a few more months, and then she'll be going on. They don't stay long. You know that."

"This one's been here less than a year, hasn't she?" Peace struggled to remember when he'd first met the girl.

"There's a reason they say Hope dies quickly," the immortal reminded Peace.

"What are you going to do then?" Peace drew another mouthful of smoke, savoring its harsh taste.

"I'm going to do what you tried to do before." Charity turned toward the man, his once mentor and the missing piece of his Four.

"That wasn't me." Peace shook his head, long strands of graying hair loose around his rawboned features. "That was another Peace and a mistake. The Four aren't evil, Charity. They exist just like the rest of us. Because mankind brought them here to serve. They're as much a part of humanity as we are."

"They've been here too long," the immortal said, nearly brushing his shoulder against Peace's in challenge. "Death and War have a hold on mankind. They're too old… too powerful. How can mankind fight against their age? I think eliminating Death and War would be the greatest blow to mankind's chains. It would allow humanity to be free of the weight of their purpose. Don't you think I'm right in that?"

"And you plan on taking the new Faith on this path of yours, once he or she arrives?" Peace snubbed his cigarette into the sand, the pleasure of the smoke lost to him. "You going to poison someone new against the Four? If it were our reason to exist, Peace before me would have succeeded with his mad plans, and I wouldn't be standing here right now watching you lick the wounds to your pride."

"The Horsemen are people, like we are. Just older, but still human. We let the legend of who they are bring us nightmares, and we cower before them. For all we know, that Peace was the last one with a clear vision of what we're supposed to achieve for mankind." Charity shrugged. "He should have succeeded. I believe we've lost our way because we aren't a Four anymore."

"And *I* believe you're full of shit." Peace's laugh was a harsh bark, scratching humor riddled with sarcasm.

"You're just afraid, old man," Charity said. "You're supposed to be a part of us. We're supposed to be Four instead of Three, and you walked away from that. Even before I came along, you turned away from us. I hope there's something of that bond inside of you that will at least let me try to make things right."

"I think you're doing this because Faith left you, not because you think the Four are evil," Peace responded. "You're going to wage a war with someone who was born to fight and another who takes souls. How do you expect to win?"

"I don't expect you to help me." Charity felt the Veil shimmer. The new Faith was nearly upon them, drawn to Charity's presence. "Can you at least keep her here with you? Until she goes?"

"Yeah, that shouldn't be a problem." Peace's keen eyes lit up at the flock of birds flying over a far ridge. "I think what you're doing is wrong. You'll be pulled back into the Veil, and for what? Nothing. And what kind of Charity can you be, plotting the demise of other immortals?"

"I'm not going to neglect my call, Peace." Charity sneered. Peace hid in the emptiness along a mountain ridge, tucked away from humanity and ignoring everything but the most insistent of pleas for his presence. "Not like you."

Hope struggled up the hill, her arms burdened by plucked daisies. A sadness lingered in her eyes, the sparkle of her wide, innocent smile nearly too brilliant for Peace to bear. Hitching his jeans up, Peace left Charity's side, dismissing the younger immortal with a wave of his hand.

"Do what you've got to do, Charity," Peace muttered, stepping onto the gravel pathway. "I hope to the gods that you don't become the first immortal Death kills. And if you are, so be it."

CHAPTER EIGHTEEN

MAL PLACED the last box of Kismet's possessions on the floor. He was trying not to show his disgust, but the place was a mess. The warehouse loft was a compromise of sorts between the young man and the Horsemen. Taking another look around, he half agreed with Min's suggestion that it could be made more habitable with a blowtorch and endless accelerant.

Kismet's refusal to live with the immortals led to long, heated arguments, punctuated by verbal jabs and angry shouting matches. Ari finally threw his hands up in surrender when he couldn't wear down Kismet's stubbornness, while Death pursed his lips, calmly outlining his arguments to persuade the young man to live someplace they could keep an eye on him. That led to a few choice words and a couple of hand gestures Mal vowed to learn.

While he didn't fully understand Kismet's violent reaction to being cared for, he did comprehend the other's reluctance to leave the shadow-infested world he'd grown up in. He couldn't imagine being without the other three.

An expanse of stacked rectangular windows spilled a hazy light into the space, heavy white paint covering most of the glass. Kismet had refused anything but the loft, his stubbornness now nearly legendary among the Four. Paint supplies and finished canvases filled much of the southern wall, horrific creatures leering up at Mal from bloodied landscapes. A few softer images lay hidden under the starkness, the float of a daisy on slate gray rain or the line of a face nearly hidden under crosshatched nightmares.

The loft's walls were a mixture of white-edged red brick and mottled drywall, its high ceilings spotted with wide-bladed fans. A kitchen had been carved out of a space by the door, a supporting column serving to anchor a long counter bristling with stacked containers. Mal sniffed at the mustiness in the air, spotting the slither of shadows collecting near the bathroom door. The wraiths were slothful, sated from a feeding off the homeless clustered around the trolley station below. Mal shoved his will at the dark masses, moving the serpentine shapes on their way.

Kismet stood at the counter, wrinkling his nose at the furry remains left in a Tupperware coffin, the fridge just starting to hum under newly restored power. After tossing the container into a black plastic garbage bag, he systematically rifled through the small cabinets, debating the worthiness of abandoned utensils and a spare pink dish.

Stacked mattresses served as living room furniture, an angled array of cushions scattered over the too-soft bedding. He'd accepted Mal's offer of a bed, the low platform boasting drawers he could throw his clothes into, the plastic still wrapped around the box spring. Hidden partially behind fabric curtains strung on framing wire, the bed area would be his haven from the chaos of his captured dreams, the pain of his images cut free from his mind and left on the stretched canvases.

"We can hire someone to take the paint off the windows." Mal picked at the flaking film, thankful he wasn't subject to lead poisoning. There was evidence of past attempts to remove the thick covering, irregular scraping along the bottom of one pane.

"Or I can just take off what I want when I can." Kismet looked up at the other man. Mal's shirt stuck to his back, beads of sweat spreading between his shoulder blades. With an appreciative smile, Kismet walked over to the contemplative immortal, his fingers briefly stroking at Mal's spine. "It'll come off with a razor blade. I might leave some of it on. It depends on how much light gets in. Hey, you can help me scrape it off and tell Death it's just another training exercise."

In the weeks since the encounter with the wraith, Mal grimly set to the task of learning how to handle a weapon, spending long hours in the practice studio or at the weights to build his strength. While the Horseman would never attain the breadth of War's shoulders, his lean body easily adapted to the regime, sculpting hard lines into his long limbs and back. Kismet appreciated the slow change in Mal's slender form, spending time watching Mal spar with Death just because he could.

"I don't like this neighborhood." From what Mal could see through the east-facing windows, the area left a lot to be desired. "It's too dirty. It's not a good neighborhood."

"Hell, Mal," Kismet replied. "For me, this is a huge step up."

A rattling iron-gated elevator grumbled up to the fourth floor of the warehouse's top level, shuddering as it passed between second and third. Outside, downtown San Diego shuffled on its way, pausing only to scream or piss into the gutters, the Veil clouded with wraiths feeding on the raucous clusters of people, dark seagulls picking fodder from the air.

"We can find you someplace better," Mal countered. "Someplace safer."

"Don't push, Mal," Kismet replied, squatting to dig through the box at the Horseman's feet. They'd raided a thrift store, picking through the battered pots and pans. He'd wondered at Mal's insistence on including a baking sheet, perhaps driven by dreams of hot cookies coming from a nonexistent oven, but Kismet shrugged, adding it to the pile. The artist thought twice about giving in to Mal's quirks, as he struggled to dislodge the more necessary dish drainer from the tangled mess wedged inside a box.

A shape danced alone in a corner of the loft, formless except for askew arms and legs flying about, its head a blank appendage missing telltale features. Kismet blissfully ignored the specter, leaving it to its solitary celebration. He'd wanted to put a lamp in that corner, a tall halogen torch they'd rescued from a trash pile, but it would have to sit a few feet away, leaving the ghost in peace. Finally triumphant over the drainer, Kismet nearly tumbled back on his rear, caught in Mal's steady hands.

The Horseman helped the smaller man to his feet, taking the drainer from Kismet. Sniffing at the moldy smell clinging to the rubber mat, Mal turned on the hot water at the sink, waiting for the faucet to run clear after spurting a rusty stream into the basin. A tint of red remained, then disappeared, the drain coughing as it struggled to swallow the rush of water.

A child's voice echoed in the spacious area, bouncing gleefully off the walls. Unseen, Chase's laughter ran along the edges of the main room before dashing into the bathroom, folding into the tiled walls. Kismet followed the sound, his eyes unreadable and clouded. Intent on Kismet's pretty face, Mal's soul saddened at the pain living there, simmering just below the surface.

"At least let us make this place a sanctuary. I might be able to if Death teaches me. He says it's just a matter of leaving a part of myself here. It'll keep the shadows and ghosts away," Mal offered. "Although I wish you'd reconsider living with us."

"Mal, come on, man. Leave off." Kismet waved away his friend's protests. "We've already had this conversation. I can't do that to Chase. Even if he's not really here. What's left of him is all the family I've got."

"We're your family." Mal saw the disbelieving glance Kismet gave him. "Okay, I'll be your family. Death too. He's good. Ari just needs some time, and Min cares. In a Min kind of way."

"Ari needs to get laid." Another set of mixing bowls lay at the bottom of one box, and Kismet wondered just how many bowls someone really needed. He set the smaller ones aside, thinking of using them for mixing paints. "You'd think that old Mustang Death got him would have done the trick."

"It did, a little bit." Leaning on the counter, the immortal grinned.

Ari nearly wept with joy when Death led him downstairs and showed him the vintage Grande Coupe he'd bought for him. He'd been offered the first ride, an honor that touched Mal deeply. Since then, he'd almost forgiven Ari for the scare he'd been given when the older immortal opened the engine up on the freeway and nearly sent them into next week.

"Yeah, now he's down in the garage waxing the car and thinking lewd thoughts about Death. Porn's much cheaper." Holding up a whisk, Kismet grimaced at Mal. "What the hell were you on when we were shopping? It looks like you were possessed by a magpie or something."

"I think I was distracted," Mal admitted slowly. He'd spent more time watching Kismet pick through the shelves than actually shopping, and he'd guiltily thrown things into the basket to look busy. He'd already discovered two sets of salt and pepper shakers, and who knew what was still lurking in the boxes they had left.

"I'm not taking you with me anymore. It's like you see something that looks halfway domestic and you toss it in." Laughing, Kismet grabbed an apron, its frilled laces dangling over the edge of the cardboard. "You've got some issues. Dude, there's more bowls in here! What the hell?"

"I like bowls." He shrugged, taking the bright Fiesta ware and placing it in the cabinet. "I liked the colors. They're kind of happy."

"Mal, bowls can't make you happy." Kismet nearly jerked his hand up, unsure if the dark, skittering shape he just saw was a wraith or a cockroach. "Okay, maybe they can make you happy, but they don't do it for me."

"I want to make things work for you." Mal opened the lid of a packing box, then pulled out unfolded clothes and an odd shoe. His hands closed over a rolled-up towel, its edge unraveling as he placed it on the battered Formica table they'd dragged up from his SUV. "Maybe if I try hard enough, I can fix everything that's gone wrong. I just don't know where to start."

A piece of tubing and syringes scattered out of the bundle, small foil packets folded into tight squares gleaming on the washed-out terry cloth. The kit lay where it fell, inert and poisonous in Mal's eyes. Kismet stood silent, watching the other as he gathered up the items, rolling them carefully into their towel coffin, and handed it to Kismet. His fingers closed over Mal's hand, holding on tightly.

"I'm trying, Mal. I haven't used in a while, but it's not going to go away overnight," Kismet whispered. "You can't fix me. I have to do it myself."

"But you know you're not broken." Mal bowed his head, resting his forehead on Kismet's temple, and sighed, exasperation heavy in his breath. He fisted his hands in Kismet's shirt, wanting to either push the young man away or hold him closer. The loneliness in his life eased when Kismet was around, his husky laugh a memory Mal brushed over gently before he fell asleep. He wanted that sense of peace for Kismet. "Everything you see is real. You don't need this shit to help you run away anymore."

"I'm a bad influence on you. I'm pretty sure you didn't swear before you met me," the young man said, rubbing his cheek on Mal's before pulling away. "Death must be so proud."

"I'm serious," Mal said. The immortal watched as Kismet placed the kit back into the box, burying it beneath old clothing he'd bought for rags. "I want to help you deal with this."

"I'm doing the best I can," Kismet assured him, dragging another box for the kitchen closer to one of the cabinets. "I'm not going to promise you that I'm going to be clean tomorrow or even the day after. It's going to take time, and there's going to be some days that I just am not going to be able to go through without it. You're either going to have to deal with that or walk away."

"I told you I'm not going anywhere, Kiz," Mal said. "Hell, we've been shot together, sort of. That's not something Death and Ari can claim."

They continued to unpack, quietly companionable, at times pulling items from the thrift-store boxes and wondering at the other's taste. Kismet dug around at the bottom of one of the boxes, finding a small velvet pouch tucked into its corner. Curious, he tugged open the ties, then shook out a leather thong strung with five dark green jade beads. Pursing his lips at the immortal, Kismet held the beads up to Mal's face, a quirk of a smile as he waited for an explanation.

"Somehow I don't think we got this at the Rags in a Box." Kismet's fingers worked over the carved jade. He traced over the kanji, then rubbed at the leather knotted to keep the beads centered on the thong. "What's this?"

"I got it for you. Well, I had it made." Mal took the leather from Kismet's hands, sliding the threaded beads around the artist's neck. The Horseman tied the thong around Kismet's throat, then took a step back. "Those are our names, the Four and you. That's Kismet in the middle. Death and War are to the left, and Pestilence and Famine are to the right."

"Tell me that Death and you are next to me and not Ari or Min." Kismet touched the beads, the jade cool against his skin. "Okay, I don't mind Min. Ari, he's just an ass."

"Yeah, we are." Mal grinned, a sense of satisfaction filling his chest at the sight of his name hanging around Kismet's throat. "I wanted to give you something so you knew that you were never alone. The Four's here for you. I'm here for you."

"Ari wanted to kill me. More than once," Kismet reminded him. "He said it was the best thing you all could do."

"I think that's Ari's way of showing affection," Mal responded. "He's been wanting to kill me for years. Death says it means he likes you."

"Then he must think I'm God or something." Running his fingers over the kanji, he blinked at the moisture in his eyes. Stretching, he brought himself up to the immortal's height. "Thanks, Mal. I like it a lot."

It was a simple kiss, the touch of a soft tongue against Mal's bottom lip and then a sigh of a breath into the warmth of his mouth. It was enough to send shivers through the immortal's soul, and he stilled, letting Kismet explore him. Too quickly, it was done, and cold air rushed into Mal's lungs when the young man pulled away.

"You're welcome." Finally able to breathe, Mal leaned in, bumping shoulders with his friend. "I'm just glad you're here."

"I'm glad you're here too," Kismet said.

A bowl leaped from the counter, spinning in midair before crashing against the far wall. Another followed, larger shards scattering on the painted floor, a chunk flying as far as the mattresses positioned around the potbellied stove set in a near corner. Chase peered out of the wall, eyes wide and shocked at the commotion. Sliding back into the shadows, he left behind a gray mist on the gypsum board, its edges creeping out like mold. Amid the busy street noises coming from the half-open windows, a woman's voice lifted into a giggle, then fell away, leaving Mal and Kismet alone once again.

"Well, lucky for me, you've got this bowl fetish." Kismet shrugged, shaking out a dish towel. "Or I might have had to reconsider that sanctuary thing."

"You should reconsider it anyway."

Kismet gave Mal a long steady look, sincere and open. Resting his elbows on the counter, he put his chin on his clenched hands and said with a smile, "Only if you could reassure me that it could keep Ari out. And maybe you in."

RHYS FORD admits to sharing the house with three cats of varying degrees of black fur and a ginger cairn terrorist. Rhys is also enslaved to the upkeep of a 1979 Pontiac Firebird, a Toshiba laptop, and an overworked red coffee maker.

Rhys can be found at the following locations:
Blog: www.rhysford.com
Facebook: https://www.facebook.com/rhys.ford.author
Twitter: @Rhys_Ford

Black Dog Blues

By Rhys Ford

Ever since being part of the pot in a high-stakes poker game, elfin outcast Kai Gracen figures he used up his good karma when Dempsey, a human Stalker, won the hand and took him in. Following the violent merge of Earth and Underhill, the human and elfin races are left with a messy, monster-ridden world, and Stalkers are the only cavalry willing to ride to someone's rescue when something shadowy appears.

It's a hard life but one Kai likes—filled with bounty, a few friends, and most importantly, no other elfin around to remind him of his past. And killing monsters is easy. Especially since he's one himself.

But when a sidhe lord named Ryder arrives in San Diego, Kai is conscripted to do a job for Ryder's fledgling Dawn Court. It's supposed to be a simple run up the coast during dragon-mating season to retrieve a pregnant human woman seeking sanctuary. Easy, quick, and best of all, profitable. But Kai ends up in the middle of a deadly bloodline feud he has no hope of escaping.

No one ever got rich being a Stalker. But then few of them got old either and it doesn't look like Kai will be the exception.

http://www.dsppublications.com

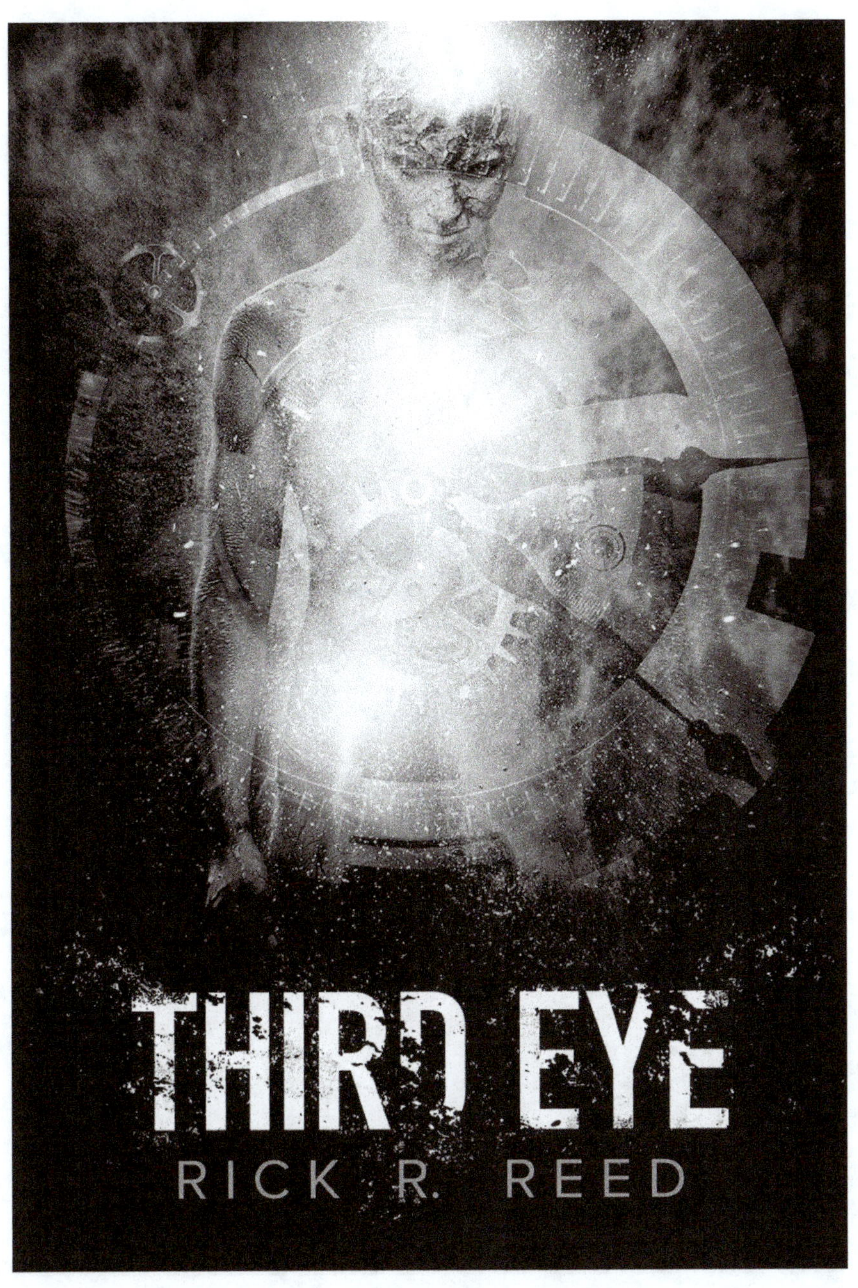

http://www.dsppublications.com

http://www.dsppublications.com

http://www.dsppublications.com

http://www.dsppublications.com

THE RELICS OF GODS

YEYU

http://www.dsppublications.com

DSP PUBLICATIONS

visit us online.

WWW.DSPPUBLICATIONS.COM